St. Helena Library
1492 Library Lane
St. Helena, CA 94574
(707) 963-5244

A Gift From
ST. HELENA PUBLIC LIBRARY
FRIENDS&FOUNDATION

CORKSCREW

The highly improbable,
but occasionally true, tale of a professional wine buyer.

Peter Stafford-Bow

THISTLE
PUBLISHING

Cover design by Patrick Latimer Illustration. www.PatrickLatimer.co.za

This first edition published in 2018 by:

Thistle Publishing
36 Great Smith Street
London
SW1P 3BU

www.thistlepublishing.co.uk

To Curly, with love.
"It smells like wine…"

Welcome Initiates, on this, the twelfth day of Dionysus!
The day of Theemeter!
Behold! The clearing of the wine.
And now this pompe arrives
Let the contest begin!
And may all win, in the manner of Dikaiopolis.
From 'The Invocation of *La Vendange*'
(Courtesy of the Worshipful Institute of the Minstrels of Wine)

CHAPTER ONE -
A RUDE AWAKENING

"**D**o you have the slightest idea how much trouble you're in?"

The man had a coarse voice. He sounded like a plain-clothes policeman. An unpleasant one. Maybe he was a particularly vicious civil servant. Was this how the Department of Health rolled these days? They'd been threatening to get tough with alcohol retailers who failed to take their responsibilities seriously.

"If you're referring to the accidental sale of a case of cherry brandy to that thirteen-year-old in Twickenham, I can assure you that it was a completely isolated incident," I croaked. "The cashier in question has been comprehensively retrained..."

"We're not interested in your cherry brandy," interrupted the woman sitting beside him. Her tone wasn't particularly welcoming either.

The man pressed a button on the tape recorder. A voice spoke clearly and loudly from the device. 'It's a Beretta 92. The best handgun in the world'.

"Recognise the voice?" he asked.

I did, of course. It was mine.

***

I'd received a phone call just two days earlier from a very nice young woman. She'd explained that the Department of Health was consulting with the retail industry on how to reduce the socio-economic and health impacts of alcohol, particularly within disadvantaged groups. As the powerful Head of Wine, Ale, Spirits and Salted Snacks for the country's largest supermarket chain, would I be willing to speak to the government's researchers?

It sounded rather dull, to be honest, despite her friendly tone. She then explained that expenses would be paid, to the tune of five hundred pounds, which kindled the public spirit within me. She even suggested a six p.m. appointment, so as not to disrupt my busy working day. How considerate, I thought. The date was set, and a couple of days later I found myself in dingy old Paddington.

Central London's explosion of fine restaurants and glass-fronted offices had yet to gild this grimy corner of the capital. It was only a matter of time, of course. Here and there a crane towered overhead, and every couple of minutes the air vibrated with the growl of a great machine, carving into the earth behind a plywood hoarding. But for now, the streets were still lined with cut-price hotels, poorly disguised brothels and tired old pubs. Quite charming, in its own way.

I found the address just a stone's throw from the station, one of a hundred identical doorways in a peeling white mansion block stretching the length of the street. Beneath the intercom sat ten buttons, nearly all anonymous. The third, however, was paired with a neat little sticker stating 'SG Consulting'. I pressed it. Nothing happened for a few seconds, then the electric lock hummed and I pushed the door open.

I'd left enough time to enjoy a couple of large Ports at a faded wine bar near the station, so there was a spring in my step as I climbed to the first floor. Before me lay a solid white door, bare but for a small number three. It opened before I could knock.

"Good evening Mr Hart. Please sit down."

There was only one free chair, in the centre of the room. It was positioned in front of a plain desk upon which lay a few files and a complicated-looking tape recorder. On the other side of the desk sat a man and a woman. He was thin faced and wore a dark suit, no tie, and a rather impatient look. She looked stern, smartly but conservatively dressed in a buttoned up blouse and plain jacket.

I dropped my bag next to the vacant chair, strode over and held out my hand. "Please call me Felix. Nice to meet you."

Neither of them moved. The man just gave a slight shake of his head and repeated, "Sit down please."

What a funny pair, I thought. Then the door shut behind me with an unusually heavy clunk. I turned and saw there was a third person in the room, a large man with very short hair. He wore a neat suit but looked like a rugby forward, a right brawler. He stood with his back to the door, arms folded, looking me up and down.

A feeling of dismay settled upon me and my stomach started to churn, the way it does when unpleasant things are afoot. "What's going on here?" I demanded.

"It would be much easier if you just sat down, Felix," said the woman.

"So, we're on first name terms are we? How about you introduce yourselves?"

I looked around the room. It was small and windowless with no other exit, just a closet door in the far wall. There were no pictures or pot plants, only a rather incongruous standard lamp in the corner with a wooden base and faded yellow shade, though most of the light came from a bare bulb overhead.

The seated man simply nodded at the empty chair.

These three were a peculiar lot. Who were they? The mafia? Was I being kidnapped? I considered making a run for it. The fellow standing at the door was a big chap but then so am I. And I was two Ports ahead. But what about my expenses – all five hundred pounds of them? I hesitated. I was definitely on the back foot.

"Felix," said the woman, "you are simply helping us with our enquiries. If you're helpful enough we may be able to look more favourably on your transgressions. Cooperation is usually the better strategy in these types of situation."

So they were detectives. But why invite me to this horrible little place? The whole setup stank and the whiff from the cheap brothel next door wasn't helping.

"I've got a better idea" I said, glancing at the silent man by the door and inhaling to reach an even more intimidating size. "You let me leave right now and I won't sue you for unlawful imprisonment."

The woman sighed and the seated man piped up again. "Do you have the slightest idea how much trouble you're in?"

And then he played his little recording of my voice and I realised that, sure enough, I was up to my neck in it.

"The crimes you have committed are extremely serious," said the woman. "They have an international dimension. The British authorities aren't the only ones taking an interest."

"Did you know you're a person of interest to the FBI, Mr Hart?" asked the man.

I didn't, and it sounded like very bad news.

"You've upset the authorities in a number of countries," he continued. "But it's the Americans I'd be most worried about if I were you. If they extradite you, which they are perfectly entitled to do, I guarantee it will be a deeply unpleasant experience. They're a lot more … direct than we are."

The woman looked down at her file. "Bulgarians, Italians, Turks, a Middle Eastern conspiracy. People smugglers, drug dealers, left-wing extremists, unidentifiable Islamists." She raised her eyebrows. "Even slave trading."

I sat down, suddenly rather drained.

"It's an astonishing list, Felix," she continued. "Barely believable, in fact. But there's enough here to have you locked away for an extremely long time."

The man leant forward, and held my eye. "We know where the bodies are," he whispered.

"Am I under arrest?" I asked, limply.

"No. Not yet," said the woman. "What we don't know is how all these activities of yours are linked. That's what you need to explain to us. Otherwise, we'll be obliged to hand you over to colleagues who care rather less about the subtleties of these things."

"But I'm just a simple wine merchant, not the kingpin of some underground network…"

"We believe that's probably true, Felix, which is why we're still talking to you. But people smuggling, drug dealing, subversion and murder are major crimes. So why don't you just take a deep breath and tell us everything? And if we're satisfied with your account, we might tell our American friends there's nothing to worry about. Oh, and we'll take your phone for now. What's said in here stays in here."

What choice did I have? God knows what other evidence they'd intimidated out of witnesses or winkled out of servers and switchboards up and down the land. And I certainly didn't fancy spending the summer water-boarding with the FBI before being locked up for the rest of my days in a maximum security stockade.

I placed my phone on the desk. The woman separated the battery and deposited both pieces in a metal box at her feet.

"Well," I said quietly, "I suppose I should start at the beginning. The story really begins several years ago. In the week before my expulsion from school, in fact."

***

The Christmas holidays were over and it was the first morning of the new term. I had the faintly euphoric sense of being on the final stretch of a marathon. I'd just turned eighteen, my friends and I were in the final year of school, the only remaining hurdle an unpleasant clutch of exams in a few months' time. And once I'd winged my way over those, the world of university and freedom beckoned.

I'd enjoyed an itinerant break, as usual, over-wintering at the homes of various friends. My own parents were no longer on the scene, my father having scarpered when I was a toddler, leaving my poor mother to bring me up single-handed in a damp council house before succumbing to a lung infection when I was eleven. A tragic tale, I'm sure you'll agree, but you get used to these things. By the time I was in my late teens I'd grown to love the freedom from adult supervision.

The day had started conventionally enough, our class of thirty boys sitting in pairs at too-small desks, catching up on holiday gossip and boasting of conquests in foreign lands, mostly carnal, the vast majority completely fictitious.

"Morning gentlemen. Welcome back. Quiet please." The hubbub died down a little. The Master shuffled through his folders, located the class register and, clicking his pen, began the roll call. When he got to 'G' there was a pause. "Golden?" No response from the sea of murmuring conversation. "Golden!" Again, no response.

I turned to the desk behind to see my good friend, aspiring musician Dan Golden, in intense conversation with his desk-mate.

"Golden! Golden! Golden! Golden! Golden!" shouted the Master, slapping his palms against his desk. Dan looked up, startled, taking in the twenty-nine smirking faces and one livid one.

"Roll call," I whispered.

"Oh, ah, yes. Here sir." A chorus of giggles.

"Thank you Golden," said the Master. Then he caught his breath. "What in God's name is that on your face?"

"A moustache sir. I became a man over the holidays." Cue howls of laughter.

The Master clenched his teeth. "Facial hair is not permitted, Golden, as you very well know. Except for religious reasons," he added, glancing at Golden's desk-mate, who had sported a magnificent black beard for the past year.

Paul Singh stroked his luxuriant cheeks. "My beard is very religious, sir."

The Master removed a handkerchief and mopped his forehead. "Golden, that's a Hitler moustache. And you're Jewish."

"I'm reclaiming the look from the Nazis sir. It's my right as a member of an oppressed race." Further titters from around the classroom.

The Master took a deep breath. "Golden. Leave the classroom now and shave it off, or I will have the entire teaching fraternity hold you down while matron personally waxes your face. She's not a great fan of yours, so I think she'd enjoy that."

Golden stood and walked to the door. "This is how the Third Reich started!" he declared and slammed the door. The room burst into a round of applause, whoops and cheers.

"Shut up" snarled the Master, surveying the room with disgust. "What a puerile shower you are. God help us." He turned back to the registration folder. "Hart?"

"Sir," I said.

"Hussein?" Silence. "Hussein!"

"Hussein's in Mecca sir. Doing the Hajj, sir," called a voice.

"He did the Hajj last year," growled the Master. "And, as I recall, the year before."

"He's very devout sir." A rumble of guffaws from around the room.

My good friend Tariq Hussein certainly was devout – fanatically devoted to investing every possible afternoon down the King's Head, that is. It was a devotion we shared. Tariq was currently on his father's yacht in the Caribbean enjoying some winter sun, the jammy dodger. While we shivered in an under-heated classroom he was probably dancing on the deck surrounded by gyrating lovelies, a half-finished bottle of Bajan rum in one hand, the other caressing a nubile, bikini-clad...

"Oh, by the way, Hart," said the Master, interrupting my reverie. "You're to see the Head of Sixth Form after assembly. Something to do with your dismal attendance record I imagine."

Sods, I thought, a rollicking within two hours of the beginning of term. Not a great start. The Master finished the roll call, making his final mark in the register. "Now get out and go to assembly, you appalling rabble."

After a soporific welcome-back speech from Headmaster Dr Pankhurst, better known as Dr Pie 'n Crust, and a dirge-like rendering of 'Abide With Me' led by the school's profoundly deaf organist, we filed out of the assembly hall. I made my way to the Old Manor House which housed the private studies of the senior staff.

Fletching Ordnance School for Boys was a minor public school founded in the late eighteenth century, set in acres of wooded grounds near Hampstead Heath. Founded by a religious zealot who made a fortune out of naval weaponry, it was established to mould muscular Christian boys who could plant God's word and deed overseas, presumably after raking the bewildered natives with cannon fire and stealing their land.

Its motto, *Carpent tua poma nepotes*, translated as 'Your descendants will pick your fruit'. The somewhat crowded school crest showed a woman kneeling behind a bearded man who, in turn, was stretching to pluck an apple from a tree. This picture of imperial bliss led to the school being known affectionately as

Felching Orchard by the pupils, though not within earshot of the senior masters.

The Old Manor House was the historic heart of the school and Reverend Parr, Head of Sixth Form, had one of the grandest studies. I knocked on the door.

"Come!" he barked.

I'd been summoned to Parr's office many times and I suspected the door was kept deliberately difficult to open to intimidate the smaller pupils. I turned the brass handle and gave the door a good shove. It swung heavily against the inside wall, the handle cracking against the wood.

"Try not to destroy the place, Hart!" snapped the Reverend. He sat behind an enormous wooden desk, an austere, bony man with just a fringe of grey hair and a flaking scalp. A light frosting of dandruff coated the shoulders of his black shirt, softening the contrast with his dog collar. "Do you know why you are here?"

Not sure I like this, I thought. Usually you have a fairly good idea why you're in the crapping-castle with the Reverend. If there was something expensive broken or missing he'd be accompanied by a member of Her Majesty's constabulary. If the Headmistress of St Hilda's Girls School was standing there, face livid and hands on hips, it would be an interrogation as to whether the CCTV footage of a strapping young buck climbing through a first floor window was yours truly. But on the very first morning of term I was stumped.

"Am I to be inducted into the school choir, sir?" I asked sweetly.

"You truculent oaf, Hart. You think you're clever don't you?" He gave an unpleasant smile and rose from his desk. "Well you're not. You are a miserable disappointment. Every privilege that God and Great Britain have seen fit to lay before you, you have frittered away." He paused a moment, looking out of his window as if for inspiration. "You are the recipient of the *Dio iuvante* scholarship, Hart, the only one in your year. It means 'With God's help'. But how do you use this gift? You flush it down the urinal like everything else that passes through those sorely abused kidneys of yours."

Parr peered down at a report on his desk. "Three GCSEs passed. An 'A' in French and you scraped a 'D' in mathematics and feminist studies. You didn't even turn up for your mock A Levels last term, Hart. Why was that?"

"I was ill, sir." In fact, the exams had clashed with the Hammersmith Beer Festival. I'm not a man to get his priorities muddled.

"You do understand, don't you, that you are a scholarship boy? That means your presence here is an act of charity on our part. A benevolence, courtesy of the trustees of Fletching Ordnance. The families of everybody else in your year are obliged to pay fees. Very substantial fees they are too."

"I'm very grateful sir, really I am." I made my best Oliver Twist face.

"We've been having this same conversation every month for the past two years, Hart. Your attendance record is abysmal. Your essays remain absent without leave. Your exam scores continue their merciless decline, through the floor of mediocrity and into the basement of wretchedness."

"I'll pull my socks up, sir."

"We could have given your scholarship to that nice Nigerian boy. By Jove, he wouldn't have let us down as you have. A good Christian family, too!" He narrowed his eyes. "What would your parents have said?"

"That's a little low sir," I murmured, eyes cast down for effect. God alone knows what my father would have thought. I didn't remember him, and my mother told me he was killed in an accident in Macao a year after absconding. It's true that my mother would have been heartbreakingly disappointed but, given that she passed away the best part of a decade ago, her influence and my shame had eroded somewhat.

I had been a model infant, scoring top marks in every little end-of-year test my primary school threw at me. Then mother's illness struck, just as I took the scholarship exam to Fletching Ordnance School for Boys. Who knows whether it was my academic prowess or sympathy for a poor little orphan, but I was immediately inducted into Hampstead's most venerable public school, rubbing shoulders with the sons of stockbrokers, well-to-do farmers and a few scions of the international super-rich.

"You're a waste, Hart. A waste of a good place at Fletching Ordnance. And I cannot abide waste." Parr paused and considered me, his jaded expression that of a treasure hunter unearthing a foil-wrapped turd. "Consider this your final warning."

Bit of a bumpy start to the term, I thought, as I encouraged the Reverend's door to swing shut behind me with an enlivening bang. But the Gods, I trusted, were still with me, even if something of an unholy grudge was curdling in the mind of their emissary on earth.

CHAPTER TWO - CACKERING HALL

The gods were bloody well not with me. As I crossed the huge, oak-panelled hallway of the Old Manor House, a woman's voice called to me.

"Felix dear, there's a phone call for you." It was Hilda, one of the school secretaries. "It's your girlfriend." Hilda waggled the receiver at me while the other secretary pretended to read a file.

I took the handset from her. "Which one?" I mouthed.

Hilda shrugged and looked down, smirking, while the other woman tittered.

"Hello? Felix speaking."

"It's Portia. I couldn't get hold of you over the Christmas holidays so I'm calling you now."

Ah, that girlfriend. I'd been quite keen on her for a while and we'd had a few fun dates, but she'd started to strike me as a little too matter-of-fact when really I was looking for more *je ne sais quoi*. It might have been because she was the daughter of a military man, they do tend to err on the side of straight-forwardness. I wasn't sure we'd be together for too much longer, though I didn't want anyone's feelings hurt, of course. Fingers crossed she was calling to end it all.

"I'll get to the point, Felix. I'm pregnant. With your child."

I felt as though I'd been punched in the stomach. "How?" I whispered.

"It's very simple Felix. You ejaculated your sperm into my uterus."

"Ah. Yes. I see."

"The question is not how, it's what. What are we going to do?"

My heart was hammering and I was feeling distinctly sweaty. "Well, should we ... er ... visit a clinic somewhere?"

"Don't be a filthy beast, Felix. I'm having the baby."

Oh Sanctus, Dominus and bloody Deus. That really did make this an F-grade, shop-soiled, brown-letter day.

I knew when it had happened. It was at a particularly well-stocked party at Tariq's place in early November. A couple of bottles of Chilean Merlot down the hatch and a few smooth words from yours truly and it was knickers off and squeals of joy behind the gazebo. No johnnies to hand but what the hell. Well, this is what – a baby! And she was having it.

"Are you?"

"Yes I am. We have to tell my parents."

"Um ... wouldn't it be better if you broke the news yourself? The wonderful, joyous ..."

"No! You did it, so you can come and explain it."

"Ah. Will they be pleased, do you think?"

"No, they won't. But when we explain we're getting married, they might calm down."

Oh God.

"Do you need a pat on the back, Felix?" called Hilda, looking alarmed. "Francis, go and get Felix a glass of water." The second secretary hurried off.

"We're going to see them at the estate near Pluckley next weekend," Portia continued. "Saturday, midday. Father will arrange for a car to meet you at the station. Don't be late – he has a thing about punctuality." She hung up.

"Everything all right, Felix?" asked the other secretary, handing me the glass of water.

"Yes, thank you," I lied. "Everything is mostly fine. Thank you."

On Saturday morning I caught the train from Charing Cross to Pluckley, an hour through Kent's bare winter fields, then twenty minutes in the car. The driver remained silent as we twisted through the narrow lanes, rows of vines either side, stumpy and black in the pale sun. A crow sat on one and watched us pass, cawing at my predicament. Then we turned between two high brick pillars onto a private road. A weathered stone plaque announced we had reached our destination, Cackering Hall.

The house was a rather fierce red-brick mansion, three stories high with towering chimney stacks. The doorbell, a white ceramic button with a large brass surround, ordered me to 'PRESS', so I did as I was told. No pealing bells sounded inside the house so I prodded it a couple more times. Eventually the door opened a crack, revealing the face of a shrunken old woman.

"Good afternoon. I'm here for lunch," I said.

She scowled and opened the door a little wider. I followed her, flinging my coat artistically over a chair in the hall, and found myself in a small kitchen with a stone floor. A large pile of wrinkled apples and a dead rabbit lay on the countertop. The woman turned and scowled at me again.

"I'm looking for Sir Balfour and his wife and daughter," I said, lamely.

She nodded toward the door.

"Thank you ever so much. I hope you don't have to wait too long for your new vocal chords." I retraced my steps and, after a few wrong guesses, located the door to the dining room. It was ajar and I slipped through. The room was huge, with leaded windows facing onto a frosty back garden. There was a sturdy brick hearth near the door and the wood-panelled walls were hung with pictures of plump men on horses surrounded by baying hounds. A chest-height wooden giraffe stood next to the fireplace, eyeing me suspiciously.

A vast dining table lay at the far end of the room, already laid with cutlery and glasses, two large antique china jugs decorated with peacocks dominating its centre. Portia sat at the long side of the table, scribbling at a Sudoku puzzle, her pert little nose and mouth twitching over the mental arithmetic. Somebody or something sat at the head of the table, hidden behind The Daily Telegraph, emitting a laboured wheezing.

I cleared my throat and Portia looked up.

"Felix!" She rose and walked over, giving me a chaste kiss on the cheek.

I could swear to God her breasts had grown. I wondered what they might look like unencumbered by her unflattering knitwear. Not that I was likely to be permitted a look. "Hello Portia."

"Daddy!" she scolded. "Felix is here."

"Tell him to put the wine on ice then check on the horses," The Daily Telegraph rumbled.

"Daddy! Felix Hart is my friend, not the butler. He's staying for lunch."

"Eh?" Sir Balfour lowered the paper. A livid red face traced with blue veins testified to a life lived liberally, with little regard to government health recommendations. "Where's your tie, boy? Where do you find these people Portia? In the fish-porters' café at bloody Billingsgate?"

"A pleasure to meet you, sir."

"Well, the pleasure's all yours. Have some wine." Sir Balfour waved at a large pewter ice-trough holding four bottles. Bit of a rough start, I thought. Hopefully he'll warm up.

After settling in the chair opposite Portia and downing a generous glass of Grand Cru Chablis, I raised my eyes to the cob-webbed ceiling. Maybe today won't be so bad, I thought. I'll give old Sir Balfour his due, he keeps a good cellar and he's generous with it too. Perhaps the consumptive old bison might help me out. Introduce me to some contacts in The City? Maybe a loan to get me on my way?

I took another look at Portia, still occupied with her puzzle. Was her belly swollen, as well as her breasts? It had been only three months since I dipped my unprotected wick – surely it was too soon to show? I imagined her naked, with a rounded stomach and taut, full breasts, her stiff nipples demanding a thirsty suck. Steady on Hart, I chided myself, that's what got you into trouble in the first place. I adjusted my trousers and glanced at the empty chair at the far end of the table. I couldn't very well greet the mother with a raging hard-on. Mind you, from what Portia had told me, I doubt she'd notice, apparently she was a legendary soak.

I leant forward and grasped the Chablis once more, pulling it from the ice trough with a rattle. Not that it needed chilling. Cackering Hall in January was absolutely bollock bloody freezing. Did they even *have* central heating?

"Pour me one before you guzzle it all, boy," growled Sir Balfour from behind the paper.

"Right-o, sir." I had just retaken my seat when the door was flung open and a butler, of Indian extraction, cleared his throat and announced, "The Lady Edith Whittington!" The lady of the house stepped into the room, resplendent in a long turquoise ball gown, the top encrusted with glittering beads, its chiffon base trailing out of the door behind her.

"Good afternoon," she called, imperiously, to the room at large.

I rose to my feet like the gentleman I am. The rest of her family remained seated. Lady Edith grasped her skirts and wrenched her long chiffon train through the door. Unfortunately, the billowing material snagged on the wooden giraffe, sending it toppling to the floorboards with a crack.

"Christ Edie!" growled Sir Balfour. "Will you watch where you're throwing your skirts?"

"Oh, be quiet Bal!" She gathered the fabric, threw back her shoulders and took a few seconds to focus on the opposite wall. Then, like a newly launched battleship, she advanced toward the table. Unfortunately, the generous cloth of her train had become entangled in the horns of the giraffe, which followed her noisily across the room.

"Good God!" bawled Sir Balfour, flinging The Telegraph onto the table. "It's like the arrival of the sodding Mahdi Army!"

"Can I help, ma'am?" I offered, in the most deferential tone I could muster. "You appear to be slightly tangled." I slid from my chair and dropped to one knee. She was nearly as tall as I and quite striking, though possibly a little too veteran for me to entertain any serious carnal thoughts. If she had insisted though, after a bottle or two, I suspected it would have been rude not to comply. And I may be many things, but I am not rude.

"Please do be careful, this is haute couture!" she warned, but stood still as I unpicked the animal's sharp features from the material. As I returned the giraffe to its proper spot, Lady Edith planted herself at the far end of the table to Sir Balfour. "So, where do you school, Felix?" she enquired, in the tone of one with limited expectations.

"Felix is taking his A Levels at Fletching Ordnance, mother," answered Portia. "It's a very good public school near Hampstead Heath."

"Bunch of sensitive sodomites, I expect," muttered Sir Balfour. "Wine Kumal!"

"And your parents?" There was a wary note in her voice.

"I'm not entirely sure where my father was schooled, Lady Edith. He was from Portugal."

"Oh dear."

"Related to the Symmingtons was he?" enquired Sir Balfour.

I suspected this might be the right answer, whoever the hell they were. "Yes, indeed, sir. A minor branch of the Symmingtons."

"Oh. Well. That's probably all right then," he muttered. "Kumal! Some red please! My glass has been empty for the past bloody month!"

The butler glided in and filled his glass. He moved to the other end of the table and filled Lady Edith's before seeing to mine.

Sir Balfour took a long sip and grunted. "Very good. What is it Kumal?" He took another mouthful, as did I.

"Argentinian, sir."

Sir Balfour choked and coughed loudly. "For the love of God!" he shouted, when he had recovered. "They're the bloody enemy!"

"Bal, really! Try to behave! We're not fighting them anymore," Lady Edith scolded. "The nice man from Majestic Wine recommended it. And anyway, I like Malbec. There was an article about it in The Times last week. Apparently they employ young polo riders as cellar hands in the off season."

"I would love to see that, it sounds fascinating," I said, giving what I hoped was my best card-games-with-wealthy-aunt smile.

Lady Edith appeared to soften a little. Looking more closely I realised her livid lip colour, not to mention that of her teeth, might have had more to do with a morning soak in Argentinian Malbec than the careful application of Dior.

"Bloody communists," muttered Sir Balfour. "Kumal, get me some claret, will you?"

"Mother. Father," began Portia. "Felix and I have some news."

My stomach tightened and I suddenly felt rather cold and sweaty. I wasn't sure this was the optimal moment.

"What's that dear?" enquired Lady Edith.

"Felix wishes to ask father for my hand in marriage."

In for a penny, in for a pound. Old Balfour was clearly a wealthy chap, and there were worse places to live than a country estate an hour from London. Maybe I'd be gifted a little cottage in the grounds. It's funny how you're trotting along quite happily one day, then life just bolts and gallops away without any warning, leaving you shaking the reins and praying for an absence of low branches. "I would be honoured, sir."

There was a stunned silence while Sir Balfour stared at me. "What the hell do you want to do that for?"

Lady Edith stretched a hand towards Portia. "Portia dear, I know he's good looking, but you can do better. I had Jeremy Spott-Hythe in mind, actually."

That struck me as a much better idea. Yes, why not marry Jeremy, I thought, I'm sure he's a regular kind of chap. He might even want the sprog too. I wouldn't dream of charging him for the privilege.

"Jeremy is eight years old, mother."

"But his father owns that huge vineyard down the road, dear." She looked at me with pity. "What land do you own Felix?"

"Not terribly much, to be honest."

"What the hell's going on, boy? You haven't made her pregnant have you?" growled Sir Balfour.

"Ah. Well…"

"Yes he has, father. I'm having a baby in July."

"Oh heaven help us!" wailed Lady Edith.

Sir Balfour rose slowly from his seat, his face turning puce with rage. "What! By God, boy, I'll have you gelded! Kumal! Get my shotgun!"

"Very good, sir."

I had a terrible sense that things were slipping out of control. "I do apologise, Sir Balfour, I didn't mean anything by it. Kumal, I'm sure there's no need for firearms. Can't we just have a civilised discussion?"

Kumal ignored me and left the room. Oh Sweet Mary, I'd have to do a runner. But I was miles from the station and I had no car. I wouldn't get half a mile before the old lunatic rode me down with the hounds.

"How could you be so foolish, Portia? How could you!" chided Lady Edith. She drained her glass in one gulp and rose, advancing on me. I was about to be caught in a pincer movement. Time to get out of here before Kumal returns with the gun. I jumped up from my chair and turned to the door but Lady Edith lunged and grabbed my left arm with both hands. She was surprisingly strong.

"Tell me you forced yourself on her! Tell me she had no choice in the matter!"

"Er … would that be better?"

Lady Edith tightened her grip and looked beseechingly at me. "Yes it would. It really would. Please tell me it was rape! It must have been!"

"Oh don't be ridiculous mother, it was all perfectly consensual," sighed Portia.

"Oh God no! The shame!" wailed Lady Edith, releasing me and clutching her head.

As Kumal returned to the room with the shotgun I realised it was time to flee the madhouse immediately. I'd gone off marriage, children and country living completely. The butler handed the gun to Sir Balfour who pointed it across the table at me. I took cover behind Portia's chair.

"Get out from behind my daughter you miserable coward!" bellowed Sir Balfour.

"Daddy! Daddy! Stop being silly and put that down!" Portia looked over her shoulder. "Felix! Get up and talk to father like a man!"

"He's got a bloody gun! You talk to him!"

Portia sighed, rose, and approached her father, beckoning for the gun. Unfortunately, that meant I'd lost my human shield. I raced along the table to Lady Edith's chair while Sir Balfour followed me with the shotgun, taking aim down the barrel.

"No Bal! Not the Spode!" Lady Edith flung herself across the table to protect the china jugs and I crouched, using her body as cover.

"Get out of the bloody way Edie!"

"They're 1815 Bal! They're our daughter's inheritance!"

God bless old Spode, I thought. But Sir Balfour was attempting a flanking manoeuvre, despite his daughter's attempts to wrestle the gun from his hands. I ducked under the table and scurried on hands and knees to the far side, only to come face to face with the business end of the shotgun and Balfour's grimly triumphant face. He'd shaken off Portia and I'd run out of hiding places. "Now you'll get what's coming to you!" he wheezed.

I raised my hands, summoned all my creative talents, and blubbed like a baby. "Please, Sir Balfour. I didn't mean any harm! I'm an orphan. My father was a soldier who lost his life in Northern Ireland and my mother died soon afterwards of heartbreak."

"Thought you said he was Portuguese?" Sir Balfour prodded the barrels of the shotgun against my forehead.

"Anglo-Portuguese!" I gibbered. "I was raised by monks and they taught me right from wrong. I've never so much as held hands with a girl before, but when I met your daughter I fell deeply in love. I saw my own mother in her face you see, I couldn't help myself."

"Don't talk to me about love, you horrible little scrotum! You're an alley rat!"

I was in a flat panic now. The tears were coming thick and fast. "I'm not! I was due to take holy orders, I swear on the Gospels sir! I promise to do the right thing, we are due to marry and I will cherish your daughter forever. I'll make you proud, sir. Please don't shoot me, I can't bear the thought that my family name will end in violence, just like that of my dear father. He would have been so proud to see his grandchild follow him into the Services. I only wish he were here now ..."

I don't know how I dreamt up that cascade of codswallop and for a second I thought I'd overdone it, but Sir Balfour slowly lowered the weapon, still frowning and wheezing. "Killed by the Mick, was he? Savages!"

Lady Edith grasped the gun and took it from her husband. "Oh you poor thing," she cried. "We had no idea your background was so tragic."

I crawled out from under the table, sniffing. "All I ever wanted was stability and a loving home." I dabbed at my entirely genuine tears of relief. Lady Edith embraced me and I hugged her back.

"Not sure I liked the thing about him wanting to shag his mother," muttered Sir Balfour, his face lightening to a marginally healthier shade of red. "Still, I suppose that's what you get when you hang around with monks."

There then followed a rather awkward, silent meal of revoltingly tough meat, accompanied by potatoes riddled with black spots. I compensated by drinking as much wine as possible.

Portia observed me dispassionately. After the meal she informed me, out of earshot of her parents, that she was having second thoughts about the marriage. Furthermore, she had decided to bring up the child along feminist principles, without the disruptive effect of rogue males, and that it might be best if we didn't see each other quite so often.

I wondered if her decision had anything to do with my hiding behind womenfolk when faced with firearms, or my whimpering cock-and-bull story to her father. Whether it did or not, this seemed like a much better arrangement all round, and I permitted myself a short burst of self-congratulation for brokering such a satisfactory resolution to the crisis. I embraced Portia and I'm not embarrassed to say I wept again, genuine tears of relief cascading down my warm, wine-flushed cheeks.

By mid-afternoon, with the beef lying resentfully in my belly like the sole of an old boot, I was delighted to take my leave of

Cackering Hall. I kissed the hand of Lady Edith, who by this time was comatose in her chair, and shook that of Sir Balfour.

"I accept you're not a scoundrel but you're a flawed man, not my cup of tea at all. I shall be speaking to your headmaster and I shall leave it in his hands as to how you are punished. I will, however, recommend a sound thrashing."

Thrashing or not, I couldn't imagine this going down too well with the Reverend. I had a feeling there were rules about procreating without completing the relevant forms. "I quite understand sir. I shall accept my punishment with honour."

* * *

'Not going down too well with the Reverend' turned out to be an understatement of Imperial Japanese proportions. The following Monday I was hauled in front of the holy trinity: The Reverend Parr, looking like an Old Testament prophet with a twisted bollock; the Headmistress of St. Hilda's, Portia's school, her face that of Boudicca avenging her daughters' stolen chastity; and the red-faced chief duffer himself, old Dr Pie 'n Crust, looking like a Victorian undertaker whose client had just requested a penis-shaped gravestone.

It was fair to say the Reverend Parr regarded the news of my fertility as the crowning turd on a multi-tiered cake of ordure. He broadcast a fiery sermon, around six inches from my face, on sexual propriety and the perils of moral turpitude, while I struggled to avoid gagging on his pea-soup halitosis.

I've no idea what qualified him to deliver the lecture. I doubt he'd shoved his sticky wick in anything other than the hole in the chapel door. At one point he demanded to know whether I was regularly troubled by temptation, to which I was able to reply, quite truthfully, that it rarely troubled me at all. It was all rather disconcerting, like experiencing a great thunder of gunfire from all sides, but there was no mistaking the coup de grâce.

"You're expelled. This is your last week at Fletching Ordnance School for Boys."

After that, it didn't seem so necessary to focus on the rest of the sermon. I'd assumed the constant threats of expulsion over the past few years were just part of the vocabulary of the teaching staff, a kind of drumbeat to keep the troops in step. I hadn't expected this degree of ruthlessness, not even from the Reverend. I would have attempted the odd plea in my defence but the air had squirted pretty rapidly from my balloon. All I could do was stand there, absorbing the odd snatch of practical information, "no need for you to disrupt any further classes" and "arrangements to transfer your funds to a Post Office account", as my future cooled from freshly-baked loaf to abandoned soup over the course of two minutes.

And so, with the Reverend Parr's hellfire words still ringing in my ears, not to mention the stench of his rotting gums lingering in my nose, I headed to the dorms to pack my old kit bag.

First though, I dropped by the office of the Deputy Head, Mr du Plessis. He was one of the few masters who liked me, a slim Afrikaner with skin grilled permanently brown by the fierce South African sun. I knocked on the door.

"Ja. Kom."

I put my head round. "Just wanted to say goodbye, sir. I've been dismissed."

"I know." He pointed to a seat on the opposite side of his huge mahogany desk. As I sat, he rose and unlocked a cabinet next to one of the many shelves of books, and I saw the glitter of crystal. He returned to the desk with a heavy decanter and two tiny glasses, and poured us each a glass.

"I think you can heff a little drop, given the circumstances," he said, his crisp Afrikaans accent still strong despite decades in England. "Here's to your rather unconventional graduation."

"Cheers," I muttered. I tasted the wine. It was strong and salty, very unusual.

Du Plessis held the glass up to the light. "They say you should not serve dry Sherry in a decanter, or at room temperature. Why do you think they say that?"

Well, if my final lesson of my school career was to be wine appreciation, I may as well make an effort. "To stop it oxidising, perhaps?"

"Exactly, Felix. So you picked up something from your studies. Good. The salty taste comes from the sea breeze that cools the barrels as they age on the coast of Sanlúcar de Barrameda." He gazed at the liquid.

"Nice," I agreed, swallowing the rest of the glass.

Du Plessis poured me a refill. "So what are you going to do, young man?"

"I'm not really sure. Work in a shop perhaps."

"What kind of shop? And don't say a knocking shop. I'm serious."

"Oh, I don't know. Something that allows me to travel and do the things I like to do." I downed the pitifully small glass of wine.

"I have an idea what it is you like to do, Felix. Unfortunately, being a drunken gigolo doesn't offer much in the way of a career path, never mind health care and a pension." He replaced the heavy crystal stopper. "You should work in a wine shop. An off-licence."

"Selling Mars bars and cigarettes?"

"Selling wine, Felix. It's hard work but you're a strong lad and I think you could be a good salesman. And if you make a success of it, you may even have a chance to see the world. The better half of it, anyway."

"Maybe I'll give it a try."

"You do that. Go down to Charlie's Cellar in Crouch End. It's a wine shop for the more discerning customer."

Du Plessis considered me for a few seconds, then opened a drawer and extracted a small cardboard box, the size of a bag of sugar. He placed it on the desk and pushed it towards me. The packet was decorated with a sketch of some orange mountains, a vast plain and a tiny town nestling in the foothills. It didn't look like the South Downs, that was for sure.

There was a title which I tried to read aloud. "Madame Joubert's Lekker Medisyne Trommel. What is it, sir?"

"It's a folk medicine, you might call it a pick-me-up. The original Madame Joubert took part in the Great Trek into the heart of Southern Africa. Her community relied on this ... remedy ... when they were escaping from the type of person who founded this school." He looked around his grand study for a second and smiled. "It's an old recipe, learnt from the ancient people who inhabited those lands for millennia, which has been kept alive by the great Madame Joubert and her descendants."

"What do I do with it, sir? Stir it into my morning cuppa?"

"If necessary, yes. But use it only at times of great fatigue or when you need a special boost. And I advise you, most strongly, never to take more than one teaspoon full at a time."

"Thank you very much, sir."

"I think you might need it. And I trust you won't abuse it. There's a kilo there – that's around two hundred doses. Depending on how frequently you burn the candle at both ends it should last you a year or two."

"I'll come back if I need some more, shall I?"

"When you need some more you can go and find it for yourself."

"And where should I find it, sir? Down the supermarket next to powdered soup?"

"Follow the picture on the packet, young man. That's the Karoo. *Die Groot Karoo* ..." He tailed off and stared into the distance.

I sensed the meeting was over. "Thank you for the Sherry, sir."

He looked back at me. "Good luck, Felix. May the gods be with you."

CHAPTER THREE - THE GREAT BRITISH HIGH STREET

A dejected walk down Crouch End High Street that afternoon brought my predicament into sharper focus. I wasn't just expelled from school and broke, I was also homeless. I could probably stay at Tariq's for a while, now he was back from his pilgrimage to the Bahamas, but sooner or later I'd have to find a place to live.

Over a pint in the Harringay Arms, I made a plan. I would take a cheap coach to the South of France where I would live by my wits, drinking hearty red wine in sun-dappled squares by day and servicing the needs of sexually frustrated duchesses by night. I'd become the muse and companion of a lonely, attractive and fabulously wealthy widow, who would buy me a vineyard of my own.

It was a good plan, with very little downside. Unfortunately, I had only sixty quid in my Post Office account which would barely get me to Calais, never mind Cannes.

So for now I would crash at Tariq's mansion on The Bishops Avenue and get a job. Tariq's place had an indoor swimming pool with karaoke, and the house was so vast that his parents would be unlikely to know I was even there. They spent half their time in Dubai anyway. The South of France would have to wait.

I found the Crouch End branch of Charlie's Cellar, an off-licence chain with stores across London and the Home Counties.

This was one of their larger branches, its wide glass facade dominating a busy road junction. Chalk boards were propped against the wall advertising various deals – two bottles for five pounds, five for a tenner – while the window was festooned with posters boasting that the chain had been crowned Wine Emporium of the Year in a prestigious liquor competition.

I walked in and nodded to the gangly youth leaning over the counter. He wore a baggy red and black striped rugby shirt.

He nodded back. "Alright mate. Can I help you with anything?"

"I wondered if you had any jobs going."

"Boss?" he shouted at the open door behind the counter.

An obese, crew-cut man, painfully squeezed into a similar rugby shirt – which appeared to be the uniform of Charlie's Cellar – waddled out of the office, a copy of the Racing Post in his hand. "No pal, we haven't any vacancies, sorry." He had a brisk Scouse accent. He turned and disappeared back into the office.

"Please, sir. I'm a passionate wine enthusiast and I'll work like a Trojan," I called through the open door.

The boss reappeared at the door, the spare tyre around his waist brushing both sides of the frame. "Like a Trojan, eh?" He tittered in a high voice, waves of fat rippling up and down his torso. "What are you, a classical scholar?" Something dawned on him and he stopped laughing. "Hang on. Are you from that posh school down the road? You're Mr du Plessis's boy aren't you? He phoned and said you might be coming down."

"Yes, that's me," I replied, in a premium department store voice.

"All right. You're hired. I like Mr du Plessis. He's one of our best customers."

"But boss, we don't have any spare shifts," whined the gangly youth, tugging at his goatee.

"Yes we do, pal. Yours. Sod off, you're fired."

"Wha … ?" gasped the youth.

"You heard me, you're fired. You're lazy, you're thieving and you're too working class for our customers anyway. I need a better-spoken arsehole round here. Get lost."

"Bloody hell!" spat the youth, shooting me a look of hatred as he marched to the door.

"Hey! And leave the shirt as well, that's company property that is!"

"Sod your bloody shirt!" he yelled, pulling his baggy top off to reveal a yellowing vest over a pale torso, tiny tufts of dark arm-pit hair contrasting with his sallow, hairless chest. He threw the shirt at his ex-boss and turned to the door.

"Hey! Have some respect you cheeky little arse!" The man-ager lifted a large bag of peanuts and hurled it at the youth's head. It just missed, splitting against the metal door frame as the boy ducked and ran from the shop.

"Right. You can wear that." He threw the ex-employee's shirt at me. "Probably fit you better, anyway. First job, clear that mess up." He waggled a sausage-like finger at the spray of peanuts. "I've got paperwork to do."

He rolled back into his tiny office and sat on a distressed chair, sponge stuffing bursting from its seat. He picked up the Racing Post and frowned in concentration.

"Yes sir. Thank you for the opportunity."

And so began my first tentative steps in the wine trade. The pay was poor and the hours were long, but with Tariq putting me up in an unused bedroom in the east wing of the Hussein man-sion in exchange for a generous discount on booze, my expenses were manageable.

The bulbous boss's name was Terry. He was from a rough estate in Liverpool and had worked as a nightclub bouncer before settling in London after an unexplained falling out with some relatives. When I asked if he ever visited back home he muttered something about a "bunch of divvies," which I understood to mean he wasn't close to his family.

There were three other members of staff, who worked alongside me in the evenings when the shop became busy. Maria was a petite art student from the local college. I'm not sure whether we were in love, strictly speaking, but I found myself irresistibly drawn to her bohemian, carefree personality and within days we were tupping vigorously over the back-office table during the quieter periods of trade.

Raj was the delivery driver, cheerful, laid back and a great fan of the muscular end of the hip-hop spectrum, the lyrics of which sometimes unsettled the more delicate of our client base. The third assistant was Harry, a struggling actor in his forties. He knew his wines and was always opening a bottle when we shared an evening shift. "Education is the key to everything my lad," he would explain, easing the cork out of a superlative Rioja and splashing each of us a generous glass. It was perfectly normal to drink on duty – we were obliged to open sample bottles for customers, and a few half-glasses of wine dotted around the shop added to the atmosphere of authority and professionalism.

After a couple of months, Terry increased my hours. As the only other full-time member of staff, I had soon taken over all his administrative functions. Terry was only too happy to leave everything to me while he studied the Racing Post, munched on doner kebabs and chain-smoked his way through his Lambert & Butler. I would place the orders on the primitive stock computer, check in deliveries and carry out regular inventory checks to see what had been stolen (mainly Lambert & Butler cigarettes).

Terry gradually spent less and less time in the store. He would amble in at around eleven, after I had received the daily deliveries, restocked the shelves and opened the shop. He'd wander around, grumble at the odd missing price ticket, then demand I put the kettle on and fetch him a kebab from the

Bodrum Grill next door. Then he'd read the paper and amble off by mid-afternoon, unless the area manager was planning a visit, in which case Terry would order me to clean the office before he squeezed into a cleaner shirt and took all the credit for a ship-shape wine merchant.

I awoke one July morning, my limbs still entangled with those of my close colleague Maria, to find a text message on my phone.

I had our baby last night. A boy. Doula and support group invaluable.

I suspected Portia was implying I wasn't part of her support group, but it was good to know the old Hart genes had been passed on, so I sent a little 'well done' by way of reply. No need to cause a fuss – I was confident the doula had everything under control.

Given that I was now a family man, not that I'd been informed what additional responsibilities that might entail, I felt it was time to approach the boss for a pay rise. "Morning sir," I chirped, as he rolled in just after midday, cigarette hanging from his stubbly jowls.

"Have you got that kettle on yet?"

A few minutes later, a cup of tea in his pudgy fist, I broached the subject. "Given all my extra tasks and superlative performance, sir, do you think a pay rise might be in order?"

He didn't look up from the paper. "I'll have a think about it. Don't hold your breath, though," he wheezed as he tittered to himself.

"I'm pretty much running the shop myself. I thought that might be worth a little extra?"

Terry looked up. He pointed a fat finger at me. "Hey! Don't get funny with me pal. I gave you this job, I can take it away. Now go and get me a kebab. That divvy Richards is coming round in half an hour."

Gary Richards was the area manager, a bald accounting type with round glasses and the air of a man who suspects something is afoot but can't quite summon the enthusiasm to uncover it.

"Can I have some money for the kebab then?"

"Put it through the till under office supplies. I'm eating it in the office, aren't I?" I left Terry giggling to himself and walked to the Bodrum Grill.

"Merhaba Mehmet."

"Merhaba Felix my friend, how are you today?" Mehmet was sharpening his huge kebab knife with expert strokes, the blade rasping against the steel.

"Good. The usual please."

"You're a bit early. I've only just switched the machine on." Mehmet nodded to the elephantine leg of glistening kebab meat on its vertical skewer, rotating slowly in front of the electric grill. A few drips of fat had started to pool in the dish beneath.

"Looks all right to me. I'm sure Terry won't mind. Can't you just nuke it a bit?"

"All right." Mehmet carved a few slices and placed it in the microwave for a few seconds. He sliced open a pitta bread, stuffed it with salad and chillies, then nestled the lightly steaming slices of translucent meat on top.

"Easy on the salad Mehmet, you know he doesn't like it too green. Don't bother wrapping it – I don't think it's going to last long."

"Two quid Felix."

"Cheers." I walked back and handed the kebab to Terry, who took a ravenous bite, the trailing meat leaving a smear of grease on his chin.

"Too much salad," he complained through a mouthful of limp flesh and pitta. "And have you put that kettle on yet?"

I flicked the switch and dropped a new teabag into Terry's Everton FC mug. As the kettle boiled I did a circuit of the store, pulling forward a few bottles ahead of the Area Manager's arrival.

Now, I'm no ruthless greasy pole climber but somehow I needed to displace Terry and have myself installed as manager. I pondered my options. Should I grass him up to the Area Manager for subsidising his cigarette habit from company stocks? Or fraudulently claiming kebabs on expenses? But there was no proof – Terry would simply blame me or another member of staff. And there was the small matter that he might just beat me to death. He wasn't in great shape but he was probably five stone heavier and a vicious devil with it. I wondered what damage he'd done to patrons of that club in Liverpool who'd been foolish enough to displease him.

"Afternoon Felix." It was Richards, the Area Manager. He was early, as usual. He liked to catch his managers out, checking who was frantically cleaning up prior to his arrival.

"Good afternoon, sir. How's business in the wider North London region?"

"Could be better. Could be worse. Just had another armed robbery in Little Chalfont. The manageress has resigned because of the stress."

"Oh dear."

He walked the perimeter of the shop, his beady eyes scanning the shelves for gaps or spots of dirt.

"Hey, afternoon Gary," chirped Terry as he emerged from the office, wiping kebab grease from his face with the back of his hand.

"Well Terry, looks like business is good in Crouch End. Is that all down to your new colleague here?"

Terry smiled and put a huge, ham-like arm around my shoulders. He smelt of very rare lamb and mild body odour. "Well, it's a team effort, obviously. But Felix isn't doing too badly. Needs his arse kicking every so often." Terry gave his high giggle and vibrated with laughter.

You dreadful tub of lard, I thought.

"Well, you're doing something right. Sales are up twelve percent. You need to get on top of that cigarette theft problem though. Any idea who's doing it?"

"I've got my suspicions Gary."

So have I, old bean. I considered making subtle eye movements to give Richards a clue but that would have been a high-risk strategy. Terry still had his arm around my shoulder and, if he caught wind of my disloyalty, could have crushed my neck in a second.

"Well, I'd like a report on that please. I want you to do daily cigarette stock-checks too. Otherwise, keep up the good work. I'll be back in a month."

"Great, will do. Always good to see you, Gary." Richards left the store. "And whistle while you're at it, twat," he added, once Richards was safely out of earshot.

Terry waddled back into the office and I smiled as an elderly lady entered the store.

"My usual please, darling."

I took a bottle of gin from behind the counter, wrapped it in paper and placed it in her shopping bag. And so a typical day went by, the patrons of Charlie's Cellar coming and going. A packet of Silk Cut for one gentleman, a case of Burgundy for another. All left satisfied and were soon back for more, thanks to the legendary Felix Hart charm and panache.

Maria sashayed in with a wink and a smile. "Hiya Felix, how you doing?" I glanced at my watch – it was just gone six o'clock.

"Better for seeing you. Painted any nudes today?"

She smirked and walked into the office, wriggling into her small-sized rugby shirt and turning up the sleeves.

"Terry's still here," I said. "He must be downstairs in the storeroom doing some work for a change. We'll have to behave tonight."

Maria sulked and slumped over the counter.

"I need some food," I added. "Can you hold the fort while I get something to eat?"

She nodded and stuck her bum out as I squeezed past.

"Unprofessional, my dear." I patted her tight behind through her jeans. "Would you like some chips?"

"I'd rather have a sausage," she pouted.

Students, I mused. It's times like these I realise it was a mistake not to attend university.

I wolfed down a large helping of Mehmet's fish and chips and returned to the shop. It was the evening rush and Maria was kept busy serving customers as I ran up and down the steps, fetching cases of beer and wine to replenish the shelves. Terry had obviously sloped off and by nine p.m. things had quietened down. It was time to cash up and go home. Maria made it clear it was to her home we were going, so I grabbed a bottle of Chilean Sauvignon, set the alarm and headed back to her place for a night of artistic creativity.

As usual, I was on the early shift the following day. So, after a quick morning shower with Maria, it was back to work. I'd done a pretty good job keeping the shelves stocked the previous night so there wasn't much to do, just a couple of cases to be filled up here and there. Maria hadn't allowed me much sleep, not that I was one to complain, so I was looking forward to a gentle day. I jogged downstairs to fetch the missing wine.

Then I noticed the appalling smell. Something between a rotting animal and the toilets at a rain-soaked music festival. Oh lordy, please don't let it be a blocked pipe or burst sewer. I couldn't imagine Terry mucking in, it would be down to yours truly to clean up the lot.

I kicked open the door to the toilet cubicle. It was very clear Terry wouldn't be helping with anything because he was sitting on the pan, his pants around his colossal, swollen ankles and an ocean of puke down his shirt. His eyes, bulging in horror, stared back at me. He was also, so far as I could tell, stone bloody dead.

I clamped my sleeve over my face, backed out of the store-room and ran up the stairs. I dialled 999, still holding my breath.

"Police, ambulance or fire?" barked the operator.

"Ambulance, I think."

"You think? Is somebody injured, sir?"

"Well, they're not tip top, that's for sure."

"Can you explain please sir? Does somebody require medical assistance?"

"Somebody requires a hearse. A large one. Charlie's Cellar, Crouch End. And you'd better send a fire engine too. I think you'll need some heavy lifting gear to hoist him out."

"Do I understand correctly, sir? Has somebody died?"

"Yes. Somebody has very much died."

"Do you require the police sir? Has there been foul play?"

"It's more than foul, it's absolutely bloody revolting."

There was a pause. "Can I take your name please sir?"

"Hart. Felix Hart. I'm … the manager, I suppose."

CHAPTER FOUR -
CRIME AND PUNISHMENT

It took the fire brigade two days to remove Terry. First, a team wearing hazmat suits sprayed the toilet cubicle and my predecessor with industrial disinfectant. Then the cubicle was demolished, the back door removed and widened, and Terry was carried out on a horse stretcher, on loan from the school of veterinary medicine.

There was quite a crowd when the oversized body bag was finally hoisted into a bariatric ambulance. As Mrs Finnegan confided the next day, it was the biggest sensation in Crouch End since 1978 when the local Budgens announced they would be stocking avocados.

An earnest little man from the Environmental Health Department came round a few days later to explain that, during the autopsy, highly toxic pathogens had been found in Terry's stomach, and that these had played a starring role in his tragic demise. He wanted to know if I was aware what he had eaten in the hours before he departed for the great feeding trough in the sky.

I didn't want to get Mehmet into trouble. Besides, his chips were delicious, and he always gave me an extra-large portion. "Terry used to bring in leftovers from his dinner the night before and stuff them in pitta bread from the supermarket," I explained, in my best recently-bereaved colleague voice. "Usually sliced meat, I think. He was very careful with his money and hated to waste anything. We don't have a fridge here, so his leftovers would sometimes sit on the side all morning before he ate them. I suppose that's not advisable?"

"It certainly is not!" said the man from Environmental Health, scribbling in his notebook.

The thought of Terry having anything left over from a previous meal was ridiculous, of course. And I made a mental note to advise Mehmet that ten seconds in the microwave might not be enough to render raw kebab meat safe for human consumption.

Richards dropped by several days in a row to check the store was open and trading properly. It was, of course, because I'd been running it myself for the past six months.

"You're doing a great job, Felix. I see you've even got on top of that problem with the cigarette theft."

"It's not so difficult, sir, when you've got a motivated and passionate workforce."

"Excellent. You must share some of your tips with the wider region. We could do with more passion in our stores."

My mind strayed to dear Maria, bending over the office table on tiptoes, tight jeans round her knees, cursing and exhorting me to pump faster. "I'd be delighted to share my technique more widely, sir." I felt it was time to seize the day and adopt a more assertive approach to my career progression. "And I would be honoured if you gave me the opportunity to take up the challenge of an official management role too, sir."

"Let's see how you manage over Christmas, Felix, then I'll consider it."

They say good things come to those who wait. But, I must confess, the fire of ambition had been lit within me. I wanted a shop of my own, and soon. "I won't let you down, sir."

* * *

I wasn't complacent – I'd heard enough about overflowing stock-rooms and queues of raging customers to know that Christmas would be a challenge. And, sure enough, the festive week hit us like a tsunami.

Raj, our driver, was on the road morning to night, delivering Champagne and Pinot Grigio to the well-heeled party animals of Highgate. In the shop itself, the punters were queued around the floor, out of the door and half-way to the Bodrum Grill. The team manned the tills while I stalked around the store, offering sage advice to one and all, for my months of wine tasting with Harry had made me a confident and knowledgeable salesman. Every customer who wanted a bottle, I talked up to a case. And those who asked for a case were easily persuaded to take half a dozen.

By the twenty-third of December I was exhausted. I'd spent every minute of the previous few days on my feet, cultivating customers and directing staff. After closing time, I would restock the shelves, assemble orders for Raj to deliver the next day, and enter replenishment orders on the stock computer. I'd stagger back to Tariq's at gone midnight, set the alarm for six a.m. and collapse into bed, rising in time to greet the Charlie's Cellar delivery truck laden with fresh stock.

When my alarm sounded on the morning of Christmas Eve it was still pitch dark. I swung my legs from under the duvet and sat up, clicking on the bedside lamp. My head was swimming with fatigue and every muscle in my arms and chest ached from humping hundreds of cases up those stairs from the stockroom. I had the busiest day of the year ahead of me but I wasn't sure I could summon the strength to even stand. I was destroyed – I could feel my head drooping even as I fought the urge to sleep.

And then I spotted the little box peeping out from my kit bag in the corner of the bedroom. The strange sketch of orange mountains and that bizarre title, Madame Joubert's Lekker Medisyne Trommel. A pick-me-up, Mr du Plessis had said. Well, that's what I needed all right.

I staggered across the room and grabbed the box. Just one teaspoon, he'd said. I tore open the top. There was a zip-lock plastic bag inside, full of white powder. I opened the seal and carefully transferred a level teaspoon into a coffee mug, filled it with tap water and stirred. The powder fizzed vigorously then vanished, leaving the water with a faint pink hue. I smelt it but, aside from a faint whiff of soda water, there was no aroma. I took a small sip and swallowed. It had a fruity, slightly chalky flavour, not unpleasant, so I took a larger gulp. Nothing untoward happened so I drained the cup. At least I was upright now. I pulled on my Charlie's Cellar rugby shirt and cleaned my teeth, noticing a warm feeling spreading through my stomach.

As I descended the stairs, I could feel the ache in my muscles had subsided. I felt lighter. By the time I shut Tariq's front door noiselessly behind me, my head had cleared and my hearing seemed more acute. There was a spring in my step and, much to my surprise, I broke into a run, covering the couple of miles in a quarter of an hour, my muscles rippling with energy. I arrived at the shop a new man, brimming with power and focus. I hurled open the steel shutters and marched into the store, bellowing a profane version of 'Jingle Bells' at the top of my voice.

That day I was a man possessed, simultaneously carrying out a live wine tasting, trading every punter up to a full case, and urging the team on to ever-greater heights of customer service. I took just one short break the entire day, when I led darling Maria into the office and gave her a huge, knee-trembling Christmas bonus, at which she screamed with such delight that Harry knocked on the door to check everything was all right.

We completely dominated the North London fine-wine trade that Christmas and, for the first time ever, Crouch End took the prestigious number-one position for sales across South East England. On January the fourth, as I restocked the shelves in the sober New Year, Richards wandered in with a little framed certificate.

"Congratulations, Felix! You're promoted to manager!"

Hallelujah! "Thank you sir! I've got a sackful of ideas on how to build sales here – we've barely scratched the surface."

"Not here, Felix. I need you to run our Little Chalfont branch. The latest manager has resigned following yet another armed robbery and the place is on its knees. You're just the man to sort it out."

I was floored. Little chuffing Chalfont? I didn't even know where it was – presumably some sleepy village, way out of town. I didn't want to sell Liebfraumilch to rural biddies, I wanted to sell fine wines to bankers and TV stars. And I didn't like the fact that the store's best customer was an armed man in a balaclava with questionable manners.

"But, what about Crouch End, sir?"

"Sorry Felix. You've done a great job but we have senior managers who have been waiting a long time for a store like this."

I was surprised to find a stab of jealousy invading my previously gentle and contented thoughts. All my schooldays I'd had the virtues of hard work drummed into me, had been assured that reward followed effort, like spotted dick followed a visit to the fishmonger's. But standing there, before the area manager of the North London region, I felt my faith in those meritocratic tales weaken. Was this to be the story of my working life, to labour like a navvy, only to be gazumped by time-servers and lettuce-nibblers?

"You don't have to go. You could stay here as a shop assistant, of course. But I should mention there's a perk that comes with the Little Chalfont store."

And what's that then? A sponge baseball bat to wave at chummy when he's next in for the contents of the safe?

"There's a property above the shop. It's huge, six bedrooms or something. You can live there for free."

A place of my own! Now you're talking. I could host parties, convert the lounge into a pub, rent out bedrooms to attractive foreign students. "That will do nicely sir. When do I start?"

I started the next day. The last manager had run off before Christmas, never to be seen again, and the branch hadn't opened since. Richards was desperate to get the store open and taking money.

Little Chalfont was a bumpy forty minutes out of central London on the Metropolitan line. I alighted from the tube at the village station, kit bag over my shoulder, and walked the couple of hundred yards to the town centre. It was a modest-sized village – a few dozen shops and a small supermarket nestling either side of a gently buzzing high street.

I couldn't wait to check out my new home. I walked round the side of the shops and ascended a steep metal staircase. There it was, a grubby number '2' nailed to the middle of a faded door. Richards had given me a bunch of keys, helpfully labelled 'shop', 'alarm', 'flat' and so on.

I tried the key labelled 'flat' but it didn't fit. I worked through the others – none of them matched either. I sighed and pulled out my chunky new company-issue phone. As I brought up Richards's number I gave the front door a couple of light kicks. Paint flaked off against my boot.

The door suddenly opened to reveal a tall, very broad young man, about my age. He had long blonde hair tied in a ponytail, was bare-chested and bare-footed, and wore a skirt. He looked like a slightly chubby Tarzan. "What do you want?" His tone was assertive but not unfriendly.

"Er ... I think this is my house. Who are you?"

"My name is Wodin and I disagree with your arrogant concept of property ownership. I live here with my fellow travellers, although we do not own it any more than we own the trees or the skies. We have squatters' rights. If you attempt to molest us we will call the authorities."

What is the best tone, I wondered, in which to address anarchists? I opted for polite but firm with no sudden movements. "Now look. I work for Charlie's Cellar. I run the shop downstairs. And I'm entitled to live here."

"Glad to hear you're opening the shop again. It's very inconvenient walking down the road for wine, and I don't approve of supermarkets. Good to meet you, what's your name?"

"I'm Felix." I shook his outstretched hand and tried to peer over his broad shoulder into my flat. A waft of warm, incense-scented air emerged from the dark hallway. I could see there was a sheet with a floral design attached to the ceiling by each corner, giving the room the appearance of a Bedouin tent.

"I see you're wearing a skirt," I said, for want of something to say.

He looked at my suit and shirt. "It's a sarong. Far superior to trousers. You should try it."

There was a period of silence as we eyed one another. "How are we going to sort this out then, Wodin?"

"I don't see that there's anything to sort out. We live here and you don't. Goodbye." And with that, he shut the door on me. This was a major setback to my dreams of upwardly mobile, independent living.

I considered my options. The most obvious was violence. But Wodin looked a fairly large chap and who's to say whether, underneath that hippy skirt, he wasn't sporting a machete? And how many others were in there? In any case, they were claiming squatters' rights and didn't appear to have damaged anything, so even if I kicked the door down and bundled them out, they would probably be able to demand re-entry, backed up by the authorities.

I pressed the green button on my phone and Richards answered. "There's a problem sir. There are squatters in the flat above the shop."

"Oh dear. That's unfortunate."

"But you said I could live here. Charlie's Cellar will have to get them out."

"You can live there but you'll have to deal with it yourself, sorry. Charlie's Cellar can't do anything about it. Do you know how much it costs to go to court and evict people? It takes years." He must have known all along, the turd.

I descended the iron stairs and returned to the shop, unlocking and pushing up the steel shutter. A pile of letters had accumulated behind the front door and the shelves were nearly bare. I locked the door behind me. It was a much smaller shop than Crouch End, just a single till and a short counter. I walked through to the office. Papers and files lay all over the floor. The manager had clearly had some sort of fit, then just given up and vanished.

I eased myself into the office chair and placed my feet on the desk. I had no staff and no customers. I didn't even have a bed. But I had my own shop. Napoleon said the English were a nation of shopkeepers. I had arrived!

I stuck a note on the door saying 'Staff Wanted' and stepped out to explore the High Street. There was a decent enough pub, the Stag & Hounds, and a tandoori restaurant, so that was my everyday needs covered. At the small, family-run furniture store I bought a cheap mattress and, balancing it on my head like an Indian bricklayer, returned to the shop and installed it in the office.

Having worked up an appetite, I took a seat in the Kabul Tandoori and waved to the waiter. It was lunchtime but I was the only customer. He handed me a sticky menu. "May I look at your wine list please?" Sure enough, a very old fashioned list of wines, all cheap French plonk, some of the names misspelt. No wonder there was something of a customer drought, I doubted the staff knew their Chablis from their Champagne. If this was to be my dining room I'd need to improve the beverage selection, sharpish. I asked to speak to the manager. An apprehensive-looking man with a superb moustache appeared from the back.

"Felix is the name, I'm the new wine merchant round here," I said, pumping his hand. "How about I re-write your wine list for you and throw in the first order for free? I'll match the pricing of your current supplier and I'll deliver wine within five minutes of you ordering it, seven days a week."

By the end of the meal I had my first customer and a free rogan josh into the bargain. I retired to the Stag & Hounds and got chatting to the landlady, a rather attractive woman whose low-cut top suggested a generous and nurturing manner. That was my second customer of the day landed and, going by the looks she was giving me by the end of the night, I suspected I'd be delivering more than a case of French dry white next time I was in.

After last orders I returned to the shop and bedded down for the night on my new mattress. As I drifted off I heard the sound of drunks fighting on the street outside and scratching from the corner of the stockroom. I made a mental note to buy some mousetraps and sighed with contentment. A skin-full of beer, the muffled sound of fisticuffs and the patter of little vermin feet – just like my old school days at Felching Orchard. I was soon sleeping like a baby.

The next day was one of action. Using a length of cord and a plastic bucket with holes punched in the base, I rigged up a workable field-shower in the toilet. Then I isolated the last dozen decent bottles of wine and spirits and placed them on a special shelf in the back for personal consumption. It wasn't misappropriation of course, it was education. How could I sell the finest wines to the good folk of Little Chalfont if I hadn't drunk them myself? It would be fraudulent to even try.

The roar of an engine and the hiss of air-brakes heralded the arrival of the Charlie's Cellar delivery truck, laden with my new stock. It was a huge order – the grunting driver and his red-faced mate wheeled in no fewer than twenty towering pallets, filling the entire stockroom. I had a hard day ahead of me unless I could quickly recruit some staff.

I hadn't had much luck on that front. The only applicants had been a teenaged youth with yellow pimples who asked if we sold glue and a shuffling pensioner with an unkempt beard who smelt as though he had recently bathed in whisky and urine.

There was nothing for it but to neck a mug of Madame Joubert's Lekker Medisyne Trommel and get stuck in myself. By the end of the day I had restocked the shelves, built several towering wine displays and the shop was ready to trade. I propped open the front door to see if I could drum up any evening business and poured myself a glass of a rather excellent Rioja Gran Reserva.

Wodin wandered in, barefoot despite the January chill, wearing his sarong and a multi-coloured ethnic jacket. "Excellent. You've got it scrubbed up nicely."

"Indeed. Are you a wine connoisseur, Wodin, or do you only drink rainwater filtered through the back passage of a local druid?"

"Very amusing, my shop-keeping friend. I do indeed partake of the vine." Wodin took a bottle of expensive Australian Shiraz from the top shelf. "What kind of friendly neighbourhood discount can you do on this then?"

Now, I was still relatively new to retail but I knew that discounts were a thing to be offered sparingly, rather as one might occasionally feed a large dog a tasty morsel of steak, lest the recipient become greedy, complacent and ultimately, when suddenly denied their treat, turn upon you in a blind and savage fury.

"I'm terribly sorry. I'm only permitted to offer discounts to customers who order by the case-load."

"Disappointing, my man. I may have to take my business elsewhere."

I had an idea. "How about a special skirt-wearing hippy discount, in exchange for a nice bed and lodgings upstairs?"

Wodin considered my offer. "Now that is more in line with the sharing economy, my friend. And as I have told you once already, this is a sarong. I am obliged to audition anyone who wishes to share our tranquil homestead."

"You want me to sing a song?"

"No. I want you to prove that you are cool and down with the kids." Wodin extracted a large joint from his pocket.

"Aren't you concerned about doing that on CCTV?"

"Your CCTV doesn't work. Which is why the local criminal fraternity keep knocking off this good shop."

It was true. I had just put in an order for a new camera system but it was unlikely to arrive for another month. "You'd better come through to the office."

So Wodin and I shared his potent spliff, and a very pleasant little number it was too. We chatted over the rest of the Rioja and I gave him the bottle of Aussie wine for free, in exchange for a promise that he would discuss, with the rest of the occupants, my application to become a flatmate.

Just before closing, I had some more luck. A presentable young Polish lady put her head round the door and asked whether she could apply for the advertised position. Since she appeared to have four working limbs, a reasonable grasp of English and didn't smell like an item of decayed taxidermy, I gave her a job on the spot.

Over the next few days the locals noticed the store was back in business and customers began to trickle in. Little Chalfont was an affluent village and there were plenty of people in the market for fine wine. I took on more evening staff and, after a couple of weeks, my complement of workers was complete, so I was able to spend most evenings down the Stag & Hounds. Angela, the landlady, was only too happy to let me stay over every so often, in exchange for a little light work around the bedroom.

Sales were increasing at a good rate and Richards was very pleased. He popped in to check the figures, nodding approvingly over the jump in profitability. "You do appear to be writing a lot of stock off against the tasting budget, however," he noted.

"Vital sir, to hook in some of those big spenders. I can't increase sales without showing the wares, can I?"

"You appear to know what you're doing, I suppose," he shrugged. "Any problems from the local criminal fraternity?"

For a moment I thought he meant Wodin from upstairs. Then I remembered the robbery problems they'd had last year. "No, nothing like that."

"Good. See you in a month or so then. Keep this up and one day you might get one of those."

He nodded towards his company car, a brand new Vauxhall Cavalier. He patted me on the shoulder and departed.

I had spoken too soon.

The following day, in the name of education, I uncorked a rather cheeky New Zealand Pinot Noir in the back office. I poured a glass, savoured the wonderful, berry-scented aroma and took a little sip. The bell sounded, informing me a customer had opened the front door, so I swallowed the wine and strode out to greet them.

For a second, I thought a particularly ugly veiled woman had entered the shop. Then, with horror, I realised it was a slender-built man with a stocking over his head.

"Do you know how much damage this will do if I fire it into your belly?" He had a rather rough voice. I suspected he had not schooled at Eton, as Lady Edith might have said. He was a few inches shorter than me, dressed in dark clothes and dirty trainers. He carried an old empty sports bag. But my main concern was the object in his other hand – a wooden stock, from which protruded a short double barrel wrapped loosely in a plastic bag. It looked very much like a sawn-off shotgun.

"A lot?" I suggested, my bowels twitching with fear.

"Yes, a lot. So lock that door before I make a mess of you!" He thrust the gun at me, aiming it at my stomach. I was too far from the office door to make a run for it and I knew it would have been a suicidal move anyway. At that range he wouldn't even need to aim – a couple of feet either side and I'd still be peppered like a Swiss cheese.

My stomach gurgled in horror as he stepped even closer. I could see his bared teeth through the stocking mask. I pulled the keys from my pocket with a shaking hand. Oh sweet Mary, please don't shoot me! Why couldn't he have held up one of the evening girls? There would have been more money on the premises then too, the idiot.

"Stop looking at me!" he shouted.

I looked down and walked to the front door. He followed right behind, shoving the barrel into the small of my back for good measure. No chance of making a quick dash outside. I turned the key in the lock.

"Now, open the safe."

He shoved the barrel into the back of my neck this time. I wanted to tell him he really didn't need to keep prodding me – I was already on the verge of decorating my pants. I had visions of his nervous finger slipping on the trigger and a red-hot cloud of lead blasting through my delicate body. Did he really have to point it right at me? For God's sake, did he not know the first thing about gun safety?

"It … it … it's on a time lock," I stammered.

"I know it is. Move!"

Ah, a regular customer. I tried to look on the bright side – at least the long history of armed crime at this store had never included a murder. But might he make an exception this time? He could be on drugs. Or maybe he wasn't on drugs and was very angry about it. I wondered if I should offer him some Pinot Noir. I also considered explaining that, despite being a big chap, I definitely wouldn't be trying any heroics.

"And don't go trying anything clever. I know where the alarm button is."

"I definitely won't, sir."

"That's better. Call me 'sir'."

I turned the key in the sunken safe lid and started the time lock. It buzzed quietly as the clockwork mechanism counted down the fifteen minutes.

"Now sit on the floor!"

He shoved the barrel hard into my thigh in a very unfriendly way. It knocked against the penknife in my pocket which I'd used to open the Pinot Noir – there was a dull clunk of metal against metal. I sat down, cross-legged, next to the safe and faced away from him, looking at the floor. Well, this was awkward. We had fifteen minutes to kill, no pun intended, and I really didn't feel like chatting. Luckily, nor did he.

Finally, the time-lock pinged, and I climbed to my feet, reaching out to detach the heavy lid from the safe.

"Careful!" he warned, nestling the barrel against the front of my trousers.

That focused my mind, I can tell you. I shivered and gave the weapon an involuntary glance. I saw the flimsy plastic bag had split slightly where it covered the end of the barrel, exposing the muzzle. It must have been when he grazed it against my pen-knife. Something about it looked strange.

"Put everything in there!" he demanded, dropping the battered sports bag at my feet.

I took another look. Instead of dark metal, the protruding barrels of the shotgun were orange in colour. Who on earth has an orange shotgun, I wondered. But it wasn't orange, it dawned on me, it was copper. And you don't make gun barrels out of soft copper – you make them out of hard steel. Our friend had simply stuck a couple of water pipes onto a wooden handle and was merrily using it to terrorise the good shopkeepers of Buckinghamshire.

I breathed a little sigh of relief – I wasn't going to get my crown jewels shot off after all. But what should I do? I started to transfer the money into his bag, reaching into the safe and lifting out the neat bundles of used notes, one at a time.

"Hurry up!" He prodded me with the barrel again.

I could just give him an almighty thrashing. That really appealed. I was feeling rather sore about having a pretend gun shoved in various parts of my body, and he wasn't a very heavily built chap. He might have a knife, of course, but one well-aimed roundhouse from young Felix and he'd be down like a sack of spuds.

But first, a little refreshment, my mouth was somewhat dry after all the drama. I walked over to the desk and downed the rest of the Pinot Noir. "Excellent! Have you ever been to Central Otago, old bean? They make quite exquisite Pinot."

"Do you have a death wish, you posh twat? Get over here and fill the bag!" he screamed.

I strolled back to the safe and was curling my right fist into a ball when I heard a key turn in the front door. It was Daphne, one of the evening girls, arriving for her four p.m. shift.

"Who the hell's that?" shouted chummy, in an even more panicked tone. The customer bell sounded, indicating the door had opened. He levelled his toy gun at my chest.

"Hiya!" called Daphne. "Why is the front door locked?"

"It's Daphne," I said, deadpan. "She's a black belt in ju-jitsu. She'll probably tear your head off and introduce it to your colon. I've seen her do it before."

"What the…?" he snarled, digging the pretend weapon harder into my ribs, causing me to squeak 'Ouch!' quite involuntarily. I'd had quite enough of chummy's aggressive massage technique for one day and I confess I slightly lost my temper.

The filthy chiseller was leaning over, trying to get sight of Daphne making her way through the shop, so I lifted the heavy top of the safe and swung it at his head as hard as I could. He didn't see it coming. The corner made contact with his skull with a rather sickening crunch and he was knocked across the stock-room floor, his useless gun clattering to the ground.

"Stay back Daphne!" I shouted. "There's a robbery in progress!" I peered at the motionless robber. He lay face down on the floor, legs akimbo, arms splayed either side of him.

I gave him a little kick between the legs, in case he was pretending. He didn't move at all. I noticed a small pool of blood next to his head and I looked at the heavy safe lid. There appeared to be a chunk of scalp and hair on the corner. It occurred to me I might have struck him a little too hard. I put my head round the door of the office. Daphne was frozen in the middle of the shop, her face a picture of terror.

"Hi Daphne. Don't worry, everything's under control. Would you mind calling the police and an ambulance please?"

"What's happening?" she whimpered.

"There's been a bit of brouhaha. We may have to close the shop for a couple of hours. Now, if you could just make that phone call, please. I feel a little weak. I think I may be going into shock."

I returned to the office and re-corked the bottle of Pinot, hiding it behind a pile of boxes, then washed out the glass and replaced it on the shelf. I'd become rather proud of the shop and I didn't want things looking sloppy when the authorities turned up.

I'll give the police their due – they arrived very quickly, and in force. Little Chalfont is not generally considered a hotbed of terror, so this was definitely a red-letter day for them. No fewer than five police cars and a van turned up, and I counted twenty coppers, uniformed and plain-clothed, in the store at one point.

The robber was carried out on a stretcher. He was as dead as a doornail. I'd pretty much knocked the top half of his head off with the great slab of steel. As the body was loaded into the ambulance, I felt a twinge of sympathy for the poor boob. Perhaps he had a brood of hungry children at home and was attempting to provide for them the only way he knew how, with low wit and brute force.

Worse still, I could imagine Richards taking a dim view of the whole situation. The shop might be closed for some time and I could see him marking me down as an unreliable and impulsive type, not to be trusted with anything larger than a small village off-licence. A promising career, just taking off, shot out of the sky at first flight.

I put my head in my hands and sighed. "Oh God. What a waste."

A female police constable placed her hand on my shoulder. "Don't blame yourself, Felix. Guilt is a common emotion in situations like this." She had short blonde hair, a sensitive, pretty face, and her blue police jumper was stretched tight over her chest. She wore a little badge stating 'WPC Anne Peters, Trauma Counsellor' over her pert left breast.

The distress of the past hour melted away, like a Marbella ice cube in the bottom of a swiftly consumed gin and tonic.

"I just feel as though I've let everybody down, Constable."

She took my hand. "Call me Anne. We'll have to take a statement from you, but we can do that in the trauma centre at the station. It's comfortable and there's no rush. You can even have a lie down, if you need to."

I have always been a great supporter of the forces of law and order, and the empathy shown by the newer generation of female police officers is a credit to the service. I took my time over the statement, lingering over the terrible threats of violence to which I had been subjected.

"You have an unusually deep emotional sensitivity, Felix," she reassured me, as we sat side by side in the trauma suite, her hand resting professionally upon my shoulder. Well, if this wasn't love, I don't know what the hell it was. She was everything anyone could look for in a woman – calm, attentive, a good listener and quite stunningly beautiful.

I suppose, with hindsight, the mental disturbance caused by the robbery might have upset my judgement. WPC Peters explained, patiently and kindly, that it was professionally inappropriate for her to stroke my manhood back to emotional health. She explained that confused sexual responses, such as my stonking hard-on, were all too common in cases of mild post-traumatic stress, though not before she'd given me a couple of friendly squeezes through my trousers. I didn't see anything wrong with that. After all, my John Thomas had been a victim of crime, too.

CHAPTER FIVE - TINTO TOWERS

"Well, we can't condone reckless behaviour, Felix." Gary Richards tapped his fingers on the counter. "Company policy is very clear – no heroics when faced with a dangerous incident."

"I understand, sir. I never would have done anything like this if it hadn't been for Daphne's sudden arrival at the front door." I paused for a second and looked at the floor. "I would never have forgiven myself if anything had happened to her."

"You're a fine man, Felix, don't worry about it." This from Clive Willoughby, the Director of Wine. He had travelled all the way from Head Office, no less.

It was a month after the attempted robbery and we were standing in the middle of Little Chalfont store a few minutes before opening time – Richards, looking slightly peeved; Willoughby, suave in his pinstriped suit; and another man, a cynical-looking ex-detective who was the company's Head of Security.

I had been sent abroad on paid study leave for a couple of weeks, to avoid the media furore that erupted following my self-less act of have-a-go heroism. I'd spent the time in Andalucía, improving my knowledge of Sherry, tapas and Spanish student life, and a rich, culturally immersive experience it had been too.

"But it was still a serious breach of policy," said Richards.

"Oh, raspberries to your policy, Gary," said Willoughby. "Felix here is one of our superstars. You told me he ran Crouch End over

Christmas, not to mention most of the preceding year, and he's single-handedly taken over this place and turned it around." He looked around the well-stocked shelves and nodded, approvingly.

"And he got rid of that slag Philips who'd been terrorising the area for the past year," noted the Head of Security. Philips, it turned out, was the name of the unfortunate robber, now at peace in a cheap urn in the 'unclaimed' section of the local council's crematorium.

But Richards wouldn't let it go. "It caused a great deal of paperwork and disruption. He might have been prosecuted for murder!"

"Oh, hardly! It's not as if he deliberately killed an unarmed man, is it?" said the Head of Security, scanning the shelf of single malts wistfully. "Done us a favour, really."

"Is Felix in the clear, then?" asked Willoughby.

"Yes. I've had a chat to the local Inspector and they have no intention of taking it any further. It's a clear case of self-defence through the use of reasonable force. The CPS has no intention of pressing charges and no jury would ever convict in a situation like this. Job done."

"Jolly good," said Willoughby. "Felix, I understand you are something of a self-educated wine authority?"

"Well, sir, I have developed a huge passion for the subject. It helps when one is trying to sell, of course, but I do find the world of wine fascinating. My only wish would be for a larger tasting budget, so I could learn even more." I glanced at Richards, who was still frowning. "But I do appreciate there are costs to control." I gave him an earnest, look-after-the-pennies nod.

"Oh, for heaven's sake! Sod the budgets. Felix, if you want to try a wine or run a tasting, you go ahead. You can charge it to my personal cost-code."

"Thank you sir! I can't wait to try those new Burgundies we've listed."

"Good man. You see Gary, that's how to make money! Invest in our people, what?"

"Yes, I suppose so," muttered Richards, wincing like a miser in a coin-operated lavatory.

"Right, well, keep up the good work Felix. You must come up to Head Office one day and say hello. And good luck with the Australian sales competition."

The three men left.

Ah yes, the annual Australian Sales Incentive. Every January, in the week running up to Australia Day, every store in the group competed to sell the most Aussie wine. The top prize was a fortnight long, all expenses paid trip to Australia, to roll around the vineyards in a state of advanced inebriation, serenading young sheilas up the billabong and generally raising merry hell.

Well, that was my interpretation – officially it was an educational visit, funded by the Australian High Commission. There were also some runner-up prizes of Aussie-themed merchandise, but as far as I was concerned you could shove your stuffed koalas up the nearest gum tree – I was going for the full monty.

The competition began the next day and I had a plan as ruthless as a marsupial with a knuckle-duster in its pouch. I hired a smart Rover Montego estate car which I filled with Australian wine, all funded by Willoughby's gold-plated tasting budget. Then I toured the restaurants, hotels and pubs of Buckinghamshire, dialling the Felix Hart charm up to maximum and selling my little socks off. I would waltz into a restaurant, find the main decision-maker and carry out an impromptu wine tasting, accompanied by a poetic, mouth-watering commentary. Any punters who exhibited even the slightest resistance would be promised a couple of bottles for free if they felt the wines weren't up to scratch.

Nobody turned me down, of course. That first day I bagged a dozen orders and plenty of potential follow-ups. The biggest order came from the landlady of the Queen's Head in Ley Hill. She bought thirty cases after I offered her a five-percent discount, a free case of tasting stock and agreed to her suggestion of a right royal docking in the tap room downstairs. Angela at the Stag & Hounds came a close second, in more ways than one, after signing up for twenty cases, and even good old Abdul down the Indian restaurant bought half a dozen, although I'm pleased to say I didn't have to drop my pants for that one.

When I returned to the shop that evening, we turned that shop into an Aussie wine theme park. Every bottle of French, Italian and Californian wine, anything that wasn't from Down Under, in fact, was removed from the shelves and hidden in the storeroom. Instead, the shelves burst exclusively with the Barossa, Coonawarra and Hunter Valley's finest.

Unsurprisingly, Aussie sales went through the roof. A couple of customers complained they couldn't buy their favourite French Chablis, but we had a dozen wines lined up on the counter for free tasting and, with a no quibble money-back guarantee, we converted even the most ardent Francophile to the glories of Wallaby Claret.

I spent the rest of the week on the road, racking up larger and larger orders. By the time I'd finished my sales blitz, nearly every restaurant in Buckinghamshire had an Aussie special at the top of their wine list. I even persuaded the local vicar to convert his communion wine to Possum Merlot.

And so Australia Day, 26 January, came and went. The following morning, we returned all the French, Italian and Californian wines to our shelves and waited to see if we'd won.

Wodin wandered in around lunchtime, picked a bottle of Champagne from the fridge and walked through to the back office. "I see the Antipodean love-fest has come to an end?"

"Yes, indeed. Nice of you to treat yourself to one of my bottles of expensive Champagne."

"Join me. We have something to celebrate." He lit a large joint and eased the cork out of the bottle. He poured two glasses, offering me the spliff with one hand and Champagne with the other. "You're moving in. It's official. We have assessed you thoroughly and are delighted to declare you a worthy addition to our community."

"I'm allowed into my own house, you mean. That's great news."

We clinked glasses. I'm not a high maintenance guy but, to be honest, I had become bored with showering under a bucket hanging from the ceiling of the staff toilet every morning. So that evening I carried my mattress and kit bag up the iron steps at the back of the shop and entered the front door of number two.

As Richards had hinted, prior to my taking the Little Chalfont job, the place was vast. It had three floors, the top two each boasting three bedrooms while the lower floor consisted of a large kitchen and lounge. Most of the windowsills were lined with pot plants of a distinctly medicinal aroma, while the kitchen contained a large black plastic tank the size of a rainwater barrel, smelling mildly of pickled vegetables.

"What's that?" I asked.

"A waste fermenter. One of our fellow residents, Fistule, is a passionate composter. All the food scraps and waste paper go in there, and after a couple of months it's used for the pot plants."

The place was rather run-down, with no central heating and ancient metal-framed windows. The lounge, however, was warm and comfortable, with a roaring fireplace and four mismatched sofas lining its perimeter. The only other furniture was a well-stocked bookshelf and a pair of low tables, both of which were strewn with torn-up pieces of cardboard, cigarette papers and loose tobacco.

Wodin introduced me to his two flatmates. Mercedes, curled up on the sofa nearest the fire, was around twenty, dressed in black combat trousers and a colourful jacket in coarse wool. She had thin, fine features and her black dreadlocks were threaded with multi-coloured ribbons and studded with silver rings. She smiled and raised a hand in greeting, before returning to her doze.

"And this is Fistule. He's the composter."

"Hi man." Fistule sat cross-legged in front of one of the tables, crumbling a small block of hashish onto the gauze atop an elaborate water pipe. He was short and stocky, with a dark bushy beard covering his pudgy neck. He was barefoot and wore a brown jacket with tassels and dark jeans, giving him the air of a benign but hairy toad in human clothes.

"Try this, man." Fistule held a lighter over the pile of powdery hashish and inhaled hard through the mouthpiece. The flame dipped and danced over the hash as thick smoke rushed into the glass chamber, where it bubbled through a grim-looking yellowish liquid. He exhaled slowly and sighed with pleasure. "Here man, don't waste it." He pointed the end of the pipe at me.

It seemed best to be polite – these were to be my close companions for the foreseeable future – so I stooped and held the mouthpiece to my lips, inhaling some of the smoke. It had an unusual but familiar taste, a hint of iodine and peat over the pungent, floral resin of the hashish.

"That's pure Nepalese hash, bubbled through a sixteen-year-old Islay single malt," announced Fistule, with evident pride.

I inhaled again, deeper this time. The smoke was cool and delicious, like potpourri mixed with a gentle breath of antiseptic. "Very nice. Fistule is an unusual name. Where's it from?"

"When I was young, I had a fistula," he said.

"What's a fistula?"

"It's a pipe between two chambers. Like this," he tapped the brass tube leading from the smoking gauze into the water chamber.

"So you're named after a bong?"

"No, it's a medical thing. I had a fistula in my intestines when I was young. I had to take lots of time off from school and, in the end, people stopped using my real name and just called me Fistule. Even my Mum."

"But you're called Fistule, not Fistula?"

"Fistule is the French translation. I think it sounds classier."

I was suddenly extremely stoned. I sank back into one of the sofas and passed out.

I woke the next day, still sprawled on the sofa, with a dry throat and a rather sluggish head. But I was pleased to have the use of a genuine shower for the first time in a month. There was no sound from the rest of the house – I assumed my new flatmates were sleeping in. I wandered into the kitchen in search of a kettle, to find Mercedes in the centre of the room practising tai chi, wearing her combat trousers and a knitted bikini top.

"Carry on," she breathed, circling her clasped hands, her body rising and falling gently as she flexed her knees.

I wasn't sure what I was supposed to carry on with. I watched, fascinated, as she slowly danced on the spot, her slim body flowing from side to side. Little tufts of bushy black hair winked from her armpits as her arms rose and fell, and her ribbon-festooned dreadlocks followed the movement of her head.

It was mesmerising and, I confess, more than a little exciting. I cleared my throat, tearing my eyes from the tiny pert breasts barely covered by her knitted top, and filled the kettle, turning so she wouldn't notice my reawakened morning glory. Being a gentleman, I left her a cup of tea and, closing the front door quietly behind me, I descended the cold outside stairs to the shop below.

As I did so, an elderly female voice called out, "Who are you? I'm calling the police!"

I turned to see a scowling, wrinkled face at the open upstairs window of number three. I gave her a wave. "Morning madam! I'm your new neighbour!"

There was a pause and I continued down the stairs. "We don't like transvestites!" she screeched back.

I glanced down to check I hadn't slipped into one of Wodin's sarongs. "Couldn't agree more, madam. You never know what's happening down there, do you?"

As I unlocked the shop door, I could hear the phone ringing. I skipped in and leant over the counter. "Charlie's Cellar, Little Chalfont. How can I help you today?"

"Felix. It's Clive Willoughby. Good to hear you're in nice and early. How's business?" I hoped he wasn't going to complain about my battering of his tasting budget.

"Business is booming, sir. The recent Australia Day promotion went very well."

"I'll say it did! I'll come straight to the point, Felix. You sold more than any other store in the entire country. You're going to Australia!"

Had there been a digeridoo nearby, I'd have piped out the Ode to Joy. Goodbye cold British February, hello Bondi Beach! "That's wonderful news, sir. I'm sure the whole Little Chalfont team will be thrilled." Not as thrilled as me, though, to be honest.

"Always thinking of the team, Felix. I like it. You must come up to Head Office when you're back from your travels. It's the educational trip of a lifetime and the buying team would love to hear what you've learnt."

Big wave surfing, how to barbecue a yabbie, and the Southern Hemisphere's top shagging positions with a bit of luck. "I can't wait to study the interaction between soil type and climate in the Coonawarra, sir."

"Good man. Enjoy the trip."

***

I did of course. I even learnt rather more about wine than I expected. The Aussies don't take things too seriously but they do appreciate a good drop, so I was plied with drink wherever

I went, from the Hunter Valley to the Margaret River. I won't give you a blow by blow account of every winery, but I must have tasted a hundred wines every day.

It was harvest time and the highlight was the floodlit, night-time joyrides on the automated picking machines, the giant tractors racing down the rows of vines, their paddles slapping at the stems and shaking the grapes onto their conveyor belts. Then, in the winery, we'd strip to our underwear and punch down the floating morass of grape skins in the great concrete fermenting tanks, the purple liquid foaming as the grape sugars turned to alcohol, yours truly getting admiring glances from the young female cellar hands, and maybe a few jealous males too.

And there was some great R&R – there's nothing like a hard day in the winery to work up an appetite. We ended each day with a massive barbecue overlooking the vineyards, lamb steaks and crayfish hissing over the coals, corks pulled and great beakers of wine poured. Then, with flattering regularity, an athletic, beach-perfect cellar girl would take me by the hand and urge me back into the vineyard for a grand nubbing between the vines.

By the time I landed back at Heathrow and caught the juddering train back to cold, drizzling Little Chalfont I had decided on the trajectory of my future career. And no, it was not that of a shopkeeper in a sleepy Home Counties village. I'd had enough of armed robbers, underage cider garglers and dribbling drunks swapping their snot-encrusted small change for flasks of vodka.

My destiny was to be an international wine buyer, a gold-card-carrying traveller extraordinaire following the vintage around the globe, sipping wine in sun-kissed vineyards, doing million-dollar deals with tanned Mediterranean aristocrats and shaping the wine drinking tastes of the world.

I marched straight from the station into the shop, through to the back office, picked up the phone and dialled Head Office.

"Hello. This is Felix Hart. I'm phoning to make an appointment to see Clive Willoughby and the wine buying team."

I had to make this count.

* * *

The following week I caught the tube into London and arrived at Tinto Towers, the unassuming North London office block that housed the head office of Charlie's Cellar.

Willoughby's secretary met me at reception and showed me upstairs. The place was cramped, decorated in shades of dark cream, and smelt of stale cigarettes. She knocked on the door marked Director of Wine.

"Come!" I entered, to see the whole buying team sitting around Willoughby's desk. He leapt to his feet and shook my hand. "Welcome, young Felix! Let me introduce you to everyone."

I shook hands with each of the three wine buyers: Gillian, a conservatively dressed woman in pearl earrings; Paul, a very tall, serious-looking chap; and Henri, a raffish-looking Frenchman.

"Enchanté Felix," winked Henri.

"And this is Benedict, our Assistant Wine Buyer."

A pale, sensitive-looking young man, around my age, with wispy brown hair, held out his hand. It was damp and limp and he looked away as I shook it. "Soon to be a real buyer, I trust?" he said to Willoughby in a plaintive, whining voice.

"Benedict is studying for his Minstrel of Wine qualification," explained Willoughby. "Fingers crossed he'll join their hallowed ranks alongside Gillian and Paul here, then we can boast a hat-trick of Minstrels!"

"Very impressive," I said.

Willoughby clapped his hands. "So, Felix, let's hear about your trip to Australia!" In a stage whisper he added, for the benefit of the others, "Felix is our star salesman – he single-handedly turned around two of our most important stores, and he won this year's Aussie wine competition into the bargain!"

The other buyers nodded and smiled. Benedict sulked and stared at the ceiling.

"I took the liberty of bringing a couple of samples with me." I'd made sure to bring home a couple of rare bottles from my trip down under – wines that would be impossible to find in England. I drew the first bottle from my bag. It was a Sangiovese from Victoria, made by a winemaker whose Italian grandfather had smuggled vine cuttings out from the old country. I poured each of them a glass and humbly suggested how it compared to a traditional Chianti which, as any wine enthusiast knows, is made from the same grape variety.

I then revealed my second bottle, a fifty-year-old Australian Tawny Port. It should have cost a fortune, but the kind sales manager in Rutherglen had taken a shine to me and, to cut a long story short, she was happy to swap the bottle for a sampling of British beef. The buyers' eyes opened wide, and even Benedict appeared impressed for a second before he remembered himself and reverted to his sickly sneer.

"You're spoiling us here, young Felix," smiled Gillian. "I must confess I have never tasted a fortified Rutherglen as old as this!" The others concurred as I poured a short measure of the treacly liquid into each glass.

"Ohh. Zat is 'eaven!" declared Henri. The others nodded and a lively conversation ensued regarding the merits of fortified wine from Portugal, Spain and Australia.

"Well, Felix," said Willoughby. "You've done us proud – we never expected to be educated by one of our own store managers!"

"Oh, not at all sir," I protested, brimming as modestly as my pride permitted.

"Benedict! Why don't you take Felix through to the tasting room and we'll join you shortly."

Benedict made a face like a man asked to sample a range of used cat litter.

Willoughby turned back to me. "We're tasting a flight of fine white Burgundy this afternoon. You must join us. It would be interesting to know your thoughts."

"I would be delighted, sir. Thank you so much."

Benedict rose and pushed open the door, as aggressively as his puny arms could manage. I followed as he marched down the corridor, making no effort to wait for me. He paused at the entrance to the tasting room. "That awful, unbalanced, loutish port of yours has quite overwhelmed my palate. I need some water."

"Oh, I do apologise. Is there a tap somewhere?"

Benedict snorted, incredulously, and pointed to his mouth with both hands. "Does this look like a palate that drinks tap water?"

It looks like a palate that needs a slap with a kipper, I thought. I had a suspicion that Benedict might be an impediment to my entry into the Charlie's Cellar wine buying team. "Would you like me to fetch you some mineral water?"

"Good idea, store boy."

Anxious to please, in under a minute I was down the brown-carpeted stairwell, through reception and into the street. As I perused the fridge in a nearby corner store, I hit upon a terrific plan.

I had never shared Madame Joubert's Lekker Medisyne Trommel with anyone. I was already a quarter of the way into Mr du Plessis's priceless gift and I didn't intend to deplete it any faster than necessary. I had a theory, however, that this extraordinary powder not only restored one's dash, but amplified the more generous and wholesome aspects of one's character. Might a generous dose not improve Benedict's temperament, perhaps inclining him to look more favourably on a humble shop boy? Might he even extend a helping hand, hauling a fellow wine enthusiast on to the corporate trampoline?

I selected a bottle of water, which boasted of gentle familiarity with the scent of forest fruits and, furthermore, was unsullied by added sugar or sweeteners. Before re-entering Tinto Towers, I fished a sachet of Madame Joubert's from my pocket and poured it into the bottle. It fizzed and foamed until it had vanished. I screwed the top back on and gave the pinkish water a little shake. I tasted it and recognised the gentle chalk flavour, now married to a hint of blackberry and redcurrant.

When I returned to the tasting room, most of the team had already assembled. "Ah, there you are Felix," said Willoughby, glass in hand, "wondered where you'd vanished to."

"Benedict asked me to find him a little palate cleanser," I explained. I turned to the Assistant Wine Buyer and held out the bottle. "Here you go. I'm so sorry, they only had lightly flavoured water."

"Oh, for pity's sake!" he moaned, as though I had asked him to sup from a horse trough.

"I checked – there are no sweeteners or nasty additives in there. I know how important it is to protect such a finely calibrated tongue."

"Don't be ungrateful Benedict," said Willoughby, rolling his eyes. "Drink the water, for goodness sake."

Benedict sniffed the bottle and pointed at me. "If this bruises my taste buds ... I shall not be responsible for my actions!"

I nodded solemnly as he drank the water.

The door opened and Henri entered, accompanied by a faint aroma of cigarette smoke. "Alors! Let us taste these wonderful wines."

"When are we going to ban smoking from this building?" whined Benedict. "I cannot bear it. I have such a sensitive palate."

You'd have a very sensitive behind if I stuck my boot up it, you dreadful little squit, I thought. I reprimanded myself. Who was I to cultivate uncharitable thoughts about a valued member of the Charlie's Cellar buying department?

"I think the senior logistics chaps might revolt if we did that, Benedict. Live and let live, eh?" Willoughby patted him on the shoulder as he sniffed and tutted.

We began the tasting, and a fabulous flight of wines it was too. To start, a series of poised Chablis crus, then we progressed to more generous whites from the Côte d'Or.

"Is everything alright, Benedict?" asked Gillian suddenly.

Benedict was staring into his glass, tears rolling down his cheeks. His face was looking rather red and I recognised the tingling flush of Madame Joubert's. "If one does not weep over Puligny Montrachet, then one has no soul!" he declared.

"You are a sensitive chap, aren't you," commented Willoughby, taking a delicate sip of his own.

We tasted on.

"What do you think of this Chassagne, Felix?" asked Willoughby.

"I'm no expert, sir, but it's very generous in body. Perhaps a little too generous?"

"Oh please!" spluttered Benedict through his tears.

"Benedict, calm down," ordered Gillian, softly. Then to me, "Please continue, Felix."

"Well, I prefer something a touch more restrained. I feel the oak is just a little too prominent."

"Thank you Felix. Good comment."

"Perhaps a couple more years will help integrate the oak," I added.

The buyers nodded to one another. By Jove, I was good at this. I noticed Benedict writhing with frustration at the attention I was receiving. Clearly, the Madame Joubert's was not calming his mind in the way I had hoped.

"And 'ow about this Bâtard?" asked Henri, an eyebrow raised as he nosed his way into a new glass.

For a split-second I thought he meant Benedict, then I recalled Bâtard was the name of a prestigious Burgundian village. It was time to turn the ponce dial up to eleven and let rip.

"If Puligny is a symphony," I began, my face turned upwards, quite possibly receiving inspiration from the good Lord himself, "then Bâtard is a string ensemble. It may not have the majesty but it has the more exquisite poise."

"For the love of God!" screamed Benedict.

"Goodness, Benedict, will you pipe down!" snapped Willoughby.

"No, I'm sorry, I will not be silenced! What does this shop-boy know of Bâtard-Montrachet? I see you for what you are! You're a blunt tool!"

"Benedict! That's enough!"

To my dismay, Benedict's opinion of me appeared to have worsened. He dipped up and down on the balls of his feet, swirling his wine faster and faster. There was a wild look in his eyes and he shook with rage. "You're nothing but … but … a slut! You're a slut! A wine slut!" He laughed maniacally, looking at each of us in turn. Then, still spinning his wine glass like a dervish, he hurled the contents at me. "Taste that, you slut!"

"Goodness," I muttered, removing a handkerchief and dabbing the fine Burgundy from my face. I feared my audition with the buying team might be shortly at an end. In the interests of full disclosure, I should confess that I'd emptied a double dose of Madame Joubert's into Benedict's bottle, completely against Mr du Plessis's clear instructions. Still, strictly speaking, he'd said that I should never take more than one teaspoon – there was no injunction against giving a larger dose to someone else – and I'd felt that Benedict could only benefit from a king-size shot of vim.

"Good God, Benedict, what the hell's got into you?" demanded Willoughby. "Felix, are you all right?"

"He's a slut! A tart! Are you all blind?"

The others had edged away from Benedict now – he was sweating profusely and had puffed up his hollow chest. "I shall be the minstrel! I shall taste and then, I shall dance!" He began to hop up and down, then to spin on the toe of one foot, arms held above his head, like a crack-addled ballerina. He emitted a single, high falsetto note as he spun faster and faster. I made a mental note never to take more than one teaspoon of Madame Joubert's.

Gillian lifted a jug of water and hurled the contents at Benedict's face. He staggered and stopped spinning, looking at us in shock. "You bitch!" he whispered and slapped Gillian's face.

"Right, you arse 'ole," shouted Henri, grasping Benedict from behind. With Paul's help he wrestled Benedict into the corridor. We piled out after them, just as Benedict broke free. He aimed a kick at Willoughby, catching him in the groin. The Director of Wine doubled over, his glasses falling to the floor.

"Slut!" screamed Benedict, and ran at me.

I caught him in the stomach with a well-timed upset punch. It seemed the kindest thing to do in the circumstances. He doubled up and collapsed, then vomited heavily. Oh well, better out than in, I thought, particularly if he suspects someone slipped him a mickey and visits a doctor.

Henri and Paul grabbed the now rather limp Benedict and dragged him down the corridor, while Gillian put her arm around poor old Willoughby, who was wheezing heavily, and helped him to a chair. I followed the others down the stairs and was shocked to hear Paul instructing the receptionist not to allow Benedict back in the building ever again.

We all returned to the tasting room where Willoughby had finally caught his breath. Gillian handed him his spectacles.

"Well, that was a more eventful tasting than I expected," he said. "What the hell's got into Benedict?"

It occurred to me that my theory regarding the effects of Madame Joubert's had been unsound. Rather than an improving effect, it appeared the wonder powder actually exaggerated the pre-existing traits of one's personality. As a reasonably upstanding and wholesome type already, I was transformed into an even finer pillar of society. But poor Benedict, with his tendency to jealousy and other base instincts, had metamorphosed into a toad of the very lowest order.

"Well, we've not shown Charlie's Cellar in the best light today, Felix. I'm sorry about that," sighed Willoughby. "We do, however, have an immediate vacancy for an Assistant Wine Buyer..."

All eyes turned to me. My jaw pretty much leapt from its hinge and bounced off the tasting room floor.

"Goodness me! It would be an honour, sir."

CHAPTER SIX - BULGARIA'S FINEST

I paused for a moment, my eyes resting on the standard lamp in the corner of the interrogation room. A tiny moth flitted around the shade. My interviewers, by contrast, were quite still. The man had made a few notes while I was talking and occasionally he fiddled with the recording machine.

"Is this the kind of thing you're after?" I asked them.

"We're after the truth, Felix," said the woman. "There's a lot of detail about your rather immature school friends and flatmates. I'm not sure how necessary that was."

"My old school friends and my flatmates play an important part later on, officers ... should I call you officers?"

"Yes, you may."

What did that make them then? Police officers? Military officers? Something else?

"There's also a lot of stuff about wine," growled the man. "We're not studying for the Minstrel of Wine exam, you know."

"Wine is central to the whole story, officers. It's the whole point."

"Wine isn't your only vice, is it Felix?" The woman pursed her lips and removed a piece of paper from a folder. Staring down at it she began to read, "Cannabis, cocaine, amphetamines, opiates, hallucinogens, barbiturates. Various legal highs ... but most quite illegal." She looked up. "Congratulations. You've tested positive for every single narcotic on our list of substances of concern. I think that's a first."

"Thank you."

"It's not something to be proud of, Felix. With test results like that you should be in a coffin, or at least a mental asylum. Nevertheless, you still appear to be able to function at a high level. How do you manage that?"

"Everything in moderation I suppose," I mumbled. "Anyway, how did you get hold of a blood sample?" I had visions of a tiny robot mosquito flitting silently through my Little Chalfont window in the dead of night, extracting a droplet of my blood and winging its way back to Scotland Yard.

"It's not difficult, Felix. Hairdressers don't earn much at the best of times."

That's the last time I visit that barber, I thought. Lordy, you can't even leave your own hair clippings lying around these days without someone taking advantage. I suddenly realised I was talking too much. "I'm incriminating myself. I'm not sure I should answer any more of your questions."

"We've been through this," warned the man. "Given the evidence against you, there's nothing you can say that's going to make things any worse for you. If I were the FBI, I'd be very unhappy with your story so far."

"You're a bright chap, Felix," said the woman, more softly. "You've already said this looks like false imprisonment. You must be aware that anything you say under duress is inadmissible in court. You haven't been read your rights, nor do you have a lawyer present. So it's impossible for you to incriminate yourself. Anything you confess here would be thrown straight out of a court of law."

I considered this for a moment. It made some perverse kind of sense, I suppose.

"Why don't you tell us about the Bulgarians, Felix?" she asked, "we'd like to know more about them."

"I was just getting to that. I met them soon after I started my new job as Assistant Wine Buyer at Charlie's Cellar."

***

Assistant Wine Buyer was, indeed, my title, but it soon became clear I was more of an assistant *to* the wine buyers. It was no great hardship – they were a genial and undemanding bunch.

Clive Willoughby was the boss of course, the Director of Wine. He would hold a sales meeting every Monday morning, make kindly suggestions to the buyers about improving sales or profit margins, then remain ensconced in his office for the rest of the week.

Gillian, the well-spoken, pearl-wearing lady in her fifties, was in charge of Italian, German, Spanish and Portuguese wines. She was a Minstrel of Wine, the most prestigious qualification in the oenological world and, although she was sweetness and light with me, her sharp tongue could put the fear of God into misbehaving suppliers.

Paul, a younger, rather intense beanpole of a man, looked after the 'New World' – wines from Australia, South Africa and the Americas. He was very quiet, happiest in a tasting room nosing his way through a hundred Napa Valley Cabernets. He too was a Minstrel of Wine.

Henri, the raffish Frenchman, was, unsurprisingly, in charge of French wines. "I do not 'ave zis Minstrel of Wine qualification," he explained, with a conspiratorial wink, "but I am French so zat is enough."

I quickly warmed to Henri – he looked like he knew which side his baguette was buttered.

And I was in charge of everything else, which left the rather slim pickings of Eastern Europe, Kosher wines, and bag-in-box plonk. Not the most inspiring portfolio but everyone's got to start somewhere. And in my case, 'somewhere' was Romanian Merlot, Bulgarian Cabernet and sweet Israeli wines for Passover.

I continued to live in the huge flat above the Little Chalfont branch with Tarzan-like Wodin, composter Fistule and dreadlocked Mercedes. As my contribution to the household budget, I provided a steady stream of barely-touched wine samples, fresh from the Charlie's Cellar tasting room.

Richards, the Area Manager, soon found a new manager for the shop below – a task made much easier after I'd sent the local armed robber to the great ex-offenders hostel in the sky – and was perfectly happy for me to remain in the company-owned flat. After all, what was one extra squatter? The new manager had a home and family of his own, and no desire to join our merry commune.

Every morning I rattled into London on the tube from Little Chalfont to Great Portland Street, and walked the last half mile to Tinto Towers. I had my own broom-cupboard of an office, formerly occupied by the disgraced Benedict, with a window that faced the pebble-dashed building next door. The whole place was a bit of a dump, to be honest – a rabbit warren of corridors and faded meeting rooms, desks strewn with piles of white and pink copy paper, the occasional yellowing pot plant accentuating the sense of slow, beige death.

Most of my time was spent running sales reports for the senior members of the team or double checking shipping orders. But I was allowed to accompany the buyers into the tasting room and wrap my tongue around dozens of samples of whatever was under consideration that day. It might be a run of Chilean Chardonnays or a line-up of fine Beaujolais crus. By listening and tasting alongside my more experienced colleagues, I soon developed the ability to tell a stunner from more ordinary fare.

Every Friday, Willoughby reserved a lunchtime table at the Royal Oak, a huge pub a quarter of a mile from the office. The five of us would sit around the same corner table and order the roast of the day. Over the food, each member of our team would bring out a mystery bottle of wine, its identity hidden inside a thick sock. Glasses would be poured and we would have to guess each wine from the aroma and flavour. The buyer who made the most mistakes had to pay for the meal.

Being the least experienced and lowest paid, I was exempt from the financial penalty but I learnt more about the factors governing a wine's character at those roaring Friday afternoon sessions than from all my time in tasting rooms and vineyards later in my career. Needless to say, Friday lunch marked the end of the working week – by the end of the day we'd be in a right royal state. I lost count of the number of times we had to carry Clive Willoughby to a taxi and send him on his sleepy way home to St Albans.

My own area of buying was concentrated on the wines of South Eastern Europe. Unfortunately, sales from this unfashionable region were in severe and long-term decline as the drinking public embraced the more glamorous, fruity output of Australia, Chile and California. It was pretty clear I'd been given the area because no-one else wanted it, and because I was unlikely to cause too much damage if I cocked it up.

My main supplier was a heavy-set Bulgarian named Georgi. He ran the export arm of Danubia Vineyards, a huge formerly state-owned winery which sold oceans of plonk to the Soviets in the olden days. In recent years, with the collapse of the Russian market, his company had been privatised, slimmed down and was attempting to sell its wines to a wider range of countries.

I met Georgi every month or so to discuss the sales performance of his wines. It was usually a fairly depressing affair. Georgi would close his folder with a sigh at the end of each meeting and, in his heavy Bulgarian accent, declare "Screw sales, let's go drink." Naturally, as an amenable and supportive customer – particularly when someone else was paying – I would agree, and we'd retire to his favourite Bulgarian restaurant, Plovdiv, for a dinner of meaty stew, sausages and pastries, washed down with frequently refilled glasses of rather good Bulgarian wine.

"These are the wines we Bulgarians keep for ourselves!" he would declare with a laugh. As the dinner progressed he would regale me with slurred but highly entertaining stories of travelling across the Soviet Union selling wine. "Good times, Felix," he would emphasise, after a couple of glasses. "Central planning! Wonderful system. I never had to even try sell! Customers were already set up for me by apparatchiks – I only had to arrange logistics. Even if they didn't want the wine, they still had to buy!"

I would nod along, soaking up the atmosphere and the free wine.

Then, one afternoon, after a particularly calamitous decline in sales, he pushed aside the wine. He beckoned the waiter, who set down a bottle of Rakia Plum Spirit and two small glasses. "Ukraine was great place. Ah!" He sank back in his seat for a moment, lost in reverie. "You think it was all cold and depressing in Soviet times but no! Some places were magnificent!" He popped open the bottle and sloshed out two assertive measures of dark spirit. He raised his glass and pointed at me. "You could always get pussy in Odessa!"

"I'm glad to hear it, Georgi." I had no reason to doubt it. We clinked glasses.

"Nazdráve." He emptied his glass. "And in Yalta too. But Sochi was my favourite, even better than Ukraine. Wow oh wow! My friend, that was crazy place in summer. There was no TV, no internet. Just bang-bang-bang-bang."

"Sounds like paradise." I trusted his bang-bangs alluded to making sweet, tender love, rather than machine-gunning the opposition.

"I met a girl there once, she had such big thighs…" Georgi let out a little burp and sighed, suddenly serious. "All gone to hell now. Unfashionable. Everyone goes to Spain, to Turkey. Same thing with the wines. So, mister clever buyer, tell me, how do we get the Bulgarian wine selling again?"

I knocked back the Rakia. It roared down my throat, settling into a fiery little pool in my stomach. "Well, you need a re-brand. Change the name of your country to Italy. And start growing Pinot Grigio."

"Ha!" Georgi refilled the glasses. "I will speak to the authorities. I'm sure they would do it for a price, like everything!" He paused and looked at me. "The British people love Pinot Grigio, yes?"

"They certainly do. It's quite the most fashionable grape variety. Easy to drink and pronounce. We can't buy enough of it. The bloody Italians keep putting the price up, though. They're making a killing."

Georgi paused, taking this in. "Well, we have Pinot Grigio in Bulgaria."

"I'm sure you do Georgi," I winked. "Unfortunately, it tastes like Chardonnay."

"No, I am serious. Bulgaria was part of Roman Empire. Thracia it was called. The Romans planted all their grapes in our country. We call it Rulandské Šedé but no-one want to buy it."

"I wonder why not? It's a great name."

Georgi harrumphed good-humouredly and poured another glass. "I think you must come to Bulgaria for the harvest. Maybe we make a plan. Not all business either, we find some fun in Varna I think."

At that I raised my glass. "To business!"

***

"Well, I'm impressed by your dedication Felix." Clive Willoughby peered at me drily over his half-moons. "Most travel requests are for desperately important multi-week trips to Tuscany or the Napa Valley. But you want to go to Bulgaria."

"I think it could pay off handsomely, sir. My sources tell me they have substantial plantings of Pinot Grigio, masquerading under some Slavic nickname. I suspect there might be a bargain to be had."

"Well, we do like a bargain at Charlie's Cellar. Very well, you can have a week. Don't go running up any excessive expenses. Two-star hotels only."

"Of course. I'll treat every pound as if it's my own." Will I hell, I thought. Georgi was booking us into a five-star pleasure palace in Varna, and I was blowed if I was going to slum it with a bunch of pubescent backpackers.

"That's the spirit, Felix. Have a good trip."

***

"Just two hours of this crap, then we do things properly," winked Georgi a couple of weeks later as we squeezed into our budget airline seats.

Sure enough, on arrival in Varna, we were met by a swarthy looking character in a peaked cap. He grinned and ushered us to a large limousine.

"This is big deal for Danubia Vineyards," announced Georgi as the limo pulled away from the airport. He leant forward and pulled open a concealed flap in the seat in front of us. A light clicked on, revealing a minibar. "We drink local sparkling wine here in Bulgaria. But for this occasion, we drink French. Vintage Pol Roger ok?"

"A spot of Pol would be excellent, thank you."

Good old Georgi. He was enjoying himself. The bottle gave a little hiss and he slopped the wine into two slim glasses, the fine bubbles overflowing the rims and dripping on the seat.

"Never mind, plenty more where that came from. Nazdráve!"

"Nazdráve."

We finished the bottle in the half hour it took us to reach the Hotel Occident, a huge pre-war pile dominating the Black Sea Riviera. She was somewhat faded, having seen half a dozen invading armies come and go, but was still majestic, "an old countess wearing borrowed jewellery," Georgi had called her.

"An hour to freshen up, then see you in the bar, ok Felix?"

I was downstairs within the hour. Through the floor-to-ceiling windows the sky had darkened and the sea had disappeared into the gloom beyond the beachfront promenade. I found Georgi lounging on a sofa, sandwiched between two women wearing excitingly immodest clothing.

"Felix. Meet my business associates. This is Sharon and this is Diana."

"Very nice to meet you."

The women smiled.

"They do not speak English. Well, maybe a few words, the important ones. Eh, ladies?"

They laughed, delicate hands stroking Georgi's enormous stomach. I sat and Diana transferred her attention to me, pawing my shoulder for no discernibly practical reason.

Georgi waved and more Champagne arrived. "Tomorrow we start early – the vineyards are long way from here. I show you our Pinot Grigio and you meet the owner."

We made short work of the bottle and were shown into a private dining room. Georgi regaled us with tales of Varna in the seventies, when firm-bodied women from across the Soviet Bloc exercised vigorously at the lido by day and among the palm trees by night. Several excellent courses of caviar and steak later, not to mention a couple of bottles of good local wine, we were stuffed and ready for bed.

I declined Diana's kind offer to accompany me to my suite. I don't think of myself as a prude, but after all that talk of the Soviet era I couldn't help wondering whether there might be a hidden camera watching, silently, through a pinhole in the ceiling. Being blackmailed by the Directorate of Two-Way Mirrors and Poison Umbrellas is never a good look. And besides, she probably had the clap.

A six o'clock alarm call and a fortifying shot of Turkish coffee later, we were on our way. After two rather unpleasant hours of pot-holed rural roads we arrived at the winery, a squat concrete block to which four classical-style pillars had been tacked, giving the impression of a cut-price Greek temple attached to a cold-war bomb shelter.

A sharp-suited man met us at the entrance and Georgi introduced us. "Felix, meet Viktor, CEO and main investor in Danubia Vineyards."

"Good to meet you Viktor."

Viktor had a firm handshake and sparkling white teeth, his Bulgarian accent softened by a subtle American twang. "You are very welcome, Felix. You're going to love your visit."

We climbed into a Land Rover and bumped around the vineyards as Viktor regurgitated facts and figures about rootstock investments and grape yields. Then he stopped and pointed to the sloping valley before him. "This is all planted with Rulandské Šedé. Or, as you Westerners prefer to call it, Pinot Grigio."

He leapt out and stooped in front of the nearest vine, breaking off a bunch of plump grapes, and handed them to me. They were ripe and golden with a faint blush of pink. "The harvest will start next month and we can have the wine ready to ship by November.

"Very good. What price can you do for us?"

"Less than half the price of your Italian suppliers."

I looked at Georgi, who was smiling and nodding. "I think we can do some business, eh Felix?"

"Gentlemen, I think Bulgaria is back!" I declared.

***

The buying team held their glasses up to the light. Clive Willoughby gave his a deep sniff. "Well, it smells like commercial Pinot Grigio. Then again, so do lots of things."

It was two months after my return from Bulgaria, and Georgi had sent a courier with the newly bottled wine.

"They call it Rulandské Šedé out there," I said, "but I've checked with the Board of Wine and Liquor and we're allowed to call it Pinot Grigio."

"And you can sell it for three quid a bottle? Well, that's a result, Felix. If you pull this off we'll take out adverts in the national press. We can give the supermarkets a bloody nose for a change." Willoughby looked round the room. "What do the rest of you think?"

"Tastes clean, good fruit, c'est bon," shrugged Henri, spitting a mouthful into the sink.

"I wouldn't serve it at a dinner party but it's fine for everyday drinking," agreed Gillian.

Paul frowned at his glass and gave it another smell. Then he spoke, in his precise, quiet voice. "There's nothing wrong with the wine. Except..."

My heart sank. Come on, old chap, I wanted to say, why not give an assistant wine buyer a chance? What's the point of picking holes in everything?

"...how do we know it really is Pinot Grigio? They have lots of other grapes out there. They could have made a mistake. Or worse."

Willoughby sighed. "Paul's right. I'm sure your wine supplier is trustworthy Felix, but we can't risk a mislabelled wine. The Board of Wine and Liquor would have our guts for garters. We'd have to withdraw the lot from sale, then you'd be on the hook for getting our money back." He peered at me over his glasses. "And however good a negotiator you might be, Felix, I suspect you'll struggle to sell a million bottles of suspect Pinot Grigio back to the Bulgarians."

I thought of Georgi, reclining in his luxury hotel, his neck nuzzled by women in miniscule lengths of elasticated fabric. And Viktor, with his flashing teeth, holed up in his mock-classical nuclear bunker. Surely they were trustworthy? Prejudice is a terrible thing, but I confess doubts started to creep into my mind too.

"You'll have to get the vines analysed and certified, Felix."

My spirits rose slightly. "I'm sure Georgi can provide all the correct paperwork."

"I'm sure he can, Felix," said Willoughby, drily. "But you'll need to get it independently certified. Go and see the Board of Wine and Liquor, they can advise you."

My spirits fell again. The Board of Wine and Liquor was a sub-department of the Department of Agriculture, Fisheries and Food, and a more spiteful, self-righteous bunch of pen-pushing jobsworths was impossible to imagine. They would creep around the shelves of the British High Street, looking for the tiniest misspelling or ambiguity on a wine label. And when they spotted one, they pounced. They had the power to demand a retailer remove everything from sale, on pain of fine or imprisonment.

I had already fallen foul of them once, when I had printed a typically lyrical tasting note on the back label of my new Romanian Merlot. 'Juicy and full bodied,' it began, 'full of the joys of a Mediterranean summer ... ' But no, that was unacceptable to the good bureaucrats of the Board of Wine and Liquor. Willoughby received a phone call the day after we launched. Romania has no Mediterranean seaboard – its coast is on the Black Sea. So it was inaccurate, not to mention criminally fraudulent, for us to associate it with a Mediterranean summer.

I'd tried to argue that the wine was merely reminiscent of a Mediterranean summer – that it evoked the generic pleasures of a sun-kissed coast, rather than the salty lick of the waters themselves – but to no avail. At substantial cost we had to re-label the entire stock with a new, officially approved tasting note: 'Juicy and full bodied, evoking the pleasurable emotions that an informed person might associate with the Black Sea and/or the wider Danube Delta region'.

I visited the Board later that week at their Whitehall head-quarters, where I sat across the table from Mr Percival Stark, a small, middle-aged man with a receding hairline and a bristling moustache.

"So, Mr Hart. You wish to sell an uncertified, unverified wine, made from unknown or ill-defined grapes, from an unreg-istered and quite possibly entirely fictitious vineyard, as Pinot Grigio. Do I have that correct?"

I imagined holding Mr Stark's head down the Department of Agriculture's toilet and flushing it repeatedly as I paddled his arse with a copy of Hugh Johnson's Wine Atlas.

Stark pored over a large map of South Eastern Europe, shaded according to agricultural usage. He compared it to a long table in another book, detailing grape plantings in former Soviet Bloc countries since 1980. He shook his head. "Rulandské Šedé you say? Plenty in the former Czechoslovakia... some in Slovenia... but I can't see much planted in Bulgaria."

"But I've seen it with my own eyes! I'm sure you'll find every-thing is completely transparent, Mr Stark. Our suppliers are utterly trustworthy and they would be delighted to provide you with any documentation you require."

"I'm sorry Mr Hart, but that's just not good enough. We don't simply accept pieces of paper from random Bulgarians, willy nilly. This is the British Board of Wine and Liquor. We have standards, you see."

"Can I obtain a certificate from a trusted third party laboratory?"

"No, I'm afraid that's not good enough either. I think, given the size of the shipment, that a member of the Board of Wine and Liquor must visit in person, namely myself."

Oh Horlicks. I had a feeling things weren't going my way. And I'd given Georgi the green light to go ahead and bottle the wine – otherwise I'd have lost it to another customer. If it turned out not to be Pinot Grigio, I'd be stuck up the Danube without a paddle. "I'm so pleased, Mr Stark. I'll call the supplier and make arrangements."

Georgi wasn't best pleased to hear our little deal might be in jeopardy. He fumed and raged at the iniquities of bureaucrats. "This is why we shoot communists these days!" Eventually he calmed down a little and said he would work out a plan.

Stark flew to Varna two weeks later to meet Georgi and Viktor. He took cuttings from the vines and samples of the wine itself, then returned to London to have them analysed.

I spent the intervening days in a state of constant tension. I could barely sleep. This was my big gig, my chance to show Clive Willoughby and others that I was worthy of the big league and a shot at being a proper buyer. I imagined being given responsibility for a major area. Spain, perhaps, or California. Yes, California would do very nicely. I could see myself cruising up the coast road to Sonoma in a convertible, surfboard propped on the back seat, stopping to ride a few waves, catching the eye of a fit young native as we raced for the same break...

Willoughby popped his head round the door and put his thumb up. "That was the Board of Liquor on the phone. Looks like your Pinot Grigio checked out. Well done, Felix! Better get cracking and ship the stuff, we don't want to miss Christmas."

I'd never doubted Georgi for a second. I phoned him straight away and he roared with delight, insisting that we celebrate that evening at Plovdiv restaurant.

"I was a little worried for a time there, Georgi. The Board of Wine and Liquor can be real sticklers for that type of thing. How did you win him over?"

"Ah, it was no problem. We had wonderful times with this Mr Stark. He loved the sights and sounds of Varna. We even took holiday snaps!"

Georgi passed me a handful of pictures. There was Percival Stark standing stiffly with Georgi and Viktor in front of the vineyard. There was another of him frowning as he dipped a measuring cylinder into a vat of wine. And there was one of him bending over a bed, wearing a lacy bra and stockings, being spanked by a naked Diana, his little moustache leaping with delight.

My mind wandered back to Diana's invitation earlier that summer, right outside my bedroom door in the very same Hotel Occident, and I offered the Lord a little prayer of thanks that He had seen fit to bless me with such a strongly magnetised moral compass.

"Mr Stark was not happy that we discover his kinky hobby. Your British Board of Wine, not to mention his wife, would be even less happy, I think. So, we came to an arrangement." He sighed. "What is this thing with bureaucrats and spanking, eh Felix? It was same in olden days. I think they make other people follow rules because they are so naughty themselves!"

Georgi was clearly a psychologist as well as a wine salesman. Not wanting to be found in possession of kompromat, I pushed the photographs back towards him and raised my glass. A vision of California popped into my mind once more. Vineyards full of tall, slim women with Hollywood looks, laughing and waving.

The next vintage was looking very promising indeed.

CHAPTER SEVEN - MONEY TALKS

C hristmas was disappointing for Charlie's Cellar. I don't mean for me personally, of course. My Bulgarian Pinot Grigio was the talk of the town – the most successful promotion Charlie's had ever seen. We'd placed adverts in the national newspapers, built tottering displays in the stores, and people flocked to snap up the finest plonk that money could buy. There was even a small article in the London Wine Trade Review entitled 'The Wine Buyer Who Came in from the Cold', describing my Eastern European sourcing prowess in breathless detail.

But our other wines didn't sell as well as hoped, while beer and spirit sales were a disaster. We were being hollowed out by the competition in the shape of the big supermarket chains. They were cheaper, you could pick up your wine with your weekly groceries, and you didn't have to wrestle a smack-addled hoodie as you left the store.

And so, in mid-January, as my thoughts turned to skiing holidays and mulled-wine-flavoured cuddles in the corners of Swiss chalets, Clive Willoughby summoned us all to his office. But there was a young man now seated in Willoughby's chair, while the Director of Wine joined us on one of the cheap, moulded plastic seats.

"Thank you everyone for joining us at such short notice," began Willoughby. But the young man grimaced and held up a hand, and Clive stopped with a little "Oh!"

The newcomer was a strange-looking fellow, no more than thirty years old but nearly hairless – as though he had yet to start shaving – with thin, pale eyebrows above sharp eyes. He reminded me of a snake, his head constantly moving, taking everyone in, while the rest of his body remained totally motionless. His delicate hands rested on the desk, a single gold ring on his pinkie. Looks like a bit of a pervert, I thought.

Then he spoke. Quick, precise words, with little context. "You're all busy people, so I'll be brief. My name is James Nelson of Canter and Farb Inc. We're a New York based hedge fund. We completed the acquisition of Charlie's Cellar and its assets at six thirty yesterday evening. I am now your Managing Director."

Willoughby stirred again. "I'm afraid they've asked me to retire. I'm very sorry to be …"

Snakey pervert held up his pale hand once more. "Not appropriate right now."

I jumped as Gillian brought her palm down hard on the table, her rings cracking against the wood. Snakey's head flicked to her in shock and I saw a flash of fear pass across his face. Not so brave now, are you, I thought. He reminded me of the wrong sort of school prefect, the type promoted for academic ability rather than sporting prowess.

"I'm not going to sit here, putting up with this! How dare you!" I could see tears welling in her eyes. Paul and Henri remained silent, their heads bowed. I wondered if she was going to hit him. I hoped so. "Come on Clive," she said, rising to her feet.

Willoughby stood, slowly, and she took his hand. They left the room, and Tinto Towers, forever.

His composure regained, Snakey looked at each of us with his little darting head. "Anyone else resigning? It would be more efficient to get everything out in one go."

No one spoke. The head flicked to me. "You did the Bulgarian deal, right?"

I nodded.

"You're doing her job. Ok?"

I nodded again. There's a time and a place for principles and martyrdom, but this wasn't it. Felix Hart, Official Wine Buyer for Italy, Spain and Germany. The show must go on. The world of commerce demanded it.

No-one said anything for a few seconds.

"Well? Go and do whatever it is you do."

We left the office and headed to the Royal Oak. We found Clive and Gillian at our usual table, she dabbing at her red eyes with a lace handkerchief. Willoughby was looking calm and perhaps slightly relieved. He was only a couple of years from official retirement and they must have given him a lump of cash to go. Gillian would be all right too, she might not be receiving any severance pay but Henri once told me she was married to a rich stockbroker and lived in one of the largest houses in Muswell Hill.

"Well chaps, the future of Charlie's Cellar is in your hands. God help us." Willoughby smiled at us.

"I'm not sure I want to work for that arse 'ole," commented Henri, uncorking a bottle of Champagne. "Maybe I will go back to France."

"I can't believe that horrible little man thinks he can do a better job than you, Clive," sniffed Gillian.

"That's very nice of you, Gill. But he has absolutely no interest in wine, of course."

"So why is he Managing Director of a wine merchant, Clive?" asked Paul.

"Because Charlie's Cellar owns three hundred prime commercial properties in London and the Home Counties, not to mention the residential apartments above them. That's worth more than the next fifty years of our annual profits. If we ever make a profit again, that is."

There was a period of silence. And there it was, my first lesson in high finance. The simple fact was that I worked for a large real-estate company that happened to have a small wine-selling operation on the side. And if Willoughby was correct, it probably wouldn't be long before our new owners sold us off, converting our stores into estate agents, nail salons and fried-chicken outlets.

Sodbags. I'd finally managed to land a real wine-buying job, only for my employer to decide it couldn't be bothered to buy wine any longer. There was also the little matter that I was living for free, together with my trusty band of anarchists, on company property. I couldn't see that arrangement continuing for long either.

"Anyway. Here's to selling wine and making money the respectable way!" Willoughby raised his glass of Champagne and we clinked glasses. "Keep the old tradition going, won't you boys? Save a space at the table for us." Willoughby wiped a tear from his eye.

There was only one thing for it, and I wasn't going to waste a moment. Until we were closed down and I was bodily ejected from Tinto Towers, I vowed to drink, travel and fornicate my way around as much of Europe as humanly possible.

***

I needn't have worried about my accommodation situation. Wodin, who was something of an authority in these matters, instructed me to lodge an official notice with the Land Registry stating I was a long-term legal occupant of the flat in Little

Chalfont. This, it transpired, gave me protection against sudden eviction by my asset-stripping employer. I thus became both an agent of global capitalism and a radical communist, simultaneously. I'd never been one for politics but, on balance, I felt I'd fused the best of both ideologies.

Our new owners took not the slightest interest in what the wine buying team got up to. There was a sales reporting meeting every Monday chaired by the snake, but so long as the cash flow was tolerable and the profit margins didn't slip, we could do what we wanted. There was a sticky moment in February, when the travel expenses budget was reduced to zero, but a week later the entire finance department were told their jobs were to be outsourced to India.

Under the circumstances, lovely Lucy, Chief Expenditure Clerk, didn't require much persuasion to transfer a few thousand pounds to my special educational cost centre, where it could sit below the radar and be productively invested in Venetian hotel bills, Barcelona's finest restaurants, and fact-finding missions up the Mösel with Stef, my mouth-wateringly beautiful German wine supplier.

***

I found myself in Naples in September, just as the harvest began. Napoli is a slightly rough old town, and the locals are over-fond of pulling out knives and waving them at anyone who displeases them, but it's great fun if you know where to look.

I had been travelling for a week with Clara, the export manager for a producer of fine white Greco di Tufo, and she had demanded, in exchange for a good price on her wines, that I give her a proper fettling in every wine district in Campania. I was reflecting on how educational our trip was proving as we killed time in a harbour-side bar, waiting for the ferry to Ischia.

I felt the chunky little Nokia vibrating in my trouser pocket and, lifting Clara's long bare legs from my lap, I answered it.

"Felix. This is Melissa. You don't know me but I work for Octane Consulting, a firm of head-hunters. Are you able to talk freely?"

I pushed away the olive that Clara was attempting to insert between my lips. "I am now. Go ahead."

"My client is a large supermarket chain, based in the centre of London. They are increasing the size of their wine-buying team and your name came up as a person of interest. May I set up an interview for you?"

Gott im Himmel! The big league! There was only one place the wine business was heading and that was to the supermarkets. They had already throttled Charlie's Cellar half to death and the high street was littered with the corpses of weaker competitors. They were acquisitive, carnivorous and utterly ruthless. All my working life, I'd seen them as the baddies, a voracious foe to be fought at all costs, a Goliath to be slain in defence of the little guy.

The word on the street, however, was that they paid rather well, and being a fair-minded chap, I'd never really swallowed all the guff about them being the enemy at the gates. "I suppose that might be of interest," I pondered, trying to sound aloof and hard to get.

"It either is or isn't. The interview is tomorrow morning, ten thirty, at Gatesave Supermarkets' Head Office. Be there."

"Ah, but I'm in Naples..."

But she had already hung up. I turned to Clara. "I'm so sorry. I'm afraid I'm going to have to cut short our study trip."

She threw an olive at my head and pouted.

"I've got a shot at a big job and if I get it, I promise I'll give you the biggest delivery of your life."

"That's-a better," she winked and smiled wistfully.

Thank God I was in Naples and not the countryside. I caught a taxi straight to the airport and the evening British Airways flight back to London.

The next morning I arrived at Gatesave's gleaming glass headquarters in Hammersmith, on the banks of the Thames. I was shown into a ground-floor meeting room and introduced to my interviewers.

Mr Channing was a huge round man. Despite this, he was dapperly dressed in a green suit and waistcoat, his tie matching the yellow spotted handkerchief poking from his breast pocket. His young assistant had her hair precisely cut in a striking black bob, setting off her pale skin and bright red lipstick.

Channing held an expensive-looking personal organiser, bound in brown fur. He stroked the cover as he spoke, as if it were once a much-loved pet gerbil, sadly departed but now immortalised, its soft hide enclosing his to-do list. "Good morning, Mr Hart," he purred, in a high voice. "We would like to ask you a few questions."

"The pleasure's all mine. Shall I run through my career and accomplishments to date?"

Channing's lips curled upwards. "There's no need for that. Our agency has already conducted a thorough background check on your employment history. An impressively rapid rise through the ranks of retail and buying it is too, which is why you have come to our attention. Nor is your technical expertise in any doubt, Mr Hart. We have pages of testimonials from your suppliers, from Lisbon to Sofia. They are fulsome in their praise." Channing held up a wad of papers to illustrate his point.

Good old, Georgi, I thought. If I pull this gig off I'll be sure to buy ten containers of his innovative Pinot Grigio.

"Rather, we need to form a sense of your personality, your ability to fit in with the Gatesave culture." Channing stroked his personal organiser. "Tell me, how do you feel about win-win scenarios?"

Sounds like my kind of scenario, I was about to say, then I had one of those flashes of Hart intuition that told me the classic playbook of management clichés, with its talk of teamwork and mutual respect, might not be welcome here. Here I was, at the head office of the country's largest supermarket, supping in the Hall of Valhalla, coiled in the very belly of the beast. Think, Hart! What's the closest thing you've experienced to tangling with a multi-national corporate behemoth?

An image flashed before me, of a rain-swept field, men bloodied and limping, some lying motionless, others weeping with the futility of it all. It had been a particularly vicious fixture against Bulford Agricultural College, a school populated entirely by bullet-headed farmers' sons, all tiny eyes and arms like hams. I was in the scrum, head down, the ball spinning this way and that beneath flailing legs, and all I could hear was Corporal Tadler, the coach, screaming, "Thrust, Hart, thrust!" from the touchline...

"I've never had much time for the concept, Mr Channing. In my experience, whether it's face-to-face at the negotiation table or on the sports field, when I go head-to-head with an opponent there can only be one winner."

"I see, Mr Hart. So you can think of no circumstances when a win-win might be appropriate?"

Thrust, Hart, thrust! "Oh, but I can. I would define a win-win as when I'm faced by two opponents simultaneously and they both come off worse." I looked the immaculately made-up HR assistant in the eye. "And when I am faced with an opponent, that is invariably the outcome."

A flush of colour appeared in the assistant's cheeks and she looked down, sucking the end of her pen.

"How very refreshing," purred Channing. "We do like winners at Gatesave, Mr Hart. Tell me, if I were to ask your current colleagues what they think of you, what would they say?"

Thrust! "They would say that Felix Hart is a man of action, whose drive to achieve is matched only by his support for his team," Thrust! "A man with his eye on the ball and the willingness to force it over the line, whatever the cost."

"Are you a steamroller, Mr Hart, crushing all before you?"

"A steamroller is slow, blunt and noisy, Mr Channing. I prefer to think of myself as a snowplough, swift and clean, cleaving obstacles aside, leaving a clear path for those who follow in my wake. The perfect combination of grip and grit."

Channing raised his eyebrows, the movement of his plump hand quickening against the fur. "Grit, you say? I like that." He leant forward and stared me in the eye. "Are you a giver or a taker, Mr Hart?"

Keep thrusting! Keep thrusting! "Both, Mr Channing! I see my role as extracting every penny from those with whom I wrestle, without fear or favour. But for my customers, I exist merely to serve, to accommodate their most ambitious demands, without complaint."

Channing nodded, clearly pleased, stroking his personal organiser even faster.

"And what would you say is your greatest weakness, Mr Hart?" whispered his assistant, pen poised above her neat shorthand.

"My passion, I'm afraid. Sometimes it can overwhelm my less engaged colleagues." The assistant's bright red lips quivered as she scribbled, open-mouthed, in her notebook.

"Well, I hope you learn to channel that passion productively," murmured Channing, making a note of his own. He looked up, snapping his fur-lined notebook shut. "And do you have any questions for us?"

Yes, I thought, have I got the job and how much cash do you intend to hose my way? "Both of you are Gatesave colleagues, so you're clearly at the top of your game," I gushed. "I'd be fascinated to know how you made it to the pinnacle of the human resources industry."

I didn't get where I am without a strong sense of empathy and emotional interest in my fellow colleagues. My interviewers swelled with pride as they delivered potted histories of their personal climb up the greasy pole. In Channing's case, I suspected, more greasy poles than most see in a lifetime. When they'd finished, I thanked them and we all stood.

"It's been invigorating meeting you, Mr Hart, thank you for your time. Ms Edwards will show you out."

I felt the interview had gone rather well and I was right. Before the end of the afternoon, Melissa from Octane Consulting called me.

"Congratulations Felix. Gatesave intend to make you an offer. Check your email."

I opened the attachment and my face fell. In fact, it did more than fall, it hurled itself to the ground and pounded its fists against the earth. It was an insult, not even half my salary at Charlie's Cellar. Is this how these supermarkets made their money, by paying their staff less than a Grimsby deckchair attendant in the off-season?

I called Melissa back, holding my trembling lip firmly, lest an expletive or two leap out.

"I'm afraid there's been a mistake. I know you lot like a robust negotiation or two but I didn't expect to be insulted. I'm afraid the answer's no, unless you sharpen your pencil and try a lot harder."

"Excellent. Gatesave respect people who know what they want and aren't afraid to ask for it. In fact, if you hadn't asked, there might have been a question mark against your name from day one. Very well, I am authorised to increase the offer by ten percent. Given your rather short career to date, that's a rather generous monthly salary. Gatesave appear to rate you quite highly, actually."

I had opened my mouth and was about to say something along the lines of 'ten percent on top of sod all, is still bloody sod all', when I realised she'd said monthly. A thick carpet of red embarrassment crept from beneath my collar until it covered my entire face. I had assumed the proposal was an annual salary.

"Jolly good," I whispered. "Can't wait to start."

The next day, I knocked on snakey Nelson's door and placed the envelope of resignation on his desk. I apologised, not that I was particularly sorry, and explained I'd been offered a great opportunity elsewhere.

Nelson's head flicked from the envelope to me then back to his computer screen. "Naff off then."

So that's what they mean by the death of gentlemanly capitalism, I thought. If any other little turd had spoken to me like that, I'd have grabbed his pants and given him the wedgie of his life. But I probably needed a reference from the grubby little urchin, and inducing a dislocated testicle might have counted against me, so I left his office without a word.

I had my farewell party a couple of weeks later down the Royal Oak. It was a legendary event. Clive and Gillian joined us, there were speeches, and there wasn't a dry eye in the house – or a dry breast, for that matter, once enough Champagne had been sprayed around the room. After some dancing on the tables we finished the day with a rousing rendition of 'We'll Meet Again' and yours truly was hoisted aloft by the stronger members of the logistics team, four pairs of knickers around my head, as half the office snogged the other half on the booze-soaked carpet.

Charlie's Cellar didn't last much longer. Most of the personnel at Tinto Towers were poached by other companies, no doubt facilitated by Melissa and her team of vultures at Octane Consulting. A few hung around, waiting for the grim reaper, as suppliers refused one by one to deliver more booze unless they were paid for outstanding debts, and the shelves of the stores slowly emptied.

When payroll announced the payment of salaries would be delayed by a week, everyone knew the game was up. Staff gathered up whatever stock remained on their shelves and flogged it to the local pub to recoup owed wages, or held all-night closing-down parties. A couple of managers did a runner to Spain with the contents of the safes but most just locked up and posted the keys through the letterbox.

Fortunately I had leapt from the inferno just in time. On a crisp, clear November morning, just one week after my farewell party, I arrived at Gatesave's head office for my first day. I paused for a minute to take in the vast, gleaming glass building, its fascia reflected in the silvery Thames. No more beige, peeling paint and out-of-order elevators. This was a workplace more in keeping with my aspirations.

I had indeed joined the premier league.

CHAPTER EIGHT - THE PINK PRIEST

Gordon Bannerman, Head of Execution for Alcoholic Beverages, Carbonated Drinks and Impulse Grocery, was a well-built man in his late fifties, nearly as tall as me. He met me in reception, grasped my hand with a loud "Ha!" and shook it firmly. He appeared an avuncular fellow, rather like a jolly bank manager, his face creased by laughter lines and an occasional flash from the gold fillings at the back of his mouth.

"Right, you. Welcome to the Gatesave family. No time to lose, you've inherited a burning ship. We had to get rid of the last buyer. Didn't really have what it took. Ha!" Bannerman grinned like an enthusiastic crocodile. On closer examination, I decided, he looked less like a happy-go-lucky bank manager and more like the zealous organiser of a badger-baiting circle.

"I can't wait to get stuck in, sir."

We entered the lift. It rose quickly and silently to the sixth floor.

"Good. So, here are your areas of responsibility. You'll be looking after Germany…"

Good stuff. I'd always had a soft spot for the misty, schloss-strewn Rhine, not to mention huge respect for their liberated and fair womenfolk. Achtung Mädchen, here comes Felix!

"Eastern Europe…"

Oh dear. Not exactly the most up-and-coming region. I thought I'd seen the last of Transylvania's pot-holed roads. Could be worse, though. Bound to be a few more rip-roaring trips to Varna with Georgi.

"Portugal..."

Ok, that's more like it. It may not be the largest wine producing country but a nice, hospitable place to visit with good food and fine-looking brunettes. The charming cities of Oporto and Lisbon, the lush Port vineyards of the Douro, the sun-kissed landscape of the Alentejo. Yes, that would do nicely.

"...and England."

Really? I didn't get into this game to stand in an Essex field sampling Chateau bloody Basildon. And now, a big, glamorous area please. California? Argentina, perhaps? Italy?

We stepped out of the lift. The Head of Execution stared at me, grinning, gold fillings glittering. "Yes? Think you can handle that then? Any questions?"

"Oh. Is that it?"

"Ha! Is that it?" Bannerman parroted me, guffawing incredulously. Then he jabbed his fist into my lower ribs. I exhaled sharply. He was quick for an old guy. I sensed I shouldn't punch him back. When it came to physical violence, the Head of Execution was clearly a giver, not a taker. "You've got a lot to prove, Hart. That's quite enough responsibility for a junior buyer to be getting on with!"

As I rubbed my bruised ribs, Bannerman walked me across the vast trading floor. There must have been a couple of hundred people on the sixth floor alone – more than the entire staff complement of grey old Tinto Towers. We weaved through the sea of desks and arrived at the Drinks Buying Department.

"Trisha! I'll leave this young man with you. Make sure he doesn't fall asleep on the job, won't you? Ha!"

A jolly looking, stout woman with an idiotically wide smile jumped to her feet. "Hello!" she exclaimed.

"Cheerio then, don't cock it up!" chuckled Bannerman. As he departed, he thumped me from behind with his tightly balled fist, his knuckles cracking into my spine. I arched my back in pain and he strode off, roaring with laughter.

"Don't worry about Gordon, he's very tactile," laughed the woman. "I'm Patricia Hocksworth, call me Trisha. This is the wine team. Everybody, say hello to Felix!" A bunch of surly-looking characters eyed me from behind their computer monitors. Nobody said a word.

"This is Joan Armitage, she looks after Spanish and South American wine. She's a Minstrel of Wine!"

I nodded and smiled to a well-dressed woman wearing half-moon spectacles. She looked me up and down for a few seconds and then nodded before returning, unsmiling, to her screen. Happy New Year to you too, I thought. Never mind, I'm sure she'll warm up when she gets to know me.

"This is George Bolus, he's the buyer for Australia, New Zealand and South Africa."

An arrogant-looking man with a face like a spanked buttock looked up, smirking. "Oh, you're the guy from that failed wine merchant aren't you? Well, watch and learn. And let us know when the pace gets too fast for you, eh?" He chuckled to himself.

Oh dear, looks like they're introducing me to the more spiteful end of the team first, I thought.

"This is Timmy Durange. He buys French and Italian wine." A pale-looking man with oily black hair peeped over the top of his screen and grimaced. I couldn't tell whether he was trying to smile or just struggling to keep his breakfast down.

"And finally, Bill Teddington, he looks after spirits and liqueurs. Say hello Bill – don't be a grump!"

Bill, a ruddy-faced man in his fifties, stared at me with unalloyed hatred. "Hello Felix. If you need any help, ask someone else. Got it?"

Well, you shouldn't judge a book by its cover but they struck me as a right bunch of weeping sores. And, not for the first time in my short career, I was by some distance the most junior member of the team. Well, that would have to change. There was no way young Felix was going to be the whipping boy for this preening collection of social skid-marks.

I spent my first couple of weeks reading sales reports and phoning suppliers. It was clear my first challenge was to rebuild Gatesave's German wine business. It was in horrendous decline and we'd lost a chunk of market share over the past year – presumably the reason my predecessor had been thrown under the bus.

The range wasn't particularly inspiring. Most of what we sold was cheap, sweet white wine – Liebfraumilch, Hock and light Moselle. At the expensive end sat a couple of more interesting estate wines, fabulous aromatic Rieslings with gothic labels and unpronounceable names, which nobody bought.

And then there was Pink Priest. This ancient brand of Rheinland rosé wine, created over a century ago, had allegedly been a favourite of Queen Victoria. The label showed an old church, in front of which stood a wrinkled old man in a long pink robe, hood half-pulled over his bald head, looking like some freakish child molester from the depths of the Black Forest. The brand was all the rage in the sixties and seventies but had fallen rather out of fashion in the last decade or so. It still sold quite well, however, to pensioners who remembered it from their youth, ironical students who used the empty bottles as candlesticks, and the more blasphemously inclined members of the homosexual community, who found the unusual bulbous bottle ideal for recreational purposes.

Pink Priest was owned by Paris-Blois Brands International, a huge luxury goods conglomerate. The company discovered, much to its horror, it had purchased the brand accidentally as they acquired a group of Champagne houses some years ago. It sat, incongruously, in their portfolio of Swiss watches, fashionista handbags, bling Cognac and premium Scotch, unloved but tolerated thanks to its profitability.

Paris-Blois Brands did not, it was fair to say, consider Pink Priest a priority brand, but for me it was the key to my whole range. I calculated if I could double the sales of Pink Priest, it would turn my entire German wine portfolio from embarrassing decline into respectable growth. And so, after several weeks of trying, I managed to schedule an appointment with Sandra Filton, Senior National Account Manager for Paris-Blois Brands International, at Gatesave's Head Office.

Until this point in my career, my suppliers had been chinless wonders stuttering their way through fine-wine catalogues, animated Italians with limited English skills, and the odd professional Sales Director like Georgi thrown in. But this would be my first meeting with a genuine multi-national, a company even more powerful and better resourced than Gatesave itself.

On the day of the meeting, reception called and announced my visitors had arrived. Descending to the ground floor, I scanned the waiting area. A supplier meeting a Gatesave buyer for the first time is usually an anxious individual, furtively meeting the eye of all who emerge from the elevator, but there was nobody in reception who fitted the bill.

"Your visitors are already set up in meeting room twelve," called one of the receptionists.

I entered room twelve. A very attractive woman, her blonde hair tied back in a ponytail, sat at the table. She wore a stylish black suit over a white blouse, against which strained an arrogant pair of breasts. She was flanked by two unsmiling men in pin-striped suits. All three had expensive laptops open before them.

"Sandra Filton from PB Brands International." She stood, gave a thin, professional not-quite-smile and held out a hand. Her grip was strong and dry.

"Felix Hart. I see you've made yourselves at home?"

"This is John, this is Matthew. They'll be supporting me in this encounter."

John and Matthew nodded to me, without the barest hint of a smile. Encounter? What was this, a boxing match? Well, it may as well have been. And I was about to find out what happens when you go into a professional fight, underweight and without training.

"Morning chaps," I began. "Right Sandra, let's get down to business shall we? First of all, we need to look at the Pink Priest cost price. Too high I think." That usually puts them on the back foot.

"Shut up Felix. I'm not interested in your opinion. We decide the cost price and it's going up."

I was astonished, though also a little excited, by her outrageous disrespect. I was used to being kowtowed to by terrified suppliers, not dictated to. I tried to regain control. "I'm appalled by your inability to negotiate in a respectful manner, Ms Filton. This is Gatesave Supermarkets and we don't take kindly to being spoken to in that tone. I shall be taking this up with your manager. May I know who that is, please?"

"Of course Felix. His name is Pierre Boulle. He's the International Sales Director of PB Brands, based in Paris. I have him on speed dial – let me get him for you now." She nodded to John, or perhaps it was Matthew, who produced a mobile phone, called up a number and passed it to Sandra. She waited a few seconds and began speaking in French.

"*Bonjour Pierre, ça va?*" Her French was easy, immaculate and extremely sexy. She explained that she was in a meeting with a recalcitrant and immature buyer who was new in his role, didn't have a clue what he was doing and wished to complain about her negotiating style. I was somewhat dismayed to hear her include the words '*merde*' and '*imbecile*'.

"Here you go, Felix. Pierre would love to talk to you."

I took the phone, feeling I was already on the ropes.

"Bonjour Felix. It sounds like you 'ave a problem?" His voice was gravelly and heavily accented.

"Yes, as a matter of fact ..."

"Shut your face you idiot. If you cause my Sandra any problems, I will cause you much beeger problems, you understand? My CEO is 'aving dinner with your CEO next week at Paree Fashion Week, at my company's expense. So 'ow about I arrange for 'im to 'ear you are incompetent and are cock-eeng everything up? Comprendre?"

The phone went dead. I handed it back.

"Don't worry Felix – you're on a learning curve. Everyone's allowed to be a bit of a tit when they've just started. The question is, are you a fast learner or not?"

I've always considered myself a gentleman, not one of these grubby, sniffing types who stares at a woman's proud form, as though she's a prize Dexter at Kilkenny country fair. But I found myself somewhat paralysed before Sandra's gaze and half a minute must have passed before I realised I had been staring, like a cobra hearing a spiffing new tune, at her excitingly assertive chest.

"Let me explain what's going to happen now," she said. "I'm going to impose a price increase and you're going to bend over and take it like a man. But I will be gentle, Felix. And I shall ease your pain with a soothing injection of marketing funding, allowing you to grow the brand and stimulate those all-important sales. How does that sound?"

I thought it sounded filthily superb. I was new to the world of top-flight brand building so I decided a short period of putty-like compliance was in order. I composed myself. "I agree in principle, but I want a clearly set out programme for the next twelve months. If we're going to get Pink Priest back on track, I want to do it properly. Let's set a target to double sales by Christmas."

"Oh well done Felix! You *are* a fast learner – I so hoped you would be. John will send you a summary of this encounter along with the price increase and our marketing proposal."

They all snapped their laptops shut and stood. Sandra extended her hand once more. "Since we're all working together so constructively, I'll send through a ticket for the Grand Prix in July. Paris-Blois is the official Champagne sponsor and we have a marquee backstage. We always invite the Gatesave directors plus a few of the more important buyers. You won't be allowed in the premier seats, of course – you're not important enough – but you can stand with the plebs. It should be a fun day out."

Excellent! My first proper junket and a Formula One race at that. This is what big business is all about, I mused. It certainly beat a plate of Bulgarian stew at Georgi's restaurant.

* * *

Two months later, race day arrived and a right orgy of glamour and over indulgence it was too. The Gatesave directors were flown in by helicopter, buzzing overhead as I crawled for two hours along the traffic-fouled approach to Silverstone. But, once there, I was waved into the Paris-Blois marquee where the Champagne and caviar were flowing. I was soon surrounded by a bevy of lightly dressed promotions girls, all anxious to explain their marketing plans for the Champagne sponsor, mainly through the medium of touch.

I was involved in a detailed discussion of brand equity round the back of the marquee when I heard a familiar voice. "Zip yourself up darling and make yourself scarce." It was Sandra, cigarette in hand, smirking at me and my companion. I helped the lady secure her top, which had indeed become rather loose during our conversation, and she disappeared back into the tent. "I heard you were a bit of a player Felix. Who can blame you when it's all laid out on a platter?"

Sandra wore a lace-trimmed, blue summer dress, her curves hovering, unsupported, a tantalising hair's breadth from freedom.

"I'm simply immersing myself in your corporate culture," I replied, blushing as I realised I was addressing her spellbinding chest, "the last thing I want to be is inappropriate."

"Unfortunately, mister junior buyer, you are inappropriate. Wildly so. Frankly, you've more chance of being appointed CEO this afternoon than ever getting your hands on these." She didn't have to look down – it was perfectly clear what she was talking about.

"Well, I aim to be CEO one day," I mumbled. I had a strong feeling I was still wallowing in the realm of the wildly inappropriate.

Sandra took a drag from her cigarette and placed the forefinger of her other hand against my chest, tracing a little circle. She exhaled into my face. "There are three things I look for in a man. One, good looks. You get a big tick there, Felix, I must confess. Two, not too bright, but intelligent enough to dress without help. Again, a tick for you, I think."

She tapped her finger against my left nipple. I remained as still as possible as a warm glow spread from the centre of my body to the extremities. I had a feeling I was about to experience something profound.

"Three, the kind of money that means he flies into Silverstone in his own aircraft." She turned and nodded at the row of helicopters parked in front of the race track. "My boyfriend owns that one. If you can point out yours, you might just be in with a chance."

"I look forward to showing you my chopper as soon as possible," I blurted, accidentally.

Sandra threw back her head and squealed with laughter. "Felix! You get an extra portion of pudding for that one. You really are très drôle, aren't you?"

She took another drag and was serious once more. "I need a favour Felix. If you do it, I'll help you with your first step toward that CEO position. Does that sound like a deal?"

"I'd be delighted to do you a favour," I replied, fighting but failing to wrench the steering wheel of conversation around another car-crash of double entendre.

"Not that sort. Your colleague, Bill Teddington, the spirits buyer. Is he a friend of yours?"

Bill had been spectacularly unfriendly to me throughout my first six months. Among a bunch of spiteful and arrogant so-and-sos, he'd stood out as almost maniacally hostile. "Not in the slightest."

"Good. He's a corrupt old loser, Felix. And although that's not unusual or even problematic in the normal run of things, his greed and inflexibility is now causing my company significant concern."

I stayed silent. I knew when I was out of my depth.

"He is making demands of us that are outside the parameters of our tolerance. He has become good friends with his opposite number at Merryfields, your principal competitor."

"I see." I didn't really see at all.

"Together, these two little birds think they can dictate what's happening in the market. What price to sell our brands at, what new products to list. That's not an acceptable situation for Paris-Blois Brands, Felix. We decide what happens in the market, not some tatty old buyer with body odour and a cheap suit." Sandra took another drag.

I hoped she was referring to Bill Teddington, not me. "How do I come into it?"

"At some point over the next few weeks you will find yourself in a situation with Bill, where you are both under pressure. You need to be ready to show him up."

"Can you give me a little more detail? That's rather vague."

"No I can't. But it will happen. We will arrange it. I will give you warning and you need to be ready and prepared. Understand?"

"Not really. You haven't given me terribly much to go on."

"We will, when the time is right. In the meantime, keep up the good work. And if you do make it to CEO and get your pilot's licence, look after these. I won't stand for poor performance."

She reached down and grabbed my crown jewels, giving them an assertive squeeze. I nearly sounded a trumpet salute on the spot.

CHAPTER NINE - STORE WALK

There were many directors at Gatesave, but only one Director. His true title was something bland, like Commercial Director or Trading Director, and he was not the most senior on the board. But everyone knew where the power really lay. It was with The Director.

All the Heads of Execution and Heads of Margin reported to him. He was tall, thin and pale, but always immaculately turned out in dark suit, white shirt and plain tie, usually red. A mean, secret policeman's smile rested upon his lips, which vanished into a taut, severe slit when he spoke. His voice was surprisingly high pitched but quiet and precise, without a trace of accent. He had never been known to raise his voice, nor to swear. He didn't need to, because everyone remained absolutely silent and motionless in his presence unless asked a question, the answer to which generally determined the immediate trajectory of one's career.

The undisputed zenith of terror was The Director's monthly Store Walk. This took place at an ungodly hour on the first Thursday of every month. A random clutch of buyers and junior managers from across the business would receive an email at four the preceding afternoon, simply stating, 'Store Walk, 4 a.m. sharp', followed by the location – generally an out-of-town superstore within fifty miles or so of London.

The Store Walk was the graveyard of many a buyer's career. The preceding evening would be spent in a cold sweat, memorising your products' selling prices, your competitors' selling prices – God help you if your product was more expensive – weekly rates of sale and profit margins.

I had just arrived back at my desk after an extended product-immersion session with Georgi, who was very anxious to start doing business with Gatesave. Rather than discuss his wine range in a dull Gatesave meeting room, I insisted on lunch at a fine Mayfair restaurant that was rapidly becoming one of my favourite eating places, so long as some other generous soul was paying, of course.

Georgi was only too happy to oblige. After all, a listing at Gatesave would be worth ten times what poor old Charlie's Cellar could ever have delivered. Five courses of exquisite seafood, pasta and ox cheek later, we surveyed the empty bottles – a crisp Gavi to match the calamari, an aromatic Barbera d'Alba to accompany the exquisite risotto, and no fewer than three bottles of muscular Barbaresco, an absolute dream with the ox cheek ragù.

We were the last lunch patrons left and the restaurant manager and staff had joined us, helping us finish off the last of the wine. As an encore, we broke open a bottle of aged grappa to wash down some gorgeously creamy home-made gelato.

At five p.m., as the first customers started to arrive for an early dinner, I embraced Georgi and wished him good night, accompanied by a vague promise to list some of his fabulous Pinot Grigio later that year. Accompanied by a cacophony of cheerful ciaos from the staff, I swung gracefully into a black cab and announced the address of Gatesave House.

"No need to bloody shout," muttered the cabbie as he pulled away from the curb at what seemed an unnecessary pace, flinging me across the back seat, my phone clattering to the floor. As I picked it up I saw I'd received a text message. It was from Sandra at Paris-Blois.

Memorise pricing of our Scotch brands in Gatesave and competitors. Tonight.

What the hell did that mean? I squinted at the dancing letters. I really was quite bladdered. Why would I need to know the price of whisky? Spirits were nothing to do with me – that was spiteful old Bill's job.

Back in the office, I sat regally at my computer and tapped in my password, managing to spell it correctly on the third attempt. I dispatched a couple of incisive emails to Trisha, pre-written that morning, just to show my manager I was on top of my game and still committed to my role well after most others had left for the night. Then I focused on the dozen new messages in my inbox, just in case something important should...

My blood froze. Embedded among automated sales reports and unsolicited sales pitches, a single message, sent at precisely 16:00, stared back at me like a rattlesnake:

Sender: Director's Office

Subject: Store Walk. 4am sharp. Oxford South.

A Store Walk. My first. There was no escape. Failure to attend, even backed up by a doctor's note certifying Ebola, would result in a rapid transfer to a 'development role' as buyer for toilet tissue and moist wipes. The blood pounded in my head and my stomach began to twist and turn quite aggressively. Even at the top of my game, with hours of sober preparation behind me, this would be a terrible trial. With a skinful of Piedmontese wine and 70 miles to travel, my cause was hopeless.

I put my head in my hands, principally to prevent it falling onto the keyboard, and cursed my luck. Oh God, why did I start on the grappa? Tears of pure alcohol dripped from my eyes. This was it, the game was up. A brilliant career as a promising young member of the wine industry was about to end in ignominy, less than ten hours from now. A bitter memory of ox cheek ragù pricked at the back of my throat.

"Oh dear!" observed Joan, my snootiest colleague, peering at me with distaste over her half-moon glasses. "A Store Walk tomorrow and you've come down all poorly." She smirked and made little quotation marks in the air as she said 'all poorly'. "I heard you were on the list, but I didn't want to interrupt your important meeting…"

Joan was not a big fan of mine. After decades in the 'proper' wine trade, as she called it, buying fine claret for wine merchants that catered exclusively to millionaire Hooray Henrys, she had washed up on the shores of the supermarket world. Her distaste at having to buy cheap plonk for the masses was tempered, just about, by the comfort of her gigantic salary.

For Joan Armitage was a Minstrel of Wine, one of only a thousand in the world, who by virtue of that exceptional qualification were able to command astronomical salaries from starstruck wineries, merchants and supermarket chains. Joan was diligent, precise and trustworthy, qualities she evidently, and quite unfairly, judged lacking in yours truly.

"I knew I could count on you Joan, you've always been supportive of younger members of the team," I muttered.

Joan's smirk faded and her phone pinged. "Ah, my car. Off to the theatre tonight." She sprayed each side of her neck from a tiny bottle of cologne. "Good luck with the Store Walk tomorrow."

I stumbled to the toilets and splashed cold water over my face. With my head only a little clearer I stared at myself in the mirror. Concentrate! Face the impending horror.

The Store Walk. I had heard tales of KGB-style interrogations on price points and margins, tearful buyers stumbling and forgetting the price of their products, the quiet Director with his watery eyes pointing to the door. I knew the prices of about half my products but I had a couple of hundred in total and I needed some serious cramming time. I also needed some sleep and a clear head.

Then I remembered Sandra's text, and her command to memorise whisky prices, as if I didn't have enough on my plate. It had to be connected with The Store Walk, but how?

It was seven p.m. and time for action. I strode back to my desk and grabbed my laptop, downloading all the range and pricing information I would need. At least there was no need to return home. I was careful to keep a change of clothes, overnight bag and a range of pharmaceuticals in my foot locker for the not infrequent occasions that sunrise found me in a bed far from home.

I hailed a taxi to Paddington station and just made the 19:22 to Oxford, pausing only to buy a large Cornish pasty to line my stomach. An hour later I was checking into a budget hotel near the station. I drank a pint of water and set my phone's alarm for two in the morning.

What felt like ten seconds later, an urgent beeping told me it was time to wake up. My head felt like a rusty bell and my mouth a camel's nosebag. Bleary with nausea, I prized open an old shoe-polish tin, in which I had secreted a few scoops of Madame Joubert's Lekker Medisyne Trommel. I stirred a teaspoon of the powder into a glass of water. It hissed as it dissolved to the familiar faint pink. I downed the liquid and almost straight away felt my dry throat soothe. Gradually, my abused head cleared, my joints loosened and the adrenaline started to pump.

For the next 90 minutes I crammed information, flicking to the websites of competitors and back to my spreadsheets. What was the price of our cheapest Portuguese red? What profit margin did it make? Was our Liebfraumilch cheaper or more expensive than the equivalent in Merryfields? In how many stores did we sell three-litre boxes of Bulgarian Merlot?

Not the most glamorous end of the wine business and, all in all, a pretty dry hour and a half, but I do have a certain talent for remembering names and numbers, particularly with Madame Joubert's help, and now I felt a lot more confident than

I did staggering around the office the previous evening. A tepid shower later, I was directing a minicab to the store, which lay three miles south of the city centre.

It was ten to four and some thirty cars were already parked outside the supermarket. The poor devils would have been up the same time as I, sweating their way through the two-hour drive from London's suburbs after cramming all their figures the night before. The rest of the retail park was shuttered and in darkness, but Gatesave was incandescent, aisles brightly lit and the shelves heaving with produce, shining like the Garden of Eden. A security guard slid the doors open and gave a grim nod as I squeezed through.

A large knot of people hovered just inside the entrance. Some were silent. Others gazed at printed sales reports, murmuring numbers to themselves. All eyes darted up as I slipped through the door but quickly returned to their crib sheets when they saw I was not The Director. You couldn't blame them for a last-minute burst of revision. The Director never forgot a number, and God help you if you didn't know your figures. Somehow the freak knew the price of everything – some suspected he had some sort of implant receiving information directly from the Head Office mainframe.

The store management were all present, looking pale and crumpled. This was a trial for them too. They would have received the same twelve hours' notice and worked all night to ensure every gap was filled, every surface cleaned, every toilet seat buffed. A poor visit from The Director would guarantee the Manager a new job as night supervisor in a grim inner-city store, ejecting drug addicts and mopping up the blood of staggering drunks who'd gashed their heads open on the confectionary counter.

And there, in the scrum, was Bill Teddington, Buyer of Spirits and Liqueurs. I recalled how I'd brushed off the hostility he'd shown on my first day and, a couple of weeks later, made the friendly suggestion that he barter some single malt from his store cupboard for a bottle of fine Port.

"Up yours," he'd said. "Wine is for ponces!"

I hadn't bothered trying to speak to him again – I can take a hint. But I thought there might be some opportunity for solidarity, given the ordeal ahead, so I strolled over. He was scowling at a pile of strawberry punnets, his big red splodge of a nose looking like a refugee strawberry itself.

"Morning Bill!" I breezed. "Have you done the Store Walk before, then? Any tips?"

Bill turned to me, contempt dripping from his blotchy face. "Yes I have. And no I haven't. Not for a snotty, over-promoted little turd like you." He paused. "Heard you were out on the lash yesterday and didn't see the call-up until last night. You're going to get your guts ripped out." He looked pleased. A faint waft of body odour and old alcohol reached my nose.

"Thanks anyway," I said. You smell of decline and failure, I thought. Maybe I'll look and smell like you in a couple of decades. But not just yet, thank God. I made an insincere promise to myself to stop drinking by the age of forty.

Why had Sandra insisted I learn the prices of Bill's products? I fumbled for my phone. Her message had been sent yesterday at 14:55, over an hour before The Director's email. How on earth did she know we were both on the Store Walk?

The low murmur suddenly ceased. I turned and there was The Director, striding towards us at speed, the little sneer playing across his lips. He had emerged from the back of the store, after a few minutes observing everyone on the CCTV no doubt. Two flunkies with large notebooks trotted a couple of paces behind him, occasionally breaking into a canter to keep up.

He passed straight by me and stopped at the front of the store, gazing out into the still-dark car park. A car turned off the main road, its headlights washing the concrete as it sped towards the store. Someone was late. Nodding to the security guard, The Director turned and faced us. The guard turned his bunch of keys and the catch clicked, immobilising the sliding doors. I glanced at my watch and saw the second hand flick past north. The car swung into the nearest free bay and the slam of its door was followed by the clicking of running heels. A mortified face appeared at the glass, eyes wide with horror. I recognised a dowdy woman from frozen desserts.

"I'm sorry," she called to The Director's back, her voice muffled through the glass. "My car wouldn't start!" Then to the security guard, pleading, "Please open the door!"

The guard didn't move. His eyes dropped to the floor.

"Morning ladies and gentlemen," began The Director in his high, nasal whine. A slight pause, a little smirk. "We appear to have a new Buyer for Toilet Tissue and Moist Wipes!"

A round of sick, nervous laughter.

The Director's smirk disappeared and he raised his gaze to a point high on the opposite wall. "The Store Walk begins!" He launched forward, the thirty of us fanning out behind, senior store and Head Office management in front, buyers behind. He scanned the bays of fruit and vegetables, suddenly seizing a lemon. "Not ripe!"

Joanna, the head of citrus, pushed her way to the front of the group. "Turkish fruit sir, the Spanish season's over early due to high demand and there's poor weather in South Africa, so the crop's short. The whole market's affected sir."

"And how have you turned this unfortunate situation to Gatesave's advantage?"

"We've negotiated a much lower price for the next two weeks, plus a big promotion once the new Mexican crop comes on stream – we'll have the best price in the country next month."

"Commercial impact?"

"We've forecast a ten percent sales decline but a margin improvement of four percentage points, so overall profit is in a good place, sir."

"I look forward to seeing that market-beating promotion. Don't let me down." The flunkies scribbled furiously in their notebooks. Next month's lemon promotion would be scrutinised closely, that was for sure.

There were questions about imported strawberry pricing, the availability of fresh basil, why our rivals had a better yoghurt promotion, why sweet corn was only available in four-packs rather than two-packs. A persistent rattle from a milk fridge, a sagging shelf in the Indian cooking-sauce aisle, an underlying smell of fish near the staff entrance. All issues were spotted, interrogated and the person in charge humiliated or reprieved, depending on The Director's whim.

"I see we have a new range of fruit juices," he declared, knowing full well the new juice buyer was present.

"Y-y-y-yes sir," quivered the young lady in charge of fresh and ambient juice.

"How is it performing?"

"Er-er-early days, sir. We expect it to exceed expectations."

"I expect it to exceed expectations too. But it is not, is it? Sales are disappointing."

"Ah, er... Yes. I mean no, it has been a little disappointing... People just haven't gone for the new pineapple and kumquat blend sir."

"And how do you intend to turn this disappointing situation around?"

"Er... we just need to educate our customers that ours are the best juices on the market."

I winced. Suggesting that our customers needed educating was not the kind of thing to float The Director's boat.

His lips turned crueller. "Maybe it is you who needs educating. Maybe you need some lessons in what our customers want and what they don't want." He turned to the store manager. "This young woman can work in your cold store for the next three months. That will help her learn what our customers like to buy and what they prefer to leave on the shelf."

"I'll arrange it right away sir."

The poor buyer stared at the floor, her eyes filling with tears. It would be a rough few months. A two-hour commute each way, every day, for three months, all for an eight-hour shift in a small, freezing room, humping heavy boxes of fruit. Still, who was I to judge? Maybe ninety days freezing your extremities off was a fair punishment for imposing a kumquat juice on the sensitive palates of Middle England.

"I'm still waiting to hear how we're going to turn our juice range from zero to hero."

The buyer continued to stare at the floor, sobbing. We wouldn't be getting much out of her now. Maybe it was Madame Joubert's recipe still coursing through my veins but I felt calmly confident and thought I'd pipe up.

"Healthy drinks sir. That's what we need and that's what is missing from the range."

The Director's head swivelled slowly, like a tank's turret. When he was facing me he raised an eyebrow, but said nothing.

"Nobody wants rich, sugary drinks these days sir," I continued. "They're worried about calories and tooth decay. They want low-sugar juice." It was so quiet you could have heard a spider wanking in the storeroom. Well, in for a penny, in for a pound. "We could create a healthier range of juices simply by diluting them with water. Then we could charge more because they're healthy."

The Director looked at me for a few seconds more. "It appears we have a marketing genius in the room." Was he being sarcastic? "Have you got that down?" he said over his shoulder. The flunkies nodded.

Victory, by George!

I felt someone barge past me hard, deliberately knocking my shoulder. It was Bill. "Brown-nosing twat," he whispered savagely.

We moved on, The Director at the tip of the arrowhead as we flew down the aisles. "Why are we at that price on Williams Gentleman's Relish? We are thirty percent more expensive than Merryfields!" There was no answer. To a flunkey, "I want the Head of Chutney in my office at midday."

Suddenly, we were in the wine and spirits section. I elbowed my way forward, tensed for the challenge.

"Why have we launched ten new Italian wines and only four French?"

An easy starter question. "The lira has depreciated faster than the franc sir," I said. "As a result we have improved margins by half a percentage point."

"Why are Findlay's Stores cheaper than us on Hock? Our biggest selling wine!" There was a more dangerous tone to his voice now and I steeled myself.

"That was a special promotion in Findlay's, sir. It finished two days ago. We will have our own, even more aggressive promotion starting tomorrow. I was with our supplier last week and gave them a very hard time, sir."

I certainly did. The export manager for our German Hock producer was tall, blond, very much into leather and I made it a priority to visit her at the winery every quarter.

"Good. I expect to see our German market penetration figures improve next week."

"I can assure you of that, sir."

The Director moved on a few paces to the whisky section. He ran a slender forefinger down a large bottle of scotch. "McDonald's Highland Blend. Who can tell me about this?"

"Yes, sir. One of our best sellers." Bill Teddington had manoeuvred himself next to the main man.

"Ah, Bill. Any good promotions coming up?" First name terms. The old rotter appeared to be well in with The Director.

"Something next month, nothing too deep, sir. A couple of pounds off. We're looking after the margin, as usual."

"Nothing going on in the marketplace to embarrass us then?"

"No sir. I'd know about it if there were."

"No doubt. And this new, young buyer that's just started at Merryfields? Might that make a difference to the market?"

Bill Teddington's smile remained in place while the colour drained from his face. Then the smile faded too. "Er…new buyer?"

"Yes, the one who started yesterday. Following the sudden firing of the previous buyer."

Teddington's mouth made a couple of false starts, opening and closing like a goldfish's. "Fired? Is he?"

The supermarket was completely silent once more. Something was happening. I didn't quite know what, but if Bill Teddington's sweaty, grey face was anything to go by, it was going to get interesting.

"Left under quite a cloud, I hear," continued The Director. "Something to do with attempted collusion with a supplier. Inappropriate to gossip of course."

"Yes," croaked Teddington.

"The new buyer's started with a bit of a bang, though."

"Yes?" whispered Teddington. He looked hunted.

"So, any idea of the price of your biggest selling whisky in our main competitor's stores?"

Bill Teddington didn't have a clue, of course. But I did. I'd memorised all the prices a couple of hours ago. "They've put McDonald's Highland Blend on a fifty-percent discount. Started yesterday," I piped up.

The Director turned slowly towards me then back to Teddington. "Well Bill. Your junior colleague appears to know more about your products than you do. Our most ruthless competitor puts on the most aggressive whisky promotion in the past ten years, on our biggest seller, and you don't know anything about it. How can this be?"

Bill Teddington didn't answer. There was nothing to say except admit to gross incompetence or dastardly criminality, of course. Thanks to the ruthless, wonderful Sandra at Paris-Blois, only I knew that he'd been colluding with the buyer of Merryfields to stitch up the market. No wonder Bill always appeared effortlessly on top of everything. I wondered what he'd done to fall foul of Sandra. Perhaps he and his mate had over-favoured another supplier. Or perhaps they had demanded too large a bribe.

"Why are you still here?" said The Director, very quietly.

The crowd of executives parted and a corridor opened. Teddington crept through it and out of Gatesave, never to return.

"We need a spirits buyer," said The Director, turning to me once more, "which implies a promotion. I do enjoy being the bearer of good news!"

A vision appeared before me, a flock of beautiful Scotch whisky saleswomen with ivory skin, freckled breasts and curly ginger hair. I bowed my head solemnly.

"I accept the challenge, sir."

CHAPTER TEN -
THE MINSTRELS OF WINE

"**H**art!" An unmistakable bark from the far side of the floor. I turned in my seat, the office hubbub silenced, to see Jim Colt, Head of Margin, leaning from his office. His head jutted forward and his wild eyes stared, like a psychotic meerkat. "Hello? Yes, you golden boy! My office, now."

"Oh dear, Felix, you haven't cocked up already, have you?" smiled Joan, peering spitefully over her glasses.

Several hundred pairs of eyes followed my walk across the vast trading floor to the Head of Margin's corner office. Colt stood behind his enormous desk, scowling down at the piece of paper before him.

"Morning sir," I started brightly.

"Shut it!"

"Right, sorry."

Colt looked up, the look of hatred undimmed. "The door Hart. Shut the bloody door."

"Right." I slid the frosted panel home with a click.

"So, you're to be promoted. Sounds like you had a good Store Walk. The Director likes you. Big round of applause. Well done." The Head of Margin gave three slow, loud claps. A master class in sarcasm.

But my spirits rose a little. This was what passed for a good mood from the Head of Margin. If I'd displeased him, I'd already be bent over the desk, being thrashed like a blaspheming camel herder on the twelfth day of Ramadan.

His head moved forward a little and the cruel eyes narrowed. "Lord only knows why The Director rates you. Because I don't. I think you're an over-promoted wet-nursed wonder."

I stayed silent and looked as grave as I could.

"But ... you have apparently been promoted. To Middle Wine and Spirits Buyer designate." The Head of Margin wiggled his head as his lips lingered over 'middle'. "But we have standards here at Gatesave, Hart. We don't just promote precocious little tarts like you for free. I'm not having you wanking round the world's vineyards, racking up air miles and spreading venereal disease on the company budget, unless you can show you've got what it takes."

He turned his back and inhaled deeply, studying the wall. It was covered with dozens of certificates boasting wins in various trade competitions. I tried to follow his gaze. I spotted 'Best Added Value Poultry Product' in the Annual Protein Awards, illustrated by a plucked chicken sitting on a throne, complete with jaunty crown resting where its head once sat. Next to it, a gilt frame highlighted a gold medal for seasonal innovation in the household care category, awarded to a rum punch-perfumed Christmas shower tile cleaner.

The Head of Margin let out a little sigh of recognition, "Ah, there it is." His finger tapped the glass of a grand-looking certificate, just above head height. I recognised the cod-heraldic detail immediately. Glasses of wine and classical instruments danced around the border, intertwined with leafy vines and bunches of grapes. In the centre, an old stringed instrument, some kind of lute, was crossed with a bottle of Champagne and surrounded by cavorting pan-like characters. 'Certificate of Honour' it began, in fancy red calligraphy. 'To Gatesave Supermarkets, for their loyal support of the Worshipful Institute of the Minstrels of Wine'.

My heart sank. Surely he wasn't expecting me to embark upon the feared Minstrel of Wine course? I had seen far too many shiny-faced young sommeliers throw themselves into the ordeal, only to emerge physically and mentally broken by the intensity of the coursework and the punishing pressure to succeed. And, of course, there was the terrifying final exam, a legendary all-night combined tasting and classical music recital in front of the thousand-strong chamber of the Worshipful Minstrels themselves.

The Head of Margin turned back to me, the smile replaced by his default look of contempt. "Gatesave don't employ light-weights as buyers, Hart. Your promotion is provisional on you taking and passing the Minstrel of Wine exam."

I nodded, miserably.

"Which I suspect, given that it's very bloody tricky, you will royally cock up."

"I'll give it one hundred percent, sir."

"That's the spirit Hart." The snarl was back. He leant over the table. "Because when you do muck it up, you're back to assistant arse-licker to the bag-in-box wine buyer. A role more suited to your miniscule talents. Now sod off."

I made my way past the banks of desks and staring eyes and re-took my seat.

"Have they fired you yet, Felix?" asked Joan sweetly, her fingers dancing on the keyboard before her.

"No. The Head of Margin was just confirming my promotion and congratulating me."

"Oh don't be silly Felix. I think we both know that's not true."

Of course it wasn't. Positivity, affirmation and respect were utterly foreign lands to the Head of Margin. Legend has it that his very first words, at his dear mother's breast, were "That milk's not bloody warm enough."

"Actually, they want me to become a Minstrel of Wine."

"Ha!" Joan let out a shriek of delight. "You? That is hilarious! You haven't got a hope."

"I was hoping you might give me a few tips actually Joan. As a kind of mentor."

"Sorry Felix. That's just not possible. Institute rules."

It was true, not that the mean old cow would have helped me anyway. The Worshipful Institute of the Minstrels of Wine imposed a code of silence, known as the *omertà di vino*. Nothing that took place in the final exam, with the exception of the candidate's choice of musical recital piece, could be revealed outside the Institute. To break the omertà would result in expulsion from the Institute and a bar on any job associated with wine anywhere in the world. Given the influence wielded by senior Minstrels, who dominated the boards of most major wineries and wine merchants, not to mention the wine-buying departments of the larger supermarkets, this was no idle threat.

All that was really known of the final exam, *La Vendange* or 'The Harvest', was the existence of a gigantic blind tasting at which the student had to correctly identify the overwhelming majority of the wines before them. No spitting was permitted – all wine had to be swallowed. Students who correctly identified enough wines then proceeded to the second stage, *Le Récital*, where they performed a piece of classical music, scored by a panel of senior Minstrels. If the student was awarded a high enough score, they were judged worthy of initiation into the Worshipful Institute of the Minstrels of Wine.

The Institute itself traced its origins back to Ancient Greece and the pagan cult of Dionysus, God of Wine, the Harvest and Theatre. Back then the grape harvest would have been accompanied by a festival of singing and dancing and, presumably, a right old orgy of shagging, hence the Institute's insistence on both a comprehensive wine knowledge and a mastery of classical music.

The latter, it was generally acknowledged, had the useful secondary purpose of weeding out the plebs and ensuring the Institute's membership remained dominated by a better class of arse-hole.

As a result of the omertà, a legend had grown around the final exam. There were tales of a befuddled student projectile-vomiting over the piano keys while tackling Rachmaninov, and another stumbling, stupefied with drink, into her own harp strings. One student, a gifted classical trombonist, was said to have nearly choked to death on regurgitated claret after confusing his breathing during a tricky passage of the Rimsky-Korsakov Trombone Concerto.

But, light-hearted moments aside, there was a darker side to the Minstrels. Such was the pressure to pass, and so huge the benefits of initiation, that many young winemakers and sommeliers who stumbled at the final hurdle had taken their own lives. Only last year, a sensitive young Chilean winemaker, beside himself with distress, had drowned himself in a vat of his own Merlot.

"What was your recital piece then Joan? I believe you're allowed to tell me that."

"Vivaldi's Flute Concerto No. 3 in D major," she replied.

I could just imagine her trilling her prissy way through a flute concerto, like a smug swot. "How splendid. Did you puke down the pipe at all?"

Joan looked up from her screen. "You're an immature idiot, Felix. Do you even play a musical instrument?"

"Is the bass guitar permitted?"

"If you can find a pre-1910 piece of classical music for the amplified guitar, Felix, then you're welcome to perform it."

"How about Morris dancing? Would that be allowed?"

"Good luck with your studies, Felix, it's been nice working with you. I am so looking forward to next January's La Vendange." She put on an innocent face. "I wonder who they'll employ in your place next year. Our Head of Execution doesn't really tolerate failure, does he?"

"Failure Joan? I don't know the meaning of the word." But my bluster was all for show, I knew it would be a long, hard slog. I sighed. That's twelve months soaked up by study when I'd rather be chugging ale and shooting pool with Tariq, Dan and the boys down the Green Lanes Billiards Club. Still, there are worse things to study than wine and, in the extremely unlikely event of my passing the exam, I'd be made for life.

***

Gatesave duly paid ten thousand Swiss francs into the Institute's offshore bank account for my tuition. By way of encouragement, Gordon Bannerman, Head of Execution, caught me a sucker punch as he passed me in the queue for the canteen and, as I fought for breath, whispered "That's nothing compared to what you'll get if you waste that ten grand."

The next few months passed relatively quickly. I was treated with a modicum more respect by Joan, despite the rather slim probability of my elevation to the rank of Minstrel. She would invite me to her selection tastings, occasionally ask my opinion of a particular Burgundy, and give a grudging nod if I supplied an articulate answer.

I attended the other wine buyers' tastings too and I became proficient at writing rapid tasting notes with one hand, while swirling and nosing a glass with the other. After a few months I could dash off a recognisably different description for fifty Australian Chardonnays in the course of an hour.

Every Wednesday evening I attended a class at the headquarters of the Minstrels of Wine, a vast stone building on Central London's Long Acre, its grand entrance flanked by two huge, naked cherubs, each caressing a bottle of wine. Students were not permitted to enter through the main door – a side entrance led directly to the *Théâtre de la Véraison* or 'Ripening Hall' where a fully-fledged Minstrel would deliver a seminar on a particular wine region, accompanied by fifty small glasses of wine from that area. One week might be Sauvignon Blanc from New Zealand, the next Pinot Noir from Oregon.

Spitting was absolutely forbidden on all Minstrel of Wine premises, out of deference to Dionysus. It was considered an insult to the gods to waste a drop of wine that had passed one's lips. One had to take as small a sip as possible, write a detailed tasting note, and swallow. At first I tended to take a rather large gulp of each wine but quickly found it impossible to write coherent tasting notes after a couple of dozen glasses, and my first few lectures ended with a copious throwing-up in the back streets of Covent Garden. Any vomiting on the premises would result in immediate expulsion from the course, a fate that befell several less robust students within the first month.

During the course of each lecture, as each wine was sampled, the tutor would choose a student to stand and describe it in detail. The student would have to fluently catalogue the wine's composition, place of origin, the variety of wood that made up the storage barrel and the species of toenail fungus afflicting the peasant who had trodden the grapes. I jest on the final point, of course, but only just. It was an intense experience and the tutors were merciless with any student who failed to give an eloquent characterisation of a wine, which of course became harder the more we drank.

One unfortunate young lady, an apprentice sommelier at a London hotel, was suddenly lost for words when obliged to describe the twenty-fifth wine in a line-up of Greek dessert wines. Stumbling slightly as she stood, and leaning heavily on the desk in front, she raised the glass to the light and stuttered "Fruity…"

"Fruiteee?" roared that evening's tutor, a limping, bearded winemaker from the island of Santorini, with all the charm of a pirate who'd just mislaid his favourite parrot. "That ees all? Fruiteee? Here is fruiteee!"

He lifted a heavy bunch of grapes from an earlier demonstration and pushed them into the hapless student's face. She staggered backwards and fell into her chair, red juice running down her chin and staining her shirt. It was an appalling piece of bullying behaviour and, I'm ashamed to say, extremely amusing. Of course, there was no chance of him being reported or sanctioned – every student was there to ascend to the rank of Minstrel of Wine and a complaint to the Institute would be a sentence of death for one's career.

Every month there would be an exam on what we had learnt to date. It consisted of a three-hour written paper accompanied by twenty glasses of wine. In addition to theory questions on methods of vine growing and barrel making, each wine had to be sampled, swallowed, a lyrical tasting note written, and the wine's region identified. Points were gained for the eloquence of the tasting note and a bonus if it rhymed.

These monthly tests were high-pressure affairs. If you failed to identify the origin of at least three quarters of the wines, or if the lyricism of your tasting notes was found wanting, you were failed and that was the end of the course for you. The class began with everyone standing and a roll call of those who had passed read aloud by the tutor. Each student was permitted to sit only when their name was called. Those who remained standing when the list of names ended were expected to leave the room, never to return.

There was no opportunity to re-sit the test, and nobody was ever permitted to re-start the Minstrel of Wine course. Inevitably, there were tears and pleas when the handful of still-standing failures were left exposed at the end of the roll call. Some students didn't even make it to the end of the list, fainting at the pressure of being among the final few standing. But any protest was to no effect. No explanations were given as to why a student had failed. The tutor would simply state solemnly that some of the assembled had failed to please the gods. And that was that.

Now, I wouldn't want you to think me a heartless wretch or immune to the pressure of these occasions. If anything, I was under greater pressure than most of my fellow students – failure implying a knee in the nuts from the Head of Execution and the end of my career at Gatesave. Many of my fellow wannabe Minstrels could at least flit back to Daddy's vineyard or a dusty career advising chinless wonders on the value of their cellars, while I would be reduced to mucking out the stables at Cackering Hall, my dreams of international travel, drinking and shaggery well and truly sunk.

But the pressure focused my mind and, though I say so myself, I found I had rather a knack for identifying wines and writing suitably flowery words of praise. I was usually pretty sure I'd passed each monthly exam, and so it proved. That's not to say there weren't a few squeaky-bum moments when we were down to the final dozen still standing in the lecture hall the week following an exam. But the tutor always called 'Hart!' before the end and, with sweat dripping from my armpits, I would sink gratefully into my seat.

***

It was early autumn when I received my annual phone call from Portia.

"Hello Felix. Hope you're well. I thought you might want to know how Woolf is doing?" She'd named our son after Virginia, the author. Her feminist support group had a list of approved names for boys.

"Of course! I'd nearly forgotten about the little tyke. Does he speak Latin yet?"

"Don't be an arse, Felix, he's only four. He's doing very well. Actually, I'm calling because one of our neighbours needs help."

"Sorry Portia, I'm not really qualified to deliver calves."

"He's not a dairy farmer, stupid, he's a wine farmer. It's Jeremy Spott-Hythe."

"I thought Jeremy was that infant you were supposed to marry? Do they allow small children to make wine in Kent?"

"Not him, his father. All the first-born males in the Spott-Hythe family are called Jeremy. It does make things confusing. Anyway, he wants to know whether he can sell his new sparkling wine to Gatesave. Will you go and see him?"

"I suppose so. I don't have to visit Cackering Hall and see your parents, do I?" I shuddered at the memory of tearing around under that dining table on my hands and knees, her lunatic father threatening to discharge his shotgun into my tender regions.

"No, that's not permitted. Woolf is at a very impressionable age and my feminist support group says he must be protected from exposure to alpha males if he is to develop into a truly empathising new man."

Fair enough, I thought, with a little twinge of pride that Portia still considered me an alpha male.

And so, on a fine September afternoon I made the journey to Chateau Spott-Hythe, a large stone farmhouse in the heart of the Garden of England. I walked up the track, the vineyards either side hanging with plump ripe grapes, and knocked on the half-door. A tall man opened the upper part. He was around fifty, tall and bare-chested, and gave me a wide grin with wine-stained teeth.

"Ears?" he boomed, in an exceptionally posh voice.

"I beg your pardon? Are you Jeremy Spott-Hythe?"

"Ears!" he boomed again.

"Ears?" I repeated. This was more difficult than I'd expected. Was it some sort of test?

"Ears. I'm Spott-Hythe. Are you the supermarket fellow?"

"Ah, yes. I am." The penny dropped. He'd been saying 'yes', not 'ears'. He really was very, very posh. "Felix Hart, nice to meet you."

"Good-o. Come on in!"

He opened the lower half of the door, revealing that he wasn't just bare chested, but entirely naked. He turned and walked back into the farmhouse kitchen, his wrinkled bottom cheeks just failing to obscure his low-hanging goblin's purse. I followed, somewhat apprehensively.

"Have a seat, old chap."

I sat at the farmhouse table which was littered with half-full glasses of red and white wine. Spott-Hythe stood at the other end, dancing from one foot to the other, his dickory dock swinging like a pub sign in a strong wind.

"I couldn't help noticing that you're wearing no clothes," I said.

Spott-Hythe looked down. "Ah yes. Fancy that. Never mind. One finds it easier to detect changes in atmospheric pressure when one is unencumbered by clothing. It informs one when it's time to pick the grapes, you see."

Good Lord, I thought, you really are a chinless bloody lunatic, aren't you.

"Right, I see. I understand you wish to sell your wine to Gatesave?"

"Well, ears, that would be wonderful." He turned and grabbed an unlabelled green bottle from a shelf. "Here, you must try our sparkling wine. This is from our first vintage, two yahs ago." He popped the cork and a little foam bubbled from the neck as he poured me a half-glass. "Lively little bugger," he chuckled as he stretched to pass me the wine, his meat and veg swinging like an unsecured wrecking ball.

I sniffed the glass and was struck by the attractive, brioche-scented aroma. I took a sip and the bubbles danced over my tongue like creamy lemon sherbet. "That's rather good, actually."

"Yippee!" Spott-Hythe beamed and gave a little jump, sending his flapdoodle spinning like a windmill. "I've just opened my rosé fizz too, would you like a taste?"

"Is that your rosé there?"

I pointed to the vessel on the table, right in front of his groin. His whirling frankfurter had come to rest in the glass, the bulbous end dunking itself in the liquid like a thirsty baby elephant.

"Oh. I'll pour you another, shall I?"

"If you wouldn't mind. I think that one might be corked."

He passed me a fresh glass of the pink sparkler. It was also excellent, a delicious riot of chilled strawberries and vanilla. Leaving aside his eccentric approach to common decency, Spott-Hythe clearly knew what he was doing in the vineyard.

"What do you call the wine?"

"My wife does all the creative stuff. She's decided to call it Cuvée Placenta."

I was taking another sip and I spluttered slightly. "That's a... memorable name. May I ask why?"

"It represents one's connection with the earth mother, or something. Let me ask her." Spott-Hythe turned and called over his shoulder. "Darling? Come and meet the nice man from the supermarket. He wants to talk about our wine."

Please don't let her be naked too, I prayed.

Mrs Spott-Hythe strode into the kitchen. She had long, straggly grey hair and, thank goodness, wore a rough, knitted kaftan, leaving just her arms and legs exposed. "So, the evil forces of capitalism arrive at our kitchen table!" she declared, in a reasonably friendly way.

"Yes indeed. Nice to meet you too, Mrs Spott-Hythe."

"Felix was just complementing us on the name Cuvée Placenta, darling."

"Yes. Our wine represents the connection between our bodies and the soil, our own offspring and the earth mother, the fluid of birth and our own, yielding flesh."

"It's a lovely concept," I lied, "but some of our customers are less progressive in their thinking. You might find a slightly more conventional name would work better."

"Like what?" sulked Mrs Spott-Hythe.

"A woman's name often makes a very attractive description for a wine. May I ask what your first name is?"

"Calathripia."

I paused for a second, slightly stumped.

"That's nice. How about Cuvée... Carolina? Or something like that?"

"I don't see what's wrong with 'placenta', but maybe we could look at it," she replied.

"Would you like to see the press house Felix?" asked Spott-Hythe. "The harvest is under way and the grapes are being trodden."

I agreed and we set out for the outlying farm buildings. Spott-Hythe, thank the Lord, pulled an old waxed jacket over his naked body before leaving the house.

"We pay unemployed youths from Ashford to tread the grapes," explained Mrs Spott-Hythe. "They find it quite liberating being out in the countryside, away from the mental pollution of urban materialism. It's tough, physical work but I read them my radical poetry to keep them motivated."

We entered the press house where a dozen bored-looking youths in shorts stomped up and down a shallow, cement-walled tank. Every so often a vineyard worker would walk in and pour a plastic crate of grapes into the mix. Their faces fell when they caught sight of Mrs Spott-Hythe.

"Good work, boys and girls, keep it up," she called. "Feel the produce of Mother Earth between your toes and rejoice that you are part of her eternal cycle!" She reached under her kaftan and pulled out a crumpled notebook. "I have written a new poem, to celebrate the glory of the vintage and your temporary rescue from the clutches of pseudo-aspiration."

A couple of the workers rolled their eyes.

She cleared her voice.

Thatcher's children!

Got no education,

Got no hope,

Destined for a life on the dole!

"She's ever so keen on all this poetry stuff," whispered her husband. "I don't really get it myself. I prefer the stuff that rhymes."

The council estate press-gang continued to trudge up and down their concrete pen, glum-faced.

Trapped in the Tory vice,

Exploited at every turn,

Who will liberate the downtrodden youth?

Not television, not capitalism, so whom?

"She can bang on a bit," Spott-Hythe confided. "Oooh, I haven't told you about my secret plan yet!"

"What's that then?"

"I'm going to make Kent's first ice-wine!"

"Interesting ..."

"We have an exposed hillside that always catches a severe frost in December. I planted it with Chardonnay three years ago and this winter I'm determined to pick the crop, frozen."

"Isn't ice-wine production quite labour intensive?"

"Yes, it's fiddly work. One has to check the vineyards every day for weeks, plucking out all the grapes that go rotten. Then, when you get the first really cold night, it's all hands on deck!

Every frozen grape must be picked individually at the coldest time, just before dawn. Can't see this lot being up for it ..."

Not your church, not your shopping mall,
Not your playstation, nor your porno mags,
The womb! The womb of Gaia! Hallelujah!
For only she can truly liberate!

"Oh, marvellous darling!" called Spott-Hythe, clapping his hands.

"Yes, very contemporary," I agreed.

Jolly hippy lunatics they may have been, but I knew an ethical and commercial opportunity when I saw one. I agreed to buy half the Spott-Hythes' sparkling wine production on the spot and convinced them to rechristen the wine Cuvée Hope. On my return to Gatesave, I asked the PR team to write a press release boasting we had created the first English wine that liberated the long-term unemployed from a life of crime.

It was a coup. The Guardian wrote a huge feature about Cuvée Hope, complete with pictures of Mrs Spott-Hythe and her team of underprivileged workers, all looking suitably downtrodden. We sent plenty of stock to stores in areas with high concentrations of concerned liberals and I was able to sell the wine at double the price I had originally intended – a feel-good fair trade premium, if you like.

The Spott-Hythes were delighted, particularly Mrs Spott-Hythe, who had been elevated locally to the status of warrior-priestess, with a two-page spread in the Ashford & Maidstone Times. By way of thanks, she arranged for a van to deliver a pruned-back Pinot Noir vine from the estate, rather inelegantly planted in a dustbin, with a note saying 'all must share of Gaia's placenta'. I positioned it just outside the front door in Little Chalfont where it thrived, thanks to Fistule watering it with the nutritious juice drained from his kitchen composting tank.

The Head of Execution even gave me a backhanded compliment – in the form of a back-handed slap to the head as I sat at my desk – snarling, "Tasty bit of PR work there, Hart. Hope you're not turning into a bloody communist? Ha!"

Who'd have guessed my first signing at Gatesave would be an English wine and a rip-roaring success? Despite my aversion to win-win situations, this *was* one – the supplier, the customer, the Gatesave shareholders and the press all loved it. I was almost dizzy with winning.

I had the hang of this game and it was time to set my sights even higher.

CHAPTER ELEVEN - THE NEW WORLD

My mouth was dry after all the talking. I was tired too. The little moth was no longer flitting around the lampshade – quite sensibly it must have gone to bed. I glanced at my watch. It had just gone two thirty in the morning.

"I need some water."

My interrogators considered me, unsympathetically.

"And I need the toilet too."

This might be my chance to escape. They couldn't refuse me a comfort break, surely? They'd have to escort me to the bathroom and I was sure I could trip the big chap over and make a run for it.

I heard the man behind me move. He walked past me, across the room to the closet and opened the doors, revealing a tiny bathroom containing a sink and a chemical toilet. He smirked.

"You can drink from the tap," said the seated man. "Be quick."

Sod it. There was to be no escape. I walked into the closet and pulled the doors closed. Between me, the toilet and the basin, there was barely enough room to turn around. There was no light switch either, the only illumination the glow from the crack between the doors. I lifted the lid of the chemical toilet and started peeing loudly. God, I was tired. I needed a pick-me-up. Frankly, I needed a drink, too.

Of course! I had my little travel-stash of Madame Joubert's. I felt in my jacket pocket and there was the old shoe-polish tin. There was only a tiny bit left – I'd been meaning to refill it. I'd have to use water from the sink. I finished peeing and reached for the loo roll hanging from a nail in the wall.

"Ooops. Made a bit of a mess in here. Sorry. I'll just mop up," I called.

I heard a sigh from the room but there was no other reply. The sink had no plug so I pulled off a wad of toilet paper and stuffed it into the hole, then turned on the tap and let water fill the basin. I eased the lid off the shoe-polish tin and poured the remaining Madame Joubert's into the water. It looked to be about one dose, although it was difficult to tell in the half-light. I used the tin as a scoop to drink from the basin.

"What you doing in there?" said the woman.

I could see the shadow of the big guy beneath the door. "Nearly done." I stuffed the wet tin into my pocket just as he swung the closet doors wide open. He frowned at me and inspected the floor, clearly unimpressed by my bathroom antics.

I manoeuvred my way out of the closet and retook my seat. The big man returned to the door, massaging his neck. It must have been painful standing for as long as that, I thought happily. I could feel my head clearing and a warm glow in my stomach as Madame Joubert started to do her work.

"Let's carry on, shall we." said the male interrogator. It was an order, not a question.

"We want to understand what happened in South Africa, Felix," said the woman. "Our records indicate you went there at very short notice for just a few days. One of our sources even has you linked with some kind of terrorist attack."

"Ah, no. I can understand the confusion but that's very easily explained."

"Then please do."

I took a deep breath.

***

"Wine! Wine! Where's the bloody wine team?"

My fellow buyers jumped as Jim Colt's dulcet tones boomed across the trading floor. George Bolus leapt to his feet, his gormless gammon face writhing in an attempt to look dynamic, while slimy Timmy Durange gave a cowardly little grimace over his monitor. Joan sighed and swore under her breath.

"Where's bloody Hocky Cocks?" he shouted. He sounded unhappy and it was odds-on that we were in for a good hiding. "Hocky Cocks!"

"Here I am Jim," called Patricia Hocksworth, our dear manager, running towards the office as fast as her comfortable, pear-shaped body could carry her. "Team!" she called over her shoulder, "Follow me! Jim wants a word!"

He wants more than a word, Trisha, I thought. He wants blood. So long as it was hers, or someone else's, that was fine by me.

The four of us followed Trisha at a semi-jog past the rows of desks. The office hum had quietened in anticipation and a sea of muted grins followed our progress to Colt's office. A couple of the more oikish supply chain boys shook their heads in mock pity.

"Good luck Blancmange!" whispered one to Durange, making a throat-cutting gesture. Timmy gave his peculiar half-angry, half-embarrassed grimace and lolloped on.

We entered the Head of Margin's office and lined up along one side of his table.

"Don't sit down." He held up a large piece of paper covered in numbers. "October's profit and loss statement. Anyone know why I might be ever-so-slightly irked by this particular document?" He raised his eyebrows and rattled the sheet in Trisha's face. "I'll give you a clue. It's to do with the word 'profit'."

Trisha's mouth opened and closed as she tried to summon an answer.

"Hocky Bollocks? Hello? Anyone at home?"

"We'll re-double our efforts sir," slimed Durange. "I have a new Bordeaux wine that will make a market-beating margin ..."

"Shut it Freaky, I'm talking to your boss," barked Colt, without moving his eyes from floundering Trisha.

"Sorry Jim, we're ... having a challenging time with the exchange rates ..."

"Holy Moly, does anyone have the slightest clue how to make money round here?" He looked at each of us in turn.

Trisha, red-faced, appeared on the verge of tears. Durange stared down, looking like a thrashed puppy. Joan stood motionless, a faint toilet-smelling expression on her face. Bolus hopped from foot to foot, dying to blurt out an incisive commercial fact, though the incisive portion of his brain appeared to be letting him down for the moment.

"What the hell are you doing, Bolus?" Colt spat, pointing at Bolus's twitching feet. "Are you trying to cha cha cha your way out of your miserable profit performance?"

"Ah ..." spluttered Bolus, "it's like this, Jim."

Colt's face darkened. If there was one thing he hated, it was an insignificant junior squit calling him by his first name. "No. It's like this, Bolus you cretin," he thundered, flapping the sheet around Bolus's face. "Australian wine – margin below target by four percentage points." He clenched his teeth. "Four whole percentage points! What the hell are you actually doing with your suppliers on your expensive overseas trips, you lamentable excuse for a buyer? Tickling their bollocks?"

"Ah … it's the exchange rates … the Aussie dollar has strengthened … grape prices have increased hugely … and … erm …"

"Oooh oooh, mister supplier," cut in the Head of Margin, eyes wild, his head just inches from the hapless Bolus. "Please let me bend over and blow you a price increase! I'm so sorry to hear about your money problems, is there anything else I can do by way of relief?"

Bolus stopped, mortified, his usually ham-hued face now pale. There was a moment of silence.

The Head of Margin looked at each of us in turn. "And? And? Any solutions or just more bloody problems?"

I decided this might be the moment for a well-polished Hart intervention. Carpe diem and all that. "Well, the rand is very weak sir. If we bought more South African wine we could enhance our margin significantly."

Colt stared at me for a few seconds. "Oh my. Goodness me. A buyer who might just know how to buy! Halle-bloody-lujah!" He wasn't smiling – the Head of Margin rarely did – but I sensed I had pleased him. He looked down at his sheet once more.

"The only countries that have improved their profit performance are Germany…" he ran his finger down the column of figures, "thirty percent up and an improved margin too… and Portugal, also improved by fifteen percent." He looked up at me. "That's you isn't it?"

I nodded humbly. A series of cracking promotions on Pink Priest, courtesy of the generous funding package from my darling Sandra, plus a cheeky little October discount on Port had sent my sales line soaring.

"Right. You," he pointed at me aggressively, finger stabbing into my chest. "You're the buyer of South African wine, right?"

Bolus, who was actually the buyer for South Africa, bobbed up and down, mouth closed, making muted whale calls from his throat.

"Er … actually George Bolus is the South African wine buyer. He's due to visit in a couple of weeks," piped up Trisha.

"Sorry? Is anyone under the impression this is a bloody committee meeting?" snarled Colt. "I've just explained that golden bollocks here is the South African wine buyer. He's going to go to South Africa and he's going to buy a tanker-load of gorgeous South African wine at a very low price. Then he's going to sell it, in our stores, at a lovely high price. That's how you make profit. Remember profit?"

He shook his sheet at Trisha and looked at each of us once more. "Does anybody have any problems? Any doubts, issues, little queries, anything whatsoever, about the efficacy of this plan?" Everybody, myself included, remained absolutely still and silent. "Then why, in the name of all that is holy, are you still standing in my office?"

We filed out and returned to our desks.

"Well done Felix," said Hocksworth, clapping me on the back. I'll give Trisha her due – she was never down for long. Must be something to do with being battered relentlessly with lacrosse sticks between the ages of four and twenty-one.

"I shan't let you down Trisha," I replied. "I already have some ideas on how we can spruce up the South African wine range. I think we can all agree it's a touch moribund."

I heard an angry snort behind me. Bolus's face had regained its livid, ham-like colour and he was smarting badly.

"It's not really fair on George, though," I said.

"Now Felix, you heard what Jim said. I think moribund, although harsh, is probably right and I'm sure George agrees a review is overdue."

"Maybe I could … no, it doesn't matter."

"What, Felix?"

"Well, I'm loathe to let the area go, when there are so many exciting things happening, but maybe I could offer George my

Eastern European area to look after? Romania, in particular, is so dynamic at the moment."

"Felix! That is a very constructive idea. It makes perfect sense from a resourcing perspective too."

"I don't want Eastern Europe," called Bolus, panic rising in his voice.

"Don't be such a grump George. I think it's an excellent idea. Felix, well done! And congratulations on your first Southern Hemisphere country. I'm sure you'll have a very productive trip."

By Christ, I thought, I shall! No more grey November afternoons tramping around the lower Danube with only a lard-infused pudding to keep me warm come nightfall. The sun-kissed winelands of Stellenbosch beckoned, Table Mountain rising majestically to the west as the surf rolled in from the Southern Ocean. Beautiful women of every race and colour hanging from my arms, unashamedly flaunting their fine bodies beneath skimpy beachwear, laughing joyfully as I tossed another sausage on the braai. By God, I had made it!

"I'll have to make it a flying visit, Trisha. I have my weekly Minstrel of Wine lecture every Wednesday and they forbid anyone to miss a single session."

"That gives you six days to find some fabulous wine. You can do it, Felix!"

"Leave it with me, Trisha. And you'll love Moldova, George," I reassured Bolus, as we arrived back at our desks. "They call it Europe's new wine horizon you know. I'm quite jealous, actually."

"Sod off, Hart," muttered Bolus, in a small defeated voice.

CHAPTER TWELVE - VAN BLERK

Two weeks later, after a deep Champagne-fuelled sleep, I adjusted the well-upholstered business-class seat to an upright position and the pilot announced our final approach to Cape Town.

Upon landing I breezed past the long, grumpy line of economy-class passengers and strode straight to the front. I made a mental note to fly business class, if not first class, for the remainder of my career. Quite frankly, it would be an outrage if a man in my position were expected to suffer queues, limited leg room and indifferent sparkling wine ever again.

"Enjoy our beautiful country," smiled the immigration official, stamping my passport.

I had to be on the road right away. I had my first winery meeting that afternoon in Robertson, a winemaking town on the far side of the Hottentots Holland Mountains. More importantly, I needed fresh supplies of Madame Joubert's Lekker Medisyne Trommel. I was down to my last couple of doses which, in case of emergency or other peril, I had smuggled out in a hollow toothbrush. True, all rather Midnight Express, but I wasn't sure of the ingredients and anything that reinvigorating had to be illegal. And spending my first big buying trip in a holding cell at Cape Town International with a bunch of Congolese crack addicts would have looked bad on my résumé.

The big problem was that I hadn't a clue where to find further supplies. I had asked every South African of my acquaintance whether they had heard of the stuff but nobody had any idea what I was talking about. There was no mention of it on the internet either, so far as I could see. Old Mr du Plessis had passed away some years earlier and taken the secret with him. Silly of me not to ask when he was still alive, but it was only in recent years that I had grown to truly depend on the magic powder, particularly at times of stress or persecution, which happened with increasing frequency as I clambered my way up the greasy corporate pole. My only clue was that Du Plessis once told me he owned a house in Prince Albert, a village hundreds of miles inland, and that he had spent his early life on a farming station called Kruidfontein, too small to appear on most maps. That seemed a sensible place to start.

I collected the hire car and was soon heading out of town. Table Mountain and the Cape Town metropolis receded into the haze in my rear-view mirror, and the sprawling townships, roasting under corrugated iron, were replaced by rolling hills braided with rows of grapevines. The Hottentots Holland Mountains lay a few miles ahead, their sandstone peaks glowing in the midday sun.

My destination was Vinkwyn Wine Cellars, a small producer on the outskirts of Robertson. I had done my research carefully back home, subscribing to obscure South African agricultural magazines, most of which needed translating from Afrikaans, poring over wine atlases and cross-referencing entries in my well-thumbed Jancis Robinson wine bible.

This particular winery was interesting for two reasons. Firstly, it had a new winemaker, a maverick named Wikus van Blerk who was conjuring incredible wines from the sandy soil and winning every gong going. A few award-winning wines always got the punters' juices flowing and I had a plan to cook up a good bit of PR back home.

Secondly, the source of his grapes was a new vineyard he had established in the barren interior of the Cape, hundreds of miles from the famous vineyards of Stellenbosch and Constantia. People said, quite openly, that he was mad, but there was no doubting the quality of his wines. The exact location of his experimental vineyard was a secret but it was believed to be in the Great Karoo, somewhere in the vicinity of Kruidfontein, Mr du Plessis's old stomping ground.

Two hours after leaving Cape Town, Vinkwyn Wine Cellars emerged from the haze on the flat approach to Robertson. It looked rather decrepit from the outside but inside I knew it would be packed with gleaming steel tanks and state-of-the-art equipment. I parked in the gravel and entered a small tasting room, moving slowly as the heat enveloped me after the cool of the air-conditioned car. It was deserted except for a small, bird-like woman behind the tasting bar, polishing a glass with a grey rag.

"Good morning. I'm Felix Hart from Gatesave Supermarkets. I was hoping to see Wikus van Blerk," I began brightly.

The bird-like woman glowered at me as she slowly polished her glass.

"Is Mr van Blerk here?"

"*Praat Afrikaans.*"

"No, sorry. I don't speak Afrikaans. Do you speak English?"

"*Praat Afrikaans.*"

"No, I don't. I don't speak Afrikaans. Is there anyone else here?"

"*Praat Afrikaans!*"

"No. As I've said a couple of times now, I don't speak Afrikaans. Sorry." I sighed and tried to recall some words from my tourist guide. "Ek praat nie Afrikaans. I don't speak Afrikaans. Is there anyone else here? Where is Mr van Blerk?"

"She's not asking if you speak Afrikaans. She's saying you must speak Afrikaans." A wiry man in loose-fitting dungarees appeared at the door. He had a bald, slightly sunburnt head, and a sullen expression.

"Ah, hello. Sorry?"

"She's saying 'speak Afrikaans'. You should speak Afrikaans."

"Right. Sadly, they don't teach it in North London, sorry about that. I'll be sure to subscribe to a correspondence course as soon as I'm back."

"Don't get clever with me, you British *kak*." He spat on the floor.

Marvellous, I thought. I've arrived at the headquarters of the Afrikaans Linguistic Defence League. I was pretty sure this guy wasn't Wikus van Blerk – I'd seen a couple of grainy photos and van Blerk was a big, bearded chap.

I decided to try a little charm. "I do apologise sir. I realise I should have a few more words of the local language. I've come a long way to visit Mr van Blerk, I'm a huge fan of his wines you see. My name is Hart by the way." I strode over and offered my hand. He considered it for a moment then shook it. He had a warm, rather oily hand. He didn't give his name.

"Good to meet you," I said. "What do you do here?"

"I do what Mr van Blerk tells me."

"Is there any chance I could meet Mr van Blerk?"

"Do you have an appointment?"

"No, I tried to phone from England many times but nobody ever picked up. And I don't think you have an email address."

He considered me for a moment. "You can't see him if you haven't made an appointment."

"Well, may I make one now?"

"No. Mr van Blerk does not make appointments."

I suspected a wind-up, but the man wasn't smirking, he just stood there with a slightly resentful expression. I wondered whether money might help. Or a threat of violence, perhaps. Probably not, everyone was armed to the teeth round these parts. "Can I taste some wines please? I'd like to buy some."

"We're sold out. Mr van Blerk's wines are very popular."

"Yes, well, that's why I'm here," I said, with a touch of irritation. Calm down Hart, I thought. Let's have a look around, see whether we can spot any clues. I wandered to the tasting bar. The bird-like woman kept her eyes on me, still polishing her glass with the same tatty rag. She retreated a step so she was backed right up against the wall. "People say he is a very interesting character. What is he like to work with?"

"He is a madman."

I looked up. "Really? In what way?"

"He only eats volstruise."

"What is that?"

"Volstruis. The big bird." He held his hand, palm down, above his head, to indicate something taller than himself.

What in God's name, I wondered, is this lunatic yokel on about? "Where does he grow his grapes?"

"In a place no-one goes. He is mad, oh yes. As mad as a cave of wet bats."

"Actually, I think the expression is 'as mad as a box of frogs'." I smiled, encouragingly.

"I know what a frog is, Englishman. And I am telling you that he is as mad as wet bats."

"I'm not going to argue with you – wet bats it is." There was little of interest at the tasting bar, nothing to taste at any rate. I sauntered back towards the strange man and tried to peer past him into the winery beyond. He drew himself up and pulled the door nearly closed. I wondered if van Blerk was hiding just round the corner and considered barging past to see. Charging through strange doors in a town where people carry guns is rarely a good tactic, however, so I resisted the temptation.

"Ok. Please would you tell Mr van Blerk that I came by and that I would really like to meet him? I'll be in Robertson for a couple of days. Here's my card."

He took my card and continued to stand there, wordlessly.

"Oh, and just one other thing." I removed the carefully folded cardboard packaging from my exhausted supply of Madame Joubert's Lekker Medisyne Trommel. I unfolded it and showed it to him. "Do you know where I can find this?"

He looked at the packaging and his expression changed – he appeared genuinely surprised. He snatched the folded box and disappeared through the door, closing it firmly behind him. At least I'd have an excuse to go after him if he didn't return, I thought. I walked back to the front door and squinted at the vineyards stretching away in the blazing sun. It was very warm and there was no air conditioning in the tasting room. A trickle of sweat felt its way down my back.

"And how did an Englishman come to be in possession of this?" boomed a voice behind me.

I wheeled round and there stood Wikus van Blerk. He was tall, close to my height but older, in his late forties I guessed. He was well-built, with tanned, lined skin and a wild mop of curly, grey hair over piercing eyes. But his most striking feature was his huge, bushy beard, streaked with broad stripes of dark grey and white, giving him the appearance of a giant badger. Van Blerk held up the flattened box of Madame Joubert's Lekker Medisyne Trommel between his thumb and forefinger and waggled it at me.

"Ah, Mr van Blerk! What a pleasure!" I beamed and strode over, arm outstretched.

But instead of taking my hand, van Blerk stretched out his other arm, finger extended, and prodded it into my chin. "I repeat, how did an Englishman come to be in possession of this?" His wild, pale eyes bored into mine and I took a step back, rubbing my chin. His finger remained pointed, menacingly.

"A present from an old Afrikaner friend of mine. Do you know where I can find some more?"

"A present?" he boomed incredulously. "Loot, more like! The proceeds of murder, perhaps. You look like the murdering type."

You can talk, I thought, inspecting his vast, multi-hued beard. It looked well groomed, however, with no evidence of the fragments of food one sees in the beard of genuine madmen. I wondered if he dyed it.

"No true Boer would share his Madame Joubert's with an Englishman!" he declared.

My spirits rose. Clearly, this lunatic was familiar with the product. The question was – how might I get my hands on more? "It was given to me by a true Boer. His name was Mr du Plessis and he grew up in Kruidfontein."

Van Blerk's eyes narrowed and his expression changed from defiance to suspicion.

A light clicked on in my head and I was struck by one of those moments of intuition that have served me so well over the years. "I was an orphan, you see. He was my school teacher and the only father I ever knew. He gave me this as a going-away present. It was the last time we spoke … he died soon after." I cast my eyes down and blinked a few times for effect. I don't know what made me think of the orphan line but it was generally a rich seam to mine, especially with older, attractive women. And, although he was no woman, it did the trick with van Blerk, too.

"*'n weeskind!*" he exclaimed, flinging his arms wide and embracing me in a bear hug, his luscious beard stroking my face. "*Twee weeskinders!* Now I understand. It is fate, it is fate."

I returned his strong, manly hug. It wasn't a complete lie, of course. If anything, it was rather more truth than fib – certainly more truthful than most of the stories I conjured up to placate authority figures, attractive women and anyone else who needed a sunbeam of Hart charm to light up their day.

He stood back, holding my shoulders in his brown, leathery hands. His eyes were wet and a fatherly smile had replaced the earlier snarl. "Kom, kom," he turned and waved towards the door, the other hand resting across my shoulders. I spotted the creepy bald assistant peering through the gap. He darted away before van Blerk reached the door.

We entered the winery, a huge old barn with a vaulted roof and a spotless concrete floor. A row of shining steel tanks, reaching nearly as high as the rafters, lined one wall, their polished skins reflecting the lights. Small chalk-boards, scrawled with indecipherable codes, hung from the taps at the base of each tank.

Just inside the door a modern, glass-topped table sat covered in glasses of wine, open bottles and a tottering pile of paperwork. Van Blerk waved to a chair and strode to a wire-fronted cabinet filled with bottles. "So, you want to taste my wines," he said, fiddling with a combination padlock.

"I guessed you might have been listening."

He turned to me. "I was not listening. Everybody wants to taste my wines. Why should you be any different?"

Modest chap, I thought. But fair play to him, he was rumoured to make the best Shiraz in the Southern Hemisphere, possibly even rivalling the great wines of the Rhône. But there was never enough to meet demand, his wines were rarely exported and customers had to beg to get hold of them.

He returned to the table, three bottles in each hand. He clunked them down in a perfect row. I saw, to my surprise, that all his wines were sealed with screw-caps rather than corks.

"Corks are for *konts*," he stated, matter-of-factly, as he twisted each of them open.

I nodded sagely.

"Some winemakers like to stick a piece of filthy, diseased tree bark into the tops of their precious wines. Call it tradition. There is always a place for tradition, of course. But personally, I prefer my wine to taste of wine, not of crotch rot." He poured me two glasses of deep red from different bottles. "Compare and contrast," he challenged, and stood watching me, arms folded.

I swirled and sniffed both glasses, then took a sip from each. The wines were incredible, dark and brooding with a riot of herbs and spices wrestling for attention. I'd never tasted anything like it. I thought back to my months tasting with the buyers at Charlie's Cellar and my more recent tutorials at the Minstrels' Institute, and racked my brains for the closest comparison. "They remind me somewhat of a warm-vintage Côte Rôtie, but they make the French look like amateurs," I declared, hoping I had struck the right balance of academic rigour and brown-nosing.

I had. Van Blerk slammed his hand on the glass table in approval. "Yes!" he shouted.

I decided to push my luck a little further. "Very different, of course. At first, I thought one might be younger than the other. But perhaps this one is from a slightly higher altitude." I pointed to the fresher, lighter tasting wine.

"Outstanding, Mr Hart! What they must teach you in those English schools!"

I cast my mind back to my lessons at Felching Orchard but it all seemed rather a blur. Funny how the passage of time wipes one's memory so ruthlessly, like an angry blackboard eraser at the end of double maths.

Van Blerk took the seat opposite and leant in. "But you are wrong. The secret is the wind, not the altitude. The gales blow in from the cold Southern Ocean and funnel through the mountain passes guarding the Groot Karoo. Our own Mistral, Mr Hart, and the secret of my wines!" He poured me two more glasses, from two new bottles. "Again! Tell me what you can taste."

Thus passed a scorching afternoon on the outskirts of Robertson, van Blerk opening bottle after bottle and pouring glass after glass as I waxed lyrical about his wines and he boasted of the ever-more lunatic methods he employed in his mission to create the world's finest Shiraz.

By the evening we were on first-name terms and the wine was beginning to catch up with me. Van Blerk too was looking the worse for wear, the lower half of his beard stained red where, leaning over the table during a dramatic explanation of irrigation, his facial hair had mopped back and forth through a puddle of Shiraz.

But nightfall did not herald the end of the educational session. On and on we went, van Blerk presenting Port-like tawnies, fortified with local grape spirit, bursting with figs and liquorice, before proceeding to dangerous ancient brandies, as smooth as liquid satin.

He declared the following morning we would travel deep inland to see his vines. Only then would I understand the true soul of vinous Africa.

If I'd had the slightest idea what the soul of vinous Africa held in store for me, I would have sprinted to my car that very second and driven like a maniac over the mountains, across the plain and back to the safety of Cape Town.

* * *

The following morning I awoke, very unpleasantly. I was lying face down on a rough wooden surface, made even less comfortable by a dusting of abrasive straw, several blades of which had crept into my mouth and nostrils. My head, as tender as an elephant's bruised testicle, played host to a modernist music concert, the type that replaces rhythm and melody with random cymbal clashes at high volume. I raised my head, very slowly, cooing gently with the pain.

I appeared to be lying in an unhitched trailer behind the winery. I was fully dressed and covered by a frayed blanket smelling of some overworked farmyard beast. The sky was already bright, the cruel sun peeping over the mountains, threatening to sear my gentle face. I inched my way from my resting place, allowing gravity to guide my feet to the earth and taking several minutes to adopt a fully upright position. I shuffled, inch by inch, round the side of the building, a hand over each eye, keeping an elbow in contact with the wall to aid navigation, as cymbals clashed repeatedly and unnecessarily inside my skull.

I walked into a large black man in khaki clothing, an assault rifle slung over his shoulder.

"Molo! Unjani?" he declared, his voice triggering a violent beating of percussion between my ears.

"Hello," I croaked, "I'm unwell."

I walked around the man, taking care not to tread on his feet and wondering if there had been a military coup overnight. I finally reached my car, opened the back and located my wash bag, emptying the contents onto the roof. I grasped the toothbrush in which I had smuggled my Madame Joubert's and, breaking off the handle, poured the last of the powder into a small bottle of airline mineral water. I waited for a second as it dissolved, then necked the whole bottle, nearly choking on the soupy, lukewarm water. I leant on the car, panting, while I waited for the Madame to work her magic.

I was suddenly aware the gun-toting African was standing over me. "I am Njongo. Molo!"

"Hello Njongo Molo," I replied, shaking his hand. He twisted and raised his wrist so our handshake became a thumb-clasp.

"No. I am Njongo. Molo means 'hello'."

"Ah, sorry. Molo. Nice to meet you."

"No," he urged, "you say unjani."

Njongo had unslung his rifle by now and was fiddling with the magazine. It was an AK47, the weapon of choice for militia, terrorists and serious criminals across the continent. I wasn't aware the sleepy winemaking town of Robertson had a rebel insurgency but I felt it best to humour the man.

"Unjani," I replied, trying to match his intonation.

"Ndiya-phila. Kulungile! Wena unjani?" he sang, shaking his assault rifle encouragingly. He paused, open mouthed and nodded quickly, clearly expecting a response.

Love a duck, I thought. How the hell do I reply to that? If I say it wrong, he'll probably use that rifle on me. No chance of running, I'd be gunned down in seconds. I wondered if I could wrestle it off him first. Possibly, if I was fit and on top of my game, but my head still felt as though it had been used for bare-knuckle punching practice by the King of the Gypsies. Thank God Madame Joubert was starting to do her work, the percussion section in my head had begun to pack up their instruments and the fermenting camel dung in my stomach had eased to a gentle glow. I decided imitation was the best policy.

"Ndiya-phila…"

Njongo smiled warmly and clapped me on the arm. I let out a sigh of relief and an involuntary burp.

"Don't bother trying to teach him, Njongo. The British are useless at languages. All they can do is speak English louder and slower, the arrogant swine." Van Blerk emerged from behind a large, open-backed pickup. He was wearing desert boots, combat trousers and a sleeveless safari jacket. "Sleep well?"

"Like a corpse," I replied. "In fact, I still am."

Van Blerk gave an amused grunt. "I thought you might like to sleep under the stars. I hope you weren't cold, that was the only blanket I could find. My dog died on it a few weeks ago, it was very sad. Anyway, have some breakfast. This will restore your strength." He reached into his jacket pocket and tossed me a long, dried sausage. "Droëwors. Survival food. As eaten by the Boers on their long march north, escaping from oppression at the hands of the evil British."

I took a bite. It had a moist texture and a gamey flavour, spiced with coriander seed. I found it very pleasant.

"You'll need more suitable clothing," observed van Blerk.

I was still wearing my office clothes, in stark contrast to van Blerk and Njongo who appeared to be kitted up for some kind of military campaign. Luckily, I had packed more appropriate clothing on the off-chance I'd end up on safari. You never know when the opportunity to spot some big game might arise, not to mention hob-nobbing around a safari lodge with beautiful conservation students who've done nothing but measure rhino dung for the past year.

I pulled on my hiking boots and climbed into the back seat. The rear was already loaded with tents, a bundle of logs, several cases of water and, I was pleased to see, a dozen bottles of wine in ice-filled boxes. Njongo clipped his rifle onto a stand in the back and sat in the front. Van Blerk took the wheel.

"We're well armed for a trip to a vineyard, Wikus," I said.

"We're heading way inland. We'll need to hunt our own food, and we may need to protect ourselves from leopards. And blacks."

I prayed this was a joke. If so, it was rather close to the bone, but I was relieved to see Njongo found it very amusing. "Hayi! It's the whites who are the real problem!" he boomed.

Van Blerk fired up the engine and gunned the pickup onto the road in a cloud of dust. The sun, now high above the mountains, continued its fiery ascent. "It's four hours to the Groot Karoo. You'd better have some water." He tossed me a large bottle. I took a long drink and polished off the rest of the droëwors. The combination of dried sausage and Madame Joubert's had me feeling halfway human again.

"By the way," van Blerk added, "you stink of dead dog."

CHAPTER THIRTEEN - ON SAFARI

We drove for hours through the savage beauty of the Little Karoo, passing through the spectacular rock formations at Montagu then, an hour later, the small town of Barrydale. As the sun climbed higher the rust-streaked mountains glowed as if red hot. If it weren't for patches of tough, scrubby bush and the occasional startled springbok pronking away from the road, we might have been on Mars.

I pulled fresh clothes from my bag and changed on the back seat. The road had long since run out of tarmac, and we now roared over unsealed, stony clay. The loose gravel made a constant, rattling din as it ricocheted off the chassis and our wheels threw up a mile-long trail of dust as we tore through the desolate Karoo.

Njongo handed me a cold beer and I stretched out over the back seat, wondering how I could persuade Wikus to sell me his wine and lead me to the source of Madame Joubert's magic powder. It would be clumsy to ask him outright and I guessed he might clam up if I were too direct. Once I'd finished the beer my eyelids began to droop, the previous night's fitful sleep claiming its price.

When I awoke, we had stopped. I sat up and saw we had pulled off the road. It was mid-afternoon and the red earth danced and shimmered in the distance. We were a few miles from a vast range of iron-hued mountains, the road snaking towards the foothills. My companions conferred a few yards away and Njongo's rifle was slung once again over his shoulder. I clambered out of the pickup and joined them.

"We need fresh food. Droëwors can only sustain us for so long." Van Blerk held a pair of binoculars to his eyes and scanned the horizon.

"Would it not have been easier to make some sandwiches?" I asked.

"Bread is the work of the devil, Felix. It makes one bloated and saggy. Real men do not eat sandwiches."

I didn't argue. I remembered his peculiar assistant and his talk of big birds. It suddenly dawned on me what he meant.

"Volstruise?" I asked, trying to match the man's pronunciation.

"There!" Wikus pointed and lowered his binoculars.

I squinted and could just make out four or five black blobs in a row, half a mile away, wavering in the hazy heat.

"Njongo! When I give the word, fire a shot in the air," van Blerk commanded.

Njongo pulled back on the cocking handle and the rifle made a metallic chunk as a round transferred to the chamber. He rested it against his shoulder, raised at 45 degrees.

"Erm … Won't that just scare them away?" I asked, putting my fingers in my ears.

"For any other animal, the answer would be yes. But these are escaped Oudtshoorn volstruise. Highly domesticated farm animals. They have been trained to associate the sound of a gun-shot with feeding time."

"That's very convenient."

"Indeed. But they demand respect, these volstruise. You have to watch them very closely. More than a hundred of them escaped just last month. Heinrich got careless."

"Left the gate open did he?"

"Much, much worse. They are strange creatures, very loving animals. They forget themselves and get, shall we say, attached to their keepers." He looked at me closely. "Very attached."

"So ... what happened?"

Wikus sucked air through his teeth. "A farmhand went to check the gates one morning only to find the fences kicked down. Then he found Heinrich dead next to the feeding trough, gun by his side."

"They killed him?"

"He had not filled their feeding troughs sufficiently. When you call a pride of volstruise to dinner, by God you had better not disappoint them. They become frenzied when disappointed."

"So ... what did they do?"

"Shagged him to death. He was found coated in ostrich spunk, head to toe."

I sensed a short period of respectful silence was appropriate. "I'm sorry. Were you close?"

"The Karoo is a small community my friend. Yes, we were close. But he died doing what he loved."

Wikus focused his binoculars on the horizon once more. "But we shall not make the same mistake as dear Heinrich." He raised his arm slowly. "Ready Njongo?"

"I am."

Wikus jerked his arm down. "Now!" he commanded.

The rifle cracked and I jumped, despite the fingers stuck in my ears. I focused on the little black smudges in the distance. They bobbed up and down and reduced in size as they fled into the distance.

"Kak," muttered Wikus, still staring through the binoculars. "Must have been wild ones. Mind you, most of the escaped ones have been shot already."

"Yes, I imagine that was relatively straightforward."

He continued to stare through his glasses. "Wait," he hissed. "I think we've got one of Heinrich's birds. A male."

He passed me the glasses and I focused on the little black smudges. The others had nearly disappeared but sure enough, one was standing still, its tiny beaked head looking in our direction. Then it broke into a run, straight towards us.

"Incredible animals," breathed Wikus. "Amazing eyesight and hearing. In speed, second only to the cheetah on the plains of Africa." The creature was narrowing the distance between us quite smartly, long legs pumping, feet throwing up little puffs of dust as they tore into the earth.

"Fire at will Njongo!"

Njongo levelled the rifle and lined up the sights. I plugged my ears and the rifle cracked again. The ostrich continued to advance at speed – in fact I swear it actually picked up pace.

"Those feet are among the most dangerous weapons in the animal kingdom," continued Wikus. "Huge claws. They can disembowel a man in a second. One kick will unzip you like a suitcase."

"Worth loosing off a few more rounds Njongo," I suggested, as I observed the bird through the glasses. It was down to a couple of hundred yards and I could see its huge thighs rippling as it powered across the desert floor. They were as broad as my waist and pure muscle.

The rifle sounded once more but the ostrich remained on course.

"Aim for the head Njongo!" called Wikus.

"No, aim for the body Njongo," I urged. "The head's very small. Aim for the body."

Another shot but the creature didn't waver for a second. I no longer needed the glasses, the animal was coming into quite sharp focus without them. I could hear its huge clawed feet thumping against the ground. Good God, I thought, it must be covering ten yards with each stride.

"Why don't you give me the rifle? I'm quite a good shot," I suggested urgently, surprised at how high my voice sounded. I stretched out a hand to Njongo.

"No, Njongo needs the practice," insisted Wikus. "He's a terrible shot."

The rifle cracked again. The beast was getting extremely close. I began to back away, my eyes fixed on the approaching horror. I could see its beak half open and the wispy head feathers above its evil, beady eyes, flattened by its sheer speed.

"Split up. We'll confuse it," called Wikus, who had already broken into a swift trot in the opposite direction. "Every man for himself!"

Another crack from the rifle and I was off like a shot myself, perpendicular to the approaching bird. I guessed it would be attracted to the sound of the gun and that Njongo would eventually manage to land a hit.

I glanced over my shoulder to see the ostrich had changed course and was heading directly for me. My bowels loosened and I broke into the fastest sprint of my life.

"Run very fast, Felix!" shouted Wikus, in the distance.

"Shoot for Christ's sake! Shoot!" I screamed, as the pounding of the bird's huge feet grew louder behind me.

I swear that, for a second, I could feel the giant bird's beak nuzzling the back of my neck. A horrible image sprang into my head. What if the ostrich did to me what it had done to poor Heinrich? Would it attempt coitus before slashing me open with its horrific talons? Would it be a demanding lover? Might it insist on oral sex?

"Fully automatic Njongo!" hollered Wikus.

There was a deafening roar from the weapon. I stumbled as the wall of noise hit me, and careered headlong into a patch of scrub, sharp twigs tearing my clothes, grit in my mouth and eyes. I screamed in fear and rolled around, fists flailing pathetically, anticipating the terrible claws slashing at my face and neck.

As the dust settled and tears washed the sand from my eyes, I peeped from between my forearms.

A great mound of feathers attached to two huge, scaly thighs, each ending in vast, twin-taloned feet, lay just a yard away. I let out a whimper of relief. Then, to my horror, with a blood-curdling hiss, the creature's head reared up on its long neck, beak wide open. Its black eyes, shining with hatred, stared into mine before it swayed, blinked its long eyelashes and collapsed onto me. I let out a yelp and scrabbled away, the back of my head bumping against a solid object. It was one of Wikus's boots.

"Good work Felix! You distracted him just long enough for Njongo to nail him!"

I blathered incoherently as Wikus offered his hand and helped me to my feet. My shaking legs threatened to give way, pitching me back into the mountain of dead feathers.

"I think he liked you, to be honest."

"Liked me?" I stammered. "Jesus wept!"

"Don't worry, you'll feel better when we've got him on the braai. Ever tasted ostrich? It's very lean and rich in iron. Good for the heart."

Njongo sauntered over looking very pleased with himself, a wisp of smoke still rising from the muzzle of his rifle.

"Great work Njongo! What a team we are. Let's get the fire going." Wikus clapped me on the shoulder. "Would you like to help me gut this *oke*? We'll camp here and eat well tonight. Then I'll make biltong and droëwors back home from what's left."

I felt like telling him what he could do with his sodding biltong, but I held my tongue. I needed to remain on good terms while we were stuck in the middle of the Karoo. Besides, I was still no closer to replenishing my store of Madame Joubert's Lekker Medisyne Trommel.

I dragged the logs off the back of the pickup and Njongo soon had a roaring fire going. He then busied himself erecting our tents. Wikus occupied himself gutting the ostrich, a task I chose to leave entirely to him. Suffice to say it involved aggressive plucking, the extraction of armfuls of ostrich guts and a great deal of hacking with a large machete.

"Squeamish eh?" he grinned, arms stained red up to his elbows. "Well, you can dig a pit to bury the remains. Make it deep, we don't want scavengers."

Grumbling, I took the shovel and dug a large hole in the stony earth a few yards from the fire, working up a fine sweat. I scooped in the sloppy guts and feathers, struggling to avoid gagging, and finished by pushing in the bird's extremities, including the fearsome claws. I wasn't even briefly tempted when Wikus suggested I take them home and have them stuffed as trophies. The head, with its hateful eyes and long eyelashes, stared up at me as I shovelled sand over the gory mess.

"Make sure you bury the bloody sand too," called Wikus as he slapped huge, glistening ostrich fillets into a cool box.

Bury your own bloody sand, I thought. But I did my best to lift as much of the carnage-soaked soil as I could find in the fading light and deposit it into the hole. I covered the grave with a pile of rocks and shuddered. I was pretty sure the bird was dead, but I wasn't going to make it easy for the randy sod to climb back out.

Wikus took a couple of the huge steaks, trimmed them with the machete and clasped them in a hinged wire grill. Njongo added a generous glug of local olive oil and balanced the grill on the rocks ringing the fire pit. The logs had burnt down to a red-hot glow by this time and the juices hissed and smoked as they dripped onto the embers.

"Go grab a bottle Felix," ordered Wikus, pouring bottled water over his bloody forearms and wiping them down with a rag.

I picked out an unmarked bottle of red from the ice-filled cool box. To my surprise, Njongo had extracted three enormous balloon-shaped glasses from a box marked 'Riedel'. I twisted off the cap and half-filled each glass, leaving half an inch of sediment behind in the bottle. After the fourth or fifth bottle the previous night, Wikus had explained that he was fanatical about not filtering his wines.

"A winemaker who filters his wine is like a burglar stealing the family silver," he declared, banging his fist on the table. "And you know what we do with burglars round here?" He made a gun shape with his forefinger and thumb and clicked his tongue as he loosed off a few shots. So that was that.

"Impilo!" declared Njongo and we touched the glasses together over the fire.

I sat back, took a cool, deep mouthful and felt I could finally relax. The steaks were bathed in another glug of oil, plated up and handed round. They were delicious, like a rich, lean beef. Farewell, you dreadful monster, I muttered to myself, and washed down the succulent flesh with Wikus's gorgeous, dark Shiraz.

"Ah, the Karoo," sighed Wikus. "You can keep your Cape Town and your fancy beaches. This is where Africa begins. The real Africa, eh Njongo?"

Njongo nodded.

"Fetch us another bottle Felix. I'm the butcher, Njongo's the chef, so you're the waiter."

And the bloody undertaker, I thought, happy those pungent guts were finally buried under a couple of feet of Karoo soil. I grabbed another bottle. Everyone's glass was empty so I did the honours.

I lay back and stared at the night sky. It was festooned with stars of every colour, far richer than anything I had seen back in

England. The air was warm and still, the only sound a soft chirping from the bush crickets.

"What do you taste Njongo?" Wikus asked.

Oh Lordy, I thought, not another sensory interrogation.

Njongo took a mouthful and drew air through the wine like an expert sommelier, his bubbling complementing the song of the crickets. He swallowed and paused. "I taste the stars, unhidden by cloud. The African earth, caressing the vine. The promise of distant rain. The breath of the leopard."

Hadn't really picked up much leopard breath myself but full marks for poetry, I thought.

"You see Felix?" said Wikus, triumphantly. "None of your blackcurrant and delicate vanilla kak there. That's an African tasting note. And that's why Njongo will inherit my estate when I'm gone!"

He'll be inheriting quite soon, I thought, if you let him loose with that bloody rifle again.

"My own children have little interest in the soil," Wikus sighed. "One is an accountant and the other," he winced, "is in real estate."

Another moment of silence seemed appropriate.

Five bottles of wine later, Wikus suggested we turn in for the night. He shovelled a heavy scoop of soil onto the dying embers while Njongo whistled and urinated noisily over a low bush. After a pee of my own I crawled into my tent, an old, square-shaped thing made of heavy canvas, presumably army surplus. The others continued to bang around for a few minutes – I heard the shovel clatter into the back of the pickup and the clink of empty wine bottles being collected. Well done chaps, I thought, good of you to clear up after your guest. I stripped down to my pants and rested my head on my backpack. Within seconds I had drifted off to sleep.

After what felt like a couple of minutes I woke to the sound of the cool box being dragged over the ground and more clinking of wine bottles. I wondered why my companions felt they had to tidy everything away that night. Probably an ex-military thing. I tried to drift off again but to my considerable annoyance, someone started sawing wood right outside the tent.

"For pity's sake," I shouted, "can't you save the woodwork for the morning?" The sawing stopped for a few seconds then restarted. "For the love of God!" I exclaimed, sitting up and feeling for my torch. I unzipped the tent and clicked on the beam.

There was a large creature, its hide pale and covered with black rosette-like spots, just yards from my tent. It had the handle of the heavy cool box in its jaws and was dragging it, with very little effort, away from the pickup. I caught a glimpse of a long, thick tail before it dropped the box and turned towards the light. I took in the huge spotted face, the long whiskers and glowing eyes. Then it opened its mouth and gave the most terrifying, bone-shaking roar I have ever heard. My ribcage rattled and my ears sang.

There was a pause as I stared at a mouth full of shining teeth, each as long as my finger. Then the leopard sprang at me, mouth agape.

I'll be frank with you, I wet my pants. I dropped the torch and by some reflex, launched myself backwards, which probably saved my life. The creature's head was inside my tent within a second, growling and biting at the torch which spun around, illuminating its face from below in a most unsettling way.

"Th … th … th … there's a leopard!" I yelled.

The creature's broad shoulders had muscled aside the tent flaps by now and, to my horror, the torch had rolled further inside, towards me.

"Don't open the zip!" called Wikus. "That's the most important thing!"

"It's INSIDE MY TENT!" I screamed, kicking at the beast's face with my bare feet.

It growled and pawed at my pedalling legs, but by some miracle it didn't catch any part of me in its mouth.

"Pretend you haven't seen it," shouted Wikus. "They don't like being stared at."

I grabbed the heavy torch and hurled it at the leopard's head. It bounced off the creature's skull and out of the tent, leaving me in complete darkness. The beast screeched in fury and I felt the air move as it lunged at me with a massive front paw.

"Shoot it shoot it SHOOT IT!" I hollered, wriggling backwards as fast as I could.

At that moment the tent collapsed. I groped at the canvas covering my face. I felt a heavy weight pin my foot and realised, to my horror, that I was caught in a dead end. There was no rear exit to the tent, not that I'd ever have found a zip in the pitch black, entangled in heavy fabric and with an enraged leopard mauling me to death.

This was it, my final moment on earth. I would never have dreamt anything could be worse than the ostrich but this really was the cherry on the cake. I whimpered and writhed from left to right in the vain hope of dodging those jaws before they clamped down on my neck.

I felt the weight on my foot lift for a second and I hurled myself backwards, bringing my knees up and over my face. I ended up doing a reverse somersault and, by some astonishing unknown acrobatic skill, found myself on my feet in a half-crouch, swaddled from head to toe in khaki canvas, no doubt looking like an Iranian war widow after one too many drags on the hookah pipe. I was completely disorientated and blind, but I didn't intend to hang around. With a roar of my own, I raced off in the direction I was facing.

Unfortunately, my legs were still tangled in the tent so I made it about a yard before tripping and hurtling through the air, unable to even raise my arms to break the fall. I braced myself for impact with the ground but instead crashed head-first into an upright object, which moved away with an appalled growl. My blood ran cold as I realised I'd dived straight onto the leopard itself. I moaned like a drunken buffalo as I lay helplessly on the earth, wrapped as tightly as a sausage, waiting for the coup de grâce from the creature's jaws.

And then a shot rang out. Njongo! Thank God! There were shouts then I felt strong hands unrolling me from the canvas.

"Fok! Are you ok?" Wikus peered at me anxiously, running a torch up and down my body. I had a look myself and was relieved to see no bite or claw marks. Other than a throbbing forehead where I had crashed into the leopard, and a bruise on my ankle where it had pinned me with its paw, I appeared to be fine. My mental state, though, left a lot to be desired.

"Did you kill it?" I blurted.

"No," said Njongo. "He ran away after you attacked him. I just fired in the air to make sure."

"That was outstanding, *seun*!" said Wikus, with a big smile. "You took on that *luiperd* with your bare hands. What a man!"

Njongo gave a big grin and nodded. "You head-butted him right on the nose. He was not happy!"

"Yes, well. I don't like having my sleep interrupted." I pulled myself to my feet, unsteadily, for the second time that day. "I think I'll sleep in the truck."

"Go ahead. You've earned your spurs my boy. As your reward, I will sell you a barrel of my finest Shiraz. And tomorrow we will visit Madame Joubert. Keep the windows closed though."

Well, every cloud and all that. Wish I hadn't been obliged to wrestle a leopard but this was progress. "I certainly will. I'll take that too." I held out my hand and Njongo passed me the Kalashnikov.

I didn't care whether the next animal I saw was a baby panda – if any more of Africa's wildlife decided to pay me a visit, the blighter would be getting it right between the eyes.

CHAPTER FOURTEEN - MADAME JOUBERT

I woke with a pounding headache, my forehead bruised and swollen. It had been an uncomfortable night on the back seat and I'd slept fitfully, waking at the sound of every little buzz and chirrup from the bush crickets.

Njongo clinked an enamel cup against the window. I sat up and opened the door.

"Coffee, for the fighter!" he grinned.

I swapped his AK47 for the coffee and took a sip. It was hot and filthy tasting. "Thanks Njongo. Any bacon?"

"When we get to Prince Albert."

Wikus and Njongo packed the tents, shovelled earth onto the embers of the morning fire, and with a spray of gravel from the tyres we were on our way. The peaks of the Swartberg mountains loomed closer, a jagged black wall topped by an orange halo from the rising sun. Within an hour we were in the foothills, boulder-strewn slopes rising steeply either side of the track. Every so often Wikus swerved to avoid a rock that had rolled onto the road and we bumped in and out of potholes constantly.

The slopes grew steeper still and Wikus changed to a low gear. We were now in the legendary Swartberg Pass, built by Thomas Bain, a nineteenth century engineering genius. He'd recruited a gang of several hundred desperate convicts, promising them their freedom in exchange for building the road. Most of them perished of course, whether from thirst, avalanche or simply plunging hundreds of feet off the pass itself. As Wikus skidded and thumped his way around the hairpin bends, wheels just inches from the stomach-churning drops below, I wondered if we'd join them. I decided to open a beer. If this was to be my last journey, I may as well die drinking.

"*Die top!*" declared Wikus and we skidded to a halt to take in the view. The green patchwork of the Little Karoo lay behind us, while a rocky gorge carried the road ahead down to the arid vastness of the Great Karoo, stretching to the horizon. An icy wind howled between the mountaintop rocks, while low, tough little shrubs peeped from cracks in the gritty earth.

"Down there is where I have planted my special vines," shouted Wikus over the wind, pointing to the gorge that marked the gateway to the Great Karoo.

We began our descent through the north-facing side of the Swartberg. It was even more terrifying than the ascent, as Wikus slid the pickup around the narrow bends. Even Njongo looked a little grim, bracing himself against the dashboard with both hands. I drank my beer quickly, attempting to coincide my swigs with the gaps between potholes.

After half an hour or so, the slope became less fierce and Wikus turned off the road onto a track. We bounced over loose rocks for a mile or so, rounded a corner and there before us was a vineyard sprouting from the rocky slopes, the vines bushy and bright green in the sun.

"The only vineyard in the Swartberg Pass," declared Wikus. "No irrigation. It's watered by an underground river that flows beneath the vines." He walked to the back of the pickup and opened a box, removing what appeared to be a cow's horn and a clear plastic container filled with soil. He took the shovel and walked into the vineyard, between two rows of vines. We followed.

When he reached the middle of the vineyard Wikus began to dig, muttering technical facts and figures as he shovelled the soil. "Seventeen hectolitres per hectare. Still too high," he puffed. "Diurnal temperature twenty-five degrees. Altitude five hundred and eighteen metres. Wind shear ..."

"What the hell is he doing?" I whispered to Njongo.

"He is respecting the vineyard. Mr van Blerk is one hundred percent biodynamic."

These days everyone knows about biodynamism, of course. Every fashionable young winemaker worth his marketing budget is skipping around a vineyard somewhere saying prayers under the full moon and spraying cocktails of armpit sweat and chamomile over the vines. But back in the 1990s this was the sole preserve of environmental fruit-loops and deranged German spiritualists.

After he'd dug a hole about a foot deep, Wikus opened the plastic box and used his hands to scoop out the contents, pushing it into the hollow cow horn. The rich aroma of manure wafted up my nostrils. I made a mental note not to let him handle the food at the next barbecue until he'd washed his hands.

Wikus placed the dung-filled horn in the hole and, muttering in Afrikaans, shovelled the soil over it.

"Next year he will dig up the horn and use it as fertiliser," explained Njongo.

"Of course he will," I replied. Still, the guy was winning wine competitions left, right and centre, so who was I to criticise?

I suddenly became aware that somebody was standing behind us. I turned to see a short African man with tight curly hair holding a bow. He had a quiver of arrows over his shoulder and wore a short animal hide skirt paired with a Manchester United top.

"There's a man with a bow and arrow here," I said to Wikus quietly.

Wikus looked up and smiled. "Ah, Jethrow. Ay-ses!" He gave a little click with his tongue against the roof of his mouth.

"Jethrow is Khoisan," he explained to me. "A descendent of the original inhabitants of Southern Africa. His people lived here first, before the black tribes migrated south from the Congo and long before the whites sailed in. His language is made up of clicks and complex nasal sounds."

"Ay-ses!" he repeated to Jethrow, with the same tongue-slapping click.

"Yeah, I'm good thanks," replied Jethrow, fiddling with his bow.

"This is a biodynamic vineyard, which means I employ only the original inhabitants of this land to watch over it," continued Wikus. "We have problems with baboons eating the ripe grapes, so Jethrow's job is to keep them under control. But he must use only traditional methods, which is the reason for the bow and arrow."

"I would prefer the AK47," sighed Jethrow, gesturing at Njongo's assault rifle.

"Ho-am ta-ra," replied Wikus, giving another lip-smacking click. "I'm telling Jethrow I agree," he explained to me, "but we must work with nature, not against it."

I don't recall you using a bloody bow and arrow to shoot the ostrich, I thought. Still, if you'd tried, we'd all have been disembowelled and rogered to death by that duck-billed sex-pest before you could say Little John, so it's just as well.

"Where do you live?" I asked Jethrow.

"Over there." He pointed to a low, round hut covered in rough thatch at the far edge of the vineyard, looking rather like a furry igloo.

"It's a traditional Khoisan dwelling, in perfect harmony with its surroundings," added Wikus.

"That must be nice," I lied.

"It's bloody freezing and there's no internet," muttered Jethrow.

Now that Wikus had buried his horn of turds and shown me the vineyard, we walked back to the truck. "Ay-sa ha-re," he said to Jethrow solemnly, with another click.

"Yeah, bye Mr van Blerk," replied Jethrow.

"A good man, Jethrow," sighed Wikus as he started the pickup, "but I worry that he has lost some of his heritage."

We returned along the rocky track to the Swartberg Pass and began the final descent into the Great Karoo. The road widened and returned to tarmac as we entered the village of Prince Albert.

"We will stay overnight at the Hotel Beaufort, and tomorrow you meet my client Mr Hudson," announced Wikus. "He is an inspirational man who loves the soil. He owns several eco-safari lodges throughout Africa and he is my biggest customer by far. He trusted my judgement and lent me the money to plant this vineyard, so I am in his debt. He is having a braai tomorrow at his family home and we are all invited."

"Very nice. But what about…?"

"I have not forgotten Felix! We will go to see Madame Joubert right now. She lives on a farm just outside town."

It took only a minute to drive through the centre of Prince Albert. We crossed a small river and turned up a gently rising track which, after a few hundred yards, ended at a large, pleasingly symmetrical farmhouse with a long open stoep and corrugated metal roof.

Wikus turned off the engine. "There is one thing to be aware of when you meet Madame Joubert," he began, but we were interrupted by a woman's voice.

"Mr van Blerk! You have come to see us again. What a pleasure! And you have brought guests, how wonderful!"

A tall, modestly dressed lady with a coffee-coloured complexion waved from the stoep and jogged down the path towards us. Wikus climbed out of the pickup and kissed her on the cheek.

"So sorry to impose, Renay," he began, apologetically.

"No problem at all Wikus!" she replied, patting his arm. She peered through the windscreen. "Who are your guests? Ah! Molo Njongo!"

Njongo smiled and waved.

"And this is Felix. He is English but less bad than most of them. An old Afrikaans friend made him a gift of the Lekker Medisyne ..."

"And he requires replenishment," nodded Renay.

I climbed out of the back seat, stiffly, and held out my hand. A little Felix Hart charm wouldn't go amiss, I decided, and I gave a flirtatious smile. "A pleasure to meet you, Madame Joubert."

Wikus snorted and the woman laughed. "I am not Madame Joubert! I am just the housekeeper. Madame is inside." She took my arm and led me up the path.

Wikus didn't follow. "We'll wait an hour for you here. Any later and we'll see you at the Hotel Beaufort. Don't let her get you drunk."

We climbed the steps to the stoep and Renay waved me to a seat. "I will let Madame know you are here." She slid the screen door open and disappeared inside, pulling it closed behind her. After a short while, she reappeared. "Madame is ready now. She is in her workshop."

I followed Renay into a hall smelling of rich polish, her sensible black shoes clacking on the wooden boards. Several huge dried protea flowers had been arranged in a vase on the sideboard. She opened a door and poked her head through, murmuring a few words of Afrikaans. She pulled the door closed and smiled. "One moment please." After a brief pause she opened the door once more. "You may go in now."

This room was much darker and my eyes took a few seconds to adjust. It was as large as the hallway but the drapes drawn over both windows left the room in a deep, red gloom. I felt carpet underfoot. In the centre of the room sat a low round table on which stood two silver candlesticks, white candles burning in each. A thin line of smoke rose from an incense stick in a dark wooden holder.

Along one wall ran shelves packed with expensively bound books, their gilt titles glittering in the candlelight. The adjacent walls were lined with polished wooden chests and old fashioned writing desks on which were scattered jewellery boxes of all shapes and sizes. I peered around for any sign of life.

"Hart is a wonderful name!" sang a low, theatrical voice from behind me. I jumped and whirled around. A tall lattice screen stood in the corner of the room. I guessed that was where the voice had come from.

"Yes, it's one I'm quite fond of," I began uncertainly, trying in vain to discern a shape behind the screen.

A tall woman dressed in a long red velvet dress emerged slowly from behind the screen. Long black hair tumbled over her shoulders and she wore a large hat in the same coloured velvet, adorned with a fabric protea flower in red and gold – a 'fascinator' I think the ladies call it. A veil hung from the hat, obscuring her face. All I could discern through the material were two dark eyes and heavy red lips.

"Then I am fond of it too!" she declared. Her accent was mangled somewhere between French and Afrikaans and had a rather alluring, throaty quality. She glided over to me and I saw the high-necked dress bulged where it restrained a generous bosom. A fern-like design of silver sequins ran across the upper part of the dress, no doubt to draw attention to her ample breasts. I was momentarily distracted and didn't spot the rising hand until it was poised right before my face.

"Madame Joubert!" she announced.

I gave a chaste kiss to the fingers and caught a scent of lavender skin cream before she whisked her hand away. She wafted past, leaving a trail of perfume, and I respectfully noted her shapely backside through the thick velvet. I wondered how old she was. From the voice, at least forty, possibly fifty, perhaps older still. But I've never been one to tolerate ageism and, in the low light, I confess she looked quite a treat.

"Enchanté," I replied in my best French accent which, I do declare, is rather fine.

"Ah, so you speak French, how wonderful! It is so long since I visited Pair-ee. I had my heart broken there, you see."

"Oh I'm so sorry Madame, that's terrible. Some men are such beasts."

"They are!" she agreed vehemently. "A despicable species!"

I wondered for a moment whether it had been good old Mr du Plessis who had done the dirty on Madame J.

"Not all, though – I see you are not." She dipped her head and looked at me coquettishly through the veil.

Steady on, first things first, I thought. How do we broach the subject of the Medisyne Trommel? I don't want the old girl leaping on me before she's unlocked the bathroom cabinet.

"I understand you are a talented pharmacist?"

"Oh, you are too generous," tittered Madame. "I learnt a few tricks from my old *Ouma*."

I bet you did, I thought.

"Would you like me to show you?" She sashayed to the door and turned the key in the lock.

If you're talking about your skill at manufacturing the world's greatest hangover cure, fatigue dispeller and all round pick-me-up, I thought, the answer's yes. If it's a wrestle on the chaise longue, probably not. Not yet, anyway.

"Tell me, Felix darling, have you ever trodden the boards? You strike me as a thespian."

"I once played the Major-General in the school production of Pirates of Penzance. Does that count?"

"It certainly does. And you are the very model of a modern Major-General! Pray, sing me a line!" She held her hand to her ear.

Oh balls. Why didn't I just say I'd been sheep number three in the school nativity play? "Madame Joubert," I pleaded, "I have travelled many thousands of miles to meet you. Ever since my dear old teacher, Mr du Plessis, gave me a sample of your magnificent medicine on his deathbed, I have made it my life's mission to seek you out."

Madame gasped when I mentioned my old teacher's name. "You knew Meneer du Plessis! He was a good friend of my Oupa! I heard he had travelled to England after the problems at his hotel, what with the police and everything. I don't know why they had to close him down – it was very popular, and all those poor girls out of work ..."

Well, the old devil. No wonder Mr du Plessis had been so accomplished at running the school's Young Entrepreneurs Club. He was clearly a businessman of rare talents.

"You come with impeccable credentials. I shall therefore prepare for you some of my family's Lekker Medisyne Trommel, for a small consideration. Sit please, darling Felix. Sit."

I sank into an antique chair and Madame Joubert sprang into action. She strode to one of the writing desks and picked up several large jewellery boxes, placing them in a row on the table. She returned to the side of the room and lifted the top of a deep wooden chest, in which sat several cloth sacks with drawstring tops. I could hear her high heels striking the floor beneath her dress as she strode back and forth. Opening a deep sliding drawer in another unit, Madame selected a huge stainless steel mixing bowl and a handful of cook's spoons, depositing them with a clatter on the table.

"This recipe was created by my great-great-grandmother. It has been handed down, mother to daughter, ever since. Each generation has added their own little twist, just to keep the for-mulation up to date."

"You have done a magnificent job, Madame. Your Lekker Medisyne Trommel has been my faithful companion for several years."

"It is kind of you to say so. How many kilos would you like?"

"Five should do nicely, thank you."

She peeled five transparent zip-lock bags from a pile and deposited them on the table. I wondered how much it would cost. I didn't want to spoil the moment with haggling, and risk her changing her mind.

"So, we begin!" Madame clapped her hands together and picked up the bowl. She danced over to the open wooden chests and loosened the drawstrings holding the sacks closed.

"Now then! *Onse poeiers…*" Holding the bowl under her arm, she drove a scoop into one of the bags. It emerged heaped with a white powder.

"We start our recipe with *koeksoda* and *versiersuiker…*" She deposited the scoop into the bowl and returned for several more. Then she moved to the next sack, taking a half-scoop.

"…*boegoe*… for the areas down below…" Another sack, another measure.

"…*miangolie*… for the areas up the top…" She danced between the chests, extracting various amounts, sometimes a heaped trowel, other times a mere pinch. In the half-light it was difficult to distinguish between the powders. Most appeared white, others a slightly darker shade.

"…*rooilavental*… improves the mind… *rabarberpoeier*… this will help your flow…" she tittered. I wondered what flow she had in mind. Drawers were opened containing smaller drawstring bags. The scoop dived in, deposited its load, only to be plunged into yet another bag.

"... *krokuspoeier* ... to calm your fever ... *bok ingewande* ... for strength ..." She danced back and forth, singing the names as she scooped.

"... *sekelbos, kameeldoring, rosyntjiebos, tsama* ..." There must have been thirty different ingredients in the mix before she returned to the table and clunked the now-heavy bowl down.

"And now, the very special ingredients." She took a metal measuring spoon and opened the jewellery boxes. Each was partitioned and every little section contained a small plastic bag.

"Some *dans van die soldate* ..." she dipped the spoon into a bag and carefully extracted a measure, the powder level with rim of the spoon, and tipped it into the mixing bowl.

"Die *ritme van die slang* ..." She took a level measure from another bag, deposited it in the bowl and looked at me. With a wink she extracted another half-measure. "For a big boy like you, a little more!"

"A little *fluister van die bosse* ..." She dipped in and out of the little bags, carefully sealing each one after use. I wondered what in God's name was going in – it could have been essence of ostrich foreskin for all I knew.

"And lastly, a little gees *van die wonderdoener.*" She selected a tiny spatula and added a heaped measure to the bowl. Then she took the wooden paddle and stirred the powders together for a couple of minutes, singing the names of African herbs under her breath all the while. She grasped the big scoop once more and filled five bags with the powder, sealing the tops with a small iron that had been warming over a tea light.

Finally, she assembled five flat-packed cardboard boxes and placed a bag in each. I recognised the sketch of the orange mountains and the desert. It was the Swartberg, the very range we had driven through to get here. And there was the village of Prince Albert. I'd come to the right place.

Madame Joubert had judged her measurements well – there was only a small amount of powder left in the bottom of the great metal bowl. "And now you must taste." She walked to a bookshelf and took down a bottle of brandy and two tumblers of orange stained glass. She returned to the table and poured a huge measure into each, nearly to the top.

"You're not a big fan of soda water then, Madame?"

She took the small measuring spoon and scooped a portion into each glass. The powder foamed vigorously and a rich brandy aroma filled the air. Madame stirred each with a spatula and lifted her glass. "Down in one, to get the full benefit. Gesondheid!"

Now, I'm all for a round of shots when the occasion calls, but the old girl had poured out half a bottle of brandy. "I may have to drive later, I'm not sure ..."

"Are you a homosexual, Mr Hart?" she asked sharply, staring down at me through the veil.

"I am not, Madame, but I am here on business. I fear my professional standards might slip if I were to drink so much."

"And is it such a problem if your standards slip, good sir?"

Steady on, old girl, I thought. Still, at least she'd mixed the medicine. If the worst came to the worst I could grab the bags and do a runner. I just had to avoid getting drugged, robbed or poisoned. I glanced over at the five boxes.

She followed my gaze, then quick as a flash banged down her glass, strode over to the boxes, scooped them off the cabinet and placed them in the cupboard beneath. She turned a key in the cupboard door, pulled the top of her dress away from her neck and dropped the key into her enormous bosom. "If you won't drink with me, there is no merchandise!"

Oh Jehovah. What was it van Blerk had said about not getting drunk with Madame? Still, it was only a tumbler of brandy, though I wondered how many I might have to drink before that key came out. "Very well, Madame. Gesondheid!" I raised my glass.

"Good! Gesondheid!" Madame Joubert clinked her glass against mine, lifted it behind her veil and demurely turned away. Then she necked the entire glass. I did the same. It was a good brandy and the dissolved medicine gave it a slightly fruitier kick.

Madame banged the tumbler onto the table and lifted the bottle. "Again!"

"Now, Madame…"

"And I want to hear the Major-General's song!"

"I beg your pardon?"

"The Major-General's song. I want to hear it!" She poured two more tumblers of brandy, emptying the bottle. I eyed the large glass of spirit warily.

"Don't worry, I have another bottle. Now, I knew you were a thespian the moment I saw you. I want to hear your stage voice."

"I'm not sure I can remember the words really, Madame. I'm terribly sorry…"

"Nonsense! Nobody forgets Gilbert and Sullivan! If you want your medicine, you will have to sing!"

Fortunately, or not, I could remember the words. I'd cut quite a dash in the school play, having grown a handsome moustache especially for the part. It was a joint production with St Hilda's next door, and by the first night, all General Stanley's daughters and the entire complement of female pirates had insisted on a tickle of the Major-General's whiskers, I can tell you. "Well, I can try, Madame." I could feel the brandy pooling in my stomach but I also felt strangely alert. I'll give the old girl her due, the medicine was as potent as ever.

"Good. Now then, follow my lead." Madame Joubert took another swig of brandy and a deep breath, inflating her already substantial chest. She raised her hand and, in a rather good soprano, burst into song, addressing an audience somewhere to my left.

"Yes, yes, he is a Major-General!" She paused and looked back at me. "Come on! You have to sing 'Yes, yes, I am a Major-General!'"

I took a breath, and in my best baritone sang, "Yes, yes, I am a Major-General ..." The words came out far richer than I expected. Madame's medicine clearly had a performance-enhancing effect on the vocal chords.

"Excellent Felix. Now, down your brandywine!" She slipped the glass under her veil once more and drained it. I did the same. It would have been rude not to. "Ready?" She burst into song once more. "He is! Hurrah for the Major-General!"

And I replied, in my new-found opera voice. "And it is, it is a glorious thing, to be a Major-General!"

"It is! Hurrah for the Major-General!" sang back Madame Joubert.

And so, I recited the entire lyrics of the Major-General's Song from the Pirates of Penzance, a piece well known to you, no doubt, with Madame Joubert enthusiastically intervening with the ensemble parts.

As I raced through 'I can tell undoubted Raphaels from Gerard Dows and Zoffanies, I know the croaking chorus from The Frogs of Aristophanes!' the good Madame hurried over to the bookshelf and procured another bottle of brandy, from which she refilled my glass.

When I finished the final line, "I am the very model of a modern Major-General," Madame Joubert shouted "Bravo!" and lifted the beaker of brandy beneath her veil. And blow me if she didn't neck the entire lot again. "And you! Down in one!" she ordered in her soprano voice.

I obeyed and down the hatch it flowed. I was feeling in very good shape indeed. My limbs were tingling and I felt a warm, energising glow from my head to my feet, though I had a strange feeling I was not in control of my body so much as it was in control of me. "Well Madame, you've had your song. I think I may have to take my medicine and depart. Mr van Blerk is waiting."

"You will do no such thing," she declared. "We have only just begun!" She strode over and sloshed more brandy into my glass.

I was starting to feel quite warm – I could feel my shirt sticking to my back. "I should probably tell my companions…"

"Your friends have gone. You will have to stay the night."

The sun had set behind the curtains and the room was now in a very deep gloom, the only light coming from the stuttering candles. Madame Joubert's silhouette looked more alluring than ever, her flowing curves exaggerated by the half-light. "I think you are feeling very hot, no?"

"Well, it is rather cosy. Have you turned the heating up?"

"In a way, yes, I have."

I undid another button on my shirt. It really was extremely warm.

"All new customers who arrive at my workshop and wish to purchase my Lekker Medisyne Trommel are required to pass three tests."

"I assume one of them is drinking industrial quantities of brandy?"

"No, it is not. The first is a musical test. You have passed that, with flying colours!"

"Jolly good."

"The second is a physical test."

That sounded good. I felt like Hercules after those brandies.

"Would you like me to lift an item of furniture and hurl it across the room?"

"No. I would like you to lift off your clothes and throw them at my feet."

Well, there's nothing like saying what you mean. And I was feeling uncomfortably hot and sweaty. To be honest, I was feeling pretty randy too – I couldn't take my eyes off Madame's fabulous bomb shells. I had a man's intuition as to what the third test might be, and I was feeling pretty damn confident about that one too. I looked around the room to see if there was a convenient rug for a bit of horizontal traction.

"Only if you do the same, Madame."

"You first, Felix. I want to see if you are the right calibre of man for me."

She took a step closer. I could smell her perfume. Her hour-glass figure was quite mesmerising. I lifted off my shirt and kicked off my shoes and trousers. I was suddenly conscious of having swollen in all the right places. Must have been the brandy. I whipped off my smalls and sprang to attention, feeling more Greek god than man, muscles rippling and nostrils flaring.

"You are a magnificent young man, Felix. How could any woman resist?"

"I don't like to boast, Madame, but they generally can't."

"You are a liberated man, are you not, Felix?"

"I certainly am."

She turned round, presenting the back of her dress. "Then unzip me, Felix."

I felt for the tiny zip, grasping it between finger and thumb and drawing it all the way down, to the top of her fine behind. The dress peeled apart, revealing her back and shoulders. There was no bra strap. She turned back, holding the front of her dress up against her neck with one hand.

With the other she handed me an object. I thought it was her brandy glass for a second but I saw in the dim light that it was a gentleman's razor. That didn't seem right.

Madame Joubert released her dress and it fell to the floor. In the same movement, she stepped close and pushed her chest against me. I felt a strange furry sensation.

"Shave me Felix," she said in a husky voice. "Shave me like a woman."

I glanced down to see that Madame Joubert's superb breasts were coated by a thick mat of hair. Furthermore, at the point where her legs met, there was what looked suspiciously like a todger, bobbing around like an orphaned sausage and fixing me angrily with its single eye.

Well, I do count myself a liberated chap but this was pushing things a little far. "Madame, things have taken a somewhat unexpected turn," I began, edging away.

"I said shave me, you strumpet!" Madame's order, barked from behind the veil, was a little closer to my baritone than her original soprano. It crossed my mind she could have done both parts of the Major-General's Song perfectly well without me.

I took another step back and felt the table nudge into my bare behind. Madame, if that was still the correct form of address, was now standing on my clothes, and I was in something of a fix.

"This is your third test, Felix. Are you up to it or not?"

"Not really, sorry. I think the deal might be off."

Madame advanced, her furry pom-poms and sausage bobbing menacingly. My hand bumped into the candlestick and I grasped it. But I couldn't very well bludgeon poor Madame Joubert, could I? I'd be arrested for grievous bodily harm. Possibly murder. If I did hit the good Madame, would it count as that most despicable of crimes, striking a woman? And what the hell was behind that veil anyway, a grizzly bear? I brought the candlestick between us, the flame wavering in the breeze. Then, in a flash, I had a plan!

"How about a Turkish flame shave, Madame?" I held the tip of the candle against her magnificent, hirsute chest and the forest went up like a wildfire. Madame Joubert screamed and slapped at her blazing baps, while I dived to the floor and fast-crawled around her on hands and knees. There was just enough light cast by Madame's flaming breasts, as she rushed around the room, to locate the cupboard concealing my medicine.

I heard a sizzle, like water on hot coals, and turned to see Madame rinsing a bottle of brandy over her incandescent butter cups. For a second the flames spluttered, then the brandy ignited, her entire torso blossoming in a soft blue glow. Madame gave a panicked whoop as the fire spread to her pubes, beating around her bush like a rabid gamekeeper. I winced in sympathy but had no time to spare. God knows where the key had ended up, but I still had the razor. I slid the blade into the crack between the doors and pushed up, hard. As I'd hoped, the catch yielded with a snap, the door swinging open to reveal my boxes of medicine. I gathered them under my arm and turned to locate my trousers.

But Madame Joubert was back in the middle of the room, staring down at me, her stupendous breasts no longer aflame but still smouldering. She held the remaining candle high in the air, looking rather dangerous, her veil and hat casting enough shadow to conceal whatever was going on down below, thank God. A strong smell of brandy, burnt hair and roast sausage filled the room.

I winced again. "I don't suppose you fancy another sing-song?"

Madame remained silent. I considered making a starkers run for the door, then remembered it was locked.

"Did I pass the third test?" I asked, weakly.

"As a matter of fact, you did," she said, her soprano voice back. "A Turkish flame shave you say? Most invigorating." Perhaps it was the combination of three beakers of brandy and a good dose of the Lekker Medisyne Trommel, but Madame appeared to have recovered from her ordeal rather well.

"Well, if you're ever in London, there's an excellent barber on Green Lanes who can do a more professional job."

"You are a most cosmopolitan man, Mr Felix Hart. Take these and I shall send my bill to Mr van Blerk – you can settle up with him."

She kicked my clothes towards me and, in her high heels, strode to the door, unlocked it, and returned to the screen behind which she had hidden when I arrived. "Goodbye Mr Hart. Good luck with your travels."

"And good luck with yours, Madame. I hope you reach your chosen destination."

I scooped up my clothes and made a sharp exit, following the lights back to the village.

***

Well, my trip so far had been a rather patchy success. True, I had enough Madame Joubert's Lekker Medisyne Trommel to last a couple of years, but I had little else to show for my efforts beyond maulings from South Africa's more muscular wildlife and womenfolk.

The problem was that I was guaranteed a very thorough beating at the hands of the Head of Margin if I returned to Head Office without an exciting and profitable new wine or two. And a single barrel of van Blerk's Shiraz, delicious though it was, would barely fill three hundred bottles – hardly a market-changing piece of procurement. I needed a bit of luck.

As fortune would have it, my luck was about to change very much for the better.

CHAPTER FIFTEEN - MEET THE PRESS

I don't know how long van Blerk had been banging on the door before he kicked it open. "By God, that's enough sleep for any man! We're late for the braai!"

I was sprawled on the hotel bed, fully clothed, still clutching my five packets of Madame Joubert's Lekker Medisyne Trommel. The sun was streaming through the window and it was already warm.

"So, you got your medicine. Madame Joubert is quite a woman, is she not?"

"She is indeed an exceptional ... lady."

"You were lucky she agreed to produce some medicine for you at all. I didn't think she would. In fact, you are the first new customer I know of who has successfully negotiated a sale. She must have liked you. She is a very shy woman, with very particular tastes, as you probably found."

"Yes, she was quite the shrinking violet."

"Anyway, kom. We must go and see Mr Hudson and his family. He always puts on a good feast."

Van Blerk threw my kit bag at me, told me to bring my swimming trunks, and left the room. I showered and dressed then, carefully wiping the boxes clean of fingerprints, wrapped my new medicine in a clean T-shirt. With the help of the nice lady at reception, the bundle was taped securely into an empty wine box and, pleading poor handwriting, I persuaded her to address it to 'Wine Department, South Africa section' at Gatesave's head office, taking care to omit my name. Leaving a fistful of Rand for the postage, I joined the two men in the pickup.

Mr Hudson, explained van Blerk, was a big cheese in the luxury eco-safari business. He owned a chain of lodges throughout Southern Africa, all of which charged thousands of dollars per night. His wealth was matched only by his devotion to the environment.

His safari lodges were built from recycled wood, held together by metal salvaged from derelict oil tankers, and powered by solar panels. The bed linen was woven from organic hemp and dyed with the extracts of indigenous plants. All the food served in his restaurants was organic, the beer was brewed using leftover crusts from artisanal bakers, and all the wine was sourced from biodynamic vineyards – including van Blerk's.

Hudson was a titan of sustainability, a man passionately in love with the soil and the air, which is why van Blerk sold three quarters of his wine to him, leaving sweet sod all, bar the odd token barrel, for the likes of yours truly.

We pulled up at Hudson's family home, an ultra-modern building constructed from wood harvested from invasive tree species – a riot of slender pine beams topped by pale thatch. As we approached the house, van Blerk kept up a running commentary on the harmony of the building with nature, explaining that Hudson always marinated his organic lamb in honey harvested from his own hives. I was on the verge of breaking out in hives myself, such was the relentless barrage of eco-worthiness.

We were shown into the house. Njongo pointed out the furniture was fashioned from earthen mounds covered by organic woollen rugs. The housekeeper offered us drinks, and I opted for a glass of van Blerk's biodynamic Chardonnay.

Hudson was a tall, earnest man in immaculately ironed linen, presumably organic fibres pressed by the feet of rescued circus elephants. "Welcome to this patch of earth, which mother Africa has seen fit to allow me to dwell upon, for this moment at least," he orated.

"And a very smart patch of earth it is too, Mr Hudson," I replied, shaking his limp organic hand.

"Everything you see has been formed by nature. I am merely the transient curator."

Well then, you can curate me another glass of this rather fine Chardonnay, I thought, waving my empty glass at the housekeeper.

"Felix, I have some business to discuss with Wikus and Njongo. Please join my family and friends in the garden and help yourself to wine. You are also welcome to take a swim. The pool has been filled with water distilled from our household sewage using solar stills."

"Wonderful. I can't wait."

I stepped into the garden, a fenced-off expanse of white sand dotted with small bushes. The main feature was the swimming pool, which I was pleased to see appeared crystal clear. A couple of dozen people chatted to one another as they partook of Hudson's generous supply of wine. I was offered another glass and was soon hob-nobbing with the upper classes of Prince Albert.

A well-tanned and rather wrinkled woman in a one-piece bathing suit floated around the pool, glass in hand, on a large airbed. She winked and called out, "You must be Wikus's friend. Why don't you change into your swimming trunks and join me?"

"Leave him alone, Diana, he's young enough to be your grandson," said another woman, to peals of laughter.

"Thank you madam, I think I shall."

It was stinking hot and despite the presence of a predatory pensioner, I fancied doing a few lengths. I took cover behind a suitably sized bush and removed my shirt. I had just wriggled out of my trousers when Hudson, van Blerk and Njongo emerged from the house.

"I hope you're all having a wonderful time in my re-purposed piece of desert," sermonised Hudson to the crowd, who repaid him with a ripple of sycophantic laughter. "After a few glasses of Wikus's exquisite wines I'm sure you've all worked up quite an appetite!" The approving buzz suggested they had.

"Which gives me the opportunity to use my new toy!" Hudson approached an object covered by a tarpaulin, a few yards from where I was changing. "Now, I must warn you, Wikus, you probably won't like this! But there comes a time in every man's life when he just can't be bothered with lighting bits of kindling and waiting for the logs and charcoal to catch."

The audience laughed again but, looking across the swimming pool, I could see van Blerk was frowning. I kicked off my underpants and rummaged through my bag, locating my trunks.

"Hey presto!" Hudson pulled off the tarpaulin to reveal a gleaming, top-of-the-range gas-fired barbeque. It boasted three separate grill areas and a dozen shiny hooks on which hung various sizes of tongs and pokers. A bright orange gas canister sat on the base. A chorus of 'Ooooh!' rose from the crowd, but not from Wikus or Njongo.

"What is this?" growled Wikus, his face like thunder.

The crowd quietened and Hudson's face fell. "Now, I knew you wouldn't like it Wikus," he called, "but please don't judge me. The steel frame of this unit has been forged from abandoned cars. The gas itself is methane, gleaned from the exhaust pipes atop landfill refuse dumps. It reaches optimum cooking temperature immediately, without all that waiting, and it's so much easier to clean. When you get to a certain age, your back starts telling you to stop shovelling ash into fire buckets..." He laughed nervously.

"Besides, real fires are just so smoky and dirty, the particulate count is off the scale ..."

"No! I will not tolerate this!" roared van Blerk.

"L-l-look Wikus ... I promise you, I've conducted a thorough CO2 audit on the energy signature of this unit's manufacture ... I've made a donation to offset the carbon footprint by 150 percent ... There's a school in Mozambique with thirty years' worth of energy-saving light bulbs in their storeroom ..."

"Gas? What kind of man cooks using gas? The flatulent arsecough of the hydrocarbon industry! The fart of the earth! THE BELCH OF SATAN!" I was getting the impression that van Blerk wasn't a fan of gas barbeques.

"This is the DEVIL'S WORK!" He was shaking now – I'd not seen him really angry. Hudson looked mortified, and the crowd were all studying their wine glasses. Van Blerk lowered his voice and turned to Njongo. "Njongo. You know what to do. This outrage must be wiped from the face of the Karoo!" Njongo nodded and strode back into the house.

"Er ... now steady on Wikus. It's only a gas barbeque. We can make a traditional fire if you prefer. I'm sure I have some pine off-cuts from when we built the children's eco-treehouse ..."

Njongo re-emerged from the house carrying his Kalashnikov. The crowd screamed and scattered in all directions.

"Fully automatic Njongo! TAKE IT OUT!"

Njongo raised the gun and took aim at the barbeque, just a few paces from my hiding place. With a flash of terror, I realised the danger I was in. I vaulted the bush and sprinted for the swimming pool, just as the gun roared to life. The world slowed down. I heard the crack-crack-crack of the assault rifle and was vaguely aware of sparks flying from the barbeque as bullets ricocheted off the metal frame.

In three bounds I was at the edge of the pool and I launched myself over the water. It was while I was airborne that one of

Njongo's bullets found the gas canister. Despite the bright sunshine, the entire garden flashed yellow. I felt the heat on my back first, like a hairdryer close to the skin. As the searing blast shrivelled the little hairs between my buttocks I felt a twinge of sympathy for Madame Joubert and her involuntary Turkish flame-shave.

The force of the blast hit me a split-second later, giving me an almighty shove and causing me to somersault in the air. I landed in a squatting position on the airbed occupied by Mr Hudson's mother – not on top of her, thank God, but at the other end. I registered her mouth, open with surprise at the airborne approach of a large naked man surrounded by fire, and her wig, which flew from her head with astonishing velocity.

My weight and speed of impact submerged my end of the airbed for a moment, probably saving my back, sack and crack from the worst effects of the impromptu flame-shave. When the inflatable jerked me to the surface a second later there was no sign of Mrs Hudson – until she fell from the sky, having been catapulted into the air by the force of my landing. She returned to earth face down, in the middle of the airbed, her face slapping into my groin at some speed.

"Jesus wept!" I screamed.

Mrs Hudson didn't reply, on account of her mouth overflowing with my meat and two veg. Small pieces of the gas barbeque were splashing and hissing into the water around us, and the rest of the party had either dived into the pool or been blown flat.

"Would you mind if I lifted your head from my lap, madam," I squeaked, raising the unfortunate Mrs Hudson's face from my groin. She looked at me, mouth agape, a haunted stare in her eyes. She seemed different somehow. It wasn't just the lack of hair – her mouth looked strange too, somewhat looser … We both looked down at my manhood. There was a pair of false teeth clamped to my flagpole, at about half-mast.

I won't lie, it was an awkward moment.

After checking for damage, I gingerly removed the dentures from my bald butler and handed them back to Mrs Hudson. I considered popping them back in her mouth myself, but I reasoned there might be a special technique and I didn't want to make a bad situation worse.

I spotted van Blerk and Njongo crouching in front of the house, nodding to each other as they discussed a job well done. I eased myself off the inflatable, wishing Mrs Hudson all the best for the future. She remained motionless on her front, dentures in hand, only her hollow eyes following me as I paddled to the side of the pool.

The wreckage of the barbeque was burning quite fiercely, as were a couple of nearby bushes. I retrieved my smouldering clothes and wrapped a towel around my waist before rejoining my companions.

"Sorry the party didn't turn out so well, Felix. I had no idea Hudson had become such a sell-out."

"Don't worry about me, Wikus. It's always a disappointment when you find someone you trust has compromised their beliefs."

Given what a poor host Hudson had been we departed without saying goodbye. Then, on the long journey home through the Karoo, fortune swung decisively in my favour.

"I need a new customer for my wine, Felix. You are a true son of Africa. You have proved it with your love of the soil, with your fearlessness in the face of danger, and with your empathy for the produce of this great continent. I would be honoured if you would buy my wines."

"The honour would be all mine, Wikus."

***

Just six days after my departure, I returned to Gatesave's wine department a hero.

Patricia Hocksworth, my ever-jolly departmental head, was over the moon, giving me a hearty hug when I revealed we were to be the exclusive British stockist of wines crafted by the great Wikus van Blerk. "Well done Felix! They will be the highlight of December's media tasting!"

The Head of Margin gave me his own special brand of support as he stormed past later that day, on his way to kick some poor buyer's arse inside out. "One swallow does not a chuffing spring make, smart arse," he spat, jabbing his finger.

Praise indeed.

The remainder of the team were green with envy. Joan, at least, raised her eyebrows and said "Very impressive Felix. How many people did you sleep with to land that one?"

Timmy Durange squirmed and grimaced in his seat as Patricia congratulated me. "Trisha! Trisha! I think the journalists will like my new Burgundies too, don't you?"

"Of course they will Timmy," she said, ruffling his greasy hair. He hated her doing that.

The former buyer of South African wines, George Bolus, was unable to look me in the face. Mind you, it may not have helped that I left a bottle of van Blerk's wine on his desk with a little note around the neck saying, 'Thanks for making all this possible, George. Enjoy!' When he saw my gift, he went purple and made a noise like the village idiot with a cattle prod up his jacksie.

A fortnight later it was time for the Gatesave Christmas Media Event. The supermarket held this every year in the executive boardroom on the tenth floor of head office. The venue was superb – the boardroom took up half an entire floor and was luxuriously appointed with thick-pile carpet and expensive art. Floor-to-ceiling windows flooded the room with natural light and presented eye-popping views of the Thames.

Only the premier league of wine journalists were invited – those who had a weekly column in the broadsheets, those who had written popular books about wine, and a handful of celebrities who had the power to recommend wines to their millions of followers.

One hundred wines lined the vast boardroom table, the mahogany protected by a plastic sheet and layers of linen, given the tendency of journalists to spill, throw and vomit wine, particularly toward the end of a tasting. Along the wall was a huge buffet, with every delicacy the Gatesave executive kitchen could conjure, from lobster and caviar to tiramisu and crème brûlée. Adjoining the Boardroom was a 'productivity space' for members of the media overwhelmed by excessive consumption, equipped with a fully manned espresso bar and a team of masseurs.

The wine buyers hovered around the room ready to respond to any question, from a wine's level of residual sugar to complaints about the absence of anchovy paste in the journalist's local Gatesave. A small army of PR helpers were on hand to charm the older, male members of the Fourth Estate, supply fresh glasses and mop up any sick – which also tended to emanate from the older, male members of the Fourth Estate.

The purpose of the tasting, of course, was to dazzle the assembled journalists with the quality of our wines, and to inspire them to write glowing reviews in their publications. When the good people of Britain read their newspapers they would be inspired to flock through the doors of Gatesave and fill their trolleys with our fine wines, rather than buying plonk from Merryfields or any other undeserving competitor.

It only worked, of course, if you had some exciting wines that got the media's juices flowing.

The tasting started at two p.m. and, bang on time, the Chief Drinks Correspondent of The Telegraph entered the room. "Afternoon folks! Got any good wines this year or just the normal swill you corporate drones churn out?"

"Simon!" squeaked Trisha, bounding over and kissing him on each cheek. "We've got loads of fabulous wines for you to taste. I just know you're going to love our selection this year!" She made a face like a deranged wet nurse and the journalist rolled his eyes.

"Right. Just leave me alone. If I have any questions, I'll ask." He began his journey through the wines, pouring, swirling, sniffing, tasting and spitting into the huge spittoons dotted around the room. We tried to encourage the journalists to spit, but some insisted on swallowing, hence the discrete presence of a nurse and an industrial-strength steam cleaner.

At least Simon was a pro, unlike the next attendee, a famous broadcaster and self-styled wine-authority-at-large. He was definitely a swallower. "Hello girls!" he announced, as he sashayed in. The crack team of PR women simpered and smiled, reserving rolling eyes for when his back was turned. He approached the buffet and began tearing apart a lobster. He wouldn't be bothering the wines until he'd had a good feed.

Then the Wine and Travel Editor of The Times entered the room. He was seven foot tall with a nose like an anteater. It had a disconcerting habit of entering a wine glass a few moments before the rest of his face arrived, and could wipe itself around the inside of the glass in a perfectly obscene manner. He was a fairly benign chap so long as nobody said anything stupid.

He was closely followed by the Wine Correspondent of the Mail on Sunday, a man obsessed with the sulphite content of wine. He would sneeze throughout the tasting, occasionally holding up a bottle and squeaking, "I'm sorry, over-sulphured. Over-sulphured!"

Next in was Jez Newman, the pugnacious author of a best-selling series of wine books. He was arguably the most important media personality in the room. Lean and shaven-headed, he tended to make his opinions known, loudly, with a sprinkle of menace. The jewel in his literary crown was *Neck it! 100 wines you'd better drink NOW!*, the annual Christmas round-up of his top tipples of the year. Inclusion guaranteed runaway sales for the lucky winery and stockist, so he was treated like a god.

"I wonder if I'll find anything worth getting my tongue round today?" he declared, spreading his arms wide and winking at a large lady journalist.

"You couldn't afford me, Jez," she sniffed, giving him a wink back.

"I bet I could!"

The room was filling up fast. The Wine Editor of a well-known restaurant guide drifted in. After a few glasses he tended to lose control of his buttocks so we had christened him 'Le Mistral', after the vicious wind that blows through the Rhone. A thin, pale journalist from a Saturday paper crept in, a fussy, high-maintenance type, forever complaining her wine glass was unclean and demanding a replacement. I kept well clear of the pair of them.

I wandered around the room, nodding and smiling to the attendees, who were generally too busy swilling wine and writing notes to respond.

"Boring boring!" declared the man from The Telegraph. "When are you lot going to put something interesting in front of me?"

Timmy Durange greased up to him. "I think you'll find my new Burgundies very interesting," he simpered. "May I show them to you?"

"Tried them. Not bad but … where's the va va vroom? Eh? Where's the kerpow?" He made a little jab with his fist. Durange flinched and squirmed, his mouth opening and closing like an oily goldfish.

"Yes, I have to agree. All very boring so far," called Jez Newman. "I've tried more than half your wines and none of them are close to making it to my top 100."

Trisha's face fell and the PR team hurried around, offering clean glasses and plates of canapés.

"Everything is just, rather ... jejune!" declared the Wine and Travel Editor of The Times in a bored drawl.

"What the hell does jejune mean, you posh twat?" shouted Jez, his lips already stained red.

"It means naïve and predictable, Jez. Just like you."

"Oh please. What's the circulation of your paper again?"

"Yes, we all know you sell millions of books, Jez, there's no need to be so full of yourself," said the fellow from the Mail on Sunday.

"Oh no! The broadsheets are ganging up on me! Help everyone! Help!"

"Be quiet Jez, I'm trying to taste," complained the lady from the Saturday Guardian.

"I wouldn't bother love. No-one reads your column anyway."

"Yes they do, actually."

"Your paper's just launched an on-line edition, I hear," said Jez. "I don't think it's got a wine section, has it? Do you know what that means?"

"Leave her alone Jez," ordered the Mail on Sunday man.

"It means you're marooned, love. Nobody's interested. They don't want to read your prissy tasting notes!"

"Don't be such a beast, Jez. At least I can write."

"Oh, cutting!"

The tasting was clearly careering off at a sub-optimal tangent. It was time for someone to take control. I cleared my throat. "Before anyone leaves, I do recommend you try Wikus van Blerk's wines. We have an exclusive agreement to sell six of his finest blends."

There was a short silence, then Jez piped up. "The genius South African guy? How the hell did Gatesave manage to get hold of his wines?"

"Mr van Blerk is indeed a passionate man," I said. "I had to work with him for … some time … to gain his trust."

"I've never tasted them, his wines rarely leave the country." The man from The Mail on Sunday peered at the bottles. "Bloody hell, you've got some of his Shiraz!" He poured a short glass, swirled and sipped, then rolled his eyes. "That is … absolutely divine."

"Let me try," said the man from The Telegraph, striding over. He inhaled deeply, then took a slurp. "Blow me! Have you tried this stuff? It's like Côte-Rôtie with a stiffie!"

"Let me taste." The man from The Times approached, his nose leading his long, purple face into the glass. "Oh goodness! I may have to cry. Exquisite! Simply exquisite!"

"Out of my way, you bunch of tossers," drawled Jez. He muscled through the scrum of tasters and grabbed the bottle of van Blerk's Swartberg Shiraz. He poured a half-glass and downed it in one. For a second, all eyes were on Jez's face. What would the sage of *Neck it!* have to say about this extraordinary wine? I held my breath.

"Holy Mary. That wine's classier than a wank in the Sistine Chapel!"

I exhaled in relief. "Mr van Blerk will be so pleased to hear that."

Jez held his finger up. He clearly hadn't finished. "That's not just good – it's great! In fact," he looked around, "that might just be a top 10 wine!"

Trisha gave a little shriek of excitement. Jez took another swig. "Actually, I think it might be number one. Number bloody one!"

Trisha squealed again and the PR team started to jump up and down. Suzy, head of the Gatesave PR team, threw her arms around me and gave me a kiss on the cheek, then another rather longer one on the mouth, to which I happily submitted.

"I'm calling my publisher now. We go to print in two days but I'm going to make a change. That wine," he pointed to the bottle, then at me, "is bloody gold. Gold!"

He pulled out a phone and dialled a number. "How many stores is the wine in?"

"Er, about thirty," I replied.

"Wrong! It's in every chuffing store. When I make a wine number one in *Neck It!* I expect my readers to be able to get hold of it. Understand?"

"Got it. Every store."

"You're going to sell out in about two hours once my book hits the shelves."

Bless you Jez, you arrogant spunk rag. This made being mauled, burnt, shot at and transexualised all worthwhile. I had just landed the number one wine in the country's biggest-selling Christmas stocking filler.

And that made me a buying god.

CHAPTER SIXTEEN - HARVEST DAY

"**W**ell, that's all very entertaining Felix, but you're not giving us what we need." The woman placed her pen on the table and sighed.

"I'm getting to it, officers. This is important context."

"If you're gulling us, you'll regret it," said the man.

I shuddered slightly. I didn't doubt it. But the Madame Joubert's had emboldened me and I felt the whole story had to be told. Then they would all see what a terrible misunderstanding the whole thing had been, and I could get back to doing what I do best – gallivanting around the world drinking fine wine and generally indulging in nature's bounty.

"I wouldn't mind a drink before I continue."

"You know where the sink is," growled the man, tipping his head back.

"No, a proper drink."

"The pubs are closed, smart arse. And you're going nowhere."

I leant down and unzipped my laptop bag, withdrawing a rather fabulous Southern French number that I'd intended to share with Wodin, Fistule and Mercedes that evening.

"You have to be joking. You're not drinking that."

"I bloody well am," I replied, "otherwise you can whistle for your information!" Reckless talk, perhaps, but I sensed I had the upper hand for the moment. They wanted to hear my story and I was willing to tell it, but on my terms. Which meant it would be accompanied by an extremely pleasant Minervois la Livinière, one of the Languedoc's finest reds.

I always carry a corkscrew and plastic goblet in my bag, in case I should stumble upon an interesting-looking wine in the field, so within seconds the cork was out and I was inhaling the heavenly scent of the French countryside. "I'm terribly sorry, I've only got one bottle so I won't be able to share," I explained.

"We don't drink on duty, Felix," said the woman, with a thin smile.

Well perhaps you should, I thought. Might stop you taking everything so jolly seriously. I took a deep gulp and cleared my throat.

***

And so, with the triumph of the Christmas Media Event still ringing in my ears, I attended the final lecture of the year at the Worshipful Institute of the Minstrels of Wine.

I sat next to Valentina, the gorgeous Argentinian winemaker with whom I'd been flirting all year, whose wine-stained pout and Spanish-infused theatrical wine descriptions made me weak at the knees. Fourteen other students from our initial class of sixty had made it this far. At the end of the lecture we spilled outside, christened ourselves 'Les Quinze', and had a joyous group hug outside the side entrance to the Institute. Valentina hugged me particularly gratuitously and gave me a long, Malbec-flavoured kiss on the lips, so no complaints there.

Heads spinning with success and red wine, we tumbled down Chancery Lane and into the Gaucho Grill, gorging ourselves on sirloin and ravaging their fine wine list. Valentina made it perfectly clear I was accompanying her back to her apartment and, given the amount of snogging in the restaurant that night, I don't think many of us woke alone the next morning.

Truly, the spirit of Dionysus was among us.

***

A month later, just a week before Christmas, an impressively thick card dropped through my Little Chalfont letterbox. It informed me I was to attend the Great Hall of the Worshipful Institute of the Minstrels of Wine, at six o'clock, on the evening of the fourth of January. This, it explained, was the eve of the twelfth day of Dionysus and thus an auspicious day for all who worship wine. The invitation was illustrated with pictures of horse-headed men with large erections and wild-looking dancing women with snakes wrapped around their heads. It looked like a right royal knees-up – just my cup of wine. Clearly, this Dionysus chap was a party animal par excellence.

I was required to inform the chief examiner of my chosen recital piece and my required accompaniment. I would have at my disposal a full orchestra or any other ensemble of musicians, so long as they were part of the classical tradition. My recital piece must not have been performed by any other successful Minstrel, and must have been composed between the years 1600 and 1910. The ordeal would take place over a period of six hours.

Absolute lunacy, I thought. A six-hour exam in the run up to midnight? How many wines were involved? It didn't say. The rumours ranged from one hundred to over a thousand. Some said an essay had to be written on each wine, others that your tasting notes must be arranged as a sonnet and sung. Other, darker rumours talked of animal sacrifice and bestial orgies. Not so keen on the dead animals, I mused, but a good orgy might be fun. The truth was nobody knew what the hell to expect. The omertà di vino was watertight and we Minstrel-wannabes were as clueless as a November turkey.

Christmas came and went. Despite an invitation from Tariq to a week-long party in his absent father's mansion, I spent the festive period alone. My Little Chalfont housemates had returned to their home towns for Christmas, so I had the place to myself for a precious interlude of study. I read and re-read my accumulated tasting notes and opened a few unusual bottles for practice.

You may think me dull but, you see, I was an elite athlete at the top of my game. I could no longer risk nights on the lash, marinating myself in whisky-scented hashish and India Pale Ale, before collapsing into bed as the sun rose. My palate and nose were finely honed precision instruments, as vital as a tennis player's wrist or a ballet dancer's ankle. They had to be protected.

I steeled myself for January the fourth. La Vendange. The Harvest.

* * *

I didn't set my alarm for the morning of the fourth. I had a heavy night ahead and reasoned a little lie-in would keep me fresh for longer. Still, I woke early. I ate a huge breakfast of plain porridge and sliced banana. Marathon food. I studied my tasting notes one last time and practised stretching. I needed to be strong and supple for the task ahead. For lunch, a vast dish of plain pasta – a reservoir of starch to line my stomach, no strong flavours to strain my palate or bruise my sense of smell.

The invitation stated formal dress so I donned jacket and bow tie. Then I departed for Minstrel Hall, my only luggage, as instructed, a transparent folder containing my sheet music. But I tell a lie – I had also secreted two tightly wrapped sachets of Madame Joubert's Lekker Medisyne Trommel in a secret pocket inside my dinner jacket, fresh from my brand-new stash. I've never been one to look down on performance-enhancing drugs, and for the ordeal ahead I needed all the help I could get.

I arrived at the Institute a few minutes before six. Which entrance should I use? I approached the colossal main doorway on Long Acre, flanked by its muscular cherubs, forbidden to all but fully fledged Minstrels. A large, unsmiling, bearded man wearing full morning dress and holding a staff topped with a carved pine cone, stood in my way.

"I am here for La Vendange. Should I use the side entrance?"

"For La Vendange, you may use this entrance, Mr Hart. If you fail the test, this will be the last time you ever use this doorway."

How cheerful, I thought. I wondered how he knew my name. He didn't move.

"May I come in then?"

"Only wine may be consumed in Minstrel Hall." He looked down at the small bottle of water I had purchased from the shop at the station.

"I see. I'll finish this off then."

I wandered down the road, retrieved one of the wraps of Madame Joubert's, tore it open and poured the contents into the water bottle. The water fizzed and turned the familiar pale pink. I drank it slowly, not wanting to get hiccups, and saun-tered back to the entrance, discarding the empty bottle in a bin. The bearded man stood aside and I pushed on the heavy wooden door. It yielded slowly and I entered the Worshipful Institute of the Minstrels of Wine.

I found myself in an atrium decorated rather like the lobby of a stately home, polished floorboards underfoot and a chandelier overhead. The walls were decorated with wooden reliefs showing cavorting animals – bulls, tigers and snakes intertwined with ivy and grape vines. Two more bearded men with pine-cone-topped staffs stood to attention next to a door.

"Mr Hart. If you would come with me, please?" I followed one of them into a small, wood-panelled security office. There were CCTV monitors on a shelf, showing various angles of the street outside, and a neatly arranged desk with a large metal safe below.

The man leant his staff against the wall, examined my sheet music folder then picked up a security wand and proceeded to stroke it along my arms and legs. It gave a little squawk as it touched my watch and twice more as it skimmed the wallet and phone in my jacket pocket. "You'll have to leave those with me," he said.

"I promise I won't phone a friend."

"No recording devices or anything that could conceal a recording device are permitted in the Great Hall."

"Right." I removed my watch and handed over the wallet and phone. The man removed a key from his pocket and crouched, unlocking the safe. After depositing my possessions, he rose to his feet.

"I'll show you to the Great Hall." As we left the office, another apprentice Minstrel arrived through the main door. It was Hervé, a studious Frenchman from Bordeaux. He smiled in recognition.

"Ah, bonjour Felix! 'Appy New Year!" He extended his arm as he approached and I did the same. The steward quickly placed himself between us.

"No touching after the security clearance," he growled. "Monsieur, please wait here while I show Mr Hart to the hall."

Hervé did as he was told. "Bonne chance, Felix!" he called as I was led away.

"Same to you Hervé, best of luck."

The man opened another door, its panels painted with twisting vines, heavy with grapes, and waved me through. I entered a short, wood-panelled corridor. A shorter man, clean-shaven, stood at the opposite end.

"Good afternoon, Mr Hart. You are about to enter the Great Hall. You are not a Minstrel so you are forbidden to view anything beyond this point until you are at the examination table. I will be your guide from here. Please put on this blindfold." He held out a black satin mask with an elastic strap. It looked rather like something a comedy burglar would wear, but without the eye holes.

"Thank you. I don't believe you said your name."

"You will refer to me as Frog."

"Pardon?"

"Frog. You may call me Frog."

"Is that your real name? Or are you French?"

A pained expression danced, just for a second, across Frog's face. "Neither. Frogs are the guides for the Initiates in La Vendange. It is a very old tradition."

"I see. Well, nice to meet you, Frog."

I pulled the mask over my eyes. It did its job very thoroughly – I was in complete darkness. Frog took hold of my wrist and I heard him turn the door handle. When you are blind, your other senses are heightened. There was a waft of warmer air and the silence of the corridor gave way to the low murmur of hundreds of voices. He led me forward and I was conscious of entering a very large room. I could feel the Madame Joubert's coursing through my veins, the energy in my tingling muscles, the clear, quick head and an intense feeling of wellbeing, as though I were glowing inside.

As Frog walked me into the room, I turned my head from side to side, taking in the waves of sound washing over me. I perceived there were many people to either side and behind me too. The voices also came from above, as though I were in the centre of an arena. I counted the steps on the wooden floor as Frog guided me forward. Twenty, thirty, forty paces then we halted, the guide giving my wrist a quick squeeze, as if to say stop.

"You are at your examination table," he spoke close to my ear. "We will wait for the remainder of the Initiates to assemble before removing your blindfold."

I tried to pick out individual conversations in the babble of noise. There were low, male voices and higher female ones. I could hear the occasional word from the nearby members of the audience, a snatch of French here, an American twang there. There were a few coughs and conspiratorial guffaws, and, from the female voices, the occasional tinkle of laughter.

"When your blindfold is removed, the examination will commence," Frog said, keeping his voice low. "You must identify each of the wines before you, stating the region and the principal grape varieties. You will tell me your answer, which you must do quietly, so as not to give clues to your fellow Initiates."

I heard some shuffling and someone came to a halt a few feet away, presumably in the tender guiding hands of their own Frog.

"If you are correct, or close enough, I will nod. If you are not, I will raise my hand and you will incur a penalty point. You will then proceed to the next wine. If you incur five penalty points, you will be deemed to have failed the examination. If you spit, or spill any wine, you will also be deemed to have failed."

"And what happens then?"

"You will be removed from the room and you will never set foot in the Worshipful Institute of the Minstrels of Wine again."

Right. Well, that's straightforward enough, if rather ruthless. "How many wines are there?"

"You will see presently."

I took some deep breaths. I was beginning to feel rather warm in my dinner jacket and my face was sweating under the mask. The Madame Joubert's was making my muscles shiver with energy. I had to fight the urge to jump up and down like a madman. A tiny drop of sweat rolled down the side of my nose and onto my top lip. I touched it with my tongue and my taste buds exploded into life.

I tasted salt, a yeasty, meaty salt, like a rich piece of serrano ham, just sliced from a leg unhooked from the ceiling of a tapas bar in Seville, at the height of summer. But also an undertone of sea salt, like a beach holiday in Anglesey... no, not Anglesey, Cornwall! Like the taste of your hair when you've spent an hour on a trawler off the coast of Cornwall, the southern coast of course, not the north, and...

Good Lord! What was happening? I wiped my hand across my mouth, smelling supermarket soap, black metallic paint and the tiniest trace of plastic from the water bottle... My God! My senses were overwhelming me, my synapses firing wildly. Had I taken too much Madame Joubert's? Or were they pumping something into the air?

"All the Initiates are now in position," murmured Frog.

I could smell his sweat and a combination of shampoo, deodorant and musky aftershave – the latter applied some days ago.

"After the Invocator has spoken, the examination will begin."

"The who?" I asked, my leg jiggling, but my question was drowned by a trumpet fanfare blasting from somewhere just ahead. It was deafeningly loud and sounded live rather than a recording. The trumpets were followed by the pounding of drums. The fanfare ended and there was silence. Then a man's voice spoke out, loud and clear:

Welcome, Initiates, on this the twelfth day of Dionysus!

The day of Theemeter!

Behold! The clearing of the wine.

And now this pompe arrives

Let the contest begin!

And may all win, in the manner of Dikaiopolis.

What in Murgatroyd's sweet name are you banging on about, I wondered. Still, at least we were about to get on with it. I felt like a sprinter waiting for the starter's gun. I could barely stand the tension.

I felt Frog's hands remove my blindfold. I blinked for a second, then gasped. I was in the centre of a large arena, surrounded on three sides by the audience. As I had perceived, the rows of seats were tiered, layered steeply from ground level to a height of several storeys. The theatre was full and I guessed most of the Institute's thousand members were present.

There was some sort of VIP box halfway up one side, in which sat an old man in a crimson robe, holding a staff – I decided he must be the Invocator – surrounded by a handful of purple-robed senior Minstrels. The audience were dressed in their finery, dinner jackets for most of the men, ball gowns for the women. I spotted varieties of regional dress too, Japanese men in formal striped kimono and African women in brightly printed dresses. Somewhere up there, I guessed, Joan from Gatesave and Paul and Gillian from the old days at Charlie's Cellar were watching.

The cream of the world's wine industry had turned out to see me sink or swim.

At the front, from where the fanfare had blasted, a full orchestra sat on a low stage. In front of them stood a bench on which lay a collection of musical instruments, for the recital section of our ordeal, no doubt.

On the arena floor, overlooked by the audience, lay fifteen long tables, running parallel to one another, the kind of thing you might have seen at a full-on medieval banquet. Each was perhaps twenty yards in length and covered in white linen. Each Initiate stood at the head of their own table, accompanied by a Frog – our personal examiner and executioner.

But the most intimidating sight lay upon the tables. On each lay a perfectly straight line of wine glasses, spaced a couple of inches apart. They stretched the entire length of the table, each containing a quarter-glass of wine. My blood ran cold as I tried to count their number.

The glasses closest to us contained pale white wine, the colour deepening to a richer yellow as the line progressed. Towards the halfway mark the colour changed to pink, then to red, with presumably the darkest, most intense wines at the end, nearest the orchestra. And we were permitted just four mistakes, the fifth bringing immediate expulsion!

I looked at my fellow Initiates. It seemed a long time since we christened ourselves Les Quinze and drank our bodyweight in Patagonian Malbec. Everyone contemplated their row of wines stretching to the horizon, faces grim. My table lay roughly in the middle of the fifteen. To my right was Hugo, a French sommelier from Paris, to my left Alessandra, an Italian buyer for a chain of upmarket delis. I spotted Valentina, my favourite Argentinian, at the far end, frowning defiantly at her table, looking wonderful in a black, figure-hugging dress.

"There are one hundred and eighty wines on the table, Mr Hart," whispered Frog, removing any doubt. "You have two hours. You may begin."

A large digital stopwatch, high in the corner of the hall, began its countdown. I don't know which of my fellow Initiates moved first – I was focused on my table to the exclusion of all else. I took a deep breath and grasped the first glass by the stem.

Before I had even swirled the wine, I spotted the fine bubbles. A quick sniff confirmed it was Champagne, a good one, probably vintage. I focussed on the aroma – it jumped with delicious brioche and biscuit, clean and creamy. I took a mouthful. A Chardonnay-dominated blend for sure, maybe a pure Blanc de Blancs. I looked around for a spittoon and with a shock remembered the no spitting rule. I turned to see Frog watching me closely. I swallowed the mouthful. Christ Felix, take smaller sips! Many more gulps like that and you'll pass out before you're half-way through.

"Chardonnay, mainly. Some Pinot Noir. Champagne region," I whispered.

Frog nodded and I lifted the next glass. Small bloody sips, Felix. I could see this one had bubbles too. A sniff conjured up a drunken evening in Barcelona's Gothic Quarter, crammed into a hot bar, a beautiful Catalan woman with long slim limbs nuzzling my neck...

"Macabeo, Parellada and Xarel-lo. Penedès region."

Another nod. Another glass. More bubbles. This one less obvious, a creamy lemon bouquet, possibly Chardonnay, but richer than the first wine, with punchier, tropical fruit. The tasting room at Charlie's Cellar appeared in front of me, one of the buying team teaching me the difference between Australian sparkling wines. Who was it? That clipped, precise way of speaking – it was Paul, probably sitting somewhere in this very audience. In my mind's eye I could see him holding up a lean Tasmanian sparkling wine next to a more generous Hunter Valley fizz...

"Chardonnay again. Hunter Valley, Australia."

The nod again. Thank God. That's three down, only one hundred and seventy-seven to go.

At that moment there was a buzz and a quiet chorus of 'Oooh!' from the crowd. I saw one of the Frogs with his hand raised. It was Fernanda, the Chilean winemaker. Poor Fernanda, she was a nice lady – though a little intense for my taste – and I felt sorry for her making an error so early on. I wondered what she had misidentified. Maybe the Aussie fizz had fooled her or was there a fiendishly difficult wine a little further down the line? Whatever, I mustn't be distracted.

Some of the audience were looking at the roof. I followed their gaze. A huge screen had been suspended from the ceiling, each of our surnames projected upon it, in alphabetical order. Fernanda Guerra's name, just above my own, was now accompanied by a big red cross. There was space for five crosses next to each name, after which... game over.

Back to the wines. Another swirl and a sniff. A green tinge to this one and only the tiniest hint of bubbles. I tasted the wine and I was sitting at a loud, raucous table in Lisbon, very late at night.

The table was piled high with seafood – salted cod, sardines, little clams and huge tiger prawns. Carolina, a pretty woman with long dark hair, rested her arm across my shoulders and laughed as she poured vinho verde from a jug into simple glass beakers...

"Alvarinho dominates, I suspect a little Loureiro. Minho region."

Frog nodded, I could see he was impressed – though not as impressed as I'd been later that night, as the fabulous Carolina writhed astride me in her tiny apartment overlooking the Cais do Ginjal... Focus, for Christ's sake Felix!

The next wine was an Albariño from the rain-blessed lands of Galicia. I recalled sheltering from a howling storm in a tiny tapas bar, nestling in the shadow of the moss-covered Catedral de Santiago de Compostela, slipping a blasphemous hand round my partner's waist and drawing her close as we clinked glasses, enjoying the way her rain-soaked blouse pressed against my chest...

Another buzz. I looked up. A cross next to Hervé, the French friend I'd bumped into at the entrance. Maybe the Albariño had foxed him. Back to work.

A peachy, floral Gavi di Gavi from Piedmont, which conjured a roaring Courmayeur après-ski session with Clémence, my stunningly athletic ski coach. A Sicilian Fiano, gulped by the carafe in a shaded square one afternoon in Palermo. Then a South African Sauvignon Blanc, spotting whales from a sunny cliff-top in Hermanus, the wind howling off the Southern Ocean.

I started to hit my stride. A quick twist of my wrist and the wine would swirl as I brought it to my nose. Then a scene would impose itself, sometimes an eavesdropped conversation between buyers in the tasting room, perhaps a moment from a lecture in the Institute's own Théâtre de la Véraison, but more often a taverna in some pretty European town and a beautiful woman, skin darkened by the Mediterranean sun, winking at me over a table heaving with local food and wine.

Then it would come to me and I'd whisper to Frog, he'd nod, and we'd move to the next glass.

Two buzzes in quick succession. Everyone looked up. There was now a cross next to Paul, the flamboyant London wine merchant, and a second against Fernanda. How far had I progressed? Maybe thirty wines. Not even one fifth of the way through. With five lives, I could afford only one mistake every thirty-six wines. Push on.

A series of Chardonnays slowed me down. A winemaker can cloak such wines with oak, obscuring the tell-tale character of the fruit, and the variation between vintages can trick you into thinking the wine is from a different country completely. I had to concentrate, hard.

The Italian Chardonnay from Friuli was elegant and lean, like the young widow who'd shown me round her picturesque hillside winery, before showing me round her home, then her bedroom. A Marlborough Chardonnay spoke of the cooling Pacific breeze, a bite of green apple and mineral-rich soil. A white Burgundy was richer but immaculately balanced, a Barossa Chardonnay less poised but rewarding if you know what you're doing, like bedding the captain of the Adelaide Ladies First XV after eight pints of Victoria Bitter.

I spotted the white Rioja straight away. A mean trick by the Institute to place such a similarly oaked white next to the Chardonnays, but there was no mistaking the hints of almond and hazelnut over the rich fruit, nor could I supress the memory of a night in Madrid when Sofia, a student of radical feminist studies, grabbed my belt with one hand and fed me salted almonds with the other, ordering me to whisper non-patriarchal filth into her ear.

Frog was looking pretty impressed. I tried to block the noise of the buzzer, which was now sounding every couple of minutes. I had to concentrate. I lifted the next glass, sending the golden liquor spinning within the crystal bowl. But a tiny speck of hubris had lodged itself in my palate. As I nosed past the rim and inhaled, a scene unfolded before me. A voluptuous young woman, with shoulder-length black hair, sat opposite, cross-legged, on a too-small bed. She blew smoke through the open window as I refilled two glass tumblers with a simple wine, a bottle of local Athenian plonk.

"Savatiano, Attica region," I said confidently.

Frog took a step back and raised his hand. The buzzer sounded and my blood ran cold. My eyes rose to the screen and, sure enough, there was now a red cross next to Hart. I wasn't doing too badly, everyone except Fritz, the most intensely intellectual of our group, had at least one cross against their name, some had two or three. But it knocked my confidence for a moment. How had I got it wrong? I took another sniff.

"No point in dwelling, Mr Hart. You don't get a second chance."

That's not the point, Frog, I thought. I was determined to work out how I'd made the mistake – the vision of my Greek *filenáda* had been so vivid. Then I remembered. A lads' holiday on the island of Ios, we'd got together with a larger group of foreigners and were having a roaring old time in a small taverna. I was chatting to the waitress, insisting on the best wine in the house while my yokel friends screamed for cheap house white. She was amused at my pretensions, and when my companions were ready to move on I stayed behind. We drank Assyrtiko, from the nearby island of Santorini. It was only later that night, as she flicked cigarette ash into an empty tobacco tin on her window sill, her breasts shining in the moonlight, that we moved onto the cheap bottle of Savatiano.

I had confused my chat-up wine with the post-coital plonk. For a moment, I was embarrassed and ashamed. Pull yourself together, Hart, I muttered. You have another hundred wines to taste. I realised I was wallowing, quite significantly, under the influence of alcohol.

I took a deep breath and pushed on. There were only a few more whites and I nailed them one at a time, carefully but confidently. A Chenin Blanc from Savennières, bright with apple and pine, a touch of wet face flannel on the finish. Another Chenin from South Africa's Swartland, more generous in fruit, rather less flannel. A star-bright juicy-sweet Riesling from the Mösel, followed by a more muscular, dry one from Western Australia.

Then the final white, an incredible, perfumed riot of flavour. It was a Torrontés from Argentina, almost certainly from the high-altitude Salta region. Frog nodded. I had drunk a similar bottle with Valentina the day before she flew back to Mendoza for Christmas. She'd challenged me to bring the highest-altitude wine I could find and promised, on that night, I could thrust into her as many times as there were metres in the altitude of the vineyard. I felt obliged to please, so a three-hour round trip to an obscure Sussex wine merchant later, I arrived at Valentina's apartment and presented her with a Salta Torrontés, made from grapes grown at 2,150 metres. She was delighted and so began our climb, Valentina counting out loud in breathless shouts. Gazing at her shapely bare derriere, I confess I reached my summit rather earlier than intended, but I do recommend it as a memorable way of learning to count in Spanish.

CHAPTER SEVENTEEN - COME ON, YOU REDS

By the time I reached the rosé I realised I had an enormous erection. I suspected I'd been sporting it all the way through the tasting. Hells bloody bells, what had Madame Joubert put in her new, souped-up blend?

I cantered on through the pink wines, knocking off the first few – a slightly cloying Cabernet from Chile, a semi-sweet juicy number from the Loire, a deep pink from Provence, generous and knowing. Then another mistake and Frog's hand shot up once more. A rosé Merlot, but I'd assumed it was Australian and, of course, it was Californian. Silly mistake, I should have spotted the influence of the Pacific fog, rolling through the Monterrey vineyards, but my rosé experience was less broad than it should have been.

I glanced at the stopwatch. Just over an hour left. The rosés were now behind me and I marched on into the reds. The first few were light, more like deep pinks than reds. There was a bubble-gum Gamay from Beaujolais, evoking an energetic, no-knickers cycling holiday around the Mâconnais with my French exchange partner. A Ruby Cabernet from California's Central Valley, a Cabernet Franc from Anjou, then straight away I spotted the cheeky, earthy notes of a Bulgarian Merlot, just like the wines I used to enjoy with Georgi at his favourite Plovdiv restaurant.

Then another buzz sounded, not me thank God, but this was accompanied by a howl and the sound of tinkling glass. The audience gave an ahh! of dismay and I looked towards the commotion. Fernanda had incurred her fifth penalty and was standing, dejected, the offending glass flung to the ground.

"Ms Guerra has sinned against the gods," intoned the Invocator. "Take her from this place," he added, rather cruelly. Her Frog stood, head bowed, as a bearded man with a staff took Fernanda's arm and led her to the exit.

And so we were fourteen. I glanced up at the board. Fernanda's name had been struck through and three other Initiates had incurred four crosses. Several more had three and most of the rest, including yours truly, had two. The exception was Fritz, the uber-focused German, who had incurred just one penalty. That must have annoyed him, old Fritz was rather a perfectionist.

But I was a long way from the finishing post. I estimated I'd knocked off around one hundred wines but I already felt more than a little unsteady – hardly surprising, considering I had swallowed one hundred mouthfuls. I prayed the pasta would do its job of lining my stomach. Fifty minutes left and counting.

A few more reds knocked off. Lots of Pinot Noir, a wine of which I am a close student. There was a cold-eyed, perfectly fruity number from Chile's Limari Valley, right on the edge of the Atacama Desert. An elegant little drop from South Africa's Hemel-en-Aarde Valley, wearing its considerable sophistication lightly. A dry, gorgeously herbaceous gem from New Zealand's Central Otago. I shuddered slightly at the memory of that one, not because the wine was bad – far from it – but because I had once followed a wine tasting in the region with a bungee jump over the Kawarau River. At the top of the first bounce I regurgitated a full spittoon's-worth of Pinot Noir and, rather messily, it pursued and caught up with me on the way back down.

The buzzer sounded twice more. When it happened a third time, within the same minute, I knew some of my fellow Initiates were starting to flag. Never mind them, Felix, stay focused.

The next couple were red Burgundies. A young Hautes-Côtes de Nuits and an aristocratic Vosne-Romanée. Maps of vineyards and soil topography reeled through my mind – this was a minefield of overlapping regions and confusing appellations. A whiff of horse stables and cough medicine announced a couple more Burgundies, then the wines grew bolder, richer, as the focus switched to Bordeaux and heavier grape varieties – a muscular Fitou, a silky Malbec, rich Rioja and assertive Chianti.

Then my Frog's hand wavered before lifting high.

I swore, loudly, like a drunken arsehole, which is exactly what I was.

Frog hadn't been too sure of that one, I must have been close. Wrong sub-region within Chianti, no doubt. Another schoolboy error but the fatigue was starting to bite and I could feel the layers of tannin building on my teeth and lips.

Another buzz and a shout of frustration, followed by a sigh of sympathy from the audience. Vicente Casales, the sommelier from Madrid, was out. He marched from the hall under his own considerable steam, a bearded staff-bearer hurrying after him.

"Señor Casales has sinned against the gods!" hammed the Invocator, gravely.

Another oaky Rioja. Then a Ribera del Duero, a neighbouring region that uses the same Tempranillo grapes. A filthy trick but I'd spotted it. Up yours Minstrels. My many days of study in the vineyards of Castile had served me well, not to mention my evenings careering through the bars of Logroño, horny as a Pamplona bull after a Viagra enema.

Another buzz and a scream like a banshee. It made me jump and I nearly spluttered my Uruguayan Tannat across the clean linen. Thank the gods I didn't – that would have meant instant disqualification. Letitia Tressingham-White, the humourless upper-class bore who loved to boast about the size of her father's wine collection, had just incurred her fifth buzz.

"Damn you! Damn you all, you beasts! How can anybody be expected to do this? It's impossible, impossible!" She burst into tears and was escorted to the exit.

"Ms Tressingham-White has sinned against the gods!"

I looked up at the board – and nearly toppled over backwards. My word, I was as pissed as a priest at Christmas! Once I'd focussed, I saw the board was a sea of red crosses. Three were now out, five were in jeopardy with four penalties apiece, the rest of us had three, barring Fritz with just one.

More wines. A Primitivo from Puglia, Italy's heel, bursting with dark, cooked plum and fig. Then a leap to the Alpine end of the same country, a stunning old Barbaresco, bubbling with rustic fruit, crushed tomato leaves and a hint of silage.

Another buzz. "Merde! Merde!" Hervé had lost his last life. But the studious young sommelier was not going without a fight. He swept a dozen wine glasses onto the floor, where they shattered and tinkled. A bearded guard ran at him, prodding him with the carved pinecone at the end of his staff. Hervé grabbed it and a tussle ensued, until two more guards grasped him from behind. He was dragged bodily from the hall, cursing in French all the way to the door.

There was quite a noise from the audience now, until the Invocator thumped his staff against the floor. "Monsieur Moreau has sinned against the gods!"

No sooner had the door swung shut than another commotion erupted right behind me. It was Alessandra, the Italian buyer. She had fainted from over-drinking, collapsing face forward onto the table, red wine pooling around her head like a particularly gruesome murder. The bearded wonders were being kept busy, and they sweated as they dragged the unconscious young woman to the door, her legs trailing behind her.

"Signora Rey has sinned against the gods!"

The wines, the wines. How many more to go? Maybe thirty? They were all hefty numbers now, full bodied and taking no prisoners. A huge Jumilla, grown just inland from Alicante, pregnant with oozing, jammy fruit. A rich young Saint Emilion, arrogantly flaunting its cassis and cigar box bouquet. A Pinotage from Stellenbosch, fat and self-satisfied like a wealthy old Boer.

Another buzz and the bang of a glass slamming against the table top. It was Calandra Kritikos, the Greek winery owner. She strutted to the door, head held high. Unfortunately, under the influence of nearly two hundred glasses of wine, not to mention an impressively high pair of heels, she stumbled and fell headlong on to her face. She picked herself up and weaved to the doorway.

"Ms Kritikos has sinned against the gods!"

"*Gamo ton Christo sou!*" she shouted, raising her middle finger to the Invocator. Good for her, I thought.

I was down to the last twenty or so, with eighteen minutes left. The Aussies were out in force now, all blockbuster fruit and hefty alcohol. Coonawarra Cabernet. Barossa Shiraz. Great wines, but by this stage it was like being mugged by a giant prune in brandy. Then another wine, deep and chocolaty. Portuguese, from the south, a Trincadeira. I was sure of it. Where had I tried it? The Algarve? No, must be from the Alentejo, all that coffee and spice.

Frog's hand went up and the buzzer sounded. Blast it! Must have been the Algarve after all.

I stumbled for a second and grasped the table. Christ on a bike, I wasn't sure I could make it. The remaining glasses swam and doubled before my eyes. Another buzz sobered me up and I heard sobbing. The audience 'ahhh'd' in sympathy. It was Enrica. She leant over the table and puked heavily through her tears. The audience changed to an appalled 'uuurgh' and several guards came running with buckets of sand, which they poured over the puddle of vomit to mask the smell. One of them offered Enrica his empty pail, which she used to evacuate the rest of her stomach, before she was escorted out.

I took long deep breaths and checked the scoreboard. There were eight of us left. Then the buzzer sounded once more. Before my eyes, Paul Unterman, the flamboyant English wine merchant, incurred his final penalty and his name was struck through.

"Oh balls," he declared, as he staggered to the door, leaning on a staff bearer. "Farewell, farewell dear Minstrels! I tried!" The audience applauded, drowning out the Invocator's florid declaration of sin.

So, there were seven of us left – five in last-chance saloon, with four crosses each, while Hugo had three and, astonishingly, the forensic Fritz had just two. I stood up straight, keeping my hand on the table for support. If only I could dose myself with my second sachet of Madame Joubert's. But Frog was hovering at my elbow and hundreds of pairs of Minstrel eyes watched my every move.

There were ten minutes left on the countdown clock and a dozen glasses remaining. With every sinew, I focused on the remaining wines. Take it steady. A Napa Valley Cabernet, a couple more Bordeaux, an aged Barolo, a Hawke's Bay Shiraz. Good work, that's five more down.

But what the Jiggens was this? It tasted funky, like a crazed cider-maker had dipped his dong in the barrel and thrown in a mouldy apple for good luck. It was cloudy and had a very slight fizz. Of course, it was one of these lunatic 'natural wines' – sulphur-free, meaning every stray yeast cell and wild bacterium was having a shag-a-thon in the bottle. Who was idiot enough to make a wine like this? It had to be French. It was relatively light, had to be from a cooler part of the country.

The Loire? Yes, that was it. A Cabernet Franc, I was sure of it. Saumur-Champigny.

Frog nodded. Thank the gods. I was down to the last half-dozen. Five minutes on the clock.

The audience burst into a round of applause. Fritz had completed the tasting with only two penalty points. Then the applause rose again. I saw Valentina with her arms in the air, shouting with glee, she'd made it too. I stole a glance at the others. Hugo, right next to me, was on his fourth-last glass, sniffing and frowning at it. Russell, an insufferably arrogant sommelier from a celebrity restaurant in Mayfair, was down to the last six, same as me. Tallah, a Lebanese lady who ran a specialist wine importer, was further behind, maybe twenty more to go. I didn't fancy her chances.

The applause faded quickly, everyone conscious of the intense pressure on the remaining Initiates. Next wine. It came straight to me, Portuguese again, from the Douro Valley. It conjured the riverfront in Porto, picking at olives and sheep's milk cheese as the sun set, watching the metro trains rattle over the old iron Luís I Bridge.

Five to go. Next was a Malbec from Mendoza, a humdinger of a wine, glistening with tarry fruit. Valentina must have smiled when she tasted that one. She'd probably made the wine herself.

Four more. I picked up the glass and gave the stem a little flick. I gave a gasp. I couldn't believe my nostrils. What a cunning, evil joke to play. It was a Shiraz, obviously. And equally obviously, it was a Rhone wine, a Côte-Rôtie. Any expert would tell you that … but I knew it wasn't, because I'd drunk this very wine sitting next to a fire in the Karoo, shortly before I was molested by a leopard. It was one of Wikus's.

"Shiraz. Swartberg Pass, Great Karoo border," I whispered to Frog, nonchalantly.

I could see he was absolutely astonished. This one was supposed to knacker everyone. In your face, Minstrels! I looked over at Hugo, he'd been nursing it for a couple of minutes and he could tell there was something funny about it. He whispered in his Frog's ear and the arm went up. Oh dear. At least he had one life left. But snotty little Russell didn't. He was on his last life and I would have paid good money to see him cock it up. But I didn't have time to dawdle – I had three wines left and ninety seconds on the clock.

I lifted the third-last glass. It was sweet and cloying. They'd selected dessert wines for the final three. This was a Rutherglen Muscat, a gorgeous Aussie number, the type I'd drunk by the gallon on my Charlie's Cellar educational trip down under.

Next was a vintage Port, no mistaking it. Single estate, I was pretty sure I knew the exact one.

Last glass. A buzzer sounded. It was Russell. Sure enough, he'd been brought down by Wikus's palate-bending wine. I could hear his whining: "Well what is it then? It's a Côte-Rôtie, dammit! Tell me what it is then!"

There was another round of applause, not for Russell's eviction but for Juliette, a French wine journalist. She had completed the tasting. I saw her stagger from the end of the table into Valentina arms, giving her a big hug. Then the applause rose again, together with cheers of bravo! Hugo had made it home too.

Quiet you sods! The clock had ten seconds to go. I summoned all my powers of perception and focused them, laser-like, on the last glass. A sniff and a little sip. A generous hint of oxidation, dried dates and burnt hair. An old memory, from way back. An elderly woman, asleep on the sofa, snoring gently, a small glass goblet on the coffee table before her. My own hand reaching out – but it's a child's hand. I was barely five years old. I grasp the copita and my eyes bulge as I savour the taste of pure paradise. The liquid coats my tongue and slips down my throat, more glorious than any toffee, still watching my grandmother in case she stirs. My tiny hand takes the bottle and turns it to read the label.

"Malmsey, Madeira, twenty years old."

Frog dropped his head, eyes closed. For a shocking second I thought I was wrong. Then the audience burst into cheers as the countdown clock ticked two, one, zero. Valentina, Juliette and Hugo rushed over and embraced me, while Fritz stood back, looking both smug and a bit green around the gills. I was knocked off balance and we tumbled to the floor in a heap, my head buried in Valentina's breasts, as the audience rose to their feet, applauding wildly.

The Invocator banged his staff and spoke again. "Herr Stich. Madame Lavigne. Monsieur Blanchett. Señora Soto. Mr Hart. You have pleased the gods!"

The audience cheered and whistled again. Sounds like they're a few gins down the road themselves, I thought, extracting my head from Valentina's chest and struggling to my hands and knees. She remained flat on her back, whooping for joy, a sight with which I was quite familiar of course.

Hugo and Juliette continued to embrace, holding each other semi-upright in drunken French solidarity. Fritz was still standing, though only just. He leant over the bench displaying the musical instruments, palms planted heavily before him. Steady old chap, I thought, don't puke on your oboe or you're in real trouble. I caught a glimpse of Tallah, the Lebanese lady, who had failed to complete the tasting, being escorted to a side door.

Then it dawned on me, as the audience quietened once more, that the ordeal was only half done. I brought the Invocator into focus as he regarded us, imperiously, from his throne.

"And now Le Récital!"

CHAPTER EIGHTEEN - LE RÉCITAL

*A*nd so via Kadmos of Tyre
And Melampos we learn.
Oh this Odeion!
Hurry! Lest Apollo rise too soon.

You've got a fine line in horse-apples, old chap, I muttered to myself as the Invocator intoned his verse. I clambered to my feet and gave Valentina a hand, dragging her to an upright, if swaying, position. I hastily adjusted her dress where a cheeky nipple had popped into view, gentleman that I am.

Frog was at my shoulder once more. "The recitals will begin shortly," he murmured. "You will each perform your piece, in the order in which you completed the tasting. You must remain standing while the others play."

That meant I'd be last. Hell's bells. I could barely stand upright for a second, let alone through four performances. Unless ... of course! My spare sachet of Madame Joubert's! But I would need to find a cunning way to consume it while Frog, the staff-wielding bearded wonders and a thousand Minstrels of Wine had me under their beady eyes.

I moved my left hand lazily to the tail of my jacket. That was where I'd created my secret pocket – a small incision in the seam of the lining. I could feel the slight bulge made by the wrap of paper. But how would I consume it? Until now, I'd always had some water handy in which to dissolve it. And given the way it fizzed on contact with liquid, I didn't fancy trying to swallow it dry. Even with the audience focused on the performer, a dinner-jacketed chap suddenly foaming at the mouth like a rabid penguin might just arouse suspicion.

Fritz stepped onto the raised platform in front of the orchestra and turned to face the audience. His Frog had already placed his music on a stand and taken a seat to his right, ready to turn the pages when necessary. The conductor stepped onto another platform and faced the orchestra, his back to the rest of us. There were a few seconds of discordant violin sounds and random horn notes as the musicians checked their final tuning.

"May I raise a glass to my fine fellow Initiates?" I asked Frog.

He looked surprised, then pleased. "Of course."

I grabbed a glass of red wine from the nearest table and raised it high over my head, in the direction of Fritz. He looked slightly surprised and nodded back as the audience burst into applause at my generous tribute. What a noble chap that Mr Hart is, he'll make a fabulous addition to the ranks of the Minstrels! I took a very small sip – it was Wikus's wine, surely a lucky sign – and kept the glass in my hand.

The lead violin bowed a single note and Fritz raised his oboe to his lips, playing a note in return, checking he was tuned. Satisfied, he nodded to the conductor and stood to attention. The violins erupted into life. The screen hanging from the ceiling informed the audience that this was Bach's Oboe Concerto in A Major. And a jolly good tune it was too, what with the violins scrubbing away melodically for a minute or so before Fritz piped up on his oboe. I'm no classical aficionado but he seemed to be doing a reasonable enough job, swaying around expressively as he tootled away – though that may have had more to do with imbibing one hundred and eighty mouthfuls of wine than channelling J.S. Bach, of course.

After five minutes there was a few seconds' pause, then Fritz got stuck into the second movement. A bit slower, this one. And it was time for me to get stuck into my sachet of Madame Joubert's. Ever so slowly, I felt once more for the little parcel. I eased a couple of fingers into the slit in my jacket's lining and clamped the paper wrap between two fingers.

Frog suddenly looked right at me and I froze. Stay calm Felix, you're doing nothing wrong. I smiled and nodded in time to Fritz's somewhat dirge-like rendering of the second movement. Frog looked away and I breathed once more. I extracted the sachet and held it in my sweating palm.

Fritz was now onto the third movement. The tempo picked up once more and the poor chap looked as though he was flagging a little, his face red and eyes staring. The rhythmical swaying had given away to little staggering steps backward and forwards. Steady on Fritz, I thought, any more of that and you'll be exiting stage left, arse over tit.

And then, with a little trill, it was over. Fritz lowered his oboe and panted, still staggering slightly. The audience applauded politely, and I gently tapped the fingers of my fist against the palm of the hand holding my glass. Fritz bowed deeply for several seconds, then stood bolt upright. It was the last straw. With a shocked, purple face and bulging eyes, he took two sharp steps backwards and collapsed into the cello section. The applause was replaced by a crash of falling music stands and splintering wood.

As various staff-bearers helped Fritz back to his feet, I could see the Invocator in deep discussion with six senior, purple-cloaked Minstrels. They returned to their seats and he banged his staff on the ground. "Herr Stich has sinned against the gods!"

Fritz had disentangled himself from the music stands and cello strings by now and lunged forward a few steps, wild-eyed. *"Was ist das? WAS?"* Fritz wasn't happy at all. In fact, it'd be fair to say he'd gone Full German.

"Your technical skill was adequate but you lacked flair," announced the Invocator, dispassionately.

"Flair? Flair? *WAS IST DIESES SCHEISSE?*" screamed Fritz at the judges, waving his oboe like a club.

A pair of well-built staff-bearers trapped him in a pincer movement and, one on each arm, dragged him to a side door. *"VERDAMMTE SCHEISSE!"*

I have to say I'd picked up more European swear words in the past few hours than in the entire previous decade. Even if I went the same way as Fritz, the evening wouldn't have been a complete waste of time.

Valentina was already up on the platform. She was seated, dress hitched up, a cello nestling between her beautiful tanned thighs. I sighed in admiration. Trust Valentina to be a virtuoso at the only instrument you had to actually mount to get a note out of. And she was a virtuoso, she'd told me she had performed with the Mendoza Philharmonic Orchestra since she was a teenager. She now held the audience rapt with a magnificent rendition of Schumann's Cello Concerto in A minor. She didn't even need the sheet music, she knew it by heart.

I remember her telling me one night in bed, after a heavy evening on the Malbec, that she played the cello. "That's a very big instrument for a delicate flower like you, isn't it?" I replied, rather stupidly.

"Let me show you how I play the cello," she shouted, clamping my kidneys between her thighs from behind. "I play *con la pasión*, like this!"

She grasped a favourite piece of my anatomy in lieu of a bow, grabbed my throat with the other hand and proceeded to demonstrate some Mozart. I can't say I remember which piece it was, exactly, but it ended with one hell of a climax.

I was spellbound, along with the rest of the audience, and when the piece was over the standing ovation was immediate.

The judges and Invocator conferred very briefly, nodding to one another. The main man in the crimson cape rose to his feet. "Minstrel Valentina Soto has pleased the gods!"

Valentina screamed and the audience erupted once more. Her Frog approached the platform and held out a purple cloak, which she flung over her bare shoulders. We had our first Minstrel!

Juliette, the wine journalist, climbed onto the platform, a French horn wrapped around her arm. I suddenly realised I hadn't yet taken my medicine. My eyelids were starting to droop and I had to keep blinking to prevent my head spinning.

'Mozart's Horn Concerto no. 4 in E flat' flashed the screen. The violins delivered their jolly intro for a minute or so, then Juliette took a deep breath and launched into her part. She started well enough, pooping and parping quite musically as the accompanying violins sawed their happy way through the melody.

I raised my fist to my mouth, as if nervous for Juliette, leaving the little rectangle of paper just proud of my curled finger and thumb. I worked the wrap between my front teeth and moved my fist slowly across my lips, tearing the tiny package open. Hopefully all eyes were on Juliette and not my surreptitious performance-enhancement.

I needn't have worried. We were over ten minutes into the piece and Juliette was looking decidedly pasty. She reached the famous third movement, the Rondo, a fairly tricky part with lots of fast, delicate little notes. She started to slow down and I could see the conductor eyeing her with concern. He tried to slow the orchestra to match her pace but she began to miss notes completely.

A worried buzz rose from the audience. A couple of judges were conferring and I could see grave looks and a shaking of heads. Poor Juliette. She was obviously very accomplished but she'd picked a dastardly tricky piece. Presumably all the easier horn concertos had been performed by Initiates from previous years.

The notes became less and less frequent, then she stopped making any noise at all. The horn was still at her lips but she simply made little jerking movements rather than blowing. I could see her eyes were streaming and I wondered why she didn't just pack it in.

All of a sudden, a huge fountain of pink liquid erupted from the end of the horn. Smaller spouts sprayed from the valves while violent jets squirted from the sides of Juliette's mouth. The conductor, only a yard or so away, caught one of these squirts in his ear and threw his hands up in horror. The audience screamed in disgust as poor Juliette staggered forward, another torrent of hot, bile-scented wine erupting from her mouth.

This was my moment. I placed the open wrap of Madame Joubert's over my wine glass and vigorously massaged the paper. I could feel the powder sliding from the little wrap into the Shiraz, and the glass trembled slightly as the magic dust fizzed and dissolved. I slipped the empty sachet into my pocket and swirled the liquid, keeping the glass down and out of sight.

A staff-bearer escorted Juliette from the platform while another, grimacing, followed with her horn, still dripping with pre-owned wine. A third sponged down the conductor, who looked on the verge of puking himself. It seemed rather unnecessary for the Invocator to inform us Juliette had sinned, but he did so anyway.

Hugo now climbed onto the platform, violin in hand, checking with the leader of the orchestra that he was properly tuned. I could see he was suffering from drunken fatigue, his chest rising and falling as he took deep breaths.

This was my moment. I raised my glass as I had for Fritz an hour earlier. "Bon chance, mon brave!" Hugo raised his bow by way of acknowledgment.

I raised the glass to my lips and, in two big glugs, swallowed the rest of the wine. I hoped to God the powder would kick in before the wine did. As I drained the glass, I felt a sludge of undissolved powder ooze over my tongue and down my throat. It crackled like popping candy and I put my hand to my mouth, stifling a splutter. Curses! There hadn't been enough wine in the glass to dissolve it all. I could feel the exploding medicine pinging its way up the back of my throat to my nose. I spluttered again. Oh Lordy, don't spill any wine, I thought. What a disaster to be disqualified at this stage!

Frog looked at me, moderately appalled. "You probably shouldn't drink any more before your performance Mr Hart."

I swallowed hard, desperately hoping he couldn't hear my crackling throat. "Very true, Frog," I replied weakly. "I just wanted to salute my friend."

Frog nodded and patted my arm. "You're a true and virtuous young man, Mr Hart."

By now, the conductor had been wiped down to his satisfaction. He raised his baton and, with a nod and a swipe, the music began. But, rather than the full orchestra bursting into life, the only sound was that of a lone pianist. After a minute of rather haunting piano-work, Hugo joined her on his violin, and a fairly mournful old tune it was too. The screen informed us this was Tchaikovsky's Méditation, Op. 42 no. 1. I tried to feign interest, though mostly I was just trying to stay upright. Come on Madame Joubert's, work your magic, I prayed.

"My God, there's blood bubbling out of your nose Mr Hart." Frog was staring at me in alarm. I could see out of the corner of my eye that a large pink bubble was inflating out of my right nostril. I whisked the handkerchief from my breast pocket and wiped it away.

"It's nothing. Just something I picked up in The Congo a few years ago. Plays up when I'm in the presence of artistic genius."

Frog stared a few seconds more then dragged his eyes back to the performance.

I tried to sniff the stray wine bubbles back up my nose. Thankfully, the crackling in my throat had subsided and I could feel the calming warmth of Madame Joubert's concoction spreading through my body. My spinning head slowed and the fatigue lifted. Hugo was fiddling away like quite the maestro, the fingers of his left hand running up and down the strings like a demented crab. I had no idea what the judges thought, it sounded rather too much like a mouse torturing session to me, but the audience were rapt.

The strength had returned to my limbs by now and I started to feel very warm in my dinner jacket. "Frog! Can I take my jacket off?" I whispered, a little louder than I intended.

"No, that is not permitted."

That's a bit mean, I thought. I was distinctly overheating. My arm and leg muscles were pumping like miniature power stations and I flexed my pectorals under my shirt. I felt as though I'd just done half an hour in the weights room at Hampstead Gym. I took a long deep breath. "La la la la la la laaaaaa," I intoned.

"Shush!" scolded Frog in horror.

I shut my mouth. Good Lord! What was wrong with me? I was feeling distinctly peculiar, although I also felt fantastic, like a magnificent animal, a fabulous beast among mere men. I started making little boxing jabs just short of Frog's head. "Give me your best shot, Frog, come on," I challenged, ducking and weaving in front of him.

"What on earth has come over you Mr Hart," whispered Frog severely. "This is most irregular behaviour."

It was indeed. Very irregular. But I couldn't stop myself. I started doing little jumps on the spot. Strewth, it was hot in this theatre. I needed a cold shower.

Hugo appeared close to finishing, slowly bowing some very high notes and rather setting my teeth on edge, if truth be told. If that was old Tchaikovsky's idea of a meditation, I dreaded to think what he did when he was worked up. Funny lot, those Russians.

The audience erupted into applause and the judges huddled around the Invocator's throne.

"Bravo!" I hollered. "More! More!" Hugo was dripping with sweat and gave me a nervous wave with his bow. "More! Yes!"

"It is your turn Mr Hart. He's not doing an encore. Please do quieten down and follow me."

Frog led me past the raised platform and we threaded through the desks of violins. A large space had been cleared in the centre of the orchestra, and there lay my instruments. I took up my position, facing the conductor and the wider audience behind him. The violins stretched away to my right, cellos to my left, with the woodwind and brass out of sight, diagonally behind me.

"Minstrel Hugo Blanchett has pleased the gods!" announced the Invocator.

Hugo had done it! The audience stood and applauded and I cheered, waving my fists. Hugo's Frog handed him the purple robe and he grasped it weakly, grinning but too exhausted to put it on. The applause subsided and the screen displayed my piece, the Concerto for Six Timpani and Orchestra by Georg Druschetzky.

The recital was always going to be tricky for me. Although I'm a man of immense sensitivity and artistic flair, I have little experience of classical music. I prefer the manly shouts of the sports field and the ecstatic screams of the bedroom to the gentle tinkle of chamber music. My only experience with a violin was an ill-advised and expensive attempt to bat a tennis ball over the Old Manor House at Felching Orchard, and I'd be hard-pressed to tell you which end of a clarinet to blow into. And, just as Gatesave's own Minstrel, Joan Armitage, pointed out a year earlier, there was sweet sod all written for the bass guitar before 1910.

But there was one instrument with which I was familiar. It was mandatory for all pupils to spend three years learning an orchestral instrument at Felching Orchard and I had chosen timpani. Known as 'timps' to the experts and 'kettle drums' to the great unwashed, I felt it was an instrument through which I could truly express myself.

So there I stood, a crescent of six timpani nearly surrounding me. The concert hall lights gleamed in the highly polished copper and the white skins stretched steel-tight over the drums, translucent with tension.

My body felt swollen in all the right places. I'm a modest chap but I felt almost impossibly handsome at that moment, as strange as that sounds. All eyes were upon me and I felt like a god. My word, it was warm though. I could feel a rivulet of sweat running down the insides of my arms.

"Leader! Your finest A please!"

The lead violin eyed me warily and bowed a note. I took my sticks and belted out a roll on each of the drums, from left to right.

"Absolutely bloody perfect!" I shouted. It suddenly occurred to me I might have overdosed on Madame Joubert's Lekker Medisyne Trommel. Would I start foaming at the nose mid-performance? Perhaps my head would simply explode, showering the orchestra in blood and gore. I laughed maniacally and looked about me at the ranks of strings and woodwind.

"By God, I feel incredible! And you all look magnificent!" I stared down at a mousy-looking woman with a fringe, sitting in the front row of cellos. "Hold onto your skirts, madam, and get ready for the ride of your life!" I roared. A look of appalled horror crossed her face and she quickly looked down.

The conductor nodded to me, looked to the lead violin, raised his baton, and we were off. The violins and cellos launched into the opening bars and were soon joined by the woodwind and brass behind me. I knew this piece backwards. The Felching Orchard school orchestra had performed it to the parents when I was fourteen. I'd had to spend two dull evenings every week over the summer, cooped up in the school hall, practising the piece with the rest of the swots, when I could have been drinking scrumpy and practicing French manoeuvres on Hampstead Heath with St Hilda's finest.

Half a minute of stirring music later, my moment arrived. I raised my mallets and belted the drum heads for all I was worth. Momentarily, I was transported back to Felching Orchard, the tinny trumpets belting out an off-key challenge and my own drums thumping a reply. But this time it was different, the orchestra was world-class and far louder. The brass section roared and I boomed back in return. The strings soared and I thundered in response, feeling like a fantastical giant raking his fists through rainbow clouds.

Then, with a triumphant horn blast, the first movement was over. I leant forward, clamping my hands over the drum heads to cut the reverberation. I felt their damp heat radiate back as they vibrated beneath my fingers, like a heaving, sweating breast in the throes of passion. Stone the crows, I was boiling alive in my penguin suit! I clutched my chest, fearing for my heart, turbocharged by Madame Joubert's Karoo marching powder. There was only one thing for it. As the orchestra turned their pages I wriggled out of my jacket and flung it over my shoulder.

"You stupid arse!" shouted someone behind me and I turned to see a tuba player struggling to free his head from my sodden jacket.

"Keep it, you brass bell-end!" I shouted, my head buzzing with pleasure.

A ripple of applause reached me from the audience. I was surprised – one isn't supposed to clap between movements – then I realised it was appreciation for my jacket trick. Well, every little helps. I wondered whether the senior Minstrels in their purple cloaks would appreciate it too. Somehow I doubted it.

But I had no time to ponder – the second movement was under way. This was a touch slower, less martial. It still required a great deal of drum-pummelling, however, and by the time it was over my white dress shirt was slick with sweat. A few seconds to catch my breath, then back to it.

The third movement starts with a rattling salute of timpani and horns, and I was soon twisting and turning, hammering the drums one side then the other, like a frenzied jungle explorer beating off an army of snakes. The sweat ran down my arms and out from under my cuffs, dripping onto the timpani heads. As I beat each skin, the sweat splashed back into my face and sprayed the nearby string sections. The mousy cellist was looking particularly damp, her sad little fringe sticking to her forehead like a homeless toupee.

Then the third movement was complete and, after a few seconds of panting, it was straight into the fourth, this one faster still. As I writhed from side to side, my sodden mallets splashing against the drum heads in front and behind me, I felt as though a wave of molten lava was creeping down my face, over my neck and coalescing around my heart. It entombed my chest and edged lower still, constricting my waist, curling round my loins, then my thighs. This is it, I thought, I'm having a seizure! I'm going to expire, right here, just five minutes from my chance of a purple cloak and lifelong wine-based adulation.

"Save me, oh gods!" I shouted out loud. Then, in a ten-second pause during the first minute of the fourth movement, as the horns blasted away behind me with a little fanfare of their own, I realised what I must do to avoid certain death. I ripped my dress shirt open, the buttons ricocheting off the timps and into the violins. A quick twist at each wrist and my cufflinks were released. Then I lifted the shirt over my head and flung it high over the conductor's head, before it landed on the staff of an astonished bearded guard. The audience roared their approval and I retrieved my sticks from my back pockets, just as my part resumed.

And a humdinger of a part it was too, the horns blasting a salute as I thundered back, then on to the highlight of the piece – the drum solo. I drummed like a man possessed, my magnificent bare chest flexing, my carved biceps gleaming under the lights. Waves of pleasure cascaded from my head to my hands and crashed off the drums, bathing my body in ecstasy. Near-orgasmic pulses surged through me and I had to resist the urge to whip out my magnificent third mallet and wop it repeatedly on the drum before me.

I'm not sure how long the solo lasted and I may have elaborated the part somewhat. The conductor gave up after a minute or so and simply stared at me, gobsmacked. And who could blame him? I was a Greek god, a drummer fit to lead a regiment into battle. My sticks had become great axes, beheading foul demons as I raced over the plains in my chariot. By the gods – I would have victory even if I had to rip it from the judges' necks with my teeth!

I became dimly aware the strings had joined me once more and I took care to focus on the notes again. The movement ended and I shook myself like a wet dog, spraying a gallon of sweat over the nearest musicians. I could see the audience were on their feet, spellbound.

The fifth and final movement began with another drum solo. I writhed like some vast, muscular python, beating the timps behind me with backward blows over my head, using my elbows for the drums to my sides. I whipped my head round and round, mainly to stop the sweat running into my eyes, but also for visual effect. The orchestra joined me for the final few seconds of the finale then with a huge drum roll, it was over!

I stood with my arms raised and sticks outstretched, to deafening silence from the audience – but only for a second. Then the entire hall exploded in a storm of applause, shouts and screams. The swinging sweat ran into my eyes and I was blinded. I groped around and my hand found the sheet music of one of the woodwind players. I wiped my face and looked up to the judges – but to my shock they were gone and the throne was empty. Had they walked out in disgust? Too much Felix beef for you, you effete trollops?

Then I saw the Invocator striding onto the stage, arms outstretched, face beaming under his crimson hood. The other judges hurried in his wake and the violins stood and stepped back, making a path for their approach. He swept past the conductor, who looked to be suffering from post-traumatic stress, and I kicked one of the timpani aside to meet him in the centre of the stage.

"Exquisite! I have never seen the temple drums so owned! Oh my boy, my boy! Tell me you are not Rostam, Lord of Zabulistan?" He embraced me passionately, nuzzling his stubbly, wrinkled face into my chest and attempting to insert the bony fingers of one hand down the back of my trousers. Thank the Holy Mary I'd fastened my belt nice and tight, I'm rather selective about who I allow to breach my peach, if you know what I'm saying.

The Invocator suddenly broke away, his eyes wide open, an even wider grin on his ancient face. His eyes looked down to my trousers and I realised, not for the first time that evening, I was standing to attention like a Regimental Sergeant Major. This Madame Joubert's was definitely a higher octane recipe than the one old du Plessis had given me.

"My boy! You have peaked!" From the look on his face, I thought he was going to grab hold and spin me around, singing the chorus to 'Here We Go Round The Mulberry Bush' but, luckily for me, Frog trotted up, a purple robe in his arms. The audience roared its approval as he placed the robe around my glistening shoulders and I raised a fist by way of salute.

I rejoined Valentina and Hugo at the base of the stage as the Invocator declared that Minstrel Felix Hart had pleased the gods. Both my fellow Minstrels gazed at me, awestruck, and the three of us were given another standing ovation as we left the hall, a phalanx of staff-bearers surrounding us as a guard of honour.

We were permitted, thank the Lord, to leave following our ordeal, rather than having to make small talk with the audience of Minstrels. We retrieved our possessions and spilled out into the cold Covent Garden night, I holding my button-less shirt closed over my bare chest. After a joyous, three-way victory hug, Hugo vanished home while Valentina and I shared a taxi back to hers.

She confessed she'd noticed the bulging trousers throughout my performance and suggested that if I could stand to attention through a timpani concerto, I could manage a little longer back at her place. Well who was I to argue? And so, like two Minstrels at the top of their game, we made sweet music until the cold January sun rose the next morning.

CHAPTER NINETEEN - ASTI SPUMANTE

The following Monday I glided into work, as smug as a Jaipur prince, a huge smile plastered across my face.

"Felix!" squealed Patricia as I swaggered up to the wine team. "You're a Minstrel! That's so amazing!" She dashed over and gave me a big hug.

"Thanks Trisha. It won't change me, I promise." I wondered whether this was entirely true. Surely another thirty grand and a more glamorous buying region wouldn't be too much to ask?

"I know, you're always so modest, Felix. We've got two Minstrels in the team now, that's so exciting!"

Joan peered at me over her glasses, a genuine smile on her face. Well well, things really had changed.

"I wish you could tell us what happened, Joan," said Trisha, nudging her.

"The omertà di vino forbids it Trisha, as you well know. All I can say is that Felix was magnificent." Joan gave me a wink and I smiled back, Minstrel to Minstrel.

"Who's next then?" asked Patricia. "How are your studies going, Timmy? George?"

Durange gurned and wriggled in his seat. Poor Timmy, he had always been the jealous type. It must have been agony for him to see how far I'd leapt in just two years, and that I now outranked him.

"It's not fair to expect everyone to pass The Minstrel of Wine qualification, Trisha," I said. "We need a mix of talents, and George and Tim perform essential roles in the team." Durange grimaced while Bolus's face went puce. I sat down, trusting my magnanimity had helped sooth any jealous, chafing sores.

A strong forearm wrapped itself round my throat and began to throttle me. "Who's a clever boy then? Ha!"

I hoped the Head of Execution wouldn't choke me to death before I received my pay rise. "Morning sir," I croaked.

"Looks like we need a little restructuring, now that Hart here's put some lead in his pencil," said Bannerman. "All of you in my office at ten sharp, right?" He released me and I massaged my bruised windpipe.

At ten we trooped into Bannerman's office and stood in a line by the wall. "Right. Firstly, congratulations to Felix Hart. You are forthwith promoted to Senior Buyer."

"Well done Felix," chirped Trisha.

"Don't muck it up!" Bannerman grinned, grabbing my shoulder and shaking it violently, as though he was attempting to dislocate it.

"I won't sir."

"Bolus, you're going to buy spirits, right?"

"But sir, I like wine," he moaned.

The Head of Execution must have anticipated this response, because a split-second later his fist powered into Bolus's stomach. "Ha! Never mind that, we've got a new buyer starting next month. She'll look after Australia and New Zealand." He grinned, gold fillings twinkling, as Bolus doubled up, spluttering. "Any more questions?"

"You've still got Eastern Europe, George," I reminded him. He straightened slowly, giving me an uncharitable look, his face even more gammon-red than usual.

"Durange! You've looked after Italy for a long time," said Bannerman.

"But sir!" he whined, holding up his arms to ward off a beating, "I'm just turning Italy around."

"Ha! You've been turning it around for three years. We need someone who's going to actually do something!" He looked at me. "Hart, you get Italy in addition to South Africa."

Hallelujah! The best wine country in the world! I made a mental note to book a flight to Milan straight away.

"In exchange, you can give Portugal and Germany to Durange."

Farewell, dear Portugal, I thought. I'll miss those motorboat rides up the Douro with my Port supplier, her long dark hair flowing in the wind. And Germany too, those chilly December nights curled up in a Rhineland schloss, fire roaring, just leather-clad Stefanie and a bratwurst for company.

"You're a Senior Buyer so you need more than just two regions to look after. Any requests?"

"How about Champagne?" I suggested. It hadn't escaped my attention that Durange got all the best invitations to the racing, tennis, polo and any fixture where there was an excess of glamour and crackling – all thanks, of course, to his Champagne suppliers. I felt such excitement was wasted on poor Timmy. He was a shy type, positively terrified of the opposite sex, and I couldn't really picture him enjoying himself at such events. Far better for a genuine enthusiast to take his place. I was looking forward to phoning wonderful Sandra at Paris-Blois Brands and giving her the news.

"Good idea. Hart looks after Champagne with immediate effect," confirmed Bannerman.

"Nooo!" shouted Durange, with surprising passion, dropping his guard for a moment during which the Head of Execution's fist made positive contact with his solar plexus. We filed out of the room and returned to our desks, Trisha giving Durange a supportive hand as he limped along, coughing and weeping.

"I think Felix should sit opposite me, now that he's a Minstrel," declared Joan a little later.

"Good idea," agreed Trisha. Poor Durange rose from his window seat, with its wonderful view of the river, and limped over to my far less attractive seat next to the walkway. It's fair to say his day wasn't working out as well as mine, though I hoped he'd see the setback as an opportunity to inject a little vigour into his attitude.

I received my salary increase notification the following week, and a handsome improvement it was too. I also received a text from Sandra from Paris-Blois Brands, inviting me to the Monaco Grand Prix.

Clearly, not everyone can be a winner. But, like the froth on a cappuccino, someone has to be on top. And, given the hardships I'd endured over the past year, I saw no reason why it shouldn't be yours truly.

* * *

I made it my business to travel the length and breadth of Italy over the following months. The vines awoke from their winter slumber, as the poets might say, canes sprouting from woody stems, pale young leaves unfurling in the spring sunlight. As the late frosts died away and the season warmed, tiny berries appeared on branches, now lush with leaves. Spring eased into summer and the berries swelled into voluptuous grapes, darkening in colour. And, before we knew it, autumn and the harvest were upon us, the vineyards a frenzy of picking and pressing, tanks of grape juice bubbling with magic as they metamorphosed into wine.

A balmy September evening found me on the veranda of Sergio Morelli's winery, nestling in the hills above the picturesque town of Asti. A few dozen miles away the vine-covered foothills rose to become the Alps, the lower slopes streaked with forests of green pine, the higher peaks capped with a crust of snow.

I raised a flute of pale, sparkling wine before the late sun, admiring its clarity, then brought it closer and inhaled, my nose nearly touching the fizzing nectar. A generous mouthful and the glorious sensation of sweet, grapey sherbet washed over my tongue.

"Classic Asti," I sighed. "Sergio, you truly make the best fizz this side of Epernay." I swallowed the wine – it was gone seven p.m. and the time for spitting was over.

Morelli beamed.

"But we need to talk pricing," I said. "More and more of our customers are buying drier Prosecco these days, and our business is ten percent down on last year."

His face fell. Poor Sergio, I thought, it's never nice to be on the end of bad news, but I owed it to him to tell it straight.

"I knew you would ask me for this, Felix," Morelli replied. "Our business is good but we live in competitive times. I must introduce our new Export Director, Signor Rizzo." Morelli beckoned to someone behind the dark veranda window and a smartly dressed, beaming man with immaculately oiled black hair stepped through the sliding doors.

"Signor Hart-a!" He grasped my hand and clapped me on the shoulder. A waft of rich, musky perfume enveloped us both. "It is such a pleasure to meet our biggest and most-a favourite customer!"

"The pleasure is all mine, Signor Rizzo. Please call me Felix." His muscular perfume started to prickle my nostrils and I felt a sneeze building. "And our businesses will have an excellent future together, so long as we can agree on a special price for the Christmas season." I looked him in the eye and he winked back, rather impudently I thought.

"Felix. Please call me Marco." Then in a lower tone, "I agree. We must revitalise our business. And we have a business proposal for you. We want to make this the biggest ever Asti Spumante Christmas for Gatesave-a!" Rizzo sounded the vowels with an Italian flourish. Amazing how the Italians can make even a British supermarket sound glamorous, I mused.

A sudden pop and a smile from Morelli signalled the opening of a Franciacorta, a rather smart looking and more serious fizz. Condensation dripped from the bottle as he poured three glasses, the bubbles frothing furiously up the glass then subsiding just as they reached the brim.

"Here's to a sparkling, market-a-beating Christmas!" sang Rizzo. "Salute!"

"Salute!" Morelli and I replied as we clinked glasses.

"Dinner at nine," purred Rizzo. "I think we should open some very special bottles."

Morelli's estate included a beautiful old farmhouse with kitchens, guest bedrooms and a huge patio overlooking the vineyards. I changed for dinner and by the time I returned, the kitchen staff had set up a large table and were buzzing back and forth, covering it with plates of salami, croquettes and metre-long grissini bread sticks. Morelli and Rizzo were already seated, talking seriously in low tones, while a dozen or so winery staff chatted noisily among themselves. Rizzo broke into a wide smile and rose, gesturing to the seat next to him.

"Felix, sit here next to me as our guest of honour, of course-a! Sergio, you go over there, the ladies, when they arrive, can go there and there ... Ah! Signorine!" he exclaimed as two excitingly dressed young women joined us at the table. "This is Anna, my girlfriend, and this is Teresa who helps me with exports. Teresa can sit the other side of you."

She slid next to me and held out her hand. "Hi Felix, nice to meet you. I am Teresa. Like Mother Teresa, but I am not really like Mother Teresa." She grinned, with a flash of white teeth.

I wondered how much grappa I'd need to drink before mistaking my companion for Mother Teresa. Several pints, I suspected, wondering whether my gaze had already lingered longer than appropriate on her liberally unbuttoned silk top, which was making a very casual, almost negligent, attempt to cover her firm, tanned breasts. Her legs, the very tops of which were covered by a short suede skirt, knocked against mine as she took my hand.

"Scusi," she said, still smiling.

"Buon appetito!" declared Morelli, and the table was filled with outstretched arms, lifting slices of melt-in-the mouth salami and scoops of carne cruda onto plates. Corks popped and the estate's own superlative Gavi wine was sloshed into large glasses.

"Salute!" grinned Teresa, bringing our glasses together, her legs still pressed against mine, not that I minded in the slightest. Teresa grabbed a grissino and broke off the first few inches. She bit the piece in two, dipped the ends in molten cheese and offered one to me.

"I could never do the Atkins diet – I just love bread too much," she confided, placing a hand on my shoulder.

I nodded, my mouth stuffed with breadstick dipped in gooey Piedmontese cheese.

"And who wants to be a sad, skinny girl with no curves anyway?" she demanded, rather leadingly.

"No-one with any sense," I replied, my charm well-oiled by the excellent wine. "You have clearly chosen the perfect diet."

Teresa moved even closer and spoke quietly but assertively into my ear. "You are a gentleman. A fabulous English gentleman.

No wonder you are so successful and powerful. I look forward so much to working with you."

She speared a fried pig's trotter with her fork and shook it onto my plate. "Here, try this. It's called batsoa. It means silk stockings." She lowered her voice and made a mock-serious face. "But it is not the season for stockings, is it?" She laid her other hand high on my thigh.

I became aware, quite suddenly, that the point of one of Teresa's breasts was pressing gently but confidently against my ribs. It is moments like this that one realises how differently various cultures interpret the concept of personal space. A fiery flush of heat began to grow in the area beneath the table top.

"So, Felix," said Rizzo. "Let me propose my business idea before the next course arrives." With more than a little disappointment I turned away from Teresa, though she politely kept her hand in place.

"We want to sell more Asti Spumante. So do you. Our problem is you have so many other wines to choose from. Prosecco, Cava, Champagne. Even those wines from Australia."

A snort from Morelli.

"The Australian wines are good!" scolded Rizzo. "The people in England drink these wines. From Australia, from Chile, from the South of Africa. This is our problem, we cannot be arrogant!" Then back to me. "So, for Christmas we will offer you the best price you have ever seen on Asti. Ever." He paused, glancing at Morelli.

"And what might that price be?" I asked, waiting for the inevitable wafer-thin discount off the normal price.

"Twenty-five cents per bottle." Rizzo stared at me with apparent seriousness.

I paused for a moment. "Twenty-five Eurocents? Signor Riz...I mean Marco...Twenty-five cents is a tiny fraction of your production price. I assume that's a joke?" I gave a thin smile. Bloody idiots, I thought, is this their idea of fun? Where's the next course anyway? I was still hungry and could see the kitchen staff hovering just inside the cucina doorway, waiting to serve. I picked up my glass and took another mouthful of Gavi.

"No Felix," said Rizzo quietly, "I am one hundred percent serious. I will offer you this price. And in exchange…" another pause and a glance at Morelli, "you will-a buy five million bottles."

My mouth was full of wine and I mis-swallowed, sending a painful lump of air and Gavi down my throat. I goggled at Rizzo, trying not to choke.

"You see," he continued, picking up his own glass, "we want to dominate Christmas in Great Britain. We want Asti Spumante to be the only sparkling wine the British people buy. And with your super-low price, it will be. When they have tried it once, they will buy more and they will never go back to dry old Cava or expensive Champagne again. The future will be Asti Spumante – the future for both of us, Felix."

He continued to look me dead in the eye. I had to admit there was logic to it, but it seemed a pretty desperate gamble on their side. "Do you even have that much wine?" I asked. "That must be half your annual production. And you're proposing to sell it all to me, ignore your other customers and lose a fortune?"

"Not lose, Felix. Invest. Yours is a healthy, growing market, people love to party, they love to drink. In this country," he waved his arm towards the town beyond the vineyards, "people are moving away from wine. We want to make our own future, create a new market. Think about it over the pasta!" Rizzo waved to the staff and they approached with the next course.

"Salute Felix," said Teresa from my right. I turned and she chinked glasses once more. The red Barbera paired the tangy, salty gnocchi perfectly, its crisp bite followed by a warming fruity body and a long finish. I took a large sip.

"The offer is *aggressivo*, yes?" smiled Teresa, "But we can offer it only to you. Only you have that buying power, the power to make a whole market. The other supermarkets, they are too small." She raised a dumpling to her lips and a drop of buttery sauce ran down her chin. She wiped it away with her napkin and grinned. "Your business would be very happy, I think, if you made such a success of Christmas. Maybe they would promote you?" She turned her face closer into my ear. "Will you remember us when you are CEO?" she breathed, a hand moving very slightly higher up my thigh.

The plates were cleared and more wine arrived, an old Barolo. "This is from our wine library Felix," called Morelli. "We usually keep this for family. But serious discussions call for serious wine."

A great bowl of Brasato al Barolo arrived – thick, moist slices of beef and chunks of vegetable, marinated in red wine and herbs. A waiter eased the cork from the bottle.

"So, what do you say? Do we have a deal?" pressed Rizzo.

"I need the cold light of day to think about this, Marco," I replied, transferring a fabulous-looking chunk of glistening beef to my plate.

"Come on Felix," whispered Teresa. "This is the most exciting deal I have ever seen. Let's do it." I could feel her breath on my neck and my blood was up again. Rizzo took the bottle of Barolo and poured me a glass. I gave the glass a swirl, an intoxicating perfume of roses and dark berries filled the air.

"What's there to think about, Felix?" insisted Rizzo. "The price is unbelievably low and you know you could sell the wine. You have hundreds of stores, put a nice big display at the front and there will be a bottle in every basket."

"Five million bottles," I muttered, shaking my head. But it dawned on me that it might just be possible. I'd be fighting for the prime spot at the front of our stores with sneaky George

Bolus and his half-price Irish cream liqueur. But nobody would have a cost price like mine. I'd have the superior margin and that would give me dominance over the other buyers' products. In retail, he who delivers the highest margin triumphs.

"And this is the same wine that we always buy, same quality of bottle and cork?" I asked.

"Naturally!" Rizzo raised his hands, palms up, making a face as if I had questioned his parentage.

I thought for a moment. The words of old Clive Willoughby at Charlie's Cellar floated through my head, 'If a deal's too good to be true, it probably is'. But this seemed watertight. They were clearly desperate, but that was to my advantage.

"I think we may have a deal," I nodded.

Teresa squealed and clasped my head in her hands, turning my face to hers. She planted a very firm, slightly open-lipped kiss on my mouth, ending with a very brief invasion from her tongue. She looked me right in the eyes. "I am so excited! No turning back now!"

Rizzo, meanwhile, had risen to his feet and was holding his glass aloft. He tugged on my arm to rise with him and I reluctantly removed my hand from Teresa's thigh, where it had found a warm and uncomplaining home.

The hubbub around the table died down and Rizzo addressed the group in Italian, announcing the deal. Before he had finished, the table erupted in applause, cheers and calls of 'bravo!' Rizzo turned to me and clinked glasses, beaming from ear to ear.

"You've made me an offer I can't refuse!" I smiled.

Rizzo broke into a grin and clapped me on the back before regaling the crowd with a translation, giving me the chance to try the exquisite old Barolo. It slipped down very easily. Everyone burst into laughter, and one of the winery workers shouted something back, upon which they roared even louder. Rizzo put his arm around me, staggering with laughter. "He just said, 'That's a Sicilian winery deal. Tell our client he can relax, we're in the north!'"

I laughed along, helped by the infectious hilarity and the barrel-load of wine I'd consumed. Funny old lot, I thought, there's something definitely lost in translation there. Still, whatever makes you laugh.

CHAPTER TWENTY - CONFERENCE SEASON

I t was the end of September. In the calendar-obsessed retail world, that meant conference season, that feverish, transitional period when the colour of product packaging changes from summer-bright to muted, autumnal tones and the rumble of Christmas artillery becomes distinct. Each supermarket chain booked a vast stadium with efficient, nationwide transport links and competed to put on the most bombastic show possible before its suppliers, boasting of thrusting sales growth, white-hot developments in e-commerce and exotic success in foreign markets. And Gatesave, with its monstrous market share, was expected to put on the best spectacle in the industry.

As a newly minted Senior Buyer, I was obliged to attend. And so, with a heavy heart, I returned from Italy to the somewhat less glamorous environs of Birmingham and joined the CEOs and sales directors of Gatesave's thousands of suppliers at a huge arena just outside town.

The basic agenda was the same every year. Gatesave's directors would take turns to mount the stage, accompanied by a burst of soft rock music, to present evidence of the company's formidable prowess, and to insist every supplier should be moist with excitement at being part of Gatesave's success.

The presentations always ended with an 'ask' – a heartfelt request for suppliers to do more, to stretch every sinew to make the mutual relationship even more successful. It was an 'ask', of course, in the same way that a machete-wielding burglar 'asks' an old lady to contribute to his weekend cocaine fund.

You might expect the normal reaction of a crowd being 'asked' to drop their trousers and take a painful rogering would be displeasure, bordering on a rock-hurling riot, but the truth was these suppliers were completely reliant on their business with Gatesave. For many, we were their largest customer by far, so the loss of their contract might mean the end of their company's existence. And Gatesave knew it.

I took a seat near the back, next to a smartly dressed woman in a red skirt and jacket. I nodded to her and she, clocking my Gatesave staff badge, gave a nervous smile back.

"Sheryl. Great to meet you," she lied enthusiastically, in a lovely Mancunian accent.

Poor lass, I thought. She's ended up sitting next to a Gatesave Senior Buyer so she'll have to be on fanatically good behaviour. I glanced at her lapel badge and was ambushed by the sight of the generous curves under her smart white blouse. Sheryl Bainbridge, Sales Director at Wigan Hardware Ltd.

"We've proudly supplied all your own-label mops and dust-pans since 1983," she explained desperately.

"Jolly good. I'm Felix, Senior Wine Buyer."

Her eyes opened wider. "Ooh. I love wine!" she exclaimed. Then, suddenly embarrassed, she composed herself. "In moderation of course."

"Well I'm a big fan of housework, actually. But also in moderation." I gave her a smile and a nudge, hoping I'd put her at ease, and was rewarded with a little intake of breath and a more knowing smile back. I wondered if she was attending the after-show party. I hoped so. But before I could ask, the lights dimmed and the murmur of the audience faded.

Quietly, a scrum of hard-faced Gatesave store managers fanned out through the arena, taking up station along the aisles. But they didn't face the front – they kept their backs to the stage and watched the massed ranks of the audience instead. Their job was to scrutinise the suppliers and catch any sign of dissent, whether a heckle or just a worldly roll of the eyes. A particularly thuggish barrel-shaped character with a crew-cut, who I recognised from the Sutton Coldfield store, took his station at the end of our row. I flashed him a grin as our eyes met and I'm sorry to say his mouth curled in hatred.

Out of the silence erupted the chorus of Starship's 'Nothing's Gonna Stop Us Now' and a cheesy disembodied compere's voice boomed, "Ladies and Gentlemen! Welcome to … the forty-fifth Gatesave Suppliers' Conference!"

The hard-faced management guards whooped fiercely and pumped their hands together, eyes daring the massed ranks not to do the same. The suppliers, pale smiles in place, unanimously joined the applause.

"And now … give a massive, target-busting Gatesave welcome to our CEO … Roland Bonnaire!" He pronounced it 'boner', holding the final 'errr' sound several unnecessary seconds. Well, that's your first and last compering gig for Gatesave I thought, as the less mature members of the audience, myself included, let out a howl of laughter.

"Behave!" whispered our tubby guard with a snarl.

Up yours, sunshine, I thought, giving him another smile. Senior Wine Buyer outranks duty fruit and veg manager, old chum. I'd love to see you try and report me for inappropriate sniggering.

Starship's lyrics increased in volume, and Monsieur Bonnaire strode from some hidden place in the wings to centre-stage,

white teeth dazzling under the spotlights. He applauded himself slowly, shaking his head with delight and mock disbelief. His
flawless orange skin shone like a genetically modified Satsuma as
he pointed and waved at a couple of random spots in the audience, each time giving a little laugh of fake recognition.

"I lurve zat song!" shouted the beaming Bonnaire, giving
a little jig, still shaking his head with incredulous delight. The
music and applause faded and Bonnaire took a couple of steps
further forward, suddenly serious. He pointed at the audience.

"I am serious guys. To understand my strategy, you only have
to listen to zis song." He raised his hand, pointing to the heavens.
Sheryl had removed a notepad from her bag and her pen was
poised.

"Take it to ze good times." I looked sideways at Sheryl's pad.
She had written 'good times' neatly next to a pre-printed bullet
point.

"See eet through ze bad times." 'Bad times' was dutifully
recorded alongside the next bullet point.

"Whatever eet takes, eez what I'm gonna do." A faint ripple
of sighs shimmied across the arena, as two thousand suppliers
prayed they hadn't invested a return rail ticket and a night's
accommodation in Birmingham solely for a French-accented
soft-rock recital. The crew-cut manager scanned our row, trying
to spot anyone exhaling disrespectfully.

"I weel leave you with zose words in your ears so you can
reflect on zem. But above all, I want you to concentrate on zis
very important message." Bonnaire closed his eyes and brought
his palms together, as if to pray. The sighing died away and the
audience leant forward, straining to hear.

"Furk us," he intoned solemnly. "Furk us!" he yelled.

After a few seconds of absolute silence, a wave of un-
suppressible farting guffaws cascaded across the arena. What
in Jehoshaphat's name is that lunatic French fancy on about, I

thought, an involuntary raspberry escaping my own lips. Sheryl looked down at her notepad, tears welling in her eyes as she tried to suppress her own hysteria.

Our crew-cut friend looked at his fellow guards in panic, eyes bulging. "Silence! Silence!" he whispered aggressively.

Bonnaire opened his eyes, sensing that the crowd's mood had shifted in an unexpected direction. "Er … we must … furkus," he faltered. Focus. We must *focus*, you gigantic Gallic tool. What an epic opening to the conference. This was priceless.

The farting of suppressed guffaws had now given way to howls of laughter and the mutiny was unstoppable. A huge bearded man three seats down was having hysterics, holding his sides and roaring with laughter. Our portly crew-cut friend barged his way down our row of seats to remonstrate with him, and as he passed I stuck out a leg, sending him sprawling to the floor, to a renewed roar of approval from the nearby seats.

Starship erupted into life once more, mid-chorus and at maximum volume, only for large parts of the audience to join in enthusiastically:

Nothing's gonna stop us now …

The music was cut abruptly and the main lights came on. The audience participation weakened and petered out. "Ladies and gentlemen," intoned the compere, "there will be a short break before the next address, by Gatesave's Sales Director."

The smiles and camaraderie of the sing-along faded, draining like water into parched desert sand – and for good reason. As every colleague who had experienced the Store Walk could attest, The Director wielded the power of a medieval sovereign. He had the ability to award or remove patronage on a whim. A wave of his hand could mean the closure of a factory and the end of a centuries-old business.

It felt like all the air had been sucked out of the hall. The guards were back in position, looking pleased with themselves once again. Our crewcut friend had dusted himself down and was staring at me vindictively, unsure whether I had tripped him on purpose. Suppliers looked down at their hands or up at the high ceiling. The big bear of a man a few seats down had his eyes closed, no doubt wondering whether his earlier, uncontrolled hilarity might count against him when his business was next up for tender.

There was no need for anyone to be told to quieten down, The Director was nigh. The lights faded and a new anthem burst into life on the great speakers. It was Scorpions' 'Wind of Change'. The eerie intro whistle and guitar chords floated across the arena. But instead of an uplifting song of liberation it sounded like a terrifying portent of disaster. The arena remained pitch black as the haunting tune played out. Then a single, pale blue spotlight illuminated The Director, already standing in the middle of the stage, head bowed.

The hairs on the back of my neck rose as the lyrics began. The Director raised his blue-bathed head and stared pitilessly at the audience. The verse continued:

Blowing with the wind… of change…

The music faded out and the silence was total, thick with dread.

"The wind of change is indeed blowing." The Director's high, cruel voice made Sheryl start. I reached out a supportive hand and to my delight, she grasped it and laid it upon her thigh.

"Change is everywhere. And it should be welcomed." A huge screen behind The Director glowed into life, showing a long, curving graph of sales versus the number of Gatesave suppliers. A click from The Director's control button and a red circle appeared halfway along the graph.

"As you can see, ninety percent of our sales come from half of our suppliers." He turned back to the audience and smiled, humourlessly. "Let me put it another way. Half of you supply just ten percent of our sales." A concerned murmur rippled across the audience. Sheryl's hand closed a little tighter on mine.

"Ladies and gentlemen. We have too many suppliers delivering too little value. The wind of change must blow." The Director smiled again, cold in his circle of blue light. "But we will not be arbitrary or unfair in this process." His voiced softened to a whisper. "The suppliers who will retain our business will be those most aligned with our core values. Our values of Tolerance, Respect, Understanding and Delivery."

He sighed. "I found it very disappointing, however, to see those values in short supply a little earlier, during our CEO's presentation." He looked down at a piece of paper. "I would like to invite some suppliers onto the stage. Mr Bennett of Kentish Beansprouts Limited, Mr Filigree of Devon Agribiz Limited and Ms Grindwell of Bagged-4-U Limited, please make yourself known to the helpers and they will guide you to the stage. Quickly please!"

The big bearded chap in our row, whose name was clearly Mr Bennett, emitted a little whimper. "Oh no," he muttered, shaking his head as he rose. Our crew-cut guard smiled. Bennett edged past us and approached the stage, head bowed, the helper guiding him with a fat palm in the small of his back.

The Director whistled the intro from 'Wind of Change' into the microphone, eyes scanning the audience, as the three suppliers were escorted up the steps to the stage. Bennett was last to arrive, joining Mr Filigree – a thin, bearded man in a tweed suit – and Ms Grindwell, a ruddy-faced lady in a plaid skirt.

The Director stopped whistling. "We have three beansprout suppliers but we only require two!" he declared in a higher-still, slightly maniacal voice. A short-skirted, red-lipsticked flunky skipped across the stage with an envelope and handed it to him, giving a wink and an air-kiss to the audience before skipping off.

The Director tore the envelope open and read the contents, smiling and pursing his own lips in mock surprise. "I'm delighted to announce that Bagged-4-U have scored the highest number of points in our internal review! Ethel Grindwell and her team have proved they live our values of Tolerance, Respect, Understanding and Delivery, every day!" He looked at Ms Grindwell, who raised a fist over her head, her face a picture of grim victory. Bennett and Filigree kept their eyes on their feet.

"Bagged-4-U will continue to supply Gatesave and can look forward to even more business in the year ahead!" boomed the compere's voice. A smattering of applause rose from the audience. The short-skirted helper skipped back to centre-stage, linked arms with Ms Grindwell and escorted her back to the steps, where she was handed over to a less attractive colleague for her relieved walk back to her seat.

All eyes returned to The Director. "There can only be two suppliers in the bagged beansprout supply base after today." He glanced back at his notes, shook his head, then looked up at the audience. "Both Kentish Beansprouts Limited and Devon Agribiz Limited scored exactly the same number of points in our review!" He held out his hands, palms up, in a theatrical gesture of confusion. "So we had to go to penalties! Not an actual shoot-out," he added with a mirthless laugh, "but a candid assessment based on behaviours right here, today, at the conference."

The Director observed the dejected, beaded duo. "One of our core values is Respect," he intoned, "but there was a disappointing lack of respect earlier when Monsieur Bonnaire was giving his inspirational speech." His voice dropped to a dangerous whisper. "There is a time for laughter, for revelry, even for … mockery. But that time is not…" his voice rose suddenly, making poor Sheryl next to me start once again, "… is not when the CEO of your greatest, most important, most inspirational customer is addressing you from the very bottom of his heart!"

Even fifty rows away I could see the little flecks of saliva winking in the spotlight as they were expelled at high velocity from The Director's mouth. Poor old bugger, I thought, looking at Bennett, who was visibly sagging. But what a show trial! I wondered if they'd actually shoot him live on stage.

"Giles Filigree of Devon Agribiz Limited, congratulations! You have retained your business with Gatesave!" Filigree's wide eyes and ashen face remained set as a prancing stage-hand led him back to his seat.

Bennett remained hunched for a moment, then his legs buckled and he slumped to his knees. The spotlight on him went out. In the half-gloom I saw two burly helpers stride to centre-stage and, each taking an arm, drag our former bagged beansprout supplier to an exit in the wings.

The Director was calm once more, alone on the stage. A flunky skipped up with another envelope. "The household category!" he declared, and Sheryl gave a sharp intake of breath.

"Don't worry," I whispered, "I won't let them take any business away from you." A rather reckless fib, of course, I had absolutely no say in the matter whatsoever, but I wanted to be supportive.

"Thank you," she whispered back, her lips just brushing my ear. I felt the familiar rush of blood down below and congratulated myself on my powers of empathy.

"Specifically, pest control for home, garden and pet," continued The Director.

Sheryl gave a little sigh of relief.

Somewhere from the back of the arena, behind the closed doors, I heard muffled bumps and raised voices. I wondered if Bennett was raising merry hell before his final ejection from the arena. Good for him, I thought. He was a big chap and I bet he could have knocked a few of those brown-shirts over before they finally bundled him out.

"We have no fewer than ten suppliers of fly spray, ant powder and deworming tablets," declared The Director, shaking his head in mock horror. "We only need five. I wonder who will be eradicated today!"

The banging and crashing became louder, and I heard a couple of screams among the shouts. A few people turned in their seats, but there was nothing to be seen. Maybe Bennett had grabbed a couple of shotguns and was going out in style, I thought idly. That would make it a conference to remember.

I scanned the side aisle of the arena noting the position of the emergency exits, just in case. I'm a robust chap, and years of blasting through the opposition's forwards with a rugby ball under my arm has given me plenty of practice for when things turn gnarly. The commotion was still only audible to the back half of the audience – The Director was oblivious.

"Helpers, please escort to the stage the following suppliers – Mr Peridew of Ants in Your Pants Control Incorporated …"

There was quite a cacophony of thumping by now, and the shouting was accompanied by the sound of smashing glass. A few of the guards, including our crew-cut friend, moved towards the back of the hall, brows furrowed.

"Mr Whelkshell of Tring Worming Limited!"

A sound of splintering wood was followed by a long low moan.

"Sounds as though the Weightwatchers conference has broken for half time" muttered a wag behind me, to a few uncharitable titters.

"Mrs McTavish of Spray It and Slay It Limited!"

There was a series of almighty crashes as the swing doors at the back of the arena were battered open. I jumped to my feet and turned, along with the rest of the audience, but it was dark and impossible to see over the sea of heads. I leapt onto my chair for a better look and got the surprise of my life.

With a bellow of angry moans and the clattering of heavy hooves, a herd of huge cows barged into the arena, like some middle-management version of the Pamplona bull run. Within seconds the beasts had reached the back rows of the audience and there was a crescendo of yells and screams as people leapt onto their seats, or clambered over the rows in front. The cows themselves snorted and tossed their heads, some of them careening into the back row in a tangle of limbs and upturned seats.

Behind the animals, a group of angry rural types shouted and flicked long whips over their heads. Panicked by the mass of squealing humans, the herd surged forward, splitting into separate lanes as they charged down the aisles.

"Mr Singh of Bolton Fleas and Worms Limited ..." tailed off The Director, eyes rising from the paper, his eyes and mouth widening in horror as an avalanche of angry beef hurtled down the central aisle towards him.

A tinny, amplified voice with an angry Welsh lilt sang from the back of the room. "Here's a little present from Pembrokeshire Dairies, Mr Director!" I spotted a dark-haired giant of a man with hairy forearms, a megaphone in one hand and a whip in the other. "Do you remember me Mr Director? You delisted me last year, so you did. Fair ruined me you did!"

The Director stood on the stage, eyes goggling, mouth opening and closing wordlessly.

"So here's me and the girls to tell you what we think of your bloody conference!" roared the farmer.

The foremost animals had broken into a gallop by this time and had covered the full length of the arena. The stage itself was some four feet above the ground and I winced in anticipation of the beasts colliding with the solid platform. To my astonishment, the lead cow leapt into the air like a prize steeplechaser and belly flopped rather inelegantly right in front of The Director, who took a couple of steps backwards, mouth agape.

With a mighty low, her legs scrabbling to get purchase on the shiny stage, the great black and white Friesian scrambled to her feet and trundled straight at The Director. As the charging animal's forehead made contact with his chest, he wrapped his arms around her neck, his winded face contorted with pain. As she pushed him to the back of the stage he gradually lost his grip and slipped until he was trailing under her hooves. He screamed a single, high, piercing note whereupon, with a bellow of rage, the cow stamped her huge hooves all over his flailing, pathetic body.

"*Coc y gath!*" lilted the farmer into his megaphone. "That wasn't supposed to happen!"

The arena was now in utter chaos, the rich smell of sweat and animal dung filling the air. Cows at the back of the herd were nosing their way along the rows of seats, their bells clanking as they herded the shrieking delegates into bunches. The back exit was blocked by livid Welshmen cracking whips, while the side exits were jammed by cattle.

I looked at the stage once more. A pair of flunkies were attempting to ward off the cow with chairs but the beast was having none of it, snorting and tossing its head, still raking the Director with her hooves. His limp body was bent into a series of improbable angles. I suspected he'd need a fair bit of physio before he recovered from that little episode.

From my vantage point I spotted a gap in the herd and jumped to the ground, wrapping a protective arm around Sheryl. "Time to evacuate," I declared in my smoothest emergency services voice. As I pushed my way to the exit I passed our crew-cut guard cowering before an irritated heifer, attempting to defend himself with a small laptop bag. In an attempt to distract the creature, I slapped its behind and shouted "Banzai!" Unfortunately, this merely enraged it further. It lowed menacingly and lunged forward, butting our guard in the chest and flinging him hard against the wall.

We reached the somewhat crowded emergency exit and I shouldered my way through the smaller, less assertive delegates, my body shielding Sheryl from the tumbling crowd. Stamping the cow dung from my shoes and gallantly removing Sheryl's for her, we climbed into a waiting taxi. "I suspect the after-show party may be cancelled. May I escort you back to your hotel?"

"It's the Hilton Metropole in Curdworth," she said to the driver, breathlessly.

"Righto," replied the driver and he had barely put the taxi into gear before Sheryl's grateful lips closed over mine. Well, you don't become the Sales Director of a Wigan-based hardware company without a degree of assertiveness, and if there's one thing I like, it's a woman who knows what she wants.

The following morning, like a true gentleman, I made two cups of tea and retrieved the paper from underneath Sheryl's hotel room door. 'Cowmageddon!' screamed the headline. 'Gatesave's posh supplier conference invaded by cattle class!'

I returned to bed and pressed the TV remote. As Sheryl's sleepy head nuzzled against my chest, I flicked to a news channel. I soon found what I was looking for. A solemn looking reporter was interviewing a worker outside the Birmingham Arena. There was a smart corporate photograph of The Director in the corner of the screen, smiling benignly, but it was the caption that caught my attention:

Executive killed, forty-three injured in cattle stampede. Farmers arrested for manslaughter, breach of the peace, multiple counts of animal cruelty.

So there it was – The Director was no more. A terrible tragedy, I mused, but never mind, I was sure his funeral would be a jolly good send off, packed to the rafters with suppliers anxious to demonstrate their grief and loyalty to the remaining Gatesave board members. And, like any ambitious young buck, my next thought was – who will replace him? There was bound to be a whole cascade of management changes. In short, what might it mean for me?

The answer, of course, was a lot. More than I could have possibly imagined.

CHAPTER TWENTY ONE -
GOODS RECEIVED

The standard lamp flickered then brightened again. I paused to check my audience were still with me. I definitely had their attention, though they did look a little stunned. The big man was now sitting cross-legged on the floor, leaning against the door.

"I think you've drunk too much," said the woman.

There was nothing left in the bottle, it was true, but I still had a full glass before me. "Wouldn't you prefer me to drink, officers? Surely it makes me looser-tongued?"

"To be honest, that's what we're afraid of, Felix."

"I think it's time to get down to proper business, don't you?" said the man. "That's definitely enough wine." He nodded to the guard behind me, who clambered to his feet.

Quick as a flash I was out of my chair. I grabbed the empty bottle by the neck and spun around. "By the gods, you touch my wine and you'll regret it!" The big man had taken a step forward but now froze, his open hands raised, eyes flicking between me and our seated companions.

"Everybody, sit back down," said the woman. The big man lowered his arms and slowly sat once more, keeping his eyes on me all the while.

I replaced the bottle on the table and kicked the chair around so I could address my interrogators while keeping an eye on the brooding guard. I took it as a good sign they were still listening and that I'd not yet been hauled to a police station.

"We're running out of patience. We're not here to hear about your encounters with wild animals and Italian fine dining." The man flicked the ring-pull on a slim can of energy drink and took a swig. I checked my watch, it was well after five. Poor little petal, I thought, he's flagging. I wasn't, though – I was on a roll. I lifted my glass and took a sip.

"You mentioned a Mr Rizzo, Felix," said the woman, tapping on the table. "He's a person of interest to us. I think you need to concentrate on him, rather than safaris and all-night drinking competitions."

I replaced my glass on the desk and sighed. "Yes, all right. Things took a darker turn after that, I must admit."

***

My desk phone buzzed. "Hart, wine department."

"Ciao Felix! It's Sergio Morelli!"

"How are you Sergio?"

"*Bene grazie.* You're still excited about our big Christmas Asti Spumante promotion?"

"Of course I am. Is everything on track?"

"Yes, everything is fine. Except one tiny thing, but I think it is no problem."

"So what's the non-problem, Sergio?"

"No big problem, I promise. We are printing all the labels for the bottles but they will not be quite ready for your very first orders. It is just the first shipments where we have the problem. For the rest we will be fine. But I have a plan."

"Tell me."

"The plan is we ship the very first orders to you with the stock already in our warehouse in Milano. The only problem is the back label – it does not have the proper alcohol health warning in English. So, we must ship them to a warehouse in England, and there we have a team of people who stick a new label over the Italian one."

"Ok. But why can't you just stick the English health warning on the wine in Italy?"

Morelli laughed. "Ah, it is embarrassing Felix, but our label printers are lazy here and it will take three weeks to print them. And the people in our warehouse will insist on lots of extra money for sticking on the new labels. In England they will do it much more quickly. We will pay for the whole thing, of course, no cost to you."

"Ok Sergio, glad to hear it. So we'll ship the stock from Italy but route the order to your own warehouse? Then when you've added the English health warning, we can collect it and move it on to the Gatesave depot?"

"Exactly Felix! Thank you for the understanding."

"No problem Sergio. What a pain. If people are worried about the risks of drinking Italian wine, they should learn Italian."

"Ha! Felix, you are so right! The problem is your English health warning says if you drink more than one glass, this wine will kill you! But in Italy the health warning says don't drink-a too much, you might-a get laid!" Morelli roared with laughter at his own joke. "Your wife will-a kill you!" he added, mirthfully. He continued to laugh for a while longer. He was a funny one all right.

"Thank you Sergio. I'll get the orders revised."

"Ok Felix, ciao!'

I sauntered over to my logistics colleagues on the other side of the floor. Flaky Fiona, who was in charge of the Italian trade lane, was munching on a bar of chocolate. "Hello Fiona, you look nice today," I lied.

Flaky Fiona, as no-one called her to her face, had been cruelly but accurately christened. A large, pale lady, who looked around forty but was actually much younger, she suffered from a wide variety of self-diagnosed food allergies. These included, but were not limited to, nuts, dairy, gluten, yeast, shellfish, non-free range chicken, oranges, several dozen food additives and all African food.

The last of these, apparently, was added to the list on her honeymoon in Egypt, where a romantic Nile cruise had degenerated into a saga of liquid bowel movements and projectile vomiting, an anecdote she never tired of telling. Her diet, so far as I could tell, consisted of fizzy cola and raw carrot sticks, although she kept a large supply of vegan chocolate bars for particularly stressful occasions, one of which I had clearly interrupted.

"Don't hassle me please," pleaded Fiona dramatically. "I have got so much on, I'm in the middle of a meltdown, I don't know how I'm going to, like, get through this day!" She took a bite of her grey-coloured, dairy-intolerant chocolate bar.

"I just need you to place some orders, today, for my little Asti Spumante adventure, please Fiona."

Flaky Fiona chewed her chocolate and stared at her screen.

"Here's the order sheet Fiona. If you could just place these orders, please?" I placed the sheet next to her keyboard. "They need to be dispatched tomorrow. The destination is a Coventry third-party facility rather than our normal depot..." Still no response. I considered balancing the order sheet atop her flabby, chocolate-filled head.

My eyes slid to the framed picture on her desk. It was a close up of Flaky Fiona's face, smiling weakly, no doubt recovering from a colonic injury at the hands of a stray clam. She was accompanied by, I assumed, her husband, a man even more massive than herself. His face was so wide that only two thirds of it had made it into the photo, the remainder lost off the left-hand edge of the frame.

"Oh my GOD," shrieked Fiona. A dozen colleagues looked round as Flaky stared, horrified, at her chocolate bar. "Oh my God, OH MY GOD!"

I sighed and looked to the ceiling, praying to the gods of gluten and nuts that her episode might soon pass.

"What's the matter dear?" asked Deirdre, the kindly old logistics planner sitting at the next desk.

"I. Have. Just. Eaten. A Fruit and NUT!"

"Shall I get you some water, dear?" said Deirdre.

"Oh my God. I can feel my throat swelling up!"

I pushed the order sheet slowly from the side of her keyboard until it covered the keys, hoping this would elevate the task to the top of her to-do list, immediately following her hazelnut-scented brush with death. "When you've recovered, I'd be so grateful if you could place these orders, Fiona. We wouldn't want to miss Christmas, would we?"

Flaky had grasped her throat and was making Darth Vader noises while squinting at the ingredients list on the back of her chocolate bar.

"Thank you Fiona. I'll be back at the end of the day to check everything's tickety-boo." I returned to my desk, banishing uncharitable thoughts of swapping her morning slice of vegan fruit cake for a nut-stuffed badger's liver.

When I returned, at quarter to five, there was no sign of Flaky.

"Fiona had to go home," explained Deirdre. "She started sweating dangerously. Oh, she was in a right state Felix."

"Oh balls. I really needed those orders placed!"

"Don't worry, I did it for you," winked Deirdre.

"Ah, you are a darling Deirdre," I gushed, winking back. What a star! If only everyone could be like Deirdre, I thought.

***

I was sprawled on a sofa at the Little Chalfont flat a couple of evenings later when my laptop pinged. The automated email was brief:

Asti Spumante ex-Genoa. 40ft container x24.

09:35 Customs cleared.

14:50 Departed Felixstowe Port bond.

16:25 Goods received: Braintree Container Depot.

"Sods." I said, staring at the screen. I clicked 'print' and my little inkjet machine sprang to life, disgorging my request.

Wodin was filling two large glasses with a fabulous Sancerre, while Fistule assembled a pile of hashish on his water pipe. Mercedes dozed on another sofa, a book over her face.

"What's up?" said Wodin.

"The good news is that my first containers have arrived. You are looking at the owner of the largest shipment of Asti Spumante in recorded human history. The Christmas sparkling wine market is mine!" After a market coup like this I deserved to be lavished with praise by management and be presented with a gold-rimmed end-of-year bonus. The Head of Execution might even pull his punches for a month or two.

But I was aiming even higher. Ever since The Director's unfortunate public demise beneath the hooves of the Welsh dairy herd, there had been rumours a restructure was due. Patricia Hocksworth, the Head of Wine, had been in her job quite a while and had let it be known she fancied a move to Fruit and Veg – which meant there might be a vacancy for Head of Wine in the New Year. If I pulled off this Christmas promotion, it would put me in pole position. Joan wasn't interested – she was perfectly happy as a Wine Buyer – and I doubted whether gammon-faced Bolus or slimy little Timmy had anything as sexy as this up their sleeves.

I raised the ambitiously large bucket of Sancerre, and Wodin crashed his glass into mine, a fat joint pinned between his enormous forefinger and the bowl of wine. "Nice one Felix. But your email sounded like bad news. What's the problem?"

"It's a long and boring story, but my logistics colleagues have sent the wine to the wrong depot. It was supposed to go to the suppliers' warehouse for re-labelling first."

Fistule exhaled a long stream of hashish smoke, his Speyside-whisky-filled bong smouldering gently in concert. "Is your Asti Spumante fair trade?"

"No it isn't. It's from Italy, not bloody Rwanda. Don't worry Fistule, all the grape pickers drive Maseratis, nobody's being oppressed."

Fistule nodded and turned his attention back to the pipe, poking at the embers.

"I'd better drive down there tonight," I said. "I want to see the shipment before it moves onto Gatesave's main distribution centre. Check whether I need to send in a team to glue politically correct health warnings on the bottles. Fancy coming along, Wodin? You can pretend to be my Compliance Manager."

My actual Compliance Manager, a rodent-like chap called Pete, liked nothing better than running covert lab analyses on my wines. If he spotted a product that deviated from the specification he would send an email to the entire Gatesave management team, trumpeting that the alcohol level exceeded the figure declared on the label. I would then have to withdraw the wine from stores and have the lot destroyed for breaching EU labelling law. Worse still, the costs were deducted from my profit, earning me a kicking from the Head of Margin – not a pleasurable experience, as I wasn't allowed to kick back.

There is a circle of hell reserved for jobsworths like Pete. As if anyone cares that a wine might be stronger than the level quoted on the label! That's not a reason for product withdrawal, it's a gift from the gods.

"Fantastic, sounds like a mission," agreed Wodin. "It's like you've just had a baby. Let's take a good bottle and wet the newborn's head." He fetched a bag of ice cubes from the freezer and emptied them into a cool box. I extracted a bottle of vintage Bollinger from the wine rack and buried it in the ice. We descended the stairs to my Vauxhall Cavalier. Not the raciest of numbers, but as a Senior Buyer I now qualified for a company car, and it was a Cavalier or nothing.

An hour later, as evening faded into night, we arrived on the outskirts of Braintree. The depot's high, razor-wire fence emerged from the gloom. There was a light rain and the skyscrapers of metal shipping containers, stacked ten high, glowed golden in the floodlights. Wodin flicked the stub of the joint out of his window and I wound mine down as we approached the security barrier.

A young Indian guy in a high-vis jacket and a peaked cap took my Gatesave ID and the printed email with the shipment details.

"Here for quality control, hygiene inspection," I said. "This is my Compliance Manager, Pete." Wodin smiled and waved. Without a word, the guard walked back to his office, an old shipping container repurposed as a guardhouse. He scanned the bar code on the email and compared my ID against his screen. His printer disgorged a sheet and he walked back, pushing his cap up for a second, squinting at my face then back to the ID.

"You're in satellite zone 6." He handed back my ID and, rather rudely, dropped two crumpled hi-vis vests into my lap. "Wait there for Bob, he'll accompany you." He pointed at a small parking area beyond the barrier. The bar rose and we nosed through, pausing for our escort.

Wodin moved to the back seat as an older guy in a hi-vis jacket and woolly hat appeared. He slung a holdall into the foot well and climbed in. "Evening lads. Let's take a look."

I handed him the newly printed docket and he held it up to catch the illumination from the floodlight. "Satellite zone 6, area H. It's at the back end of the park, that way." He inhaled conspiratorially. "And I'll have a bit of what you boys are smoking, if there's any left."

"There certainly is, my friend." Wodin snapped open his spectacles case and extracted a large joint.

"Give it a minute – let's get clear of Hamas first. He's a bit of a puritan." He inclined his head towards the guardhouse, into which his colleague had disappeared.

We cruised past the vast towers of containers, each stencilled in giant letters with the names of Chinese shipping companies. Wodin lit the joint, took a deep draught and passed it to the warehouseman, who did the same.

"Grotty bloody night," he gasped. "Nice grass though. Turn right here." After a few minutes crawling along the canyons of metal, Bob pointed. "Area H. That's your shipment there. Park in the yellow striped area."

I turned off the engine and wound down the window. My twenty-four containers lay in two neat lines of twelve. "I need to check a couple of the loads. We might have a problem with the labels."

"Take your pick," waved Bob as he slowly exhaled smoke. "Got a job-lot did you? Bet you did. You buyers drive a hard bargain, I'm sure."

The rain had slackened to a fine drizzle. I left the car and walked along the row of forty-foot containers. I couldn't help smiling – there were another 392 of these beasts leaving Italy over the next few days, destined for Gatesave stores across the length and breadth of Britain. The trade would be flooded with

Asti Spumante, at an unbeatable price, and market domination would be mine!

At this rate, the Head of Margin should be giving me a knighthood. Surely I'd get the Head of Wine gig after such a coup? By Jove, think of the travel, not to mention another tasty salary hike. And think of the young saleswomen across every wine producing region in the world, from Argentina to New Zealand, quivering with excitement at gaining a listing with one of Europe's largest supermarkets.

"You little beauties," I grinned and gave a double knock of joy against the nearest container. There was a double knock back. I jumped out of my skin and gave a little yelp of horror, my stomach churning.

From behind the steel door came a heavily accented, anxious voice. "Hello?"

I looked back at the car, a few yards away. The orange glow of the joint shone brightly for a moment as Bob anaesthetised himself against the night shift. I turned wildly back to the container. "Who's that?" I mouthed into the crack where the container doors met.

A pause. "I am Galad. Help please."

"What the devil are you doing in my container?" I demanded, aghast. I checked the seal securing the container doors. It was intact. Shipping containers are usually secured with a metal bolt, requiring heavy-duty cutters to remove, particularly when they contain something worth stealing – like booze. There was no doubt about it. Whoever my squatter was, he'd been there since the container was loaded and sealed.

"Hello?" the deep heavily accented voice again. "Please, we need water."

I caught my breath. We? There's more than one? And then the penny dropped. My beautiful shipment of Asti Spumante had hitchhikers. They must have sneaked on board at the winery before the container was shut and sealed. The security would have been fairly lax and it was much easier than scaling the fence at Calais and trying to board a lorry. Cheeky sods, I thought, though you can't criticise them for lack of determination.

"Wait there. We'll have you out in a minute." Stupid thing to say, I thought. They're going nowhere unless they've got a welding torch handy.

"Bless you sir. Please, are the others ok? We have your package."

The others? My package? I walked back to the car, my mind racing. Bob, the warehouseman, wound down the window a few inches and a fug of smoke rolled out.

I tried to sound nonchalant. "We need to check a couple of these loads. Happy to do it ourselves. Done it enough times." I peered into the car and looked Wodin in the eye. He was still lounging across the back seats. The radio was tuned to Classic Eighties, and Genesis warbled from the speakers.

"Wod … Pete, how about we save Bob from getting wet and sort him out with another toot?"

"Well gentlemen, that's the kind of offer I can't refuse," smiled Bob. He opened his door and nudged his holdall towards me with his foot. "Bolt cutters are in there. Replace the metal seals with plastic ties and note the number down. There's a torch in there too."

"Right. Pete, bring that bottle of water."

"Have a taste of this sir," Wodin said to Bob, passing him another joint discreetly tucked under his plate-sized hand. "My finest home-grown. Don't smoke it all at once, it's a strong one," he winked.

"Cheers boys."

Bob turned up the music and wound the window closed. As we walked towards the row of containers I glanced back. He'd already tipped the seat to forty-five degrees and closed his eyes, the joint protruding from his happy lips.

"We've got a big problem, Wodin," I whispered urgently. "I think there are illegal immigrants in my containers."

"No way! Do you think they've drunk all your wine?"

"I bloody hope not. They've probably been to the toilet all over it though. It takes a week to ship from Genoa and that's a long time to keep your legs crossed." We stopped at the doors of the container I'd knocked on. I glanced back at the car but Bob was already invisible behind the steamed-up windows. I knocked again. "Galad? Are you there?"

"Well that's nice – you already know his name."

A pause, then the heavy accent. "Hello?"

"We're opening the door." I pulled the bolt cutters from the bag and handed them to Wodin.

"Cut it there." I focused the torch on the seal. Wodin lifted the cutters, which carved through the metal in a second and the bolt clattered to the floor. I lifted the slider and, with the torch held next to my head, pulled open the door.

At first, all we could see was a wall of wine boxes, neatly stacked to shoulder level. Then an eye-watering wave of warm foulness washed over us – a humid cocktail of body odour and faeces. I gagged and Wodin took a step back, covering his mouth.

"God almighty! That is revolting!" he spluttered from behind his hand.

Holding my breath, I opened the other door and saw the front left-hand pallet of wine was missing. In its place was a deep pile of crumpled sheets and dozens of empty soft-drink bottles. And further back, leaning against the wall of wine, five seated bodies swaddled in blankets, black hands hiding their faces like naughty children caught in the act.

"Kill the torch, Felix, they've been in the dark for a week."

I switched it off and, as our eyes adjusted to the gloom, the hands moved aside to reveal five black faces with bright white eyes. I noticed a bucket in the corner of the tiny space splattered with something dark and unspeakable.

"Well, fancy that. Where are you boys from, then?" asked Wodin.

A short silence then the same voice I'd heard through the doors piped up. "Somalia."

"Well you're in Braintree now. Not sure that's an improvement to be honest."

The stowaways started to stretch and one of them – I was guessing Galad – winced as he stood up. His dark skin was smooth, drawn tight over prominent cheekbones and a high forehead. He took a step forward and squinted at the drizzling sky and yellow floodlights, lips parting to reveal buck teeth.

"Christ man, get back in!" I exclaimed. I glanced back at the car but it was obscured by the open container door. I looked up and around frantically for CCTV cameras. There were none close by, but if the guardhouse controller became interested it would be quite straightforward for him to zoom in on us. "You have to stay there or they'll call security."

Galad's eyes widened and he stepped back, though not before taking a deep breath of the damp night air. "We are in England?"

"Yes, you're in England. But you're not safe yet."

He smiled and looked at me. "We are safe."

I suddenly had a terrible thought. I swallowed. "How many of you are there?" Please let it be just these five, I prayed. Please God.

"Forty-two."

"Oh Lord! Thou hast forsaken me!" I cried, sinking to my knees. The dream was over. I closed my eyes and imagined how the next few hours and days would play out, security guards snipping seal after seal, dozens of Africans stumbling, wide-eyed and blinking into the drizzle, kneeling to kiss the puddle-strewn concrete of an Essex industrial estate. Then vehicles full of police and immigration officials roaring into the depot, leading the confused stowaways into the backs of vans. And my precious stock would be impounded – not just this lot, but the hundreds of containers arriving over the next few days – as the police investigation into the smuggling route took hold.

There would be an awkward, probably quite violent conversation with the Heads of Margin and Execution, where I'd explain I was terribly sorry but Gatesave had not only no market-beating Christmas Asti Spumante deal, but no sparkling wine at all. It was far too late to find another winery capable of producing the volumes we needed. And that would be the end of my glorious career in wine and the beginning – if I was lucky – of a new career mucking out the stables at Cackering Hall.

"This is an interesting logistical challenge," said Wodin, matter-of-factly.

"Yes, you could call it that," I spat, "although I'd call it a gigantic, spunking dog's dinner."

"Well, we can't just leave them here for the Old Bill."

"What the hell are we going to do? Drive them out in the Cavalier? We'd need a bloody bus."

"Yes, we do Felix. That's exactly what we need."

I looked at Wodin's smirking face. "Have you finally smoked too much of your rhino-anaesthetising marijuana?"

Wodin pulled out his phone and started pressing buttons. He had a confident smile on his face. "We need a bus. Which means we need Carlos."

CHAPTER TWENTY TWO - HARLOW SUNSHINE TOURS

I t was a lunatic idea. But our only solution was to smuggle the migrants on their final leg to freedom before the containers were moved to Gatesave's huge distribution centre. If they ended up there they would be discovered for certain, heralding the end of my plan for Christmas sparkling-wine dominance, not to mention the end of my career.

We snipped through all the metal seals and laid out a replacement plastic seal alongside each container, old and new security numbers dutifully entered in the log book. We opened the doors of each of the twenty containers, checking them carefully by torchlight. Ten contained stowaways, all Somalis as far as we could tell, mostly men but a few women too. Just don't start bloody wailing and bring security down on us, I prayed.

We resealed the containers without stowaways and left the doors of the others ajar to allow fresh air in. All our Somali friends appeared conscious and mobile, though most looked pretty terrified. Unsurprising really, considering their first sight after a week in the dark was a gigantic hippy in a high-vis vest holding a massive pair of bolt cutters.

With a combination of gestures and pidgin English we told everyone to stay put for the moment – Wodin's alarming appearance helped. We took turns removing the slop buckets and foetid blankets and litter, dumping them in a skip some distance away. I couldn't afford to leave any evidence of stowaways inside the containers. The first warehouseman to re-open the container and find a lovely bucket of turds would be straight on the phone to immigration.

As we checked the containers nearest the car, I crept over and peered in at Bob. It was impossible to see through the condensation-coated windows but I heard a deep snoring. Wodin's home-grown herb had done its job. I just hoped he hadn't passed out with the joint between his lips – the last thing we needed was the old fool waking up screaming with his crotch on fire, surrounded by half of Mogadishu.

Wodin's phone beeped. He nodded to me. "Carlos is on the outskirts of Braintree, better get to the gate."

Rather than wake comatose Bob, I jogged the half-mile back to the main gate, leaving Wodin to keep our stowaways in place. I knocked on the guardhouse door and poked my head round. I was pleased to see the guard playing poker on his computer rather than watching the CCTV. "We need to take a few samples away with us for analysis."

He waved his approval without taking his eyes off the screen.

"Quite a few samples actually, there's a problem with the labels. Can't fit them in the car so we've got another vehicle coming."

He turned around with a faint look of irritation.

"We requested a van but can you believe it, all they could send us was a bloody coach!" I gabbled.

He scowled at me. I could see I was annoying him.

"It'll be a pain in the arse loading those cases up the steps." I started to sweat. He wasn't buying this at all. Who ever heard of a coach picking up cases of wine from a container depot? I gave a weak smile. Please, please, say it's fine, I thought.

"Well I ain't helping you, man."

A wave of relief broke over me. "No, of course not. We'll manage."

It was close to midnight and the background hum from the motorway had quietened. I strained my ears and sure enough, there was the growl of a coach-engine, growing louder as it gunned along the approach road. Carlos's bus rounded the corner and slowed as it approached the guardhouse, coming to a stop at the barrier with a hiss of brakes. I opened the door and bounded up the steps.

Carlos, dressed in a thick lumberjack shirt and jeans, gave a cheerful smile. "Felix darlin'! What an effin' pleasure."

"Carlos, thank God you're here. Have we got a job for you!"

"Yeah, Wodin said you had a few people to pick up. Funny effin' place this. What is it, a rave?"

"Shhhh!" I looked through the windscreen beyond the barrier. The guard stood in the doorway of his office, observing us balefully.

"It's a bit sensitive. You're picking up stock, not people, ok? Say as little as possible."

I jumped back out of the coach. "Does he have to sign in?"

"Course he does."

Stupid thing to ask, I thought. Play it cool.

The guard walked over to the driver's side and, with an unfriendly expression, handed a clipboard up to Carlos. "What's all this then?"

"It's an effin' coach mate," replied Carlos, signing the clipboard with a flourish.

The guard walked the length of the vehicle, which was proudly branded 'Harlow Sunshine Tours' in large letters, complete with a cheerful cartoon sun holding a bucket and spade. He walked back to the driver's window, his distaste clear. "I've never seen anyone pick up stock in a coach man."

"First time for everything isn't there," said Carlos brightly, popping in a stick of gum. Then, nodding to the barrier, "You going to raise that, then?"

The guard looked warily at me then lifted the barrier. I jumped back on board and sat behind Carlos. "Cheers mate!"

Sullen-faced, the guard watched us pull through the entrance and nose the coach into the depths of the container park.

"He was a bit of a tool wasn't he!" said Carlos brightly.

"Yes. Yes, he was." My stomach started to churn again. That was the easy part. How the hell were we going to load forty-two confused Somalis onto the coach and get back out through security? Our unfriendly guard was likely to be zooming his cameras in on us even now, maybe even dispatching a mobile patrol to check us out.

"We need some privacy." I leapt up and scurried down the coach aisle, leaning over each pair of seats and closing the curtains across the windows.

"Darling! I never knew!" laughed Carlos, taking the whole situation far too bloody lightly in my view. Mind you, he didn't know the half of it yet.

We reached the far end of the park and approached my row of containers. All seemed quiet. I'd had visions of security personnel running around like Keystone Cops, trying to catch dozens of fleeing Africans, but I was relieved to see Wodin standing alone in the drizzle.

"Pull up here, Carlos, alongside the doors of those containers." We could use the long, high body of the vehicle to shield the stowaways' embarkation from any nosy cameras. I jumped out of the coach. "Let's go."

Wodin swung open the first container door and gestured to the occupants. "Go guys, go!" Four dishevelled men emerged, stiff-limbed, blankets around their shoulders. Grimacing at the dark, drizzling sky, they limped up the steep stairs to the coach.

"Down to the back!" I urged, making pushing movements with my hands.

"What the effin' hell is this!" screamed Carlos.

"Chill, man," called Wodin. "We're just helping some fellow humans."

"Where the 'ell are this lot from?" Carlos's face screwed into a visage of horror. "And, love a duck, what's that effin' smell?"

"They haven't washed for a while. And a couple of them might have soiled themselves," called Wodin breezily.

"Oh no, no, effin' no! No way!" warned Carlos. "Deal's off mate, I am not having these stinking bums on my bus. I'll have to get it deep cleaned." The next few stowaways were trying to board the bus but Carlos raised his hands. "Sorry mush, deal's off." He made flicking movements with his fingers. "Offa del bus, gracias!"

Wodin mounted the steps. "I don't think they speak Spanish, Carlos. Mind you, nor do you."

"Not happy mate. Not effin' happy."

"Well, maybe this will make you happy."

Wodin held up a large wad of banknotes, most of which appeared to be fifties, and lobbed it into Carlos's lap. Carlos's eyes popped.

"Blow me, how much is this?"

"Two grand. Plus we'll cover all your cleaning costs and buy you a slap up meal. Felix will chip in with a case of Champagne too, won't you Felix?"

"Er...yes. Yes I will," I replied slowly, looking from Wodin to Carlos and to the wad of red notes. Wodin often carried large amounts of cash, which was par for the course when one was involved in the wholesale marijuana trade. I didn't have time to dwell on why Wodin had suddenly turned into a one-man humanitarian aid agency, but it did the trick.

Wodin gestured to the group waiting to board. "Up you get. Galad, you can help me."

I recognised Galad, my first stowaway, by his buck teeth. He accompanied Wodin to each container and, in his native tongue, cajoled the occupants out and onto the bus. Some were limping and the women were very nervous – I doubt we could have done it without his help.

"Move the coach forward Carlos," I said. "We need to shield them from the cameras."

Carlos, very much back to his chirpy self, kept the engine running, nosing the vehicle forward a few yards each time, allowing the residents of each container to climb aboard. I sealed the steel doors with the plastic security ties as each was vacated.

"Last few, let's keep up the pace," I urged.

"Felix," said Wodin, tonelessly.

"Yeah, I'm nearly there." I pulled the security seal tight on the penultimate container.

"Felix."

I looked up to see Wodin and three Somalis standing still. They were staring at a swaying, woolly hatted figure next to the door of the coach.

"Oh bollocks," I muttered.

"What. The hell. Is happening?" groaned Bob, very slowly and unsteadily. His eyes were bloodshot and a long thread of drool ran from his pouting bottom lip to the paunch of his high-vis jacket, where it pooled before making its way down his leg.

"We're ... checking the load," I started cautiously, wondering how the hell we would get out of this one, short of murder.

Bob turned to me very slowly. "Do you have? Any crisps?"

Carlos poked his head out of the coach door. "Here you go mate." He handed Bob a half-eaten tube of corn snacks.

Bob turned his attention from the refugees to the crisps and inverted the tube, grasping an inch-thick wad. He raised them to his mouth and pushed the lot in whole, crunching slowly. He groaned in ecstasy and tiny fragments of crisp abseiled down the shining thread of saliva to the pool of ooze on his stomach.

"Go! Go!" urged Wodin quietly to the remaining stowaways, who clambered aboard.

Bob turned and shuffled back to the warmth of the car.

"Ok, that's everyone," said Wodin.

Galad was the last on board and took his seat with the others – all the seats were now filled except for the first three rows.

"Stone the crows. Right, let's get some stock on board," I shouted.

Wodin, Carlos and I formed a human chain, transferring cases of Asti Spumante from the last container up into the coach. We stacked the boxes on the second row of seats and in the aisle, building a wall of wine to obscure any view of our passengers.

Before we bricked up the aisle completely, I leant through and warned Galad, "Keep the curtains shut, don't let anyone look outside. And don't make a sound. If we're seen or heard, we're all dead, ok?"

"I will tell them," said Galad quietly. "Please do not hurt us."

"Er...no, well just be quiet then." I jumped off the coach to confer with Wodin. "Here's the key to the car. You'll have to drop off our munchie-crunching friend somewhere, preferably the other side of the depot. Hopefully he'll put it all down to a dream. See you back at the house. By the way, thanks for paying off Carlos, I appear to owe you a substantial sum of money."

"Not a problem, see you later."

I climbed aboard and Carlos nosed the coach away from our row of containers and back towards the main gate. This was the final hurdle and an olympically high one it was, too. As we approached the gate I motioned to Carlos to pull up short. I jumped out and, striding purposefully to the little office, presented the log book and ID once more.

"We had to load forty cases from one of the containers for analysis at Head Office. My Compliance Manager has concerns about the label," I said, in as bored a tone as I could muster. "I've filled in the log book with the transfer quantity, of course." Don't check the bus, please don't check the bloody bus, I prayed. Take my lying word for it, for the love of God.

"Where's Bob?"

"Back in the car with Pete. They should be along in a minute, just securing the last container."

"I'll have to check the stock you've taken."

I felt like I'd been punched in the guts. We approached the coach with its closed curtains, a grim-faced Carlos watching from behind the wheel. The guard knocked on the door and beckoned for Carlos to open it. I wondered if we could make a run for it – just gun the coach at the barrier and we'd be free. The panic mounted in my throat. The door hissed open and he climbed the stairs. I followed behind.

"Forty cases, as you can see," I said brightly, waving at the wall of Asti, trying to keep the dread out of my voice. There wasn't a hope in hell that we'd get away with this. As soon as he dislodged a box, or got close enough to squint through the cracks, he'd see forty-two terrified Somali faces staring back at him and all hell would break loose.

"What's that sound?" he asked.

I froze, and my heart sank. There was the unmistakable sound of someone in distress. A low, repetitive moaning and laboured breathing. Must be one of the women, overcome with relief or fear. Or in bloody labour, more like it. Oh, balls! Of course this was never going to work!

I wondered, wildly, whether I could persuade Carlos to lend me Wodin's wad of cash to bribe the guard. Then I spotted another man watching from the door of the office, and a pair of CCTV cameras mounted on posts flanking the barrier. The game was up!

"Oh ja. Das ist so gut!" said a female voice, between moans. The sound came from above my head. We all looked up slowly and focussed on the coach's TV screen, where a voluptuous, panting black lady slowly thrust a huge, pink strap-on dildo between the legs of a gigantic-breasted, groaning blonde. The guard looked back at me in disbelief.

"Interracial Lesbian Sex Fest," stated Carlos matter-of-factly, reading the title from a video cassette case. "Apologies. Drove a rugby team back from Tring yesterday. Must have started automatically."

The guard's look of disbelief turned, slowly, to absolute horror. "And what is that disgusting smell, man?"

I didn't understand what he meant for a moment – we'd become used to the stench.

"Ah, the toilet's screwed," said Carlos. "Did a tour for some old age pensioners earlier today and a few of them got runny tummies. Completely overran the chemical toilet. It's like the effin' black hole of Calcutta down there mate. Not pretty."

The guard turned back to me, incredulous. I wrinkled my nose. "I'm sorry, it's not very pleasant, is it?" I mumbled.

"Get me off this loony tunes bus, man." He descended the stairs at pace and walked round to Carlos's window, holding up his clip-board. "Sign here, and get this vehicle out the yard."

Carlos signed and the guard raised the barrier. The engine revved to life and we drove past the guardhouse and onto the public road beyond.

We were free!

***

As Carlos's coach eased onto the quiet motorway, my heart rate slowed from rattling panic to mere high distress.

"Where're we taking them, Felix?" asked Carlos.

We hadn't really developed the next stage of the plan, given the astonishing improbability of escaping the depot. "Just pull into South Mimms Services and drop them off."

"Are you having an effin' laugh mate? I ain't doing that! Place is full of cameras and Old Bill. Even if we get them off without being spotted, they'll have my licence plates on film and my guts for garters. Why don't you ask them where they're going?"

I edged my way down the aisle to the wall of Asti Spumante and pulled a couple of cases aside. "Galad!"

"Hello?" Galad's wide eyes and toothy face popped into view.

"Where shall we drop you off then?"

Galad's face remained blank.

"Where do you want to go?" I pressed.

"We go to … London?" he asked cautiously.

His eyes looked past me, down the aisle and through the coach's windscreen to the wide, glistening road and the blackness of the farmland either side. I spotted a couple of his fellow passengers peeping through the curtains, faces illuminated by the yellow streetlights flashing by.

"For pity's sake, no looking!" I shouted, panic rising. "If we're spotted we'll be bloody murdered!"

I had visions of a pair of bored traffic policemen parked on the hard shoulder, their dinner of donuts suddenly interrupted as a coach full of blanket-wrapped black faces on a three a.m. Sunshine Tour from Harlow cruised past. I suspected it would take more than an interracial lesbian sex fest and a robust smell of faeces to discourage Her Majesty's Constabulary from asking some very awkward questions.

Galad turned round and barked urgently at his colleagues. *"Qarin ama aan dhiman!"* It did the trick and the curtains were hastily pulled back into place, fearful eyes all back on me.

"Where are you going? Do you have an address?" I asked slowly.

Galad looked confused. "We work for you. You take us to work."

"Ah. Right." I returned to my seat.

"Looks like they're staying at your place then, matey!" chewed Carlos as he popped in another stick of gum.

Christ, I thought. What will the neighbours say? At least we can get them in under the cover of darkness.

I looked back at the wall of Asti Spumante, white boxes with a large blue crest stating 'Consorzio Asti Spumante DOCG', the governing body of the wine region. There was a picture of a castle and, along the bottom of the case, the words 'Export to the United Kingdom' in English. I gazed idly at the wording for a minute or so before turning back to the front. Strange, this was supposed to be stock destined for sale in Italy – why would it already be labelled for export?

An hour later we pulled off the motorway and travelled the few remaining miles along dark country lanes into Little Chalfont. Carlos pulled up behind the parade of shops. I had dismantled the wall of wine across the central aisle, and Galad had been briefed to disembark his fellow travellers at speed and usher them up to the apartment.

I dashed up the iron stairs ahead of the group and let myself in. A warm, herbal fug of hashish washed around me as I barrelled through the hall and into the lounge. Mercedes lay curled and dozing on a sofa. Fistule looked up from his computer golf, Sega controller in hand, whisky bong smoking gently on the table before him.

"Where did you guys get to?"

"Fistule, listen," I said urgently. "We're putting up a coachload of Somali refugees for a couple of nights. I need you to help clear the bedrooms."

"Right."

"Now! They are entering the house right now. I need you to get up and help."

"Wow."

I jogged back to the front door as Galad stepped inside, warily. A long queue of Africans snaked down the stairs and into the car park, shivering in the winter air under their damp, foetid blankets.

"Go! Go! Go!" I whispered loudly, gesturing violently up the stairs to Galad.

Fistule padded up behind me. "Oh, man. We really are putting up a coach-load of Somali refugees."

"Yes we are. Go up and distribute them evenly among the bedrooms. Separate the women from the men."

The migrants tramped up the stairs. It was the first time I'd had a close look at them. Apart from looking exhausted and terrified, some had nasty cuts and bruises to their faces. All were very dark skinned and most quite tall and slim. There was one absolute giant, he must have been seven feet tall, with huge shoulders and an unsettlingly piercing stare. Wouldn't like to get in a scrap with that one, I thought.

"I see we've become the Little Chalfont High Commission for Refugees," Mercedes drawled, leaning on the lounge doorframe, a few ribbon-festooned dreadlocks hanging in front of her face. A couple of the migrants widened their eyes at the sight of her and the line snaking up the stairs picked up its pace.

After five minutes they were all in. I shut the door quietly and rested my forehead against it, eyes closed. Carlos had long since steered his bus out of the car park and into the night, no doubt planning a holiday to Ibiza with Wodin's two grand. We let him keep the Asti.

What in pity's name were we going to do with forty-two destitute, soiled Somalis? How would we feed them and wash their clothes? The main thing was to get rid of them as soon as possible, of course. Where did London's Somalis live? In the East End I guessed. Maybe we could take them there in small batches and set them free, once they'd been cleaned up. Like a team of animal lovers rescuing stricken sea birds from an oil slick, we would wash them and release them into the wild. Yes, we were humanitarians! For a moment, I felt quite virtuous.

"They're all in the bedrooms. Smelling a bit, to be honest," reported Fistule as he trotted back down the stairs. "There's already a bit of a queue for the bathroom and I need a pee," he added unhappily.

Oh Jesus, I thought. We've only got one toilet. How the hell am I going to have a wee in the morning? We'll need a rota. It occurred to me that I hadn't really thought this one through at all. I jumped at the sound of a key in the front door. Wodin stepped inside and swung two bulky black canvas bags into the hall.

"There's two more of these," he said breathlessly, disappearing for a minute then returning even more out of breath, his arms straining under the load. He dropped them and closed the door. We stared at the bags. They looked like the luggage of a gang of large burglars.

"What are these?" I asked.

"They were in one of the containers. Our friend Galad pointed them out. They appear to be part of the consignment."

"What's in them?" I asked quietly. My stomach had started to knot in that familiar, unpleasant way.

"Something very interesting!" declared Wodin brightly. "I've only taken a quick look. Let's get them into the lounge."

We carried the bags through. Wodin crouched and unzipped one. He reached in and brought out a dark shape, somewhat larger than a house brick, completely sealed in a smooth, transparent plastic envelope. He placed it on the table with a dull thud.

He looked at me happily. "That, my friends, is a kilo of hashish. This bag contains twenty of them. And we have four bags."

Numbers ran through my head. An eighth of an ounce of hash cost around ten pounds at retail price to the ordinary consumer. Thirty-five ounces in a kilo and we had eighty of them. Not far off a quarter of a million pounds. Very nice. But not really, because it wasn't ours. And whoever owned it probably wanted it back. Badly.

"Guys. Look at this." Fistule extracted another object wrapped loosely in a zip-lock bag. Instead of a dull thud, it made a metallic clunk as he placed it on the table. It wasn't a block of hashish. It was flatter and had a clear right angle to it. It was, unmistakeably, a pistol. A Beretta 92, to be exact.

I felt slightly light-headed, as though reality was slipping away. Another thought occurred to me. "When did you discover the bags were full of hash, Wodin?"

"I checked them out while you were fetching the coach."

Wodin's generosity with Carlos suddenly made perfect sense. "So, you've brought a quarter of a million pounds' worth of hashish and a gun home with you? How wonderfully gangster."

"Two guns actually," said Fistule, clunking another bag on the table. "And some ammo, I assume." He stacked several smaller boxes next to the guns.

"And forty-two Somali refugees," said Mercedes. "Don't forget them."

I had forgotten. I leapt up and dashed up the stairs. There was a queue of a dozen people waiting patiently, if awkwardly, next to the bathroom door. I poked my head around the first bedroom door. A group of eight men were huddled together sleeping, sharing a couple of our spare blankets between them. The other bedrooms were a similar picture. My own room contained the women, sleeping peacefully under a collection of duvets, my bed pushed on its side against the wall to make room.

Fabulous, I thought. I've got a house full of refugees, drugs and guns, and no bed for what was left of the night. I sloped back down the stairs and into the lounge. Wodin and Fistule had unpacked all four bags and built a pile of hashish bricks on the table. I was pleased to see there were no more firearms. And quite relived there were no rhino horns, pickled foetuses or lumps of Semtex, for that matter.

Mercedes had slit open one of the bricks with her pocket knife and sliced off a small corner, which she heated and crumbled onto the gauze of Fistule's water pipe. The sweet, herbal aroma of high quality cannabis permeated the room. Not an unattractive aroma at all and I felt myself relax slightly for the first time in a while.

"Looks like we're sleeping in here then," I said, to nobody in particular. "All the bedrooms are full of destitute East Africans and there are no blankets left. Better get that fire going."

Fistule shuffled to the hearth on his knees and tossed three logs onto the embers. Mercedes scooped her dreadlocks out of her face, held a lighter to the pile of crumbled hashish and inhaled on the water pipe. The gentle bubbling coincided with the crackle of the logs bursting into flame, then a pop as Wodin uncorked the vintage Bollinger we'd packed so many hours earlier.

I sank onto the sofa next to Mercedes and gave a long sigh as a wave of exhaustion broke over me.

Wodin passed a flute of Champagne to each of us and raised his. "To a superb piece of procurement!" he said. We clinked glasses.

"Cheers Wodin. For one night only, ok? We get them – and all that," I gestured at the foot-high pyramid of hashish bricks and the pistols in their wrappers, "out of the house tomorrow. Throw the guns in the river or something."

Wodin nodded vigorously.

I took a deep draught of the Bollinger – by God it tasted good. I made a mental note to drive straight to Reims when this was all over and to stock up on a few cases, all negotiated with a tasty Felix Hart discount of course.

I finished the glass and Mercedes passed me the smouldering water pipe. It took just one short puff of the musky, water-cooled smoke before I surrendered to the sweet embrace of sleep. I lay back and drifted off, the warmth of the fire playing on my face.

***

When I woke, all was silent. I could see the faint outlines of Wodin and Fistule on the opposite sofa, and a red glow in the fireplace. I guessed it was around five in the morning. Mercedes had curled up next to me, her head in my lap. As the fug of sleep cleared and my hearing became more acute, I heard a light fizz of drizzle against the window. My thoughts turned back to our goods-yard escapade.

There was something bothering me about those containers and those stacks of wine. If it hadn't been for the late-night Bollinger and hashish it would have nagged at me earlier. The cases I'd loaded on the coach already stated 'Export to the United Kingdom'. They didn't need re-labelling at all. And the pallets in the containers were all perfectly stacked and shrink-wrapped by a production-line robot, they hadn't been thrown around haphazardly, as you'd expect if a bunch of opportunist stowaways had sneaked on board.

This wasn't some dodgy night watchman unlocking the winery gate and letting migrants dash into unsecured containers under cover of darkness. It wasn't even an organised gang intercepting containers at the docks and shoving a few cases around to make room for illicit passengers. It was the winery itself. They weren't the unwitting victims of this racket. They *were* the racket.

And the price I'd so cleverly negotiated over dinner at Sergio's winery? The real cargo was forty-two smuggled immigrants, a large consignment of recreational drugs and a pair of pistols. The wine was quite incidental, though no doubt it provided a convenient way to launder their profits.

Then the final piece of the puzzle slid into place. Of course, those containers were never intended to pass through dismal old Braintree depot! That was a mistake! They were supposed to go to the supplier's own UK warehouse in Coventry, where the illicit cargo would have been offloaded before the wine was sent on to Gatesave. The cock-and-bull story about the need to re-label the bottles was simply an excuse to re-route the shipping containers.

Gatesave had placed the order and organised the shipment. And, with our respected name on the manifest, the containers would be considered a very low risk by Customs and Excise – a search was extremely unlikely. But Flaky Fiona had gobbled the wrong chocolate bar, gone home sick, and her replacement, not knowing the supplier's special instructions, sent the load to Braintree.

Right now, in a rain-swept depot on the outskirts of Coventry, I imagined a number of unsmiling gentlemen with thick necks waiting for their containers of Asti Spumante. I imagined them becoming impatient, then extremely angry. It wouldn't take them long to find where the load was sent – just a phone call to Flaky Fiona in a few hours' time. I'm ashamed to say I prayed to the good Lord that allergy-averse Fiona, in blurry-eyed morning confusion, might confuse her goat's milk yoghurt for a toxic bowl of crunchy nut cornflakes.

CHAPTER TWENTY THREE - YOUNG ENTREPRENEURS CLUB

As it dawned on me that I had a new career as a drugs, refugees and armaments smuggler, the sky outside lightened. I rose from the sofa, lifting Mercedes's sleeping head from my lap and replacing it on a cushion. My bladder was fit to burst. I padded out of the lounge and climbed the stairs. Four Somalis stood in a line before the closed bathroom door.

"Terribly sorry chaps, I'm desperate and I'm going to have to cut in here. House rules." I knocked smartly. "Hurry up, there's a queue out here."

"He sick," offered the man at the front of the queue.

I froze for a second. Images of villagers rolling on the floors of their huts shivering with bubonic plague ran through my mind. Oh, Livingstone! What godforsaken diseases had our friends brought with them? I thought of the roll call of horror listed in the Rough Guide to Africa. Malaria. Schistosomiasis. Ebola.

"Still engaged is it?" called Fistule from the bottom of the stairs.

"Yes. I need a slash and a shower too. I've got to get to work."

"I think it's a bit rough in there, to be honest. You might want to go in the garden. Urine makes good fertiliser."

"Does it, Fistule? That's great to know. Who's going to clean up the bathroom then?" There was no reply. I descended the stairs, opened the front door and peed off the balcony onto the weed-strewn garden below. At least I could shower at work. I changed and headed for the tube.

As I pushed through the revolving door I could see Morelli and Rizzo, my questionable Asti suppliers, waiting for me in Gatesave's huge, marble reception area. Their expressions were grim. My stomach tightened but I didn't break my step. It was just turned seven and only a few early birds were filtering into the building. The Italians quickly spotted me.

"Marco! Sergio! Ciao! What brings you to our office so early?" I said in my most business-like, early morning voice. "Do you have a meeting with logistics?"

The two men did not react at first. Rizzo remained unsmiling and Morelli glanced at him nervously before turning to me. "Ah, no Felix, we came to see you."

"I'm sorry, guys, I wasn't expecting you and I have an early meeting. I'm afraid you'll have to make an appointment for next week."

"Ah, we have a problem with the load I think, it was sent to the wrong depot?"

I was conscious of Rizzo's unsmiling eyes. I chose not to return his gaze. My stomach knotted just a little tighter. "Not really a problem, Sergio," I kept my tone light. "There was a mix up with our team and the wine's in another depot. We'll check the stock ourselves and send it on to you if we need you to re-label it."

I stepped towards the security turnstile but Rizzo moved suddenly to block me. I raised my eyebrows and raised my voice just a touch. Now was the time to act the arrogant buyer if ever there was one. "What seems to be the problem here, gentlemen? I fail to understand why you're ambushing me with a seven a.m. conversation about a shipment of sparkling wine. I have business to attend to."

Now Rizzo spoke, gently but unsmilingly, his eyes boring into mine. "Felix, we were just concerned that the shipment did not take place as we arranged. We want this project to go perfectly, so it is very important that we re-label that stock properly. We do not want a problem with your law."

Problem with the law indeed, I thought. What was that, a trick to see if I looked nervous? Despite the twisting fear in my guts, I kept up my act. "I'll ask our depot to check the stock. Then I'll inform you if we need your services. We might be able to re-label it ourselves."

I made a move towards the turnstile once more but Rizzo placed a hand on my shoulder. He gave a little smile of frustration. "Let us take care of this Felix. Please, it is our problem."

I looked at Morelli, who was looking in turn at Rizzo, his face rather grey. Then I put my hand on Rizzo's and summoned my most self-important tone. "The meeting is over gentlemen. Thank you for your concern. I'll be in touch."

I broke free of Rizzo's hand and strode to the turnstile, waving my pass over the sensor and moving through without looking back. I headed down to the gym, feeling like I was about to puke, and took a long shower.

When I returned to my desk I banged out a brief email to Morelli: 'Good news. Our depot has checked the stock and the labelling is compliant with UK legislation. No action required from your side'.

I jogged over to the logistics department. There was no sign of Flaky, but Deirdre was on the early shift, just returning to her desk with a cup of tea. "Hi Deirdre. Could you check on the status of my Asti shipment please?"

"Oh, hello Felix. Goodness me, you are in early. What's in those containers then, gold bullion?"

I froze for a second. Maybe Deirdre was in on the scam too? No, it was her who'd sent the stuff to the wrong depot. Christ, calm down Felix, you're going to have a coronary. Deirdre chuckled and dabbed at her keyboard. A page of glowing green figures scrolled down her screen.

Deirdre adjusted her glasses and peered at the display. "Twenty-four containers of Asti. Arrived at Braintree third-party container depot yesterday afternoon. Due to be shipped on to the central distribution centre at nine a.m. tomorrow. The other three hundred and ninety-two containers are now with our hauliers, due to leave Genoa over the next couple of weeks."

Tomorrow morning. That meant I needed to keep Rizzo and company in the dark for twenty-four hours on the location of the shipment. After that it would be moved to our own secure warehouse and distributed around the country, along with any clues to the fate of the contraband. In theory, Rizzo shouldn't be able to access the Braintree depot but, given that I had waltzed in with a stoned, pony-tailed hippy, bluffed in a pensioners' tour bus, and exited with forty-two blanket-wrapped Africans, I suspected his organised crime syndicate wouldn't find it too tricky to get in either.

"Deirdre, the suppliers are being a bit funny about the shipment. If they phone you, please can you tell them it's already been moved to our main warehouse and distributed to the four corners of the world?"

"Oh Felix. You haven't done some sort of dodgy deal have you?" Deirdre winked.

"To be honest, Deirdre, they're getting cold feet about the price. But once it's in the stores it'll be too late."

"Oh Felix. You are naughty! Your secret's safe with me."

"Thank you Deirdre. And what about Flake ... I mean Fiona? Is she in today?"

"Oh, terrible news. She phoned in to say she was scratched by one of her cats this morning and it's come up in a massive weal. She had to call the paramedics. She's inconsolable. She thinks she may be allergic to animals and she'll have to let the cats go."

"That's awful," I lied. I made a mental note to pray to the good Lord more often. If He was on my side, then perhaps Rizzo would assume his stowaways had escaped of their own accord, taking the dodgy merchandise with them, and chalk it down to experience. Hopefully Wodin would have abandoned the Somalis at a local mosque and disposed of the contraband too.

Which goes to show that hope, on its own, is rarely a good strategy.

$$* * *$$

It had been dark for a couple of hours by the time I returned home. I unlocked the front door to discover a powerful smell of faeces, presumably human, pervading the house. I held my sleeve over my mouth and climbed the stairs. A line of eight Somalis queued patiently for the bathroom.

I noticed they were all wearing new t-shirts and sweat pants and a long row of trainers lined the hallway. Without the grubby jeans and cheap jackets, they no longer looked like desperate refugees – more like a bunch of inner-city Londoners queuing for the gym.

I jogged back down and into the lounge. Fistule was arranging clothes, which clearly belonged to the migrants, on a drying rack in front of the fire. Wodin was stretched out on a sofa, a large chunk of hashish on the table before him and an enormous spliff in his mouth.

"Guys," I said, "it's come to my attention that this house is still full of African immigrants and," I pointed to a large stack of something in the corner, covered rather unconvincingly by a bright Hawaiian shirt, "commercial quantities of illicit drugs."

"Admittedly, there's some good news and bad news," said Wodin.

"I'm pretty clear on the bad news. Pray tell me the good news."

"Actually, there is some more bad news," volunteered Fistule.

Wodin passed me the joint. I took a deep draw and held my breath.

"The other bad news," continued Fistule, "is that the toilet is blocked. It's gone a bit Glastonbury in there."

"Oh good," I replied, exhaling. "So what are they queuing for?"

"They're taking their dumps in the bath."

My throat constricted and I began to cough, uncontrollably.

"But it's fine," added Fistule, patting me ineffectively on the back, "we've filled the bath with compost."

"Oh fabulous," I spluttered. "I'll look forward to taking a shower in the morning then. At least they've got some decent clothes." I passed the joint to Mercedes and flopped miserably onto a sofa.

"Yes, Fistule and I went shopping and bought them a load of stuff," she said, taking a drag. "They look much better, don't you think?"

"We also made some soup for everyone," said Fistule. "It's tasty, man. Do you want some?"

There was a large pan of vegetable broth on the table. Fistule ladled some into a bowl and handed it to me. It was mid-November and, with the heat from the fire blocked by drying clothes, it was chilly in the room. I spooned up the soup noisily. I'll give Fistule his due, he was a good cook.

"I've worked out a vegan food rota," said Fistule, peering at a notepad. "Each week we'll need 10 kilos of fair-trade mung beans, twenty kilos of organic carrots, fifty kilos of chopped tomatoes…"

Each *week*?

"Also, we need more bedding," said Mercedes. "And most of the guys still need more clothes and shoes – they haven't really packed for a British winter."

"Maybe the autumn/winter collection hasn't hit Mogadishu Marks & Spencer yet," I muttered.

"And we're going to need two new washing machines and two tumble dryers," said Wodin.

I'd seen a large pile of festering rags next to our ailing washing machine. From the volume of clothes hanging up, and the stack of laundry still to be done, it was clearly in constant use.

"We also need medicines, man. And dressings, laundry detergent, soap …" read Fistule, running a finger down his list.

"Hang on," I protested, "this is going to cost a fortune."

"We've spent nearly two grand on clothes and food so far. We need to spend another five thousand right now, then it's a grand a week," confirmed Mercedes.

"Holy Cow! Tell me your busking career has recently taken off, Mercedes. I don't have that kind of cash."

Mercedes shook her head.

"And since when did we decide to house and feed the Somali diaspora? Surely we just need to drop these folks off at the nearest refugee centre."

"We took responsibility when you shipped them over here, man," said Fistule, sparking up his water pipe once more. "You can't just kick them out."

"Why not? Why can't I? They're crapping in the bath!"

"You just can't, man. Human rights."

"I didn't ship the poor sods over here on purpose, did I?"

"Don't worry Felix. We have a plan," said Wodin.

"Is this plan as good as filling our bath with compost and having forty-two Somalis defecate in it?"

"You haven't heard the good news yet," said Wodin, smugly.

Fistule whisked the floral shirt off the pile of drugs with a flourish. "Half of these are actually cocaine, not hashish," he smiled, holding up a paler-coloured brick.

Having never worked in the artistic or creative sectors, I confess I was unfamiliar with the healing properties of cocaine.

"Is your plan to become so paralytically wasted that we don't notice we're paddling in a pool of turds when we shower?"

Wodin took another long drag and smiled. "No, my friend. Our plan is to sell it."

I looked at him through his halo of smoke. "You'll be arrested before you've sold five percent of it. Not to mention knifed by the competition, and I don't mean that figuratively. I suggest we burn it – apart from a small amount for personal consumption."

I stood and approached the wine rack. "And on the topic of personal consumption..." I drew a superlative Rioja from the shelf. Using the small blade on my waiter's friend I sawed through the thick foil protecting the top, then inserted the corkscrew. Each turn made a nice little squeak as the metal coil burrowed into the old cork. My mouth began to water in anticipation.

"That would be a criminal waste," said Wodin, pointing his joint at the large pile of drugs.

"Not to mention bad for the environment," piped up Fistule.

"You'll still be shot before you've sold even one of those bricks of coke," I said. "Who do you think you are? Scarface?"

"I'm not suggesting we sell it in bits," said Wodin. "We sell it in one go, to the big man. Father Turk."

I stopped turning the corkscrew. Wodin was well versed in the local narcotics supply chain, being a small-scale purveyor and a rather large-scale consumer. But Father Turk was a feared gangster and the lynchpin of North London's drugs trade. "You want to sell it to Father Turk? And how are you going to avoid having your little stash taken from you and being gently murdered?"

"Father Turk is a man of his word," replied Wodin breezily, directing a long column of smoke at the ceiling.

"He's a man of considerable viciousness," I corrected. "Didn't he throw one of his henchmen off the roof of the Green Lanes Billiards Club last summer?"

"He has a robust approach to performance management, true," conceded Wodin. "But business is business, and we've got something worth buying."

I returned to the Rioja, easing the cork from the bottle's neck with a satisfyingly deep pop. I poured a generous measure into four balloon-shaped glasses, emptying all but the sediment-filled final half-inch of the bottle. After a deep snort, I handed Wodin, Fistule and Mercedes their glasses. Thanks to its age, the wine was tawny in colour. The nose was deep and fruity, seasoned with delicate notes of old leather.

"Here's to our next transaction," said Wodin.

I grunted and clinked glasses, taking a mouthful and drawing air through the wine, savouring the palate. What a fantastic Rioja, I mused, allowing the glorious, rich liquor to flow down my throat. It nearly masked the smell of the overflowing khazi upstairs.

"We're selling it tomorrow," Wodin added. "I went to see Father Turk myself, this afternoon. I'll need you to come with me, Felix. We need to look as though we have some…presence."

If I hadn't swallowed the Rioja, I'd have blurted it across my lap. "Are you bloody mad? You've actually lined up a deal already? If you think I'm joining your little French Connection adventure, you can nick off. There's no way I'm wandering into a Turkish crack den and negotiating a business transaction surrounded by a dozen of North London's most vicious hoodlums."

"Half a million."

"Pardon?"

"Half a million quid. In cash. These little chaps are in quite serious demand," Wodin tapped the paler-coloured bricks of cocaine. "That's a huge discount on the normal wholesale price, of course, but as new entrants it was the only way to get his attention."

Truth be told, I've always had a soft spot for large quantities of cash, mainly because I've never had much. Half a million, even if I split it with Wodin, would go a very long way. I could buy my own apartment and still have plenty left over for some seriously high-class wining, dining and hell-raising.

"How can we trust him?"

"We can't ever really trust him," Wodin admitted, "but if several of us turn up and we look professional enough, he won't be so inclined to rob us."

"I'm more worried about being beheaded in a back room off Green Lanes than being robbed, to be honest."

"That's why we need to go in force. He can't behead all of us. Not quickly, anyway."

"Good Lord, Wodin. Are you seriously dragging Fistule and Mercedes into this? No offense, but I don't think they're going to intimidate Father Turk."

"No, Fistule will stay here and look after things. We're taking two cars – nice smart SUVs. I've hired them already, they're parked outside. I'll drive one, Mercedes will drive the other."

"So who else are we taking?" I thought about my old school friends. Tariq would be handy, he was a big chap and with that beard he looked quite piratical. But he was already heir to a multi-million-pound fortune, so I couldn't see him putting himself in harm's way. Dan Golden? At five foot four he was unlikely to intimidate anyone over the age of eight, even with his Hitler moustache.

I took another gulp of Rioja, my mind whirring. The taste was incredibly intense. I felt slightly strange, as though my mind was running ahead of itself. "I can't imagine many of your hippy mates tooling up and looking like they mean business."

Wodin smiled and pointed upwards. What the dickens was he on about? Divine intervention? Then it hit me. Our migrant friends! Yes, the big one was the size of a house – he'd scare the tits off anybody.

"I've already picked half a dozen out. The huge one's called Sharmarke. We'll take Galad too, to reassure the others. Fistule measured them up and we bought them all suits from M&S. Except Sharmarke, we had to go to High And Mighty for him. He's got a fifty-five inch chest."

I swallowed another mouthful of wine. "How does Father Turk know he can trust us? We could be a police sting."

"His people know me – I've been buying grass from them for years. And a couple of his people will recognise you from the Billiards Club. I doubt they'll think you're a copper."

"They still might think it's a set up. How do they know the drugs are real?"

"I've given him a brick already. As a free gift."

"Where are the guns?"

"Tossed them in the River Chess this morning, along with the ammo. They were making me nervous."

"Me too. Good riddance. If we're busted I don't want them hanging around – we'll be pensioners before we're out of jail."

"So, we're on then?"

"I don't like it."

"But you like the idea of half a million pounds?"

"Maybe I do. But it's still an idiotic idea. You're all idiots! And why do I feel so strange? What the hell is the matter with me? Why am I so hot? Why is the bloody table rippling?"

"Don't get stressed, man," murmured Fistule, "I put a few magic mushrooms in the soup. We went foraging today, it's mushroom season."

"You dosed me? Hells Bloody Bells! We've got a house full of illegal immigrants, a bath full of turds, half a million pounds' worth of drugs ... This is not the time I'd have chosen to skip through the bloody Doors of Perception!"

"We thought you needed to chill, man."

"Yeah, you're a bit on edge, Feel," said Mercedes gently. "Just go with the flow."

I felt very hot, like a badger in an oven. I needed some air. I walked to the front door. It was full and firm, so solid. I wondered how many trees had died to make it. Surely they wouldn't have killed more than one tree? I knocked my fist against it. Only one tree, I was sure. I could feel its soul. Better to be an outside door, where you could feel the elements, than an internal one. We shouldn't paint the door, either, even though it was peeling. It wanted to take its clothes off. Let it breathe.

I opened the door. A small Indian child looked up at me, her face streaked with tears. Another immigrant. They probably all had our address by now. She looked down at her knee, which was bleeding. "Wait there little girl." I floated back to the kitchen and lifted Fistule's first aid kit from the wall. He was fanatical about keeping a properly stocked medicine cabinet in case of emergency. I found a sticking plaster and antiseptic wipes, and returned to the child. "Don't worry. We'll fix you up." I wiped the graze clean and applied the plaster.

"You see. It's good to be righteous, Doctor Hart." Wodin's voice floated from somewhere behind me. The girl ran away into the night.

I remembered there were forty-two Somalis in the house. I turned and ascended the stairs, my feet barely touching the ground, and entered the first bedroom. The air was still, the window open. All was silent, the road outside deserted. The yellow streetlights illuminated the faces of the sleeping men, huddled together. They were so black, their skin so smooth, as if they were carved from a dark wood. Had they killed trees to make these men? How could anyone be so black? I felt as if I could fall into them – fall all the way to Somalia.

One man stirred and I tried to snap out of it. I could see the carpet rippling beneath me, like little waves. The ripples washed out to the sleeping men, disappearing under their white sheets. Would those waves carry the men away, wash them down the street and into the River Chess, then the Thames, into the sea and back to Somalia? Would they wake, see that they were being carried away, reach out their arms and cry for help? If I held out my own arm, could I catch one of them, grab hold of one those strong black arms?

I saw the sinews, the dark, mahogany skin, like an ancient carving, so strong. Mahogany would float, wouldn't it? It was a wood. It would float back to Somalia, wash up on the beach, beautiful pieces of deadwood, snagging on seaweed that would dry and shred, like skin. They would be bleached by the sun, worn by the wind and the blasting sand. A man would collect the limbs and make a fire on the beach, after the sun had set. He would be shivering – he was only trying to keep warm – but he was burning them, burning their limbs, just to keep the cold away. I heard the gas escaping from the burning wood, a high whistling bubbling sound, unnatural, like screaming.

I felt hands on my shoulders then around my waist, something soft and hard against my neck. It was Mercedes, her dreadlocks and their cold rings next to my skin. Her lips brushed my ear.

"They have to stay."

CHAPTER TWENTY FOUR - TURKISH DELIGHT

I pushed through the revolving doors of Gatesave's HQ the following morning. It was a quarter to seven but Rizzo was there again, waiting for me in reception. He was accompanied by a man in a black suit and dark polo neck. There was no sign of Morelli. Their eyes followed me as I neared reception. My stomach tightened. They had to be onto me. Play it cool, Felix.

"This is becoming a habit, Marco. What brings you to Gatesave's office this time?"

"Braintree container depot," said Rizzo, softly. "Why did you send our goods there?"

"Oh, I think it was a mistake by my logistics colleagues," I said breezily. "They didn't realise we'd made a special arrangement. Anyway, no harm done. I understand the stock will be in stores later today. I sent an email to Sergio confirming everything is fine."

"Sergio is no longer involved," said Rizzo. The other man said nothing, just stared at me. Not with menace, just an unflinching stare. He was slim and fit-looking, with close-cropped hair.

"What have you done to him?" I asked.

Rizzo paused and looked at his companion. "He is back in Italy, supervising the winery."

"I see. Well, let's look forward to a bumper season of Asti Spumante sales then!"

I walked away quickly, scanning myself through the security turnstile. For the second time in twenty-four hours I took the lift down to the gym, my stomach churning with fear, and stood under the shower.

I was home by six that evening and I'll give Wodin his due, he had used his day productively. Not only had he suited and booted Galad, the giant Sharmarke and four more of the larger Somalis, he had also purchased a banknote-counting machine that detected counterfeit currency. It was around the size of a large shoebox. Wodin unpacked it and plugged it in. We tested it on some real notes mixed with pieces of paper. The digital display faithfully counted the real notes as they were fed into the machine then stopped and gave a little beep of complaint when it encountered a piece of paper.

By seven o'clock Galad and his five friends were lined up by the door, looking rather apprehensive, though very smart and business-like in their dark suits and white shirts. Only Sharmarke, the giant, kept a blank face, his sad eyes following Wodin as he zipped the counting machine into a holdall. The contraband, still in its wrapping, had been carefully wiped clean of fingerprints and placed into several separate bags earlier, well out of sight of the Somalis.

We walked briskly to the hired SUVs, two new-looking black Land Rovers with tinted windows. Mercedes, who had tied her dreadlocks back, took the wheel of one, Galad beside her and three other Somalis in the back. Wodin climbed into the driver's seat of the other and I joined him in the front, while Sharmarke took up most of the back seat alongside the final Somali, a tall, wiry but strong-looking chap called Amiir.

The contraband was packed in the boot of Mercedes's vehicle – she drove ahead while we hung a hundred yards or so behind. Our main worry was that one of us might be stopped by the police, so we minimised the risk by placing all the contraband in just one SUV. If her vehicle was stopped and searched, the plan was for Galad and the other Somalis in her car to grab the legs of any police officers and hang on, allowing Mercedes to drive – or, if necessary, run – away as fast as possible.

It wasn't the most sophisticated plan and, I'm slightly ashamed to say, our Somali friends had not been fully briefed. Wodin and I told Galad that we were travelling to an employment agency to arrange jobs for all the migrants. We had to take the strongest-looking men to give the impression that everyone was fit and able to do physical work. We would be paid commission up front by the employment agency, hence the need for the counting machine. The only truthful bit was that the police would take a dim view of us if we were intercepted, hence the need to gently obstruct the forces of law and order while we did a runner. We assured Galad that, so long as Mercedes escaped, we could easily arrange the release of his friends from custody by paying bribes.

God alone knows what would have happened to Galad and his friends if we'd actually been stopped. They'd have been arrested and the contraband discovered, of course. Hopefully, it would have been obvious they were mere pawns in some sinister high-level plot, and they'd have suffered nothing worse than a short spell of imprisonment followed by deportation. I've no idea whether Galad believed our cock-and-bull story, but buying everyone clothing and food and treating them well had endeared us to our guests, so the plan had been accepted without argument.

I've always felt fortune smiles on the righteous, and sure enough we completed our journey into London without a hitch. Wodin had procured a brand-new pay-as-you-go phone and rang one of Father Turk's lieutenants as we turned onto Green Lanes. "Be outside in two minutes," he said.

Mercedes pulled over so we could catch up, then we slowed as we approached the Green Lanes Billiards Club. A pair of frowning Turkish men stood outside the entrance, observing our approach. We wound down the front and back windows of both SUVs so they could see we had arrived in force. Then Mercedes drove off, parking a mile away in a pre-agreed spot behind a row of shops. We pulled up on the pavement at the side of the Billiards Club and the four of us climbed out. The two Turkish hoods approached and I saw their eyes widen at the size of Sharmarke.

"Stay with the car Amiir," ordered Wodin, clapping him on the shoulder. Amiir climbed into the driver's seat and I lifted the holdall containing the note counting machine out of the boot.

Wodin turned to the Turkish men. "Where's Father Turk?"

One of the men, olive-skinned with a bushy moustache, tilted his head to a side door, which they opened and entered. The three of us followed, Wodin first, then Sharmarke, stooping low to avoid banging his head on the frame, then me with the bag. The Turks ascended a set of steep, narrow stairs and we followed them. I heard the door close behind me with a solid clunk – when I looked back a thin, unsmiling man returned my stare and took a seat inside the door.

My stomach started to tighten. We were clearly trapped inside the building and, no doubt, heavily outnumbered. Our little adventure suddenly seemed a much less clever idea. I hoped to God that Wodin knew what he was doing.

I started to run through scenarios. I was the one holding the bag so I would probably be the first to get a bullet in the head. Or maybe they would open the bag first, find the cash-counting machine and torture me to find out where the drugs were. Oh God, what kind of sick torture would they inflict? Probably drill into my knees first, just to soften me up. I thought of the hapless gangster hurled from the roof of this very building into the road. The rumour was that a billiard cue had been stuck up his backside before he was thrown off, so that when he landed on his arse it was driven all the way up and out through his mouth. They called it 'kebabbing'.

The stairs ended in a small landing. A young, acne-afflicted gangster stood guard in front of another door. He looked us up and down, lingering on Sharmarke and my bag, then said something in Turkish to the other two. They folded their arms and waited.

"He stays here," said the acned youth, in a London accent. He gestured at Sharmarke, who gazed at the gangsters with unnerving blankness.

"That's fine," said Wodin, "but don't provoke him. He's very emotional." All three men kept their eyes on our giant as the youth pushed opened the door and jerked his thumb.

We entered a very large room, windows covered by venetian blinds running the length of one wall. The only sign of the world outside was the amber glow of street lights through the slats. A full-size snooker table stood in the middle of the room, on which sat a billiard cue and ball.

At the far end of the room sat a glass-topped desk. Behind it, seated in the only chair, was Father Turk, watching from beneath hooded eyes. He was not alone. A thin, vicious-looking man in a tracksuit stood with his back to the windows, his stubble not quite obscuring the prominent scar across his chin. He stared at me with undisguised hatred.

We stood still. Tracksuit walked forward and pointed at my bag. "Put it there against the wall and step away."

His accent was Turkish, not London, and I spotted the flash of a gold tooth. I did as I was told. The man patted me down roughly, checking every nook and cranny, then did the same to Wodin. He nodded to Father Turk and retook his position by the window.

Father Turk beckoned us closer. He was not particularly old, perhaps mid-forties. His face was deeply lined around the eyes and he had a small, neat moustache over a rather sorrowful mouth. He looked quite ordinary – an unremarkable, middle-aged Mediterranean man. A lit cigarette lay in the ashtray before him, sending up a long unbroken line of smoke.

As we reached the table, he spoke. His voice was deep and heavily accented. "I know you. But I do not know you." He looked from Wodin to me. "Who are you?"

"I am Wodin's business partner. I played snooker here when I was at school. It's a very nice billiards club." I smiled, encouragingly. Father Turk did not smile back.

"Where did you steal these things?" It was clear what things he meant. We had rehearsed this and our plan was to stick as closely to the truth as possible. I didn't like his use of the word 'steal' though.

I cleared my throat. "They are not stolen…" Father Turk raised his hand again and I closed my mouth, my stomach giving a little lurch.

"Do not take me for a fool. What is in the bag?"

"A note counter, for the money," I murmured, my mouth now dry.

"Money? So you steal and I pay you money? I do not pay thieves, I punish them." He raised his voice slightly. "My cousin?" Tracksuit took a step toward us and put his hand into his pocket. When he removed it I saw he was holding a small snub-nosed revolver.

The tightness in my stomach leapt to my bowels. How the hell was I going to get out of here? At least Wodin was standing between me and the armed hoodlum. With a bit of luck, he'd take the bullet and I could rush for the door. But there were three men on the other side and, even if I made it without a bullet in my back, I doubted Sharmarke would be of much use – he'd probably just stand there. Even if he could fight, why would he? He was under the impression we were in a North London job centre, applying for work in a local restaurant.

The only other way out was through the windows but I didn't fancy hurling myself through the glass and into the Green Lanes traffic below. My eyes settled on the snooker cue. Oh Sweet Jesus, no. Might its next home be my tender rear, shortly before I was hurled from the roof, the latest in a long line of unfortunate, kebabbed criminals to have incurred Father Turk's displeasure?

"If you're going to shoot us, you may as well do it with a decent weapon," said Wodin. Tracksuit frowned and hesitated as Wodin pointed towards the bag. "We brought you a present, sir. We don't mean any disrespect. Quite the opposite."

I goggled at Wodin. What the hell was he talking about?

"A present," stated Father Turk in a dead tone. "What is this?"

Wodin raised his hands. "If I may?" Tracksuit pointed his weapon directly at Wodin and followed him as he approached the bag, hands aloft. He crouched, unzipped it and put his hand inside. The gangster stood over him, pointing the revolver directly at his head. Wodin very slowly removed a white fabric shopping bag, in which something had been wrapped.

It dawned on me what Wodin had done. I closed my eyes in despair. How the hell was this going to get us out of here?

Wodin placed the bag on the desk with a dull clunk and took a few steps back. Tracksuit kept his gun trained on Wodin, unfolding the bag with his other hand. He gave it a shake and one of our smuggled guns clattered onto the table. All eyes turned to the weapon.

"It's a Beretta 92," I blurted. "The best handgun in the world." Tracksuit picked it up and looked it over, excitement in his eyes. I realised my hands were raised and lowered them slowly.

"Is a Beretta 92 S," Tracksuit corrected, running his finger over the frame. He took aim down the barrel, thankfully not at me, and looked at Father Turk, who had a very slight smile on his face. "Can I keep this, *Amca*?"

"No need to worry, we've brought you two," said Wodin gently. "The other is with the stuff."

Father Turk sat back in his chair. "So you have two of these things. And then there are the other things. You tell me now where you got them."

It was my turn. "I work in the importing business, sir," I gabbled. "I don't want to bore you with the ins and outs of my business, but sometimes my suppliers offer me a bargain. Often a warehouse somewhere has some, how should we say, surplus stock."

Father Turk nodded slowly, his smile had gone and his eyes bored into mine.

"So, one of my contacts found me some sparkling wine," I continued. "Several containers. It is Christmas soon, so this is a very popular product, you see. The price was very, very cheap. My contact insisted I had to buy it quickly before someone else took it. So, I paid, I arranged collection of the wine and delivered it to my warehouse. When I opened the containers, I found there was some stock missing. There was also – how can I put this – a horrible mess in some of the containers. As if someone had lived in there and gone to the toilet."

Father Turk's face was completely still, his eyes focused intently on mine.

"I had to write off some of the wine," I went on, "but I knew I couldn't complain and expect any money back – these kinds of deals are not refundable. But then I found some additional things in the delivery, you see. So, this brings us to you. And here we are," I finished, slightly feebly.

Father Turk paused for a while and took a drag on his cigarette. Finally, he looked at me, then Wodin. "Sounds like bull," he said.

I tensed, wondering if I should make a run for it.

"Your wine shipment had illegals inside. That is why they sold it to you cheap. Your supplier would have lots of trouble from the police if they found out." He considered us once more. "You are hiding something from me, but it is not important now."

He said something rapidly in Turkish to Tracksuit, who walked to a steel cabinet and unlocked the door. He removed several plastic supermarket bags with their tops tied and dumped them at our feet.

"Now you can use your counting machine."

I crouched and untied one of the bags. It was full of cash, all odd notes crumpled together.

Wodin looked down at the bag and met my eyes. It was far too early to relax but things were looking a hell of a lot better than five minutes earlier. He lifted the counting machine from the holdall and emptied a bag of cash onto the floor.

I looked around for a plug socket. "Er, do you have a spare socket anywhere?"

Tracksuit was playing with the Beretta, cocking it then pulling the trigger, letting the bolt fly forward with a satisfying chink. He looked up and waved the gun impatiently at the opposite wall. I plugged in the machine and switched it on.

We began to feed notes into the top. The machine whirred and rattled, spitting them out into tidy wads at the front. Every time we got to one thousand we tied a rubber band around the bundle and placed it in our holdall. Every so often, the machine gave an annoyed beep and we extracted a counterfeit note, which I placed in a separate pile. Fifteen minutes later, we were done.

The display stated ninety-eight thousand, one hundred and twenty pounds.

"I thought you said we were getting half a million," I whispered.

"One lie deserves another," called Father Turk from behind the desk. "One hundred thousand pounds is enough. Now your side of the bargain."

"And the other one, and the ammo," called Tracksuit, waving the empty Beretta.

"The stuff is in our other car. Where do you want it?"

"You will deliver it to my other cousin. Here is the address. Do not say it out loud. You must text your colleagues." He handed Wodin a scrap of paper.

Wodin phoned Mercedes, explained the process and told her to expect a text, which he tapped out after hanging up. Then we sat and waited. Every so often a text message would ping onto Tracksuit's phone. Sometimes he read and ignored it, other times he said something in Turkish to the older man, who remained silent, chain smoking his way through a pack of foreign cigarettes.

For the next hour, my mind raced as we paced up and down our end of the office. Mercedes was supposed to text Wodin when she arrived, and call us back when the other side were satisfied, but we heard nothing. Were they all lying dead in a ditch? And, more importantly, was the same about to happen to me? It would be quite straightforward for them to take the contraband from Mercedes and the oblivious Somalis. I started to wish Wodin had sneaked in the other Beretta and some ammunition – at least we might have shot our way out.

Then Tracksuit's phone rang. He answered and spoke rapidly in Turkish, looking agitated and giving us filthy looks. Father Turk rose from his chair for the first time. He moved surprisingly quickly, crossing the floor like a cat and snatching the phone from his young lieutenant. He said a few words then listened for a while, all the time watching us.

Suffice to say, I was close to soiling my pants. There was clearly something wrong and I strongly suspected we were being double crossed. I felt it was time to make our escape. The younger gangster was watching his boss and held the unloaded Beretta in both hands, having replaced the snub-nosed revolver in his pocket. If I could cross the ten yards between us quickly enough and overpower him, maybe Wodin could deal with the older guy. Then I could take his weapon and we could shoot our way out.

Then Father Turk addressed us. "It looks like we have a problem. Your lady friend is making life difficult for everyone. You must talk to her." He placed the phone on the desk. Wodin picked it up.

"Hello?" He listened and his eyes widened. I could hear Mercedes's voice shouting urgently but couldn't make out the words. Wodin looked over at Father Turk, who stared straight back, unsmiling. Still listening, Wodin walked to the corner and beckoned me over. "Ok, ok, don't worry, just hang on, I'm talking to Felix."

My blood ran cold. God only knew what horrendous cock up was under way.

"Felix," he whispered urgently, "they're trying to rip us off. Mercedes handed over the stuff, they tested it, everything was fine. Then they pulled a gun on her and Galad, telling them to sit tight and send a false message that everything is ok."

My bowels tightened in horror. My very worst fears had come true. Doubtless they would force us to surrender the money and probably our lives into the bargain. After all, we now knew the location of their safe house. I looked at the two men standing at the table, observing us. But why were they just standing there? Why weren't they taking the money back? Why were they letting us speak to Mercedes?

"What's happening there now?" I whispered.

"It appears Mercedes pulled her own gun and shot one of them."

My mind went blank for a moment. Mercedes had her own gun? Of course – the other Beretta. And all the ammunition. "Christ on a bike! Where is she now?"

"She and Galad have got them all sitting on their hands. Galad's got the other guy's gun. She's telling us to get the money and get out of here."

I thought that sounded like an excellent idea. I turned to the two Turkish men. "Well, it's been nice. But I'm afraid we have to pop off now."

Tracksuit put the Beretta on the table, took the snub-nose out of his pocket and pointed it at me. I froze my stomach cramped in terror.

"Our friend says that if you don't let us leave with the money, she'll take the stuff away," called Wodin, "and shoot your cousin in the balls."

"She's mad," I added, helpfully.

Father Turk pushed Tracksuit's gun down until it was pointing at the floor. He patted the younger man's shoulder, said something quietly and the gun went back into his pocket. "Good doing business with you," he drawled, grimly.

I scurried over to the holdall full of cash and picked it up, leaving the counting machine on the floor – they could keep it as a memento. I walked backwards, watching the two men carefully. Wodin also backed up and we reached the door. I could hear Mercedes still shouting over the phone. "Don't worry, we're leaving now, give us a minute," he muttered.

I wrenched open the door and piled through, running straight into the young, acne-ridden hood. He shouted angrily and pushed back at me. The other two jumped to their feet and blocked the staircase, one of them reaching into his inside jacket pocket. It suddenly occurred to me they were ignorant of their boss's recent change of heart. I swung my fist wildly at the gangster's head and knocked him straight over.

"Get out of my bloody way," I yelled. I was aware of Sharmarke standing silently by the wall. To my delight, he suddenly launched himself forward, colliding with the other two men and sending them tumbling down the steps. Like a human steamroller he charged after them, flattening them as they tried to get to their feet.

Wodin barrelled down the stairs after Sharmarke and I followed close behind. The thin, unsmiling man guarding the exit rose from his chair, his face a picture of perfect terror as Sharmarke careered towards him. The giant Somali grasped the handle and wrenched it open, crashing the heavy door against the hapless guard and sending him flying against the wall. The three of us spilled into the night.

Amiir was leaning nonchalantly against the Land Rover. "Get in Amiir!" shouted Wodin, then into the phone, "Mercedes! We're out! We're out!" He fired up the engine, tossed Father Turk's phone out of the window and U-turned the vehicle back onto Green Lanes, heading north.

As we sped back to Little Chalfont I stared at the wing mirror, trying to see if we were being followed. We weren't, but after we'd left the motorway we pulled onto a farm track and waited for five minutes just to be sure. We arrived home just after midnight and collapsed, exhausted, in the lounge, joined by Sharmarke, who had so magnificently aided our escape from Father Turk's headquarters. He took up an entire sofa and was soon snoring away.

Wodin sparked up a large joint and I recounted our story to a stoned and astonished Fistule as we waited for Mercedes. I'd called her when we were clear of Harringay – she had successfully extracted herself and Galad from the drop-off point without further incident, though I was slightly disappointed she hadn't shot Father Turk's cousin in the balls anyway.

Mercedes arrived home a full hour after us. Such was her paranoia at being followed, she'd driven an extra junction north on the motorway before doubling back. She flopped onto the spare sofa and buried her head under a cushion, groaning. Galad joined us in the lounge too, Wodin and I moving up to make some space for him. Together with Mercedes, he had well and truly saved our sorry hides. The other three Somalis, who had remained in the SUV during the stand-off, and Amiir were largely unaware of what had transpired and, after a few reassuring words from Galad, they headed upstairs to bed.

"That was a lousy plan, guys," Mercedes called from under the cushion.

"Nice work with the Beretta, though," I said. "I think this calls for a bottle of something special." I perused the wine rack and found a bottle of Gevrey Chambertin.

Mercedes emerged. "Make mine a very large one."

I poured four glasses and looked to Galad. He gave a little smile and held up his fingers to suggest a small measure. I poured a fifth glass. As I handed Wodin his wine I asked whether there was any chance Father Turk and his gang knew where we lived. He shook his head and stayed pretty quiet for the rest of the night, taking long sucks on his joint as Mercedes regaled us with her side of the story.

It turned out that I was the one who'd been kept in the dark. Wodin had always intended to trade the two guns along with the narcotics and convinced Mercedes to go along with him. It's difficult to get hold of high quality, unused firearms in England and he knew it would help seal the deal. But, somewhat naively, he had not bargained on just how devious Father Turk might be.

Mercedes's surprising familiarity with automatic weapons dated back to her convent school days. Despite being girls-only, her school had a thriving Combined Cadet Force run by a lunatic ex-Royal Marine who kept an illicit gun collection in his lodgings. He allowed a chosen few cadets, who knew how to keep a secret, to practice firing the weapons on field trips.

Mercedes had not trusted Wodin's plan at all, and had loaded her Beretta before approaching the drop-off point. When the double-crossing cousin held her and Galad hostage, she'd bided her time until the gangster was distracted, then drawn her weapon and shot him in the leg. If she hadn't, we'd probably all be at the bottom of Stoke Newington Reservoir by now.

Despite the bumpy transaction, we were now in a significantly better financial position. We had one hundred grand in used notes and we'd got rid of all the contraband, with the exception of a thick slice of hashish for personal use.

I raised my glass. "Here's to convent school girls and the Royal Marines."

I drained the Gevrey Chambertin in one gulp. I have to say, it was drinking excellently.

CHAPTER TWENTY FIVE - SUSTAINABLE LIVING

The next day, Fistule prepared a giant pot of goulash for lunch. The Somalis queued down the stairs and into the kitchen for a generous bowl-full and a hunk of bread, before returning to their rooms. When everyone had been fed, the four of us shut ourselves in the lounge and tipped the bundles of cash onto the floor. I selected a well-aged Priorat from the rack and poured everyone a glass. Fistule poured a fine Islay single malt into the water pipe and heaped it with hashish.

"Right, team," I announced. "Please submit your applications for capital expenditure."

"Five grand for new kitchen appliances," said Wodin. "Our washing machine is in critical condition and we need a bigger stove."

"Approved," the rest of us chorused. I tossed him five bundles of notes.

"I need some money to stock up with fair-trade quinoa, organic pasta, fresh vegetables from the farmer's market..." said Fistule.

"Approved! Take a couple of grand." I passed him two bundles.

"Cool, man."

"A couple of grand for clothing and bedding," said Mercedes.

"Done!" Another couple of bundles changed hands.

"Most importantly, we need to upgrade our wine library," I declared, eyeing the seriously depleted wine rack in the corner. "I suggest we install shelving along the back wall of the lounge, floor to ceiling, and fill it with extremely fine wine."

"Excellent idea," agreed Wodin who, along with the others, had developed quite a discriminating palate. "How much do you need for that?"

"Twenty grand should do it. Everyone ok with that?"

"Agreed!" was the unanimous decision. I separated twenty bundles from the pile.

"We also need some aged single malt, man, for the bong."

"Take a grand, Fistule, and get yourself down to Milroy's of Soho."

We agreed everyone should have five grand to spend on personal items, then we levered up a couple of floorboards and hid the remaining fifty thou underneath.

"What else do we need?" I asked.

"I was trying to take a pee this morning, guys. It wasn't great," sighed Mercedes. "It's DEFCON five in the bathroom. The toilet's bust, the bath is an extreme biohazard. I'm amazed we haven't attracted hyenas."

"Mercedes is right," I agreed. "I'm sick of balancing on that plank and pooing in the bath, not to mention squirting fly-spray around my head every 30 seconds. I'm an international wine buyer – I shouldn't have to live like I'm permanently at a music festival. Besides, the bath will be full in a couple of days, then what are we going to do?"

I sighed and poured another glass of the Priorat. It was showing very well.

"We could use the loo in the local library. It's twenty pence for non-visitors so we'll need to convert one of those bundles into small change," suggested Wodin, unhelpfully.

"Useless idea but the best one so far," I replied. "Seriously, though, what the hell are we going to do? We'll have to use buckets or something. Slopping out, like in prison. We'll have to draw up a rota. Every day, someone will have to carry a bucket outside and dispose of it."

"Where?" demanded Mercedes.

"Can we bury it?" asked Wodin.

"We should compost it, man," said Fistule.

"We don't really want people queuing in the kitchen to poo into your home composter, Fistule," I said. "It'll put everyone off their lentil stew."

"But they do it in Africa, man – I read about it in National Geographic. We need to dig a composting toilet. I was talking to Galad about it – his friend knows how to do it. We could excavate one outside, in the garden."

I dashed upstairs and found Galad. "Come and tell us about your toilet idea."

"Yes," explained Galad, after joining us in the lounge, "it is called an Arborloo. Invented in Zimbabwe. Cawaale can help build it. He is an engineer."

We all looked at him.

"What, you think we can actually dig a hygienic, functioning toilet?" I peered out of the window at the back garden. "Not very private, is it? And what happens when it rains?"

"You have a tent over the top," he said. "This is a common thing in rural areas."

"Right Fistule," I declared, "you and Cawaale build your toilet. I hope it works, because Plan B involves sneaking into the graveyard under cover of darkness to do your number twos."

The next morning the garden was a hive of activity. Wodin took a couple of grand from the reserve fund, hired a van and drove to the garden centre with Fistule and Cawaale, returning with a huge pile of bamboo canes, fence posts and several sacks of activated bokashi sawdust. Fistule bought a child's Wendy house, the shape of a small circus tent, bright pink and festooned with pictures of fairy princesses, floppy-eared elephants and happy dwarves.

"Could you not have bought something a bit less conspicuous, Fistule?" I asked.

"Hiding in plain sight is the best strategy, man. Plus it was the tallest tent we could find, we don't want to be shuffling into the privy on hands and knees."

An hour later I became aware of a chugging and grinding sound from the car park. I leaned over the outside steps to see Wodin at the wheel of a small JCB digger. He guided it along the footpath, round the side of the building and parked it on our little patch of garden.

"What in God's name is that for?"

"We're not digging with spades, Felix. Cawaale says we need a trench six-foot deep and twenty-feet long."

Cawaale stood at the edge of the garden and directed Wodin as he, somewhat incompetently, began to dig the pit.

"Hello boys," called Mrs Hodfurrough from the house opposite. "What are you doing?"

"Hello Mrs Hodfurrough. Sorry for the disruption. We're just digging an allotment. We want to grow our own vegetables."

"Why do you need a mechanical digger?"

"It's a university project, Mrs Hodfurrough. We have to prepare the ground with a special fertiliser first. We're going for first prize in the Rickmansworth marrow festival." I prayed there were no electrical cables or water mains in the garden and returned to the flat.

It was Saturday, and Tariq and Dan had travelled up to watch our latrine-digging adventure. I suspected they'd come to drink my wine too – I'd now installed the wine racks and spent several thousand pounds at three rather upmarket London wine merchants. I'd also purchased a very expensive refrigerated cabinet so I could keep a selection of whites and lighter reds at the perfect serving temperature.

The toilet construction team were taking their mid-morning break and Galad warmed his hands around a cup of tea. "We must pray. My people want to go to the mosque."

"Yeah … not sure Little Chalfont has one of those, Galad."

"Hey, man," said Fistule. "They could go to St Peter's, round the corner. Churches face east, just like mosques. I learnt that in religious education. I got a B – my best subject."

"Well done Fistule. But forty-two Somali migrants kneeling round the font might just raise eyebrows at Evensong."

"It is no problem if we pray here," Galad said. "Madar can lead the prayers. He has a good voice."

"Fine, just don't make too much noise."

Galad disappeared, and a few minutes later a haunting melody floated down the stairs.

"Better than the imams in Dubai," sniffed Tariq. "Musical, these Africans, aren't they?"

We listened to Madar's voice and the softer reply from his congregation.

"What wine best accompanies the call to prayer, Felix?" pondered Dan, surveying the wall of bottles.

"That would depend on the time of day. For mid-afternoon, I suggest an Orvieto."

I pulled a bottle of white from the temperature-controlled cabinet and popped it open. I was pouring Tariq a glass when there was an urgent knocking at the door. I peeked round the net curtain and saw Mrs Hall from number three, in her dressing gown, hands on hips, looking even more vicious than usual. I opened the door a few inches.

"What's going on down there?" she screeched, pointing at the hole in the ground.

"Just landscaping the garden, Mrs Hall, nothing to worry about."

"Why can't you employ English builders?"

"They are English, Mrs Hall. They're just a bit muddy."

"And what's all that wailing coming from your house? I can hardly hear myself think!"

"Wailing?"

"Horrible singing and chanting. Like devil worship."

"Ah. That's our bible-study class, Mrs Hall. We're spreading the faith here at number two, you see."

Mrs Hall tried to peer through the door and I drew myself up to block her view. Her face broke into a mean smirk.

"They aren't Christians. I can hear them singing allahu akbar!" she declared, triumphantly.

"Yes. Well, it's a remedial class – they've picked up some bad habits. We're trying to beat it out of them."

She scowled at me.

"Oh, while you're here, I have a favour to ask," I said. "Our toilet's broken and we're having to use a bucket. Would you mind if we came round and emptied it down your sink?"

Mrs Hall's face fell.

"Thank you so much. Tootle pip." I smiled brightly and closed the door. "Can you pray more quietly please, guys?" I called up the stairs. "I'm sure God will still hear you."

"Ok," Madar called back.

Once we'd polished off the wine, Tariq, Dan and I headed down to check how the latrine construction was going. I must say, it was pretty impressive. Wodin had finished carving out a deep but slightly eccentric trench, and Cawaale and Fistule were busy driving slender wooden poles at spaced intervals into the bottom of the pit. Two more Somalis were tying garden canes together with twine, while another sawed at a fence post on a workbench. There was a huge mound of soil and rocks at the side of the garden.

"You've made a splendid bloody mess of the garden, old chap," observed Tariq.

"We'll turn it into a rockery, man," said Fistule, waving at the pile of earth and stones.

By nightfall the toilet was complete. Fistule and Cawaale gave us a tour. Pride of place was the pink circus tent, looking somewhat surreal in the centre of the muddy garden, its smiling cartoon characters gaily welcoming anyone in need of a good dump. A gangplank pointed to the entrance of the tent and the rest of the long trench was covered by a tarpaulin. Fistule unzipped the door and proudly flung it open, clicking on a light suspended from the tent ceiling.

"Solar powered, man. It charges up from a panel on the top of the tent during the day."

A ceramic toilet bowl, with the bottom knocked out, sat on planks over the abyss.

"Ok, this is how it works, man," explained Fistule. "The trench has been partitioned into several sections. When we've filled one, we move the planks and the tent over to the next section."

I peered down into the depths. I could dimly see dead leaves and a lattice of bamboo canes in the base of the pit.

"Whenever anyone takes a dump or a pee, they have to cover it with a measure of activated sawdust and a shovel-full of soil from these buckets, ok?" He tapped a trowel against a pink bucket full of earth and a blue tub sealed with an airtight lid.

"Whatever happened to good old flush and forget?" I muttered.

"This is organic and sustainable, man. Every day I'll be adding the food waste from the kitchen. Then we'll add a lattice of bamboo canes on top of every twelve inches of waste, to provide structure." He looked at Cawaale, who nodded. I recalled the Somali guys weaving their grids of canes and twine, the day before.

"Well, sounds like it's all under control, Fistule. I can't wait to get started."

"But there are some important safety rules," cautioned Fistule.

"Let me guess," I said. "No diving into the six-foot pit of fermenting turds?"

"Yeah, man. That's the main one. Thing is, sewage takes six months to break down. During that time it isn't solid, so we mustn't walk over the full pits. We'll have to fence them off or something."

"Ok, sounds good. Where's the toilet roll?"

"Actually, I was thinking of rigging up a rainwater barrel and a shower head to make an Indian bum-washer. Much more environmentally sound than bleached toilet paper, man."

"Yeah … I think I'll stick to loo paper for now, thanks. How long will this set-up last us?"

"We'll probably fill a section every week or so. We've already half-filled this one with all the mess from the bath. In two months we'll need another trench."

Ok, so we've got until February, I thought. Then what? Never mind, let's get through Christmas.

"Great work, guys," said Tariq. "Anyway, I gotta head home. Just taken delivery of my new, top of the range Japanese arse-spa. Did you know, it actually massages your buttocks as you take a dump, then sprays your starfish with warm, soapy water? Can't wait to try it. But you guys enjoy yourselves in your tent. I'm sure it'll be special. Cheerio!"

CHAPTER TWENTY SIX -
THE INSPECTORS CALL

'll give them their due, my interrogators didn't appear outraged
or even remotely appalled. I couldn't tell what they were thinking. "You don't seem very shocked. I suppose you spooks have
heard this kind of thing before?"

"Don't call us spooks, thank you," barked the man, clearly
irritated. "'Officers' is just fine." He turned to the woman. She
looked down and pursed her lips, moving one piece of paper over
another.

"Well ..." she said slowly, "it does make some kind of sense."

"You see!" I declared. "I'm cooperating!"

"Yes. It took a while, though, didn't it?" she said. "I don't
think we needed to hear quite so much about toilet construction."

"On the contrary, officer, it's part of the circle of life. You
demanded an end-to-end story, and you're getting it." I'd given
them a lot and I felt it was my turn for some answers. I lifted my
glass and finished the wine. "How's Father Turk doing? Friend of
yours, is he?"

She looked up quickly. "He's dead, Felix. You see, you and
your friends rather upset the delicate balance of the London narcotics trade with your little transaction. Caused a major conflict
between the Turks and the Italian gangs. A price war, you might
call it. Eight people dead, Felix, including all three of Father

Turk's sons. He shot himself, in grief. With a brand new Beretta." She gave a grim little smile and looked me in the eye. "Now, are *you* shocked, Felix?"

Rather relieved, quite frankly, I thought. Now that she'd mentioned it, I vaguely remembered reading about an uptick in North London gun crime, though I'd not paid much attention now I lived out of town. Anyway, a bit of violence on the Tottenham borders was hardly out of the ordinary. If memory served, it wasn't a proper Saturday night out down Green Lanes without a little light machine gunning.

"That's tragic," I agreed, attempting to look morose.

"It kept Scotland Yard very busy," growled the man, leaning in. "I'm sure they'd be fascinated to know who caused them all that overtime."

I wasn't out of the woods yet, clearly. Would I ever be?

"Let's talk more about your Italian friends. Signor Rizzo is a senior member of the 'Ndràngheta, Felix. Ever heard of them?"

I had. They were the wealthiest, best-connected and most psychotic bunch of cut-throats in the Mediterranean. They made the Sicilian mafia look like a self-help group for insecure Buddhists. "I always thought he was a bit dodgy."

My interrogators looked at one another then back to me. "A bit dodgy?" spat the man. "The 'Ndràngheta run half London's drug trade. Or they did until your little intervention created a power vacuum. We believe the Bulgarians moved in to fill it."

"You know all about Bulgarians, though, don't you Felix?" said the woman, eyebrows raised.

I wondered whether Georgi might have diversified from Pinot Grigio into cocaine. Good for him, I thought. If he had, he owed me. That had to be worth more than a plate of stew at Plovdiv restaurant.

The man continued to lean forward, looking me right in the eye. "But Signor Rizzo disappeared. Where is he?"

It was a shame my glass was empty. I needed another drink.

***

The days ticked by in Little Chalfont. November became December, and our busy flat settled into a rhythm of semi-normalcy. We bought a couple of televisions, installed a satellite dish and subscribed to a handful of Arabic TV channels. The Somalis were happy to watch Egyptian soaps in the bedrooms, filing in and out of the kitchen to do their washing and cooking. The largest bedroom was cleared so they could have a good old communal pray every so often, led by musical Madar.

The outside toilet appeared to work. Cawaale the engineer had known exactly what he was doing. Astonishingly, it didn't smell bad at all, though the seat was cold enough to freeze the gonads off the proverbial alloy primate, especially at night. On top of our unmentionables, Fistule added kitchen vegetable peelings and fallen leaves from the garden. Every week, the pink tent was moved a few feet further along the pit and the newly filled section covered with a layer of compost and planted with butterfly-friendly seeds. Fistule stuck a few bamboo canes in the ground, linked with garden twine, and hung a little sign saying 'Keep Off, Wildflower Zone'.

It was Saturday morning and I'd wandered down to the local Gatesave to replenish our tea and sugar. I became aware of a presence beside me as I inspected the wine section.

"So this is where you spend your time, when you're not ruining yourself?" It was Dr Shah from number one, next door.

"Hello Dr Shah. Yes indeed, I am a student of retail and of the vine," I replied breezily, sounding slightly more of a smart arse than I'd intended.

"A student of debauchery and an early grave, I would suggest." He considered the shelves and frowned.

"Would you like me to recommend a bottle?" I asked. Once a shopkeeper, always a shopkeeper.

"I do not drink, young man. For one thing, intoxication and losing control do not appeal to me. For another, Islam forbids it."

Doesn't stop the Muslims I know, I thought. I pictured Tariq dancing on the deck of his boat in the Caribbean, or the fun-loving Turks of Green Lanes downing Efes Pilsner by the crate. Not the best examples of medieval piety, but who wants to be medieval, unless you have a fetish for black teeth, bubonic plague and expiring during childbirth?

"Right. So, what brings you to the wine aisle of your local supermarket, Dr Shah?"

Dr Shah turned to face me. "To say thank you, Felix."

"What for?" I exclaimed, genuinely surprised.

"My granddaughter fell and grazed her knee last week. You and that man who wears a skirt cleaned and dressed the wound."

"Ah, yes ..." I attempted to recall the episode but the fog of hallucinogenic mushrooms had left me with only disembodied snapshots, as if it had been an ancient dream.

"Not many would do that for strangers in this day and age," he added.

"Well, we try to be good neighbours. We're not all bad," I replied, hopefully.

"No, perhaps not all bad. But room for improvement, I would suggest." Dr Shah paused again and turned back to the shelves of wine.

"One good turn deserves another, Felix. Two men in suits have just visited me. They were very interested in what's going on at your property."

My blood ran cold. Were the police onto us already? We still had enough hashish in the house to get us sent down for dealing. And what had Wodin done with the other gun? He'd promised he'd got rid of them once before, but that was a lie. How long would you get for possession of a firearm? Not to mention people-smuggling and slavery? Ten years in the Scrubs? I'd have to do a runner right now – there was no way I could go back to the house. Wodin and the others would have to take the heat. It was their idea to host the Somalis anyway, the reckless tossers.

"Oh. What did they want?" I asked, as nonchalantly as possible, my mouth dry.

"I imagine they were curious as to why you have several dozen dark-skinned people sharing your apartment. I suppose Mrs Hall in number three reported you."

Mrs Hall. Of course, the leprous old hag. I uncharitably considered burning her house down, picturing the wrinkled old fascist hurling herself from the upstairs window, nightdress ablaze. But I discounted the idea – there would be no way to stop the flames spreading to our property. Besides, burning witches probably carried an even longer prison sentence than smuggling drugs, guns and refugees.

"How strange," I lied, in a small voice. "What did you tell them?"

"I told them I didn't know anything. I said it was none of my business and they should ask you."

"Thank you."

"I have no idea what you're doing with those foreigners in your house. I suspect you're earning a bit of extra money by subletting your spare rooms. So long as it doesn't cause a problem, I really don't mind. I hope you're not treating them badly?"

"No. We're treating them very well. It's just a few distant relatives staying for a week or so, they'll be off soon."

But not before I'm off, I thought. Thank God I've got my car keys and credit cards on me. I'll jump in the Cavalier and drive over to Tariq's, then lie low while the Old Bill turn the place over and march poor Wodin, Fistule and Mercedes off to their new lives behind bars.

"Distant relatives…" pondered Dr Shah. He turned back to me. "That would be the Muslim side of your family then? I can hear the prayers through the wall, you see. It doesn't bother me – in fact it reminds me slightly of my youth in Bombay – but I suspect Mrs Hall in number three finds it slightly unsettling."

"Yes. She probably does. I'll ask them to tone it down a bit."

"And you probably need to talk to the men from the council. They're waiting outside for your return."

The council! Not the police. Thank goodness for that. I started to breathe a little easier. But still a problem. One sniff of what we were up to and the police wouldn't be far behind. "Thank you Dr Shah. I'd better go and reassure them that everything is above board."

Dr Shah didn't reply. I hurried out of the store and down the street, bringing up Fistule's number on my phone.

"Hello?" whispered Fistule.

"Fistule! Listen. We have a problem. The council are sniffing around."

"I know," he whispered.

"Why are you whispering?"

"They knocked on the door. We're in lockdown."

"Where are you?"

"I'm under the kitchen table. We've killed the power and I'm composting all incriminating documents."

"Are you stoned, Fistule?" What a silly question.

"I've dropped some mushrooms." Oh Jesus. Thank God he didn't answer the door.

"Where's Mercedes?"

"She's upstairs, teaching the Somalis tai chi."

"Stay where you are. Don't let anyone in." I flew up the road, breaking back to a fast walk as I rounded the side of the shops. I spotted the two self-righteous-looking council workers on the walkway as I bounded up the outside stairs. One was trying to peer through the window which, thankfully, was obscured by a grubby net curtain. The other was standing with his back to our front door, arms folded, like a cut-price bouncer. They wore cheap-looking suits but no tie, presumably to minimise the risk of throttling by frustrated taxpayers.

"Morning chaps," I said brightly. "How can I help?"

"Do you reside at these premises sir?" This from the arms-folded man. He had an untidy little moustache and the air of a school sub-prefect who'd just been granted the power to issue punishment essays. I took an immediate and splendidly strong dislike to him.

"I certainly do. At last. I hope you're here to evict my squatters?"

"We have no powers to evict persons living legitimately on the premises," whined the other man, turning from the window. "Squatters have rights you know." He was bearded and weedy-looking, with a strange, semi-aggressive demeanour, half-way between a truculent schoolboy and a recently beaten dog. I suspected he might be a passionate socialist.

"Well that's a shame," I boomed, in my best golf-club-bar voice. "An appalling bunch of lefties they are too, always going on trade union marches and that type of thing. They won't pay me rent and they're always inviting blacks round. Shouldn't be allowed."

The weedy man bristled. My intuition had been correct. In my experience, public servants prefer to pick on the conservative and generally law-abiding. The more I could paint our residents as a conspiracy of political rebellion, the more likely we'd be left alone.

The moustachioed man piped up again, self-importantly. "We have reason to believe you have converted this housing into premises of multiple occupancy. We request that you allow us inside to inspect the property."

"Your information is incorrect. And no," I replied, smiling tightly and slightly desperately. How the hell was I going to get rid of these interfering toads?

"Furthermore, we have reason to believe there may be health and hygiene issues at these premises."

"Wouldn't surprise me, these foreigners have awful eating habits," I said, conspiratorially. "Mrs Hall next door and I were saying just the other day we'd prefer this to be a whites-only road."

The two officials looked appalled, as was I, to be honest. Maybe I'd been a fascist rabble-rouser in a former life. Anyway, it did the trick. It was foul old Mrs Hall who called them, as Dr Shah had guessed. My nasty little comment had clearly damaged the credibility of her official complaint.

"Come on George, there's nothing to detain us here," said the bearded official, curling his lip.

His colleague considered me, his moustache twitching as he pondered his next move. His eyes slid off me and surveyed the garden below, coming to rest on the pink tent, iridescent in the evening gloom.

"What is that?"

"Oh, the squatters are growing vegetables. They're in to all that sustainability nonsense," I said airily. Damn it! I was pretty sure digging a six-foot deep latrine in your back garden was against some hygiene law or other, even if it was constructed by one of East Africa's finest toilet engineers. If they examined it closely they'd probably have grounds for a warrant, then the game would be up.

"Doesn't look like a vegetable patch to me. I think we'll take a look."

The two of them moved towards the stairs. I stayed put, blocking their path. "There are no vegetables there yet, obviously. It's still winter. The tent's just protecting the earth from waterlogging."

"We'll take a look anyway. These gardens are council land and ultimately our responsibility. It might be a health and safety hazard." They brushed me aside and descended the metal steps. I watched them, miserably, as they picked their way over the muddy ground and approached the tent.

"Don't tread on the tarpaulin areas, you might trip," I called, helpfully. I followed the pair down, frantically trying to think of a way to discourage them.

To my dismay, the moustachioed official pointed at the sign hanging over the entrance stating 'Vacant'. He crouched, searching for the zip at the base of the canvas.

"Don't do that," I called, catching them up.

"Why not?"

"You'll disturb the seedlings," I blurted, idiotically.

"Why should you care? I thought you didn't like all that sustainability rubbish."

He located the fastener and unzipped the front flap. A breath of warm, yeasty sawdust and fermenting leaves wafted from the tent's interior.

"What's that funny smell?" asked the bearded one.

"It's winter fertiliser," I improvised, pathetically.

"Pass me your torch, Gary," ordered the moustache. "I'm going to check for vermin." Beardy fished a slim flashlight from his jacket pocket.

"There's nothing to see," I pleaded.

"I'll be the judge of that." Moustache clicked on the flashlight and, before I could warn him, stooped and placed a foot inside the tent, without looking. There was a snapping as the slender canes covering the pit gave way. With a squelch, his leg plunged thigh-deep into the pit and his body pitched sideways. I heard his head chime against the toilet bowl, his other leg still protruding through the tent flaps.

An appalling stench rolled from the tent's interior. "Arrrghhhh! Jesus!" he shouted.

"Are you all right George?" called the other man.

"It's just organic fertiliser," I reassured him through the tent flaps. "It's non-toxic but a little pungent if you stir it up."

"Get me OUT OF HERE!" he screamed.

We grabbed Moustache's available foot and with a huge effort, accompanied by an obscene sucking sound, pulled him clear of the fermenting mash of turds and vegetable matter. His buried leg was shiny with a slick of foul brown slime, as was one arm and the side of his jacket. He also appeared to have lost the shoe from his immersed leg. The smell was mind-blowingly revolting and I staggered backwards, trying not to retch.

The official bawled like a toddler, his moustache bouncing as he goggled at his shoeless, poo-slicked leg. With his fouled hand, he grabbed hold of his colleague's jacket, attempting to stand. Beardy wailed and hammered his fists on the stricken man's arm, frantically trying to loosen his grip. Little droplets of ferment-ing crap splashed from the sodden fabric onto both men's faces. Beardy suddenly stopped his hammering and made an ominous, low gurgling sound, his face white against his dark beard. Then a wave of puke exploded from his mouth, covering his colleague's shirt and clean arm.

Holding my breath, I retreated from the garden and up the stairs to the front door, feeling I had little of value to add. I watched the two men limp back to their car, pausing now and then to empty their stomachs. That would be a fun drive back to the office, I mused.

I let myself into the flat. It was as silent as the grave. I crept into the kitchen and spotted a naked foot under the table. Crouching, I found Fistule sitting cross-legged in front of the composting bin, into which he had stuffed various utility bills and the instruction book for the central heating.

"Fistule!"

He looked up. "We're still on lockdown," he whispered.

"We can call off the lockdown, Fistule, we're clear. And you can separate the electricity bill from those vegetable scraps, we need to pay it."

"Lockdown is lifted. We are now clear. I repeat, we are now clear," stated Fistule, in a small robotic voice. I wondered how many mushrooms he'd imbibed.

I climbed the stairs to find Mercedes demonstrating tai chi to the fascinated Somalis. I have no idea what they made of it but it had certainly kept them quiet. "Cawaale, I'm afraid there's some damage to the toilet," I said. "Please could you take a look?"

Fortunately, there was nothing that couldn't be repaired with a few bamboo canes and a couple of shovels of soil. We'd had a narrow escape, but nothing could prepare me for the horror that was to come.

***

Christmas raced closer and it was all-hands-on-deck at Gatesave. My time was spent ensuring our supermarkets were stuffed with industrial quantities of Asti Spumante. Running out of stock before Christmas would have resulted in a public hanging, not to mention drawing, quartering and a swift kick to the nuts, in no particular order.

I'd had a good day – my Asti Spumante had broken the all-time record for sparkling wine sales – and I'd had an even better evening, snogging recently divorced Felicity from Credit Control round the back of the Kings Arms, where she'd insisted on an early start to her scandalously filthy New Year's resolutions.

I tumbled off the train and strolled the final few yards home. If I'd been sober, perhaps I'd have spotted the shadows lurking at the corner of my building, but I was sozzled and as I reached for the stair rail to hoist myself up to the flat it was too late.

"Felix-a."

I recognised the lilting accent and my blood ran cold. Rizzo stepped from the shadows. There was no attempt at a charming little smirk, his face was cold. The hard-looking polo-necked man, who'd accompanied him on our last encounter, stood beside him.

I drew myself up to my full height but I knew my chances of bluffing my way out of this one were slim to none. It didn't stop the self-righteousness rising in me though. He had a nerve showing up at my house. "What the hell…"

"Save-a your breath!" snapped Rizzo. He studied me for a second. "You are a good liar, Felix. For a young man, a very good liar. I'm sure you have a lot of practice, telling your suppliers how poor your mighty supermarket is, how you can't afford to pay so much for their goods. To be able to say this when everyone can see it is not true requires a special skill." He gave a little smile. It wasn't warm.

"But you are not good enough. We know what you have done. We know you have stolen the goods we shipped…"

"I don't know what the hell you're talking about, Marco, and I resent being ambushed outside my home. How dare you! If you don't leave I shall call the police."

Rizzo glanced at his companion who removed a large knife from his coat pocket. It was fat and broad with a serrated back, the kind of knife that unhinged survivalists use to kill grizzly bears. My bowels turned to water.

"This is Franco. If I tell him, he will push this knife into your guts for a few seconds, then remove it. You will die, but it will take around ten minutes as you bleed to death inside. It will be extremely painful."

I had no intention of testing Rizzo's blood-curdling hypothesis – I trusted him completely. My stomach groaned in panic as I glanced around, trying to spot an escape route.

"Franco followed you home last night from the Institute of Directors, Felix."

That wouldn't have been difficult, I'd been thoroughly trolleyed last night, too. I'd been to the annual awards ceremony for the Anglo-German Wine Institute – a small affair but prestigious in its own way – where I'd received a gong for 'The Most Promising New Talent in the Field of German Wine Exports'. But it was all for nothing. I would die in agony tonight, behind an obscure parade of shops in Little Chalfont, cut down in the prime of a glittering career in international wine buying.

"So we know this is a dead end, the only way out is past us. You are a big man, Felix, and I'm sure you are quick. But not as quick as Franco, I think."

I stared at the knife, glinting dully in the low light. I was rooted to the spot. I had no doubt that Franco was quick, and I had no intention of running towards his knife to find out.

"Do you know how we know you are a liar, Felix?"

I remained silent.

"When we last saw you at your Head Office you asked what we had done to Sergio. Why would we have done anything to him? Only someone in fear would ask a question like that."

He was right, of course, the cunning fox. I'd have to remember that for next time…except there wouldn't be a next time. This was it. I shuddered as I imagined Franco's knife julienning my innards.

"So Sergio is ok?" I gibbered. If Morelli was all right then maybe they weren't so bad. Perhaps they were just trying to scare me and we could come to some kind of grown-up arrangement.

"No, Sergio is-a dead," stated Rizzo, flatly. "He had a simple job to do and he messed it up."

Oh misery! Oh Lord have mercy! This wasn't sounding good at all.

"We visited Braintree and talked to the security guards. It does not take much to persuade a security guard to talk, Felix, they are not paid very much. They told us an interesting story about you arriving at the depot with a colleague, then leaving in a bus. I wonder what was in that bus?" Rizzo didn't look as though he was wondering at all. But he certainly looked extremely peeved.

"And we spoke to your neighbour earlier. A strange woman. She accused us of being Polish, I don't understand why. I do not look Polish, neither does Franco." Rizzo shook his head and glanced at Franco before turning back to me. "She confirmed that you have our people in your apartment. They will be coming with us, they belong to us."

"Fine," I replied in a small voice.

"No, not fine. The other things that belong to us. Where are they?"

Coating the nostrils of half London's dinner party guests, I thought. But I sensed my answer might determine whether I lived or died. Play it cool, Felix. Very, very cool.

I glanced at the dilapidated shed at the end of our patch of garden, then looked down. I had to look defeated, my life depended on it. "In there," I said, miserably.

"All of it? In there?"

"We wanted to sell it but we didn't know how," I muttered, my eyes downcast. That part certainly wasn't a lie.

Rizzo removed the left hand from his coat pocket. It held a small silver pistol, which he pointed at my chest. My stomach turned a somersault. He had me with Franco's knife, why the hell did he have to pull a gun as well? "Show me. No tricks, Felix."

Franco stepped forward and poked the end of his knife at my stomach, piercing my coat. I yelped involuntarily.

"Shut up!" hissed Rizzo. "And get moving!"

"Follow me," I said, my voice quavering. I didn't have to fake the fear. I turned and strode across the muddy ground, taking care to avoid the 'Wildflower Zone' inside the bamboo canes. The pink tent stood like an absurd giant nipple in the centre of the garden, its 'vacant' sign swaying in the frosty breeze. In the half-light I could just see the knee-height strand of wool marking the perimeter of the filled-in pit.

"We're trying to grow flowers in the garden and we've just planted seeds. Come around the outside, we don't want them damaged." Maybe it was the fear, but my tone had become even prissier and more condescending than I thought possible.

Rizzo's face turned dark, he looked at Franco and jerked his head towards me. "Screw your stupid flowers!" he snarled. The two men marched towards me, snapping the woollen boundary thread, Franco holding his knife as if he meant to thrust it into my guts the second he reached me.

This was it! The end! My last throw of the dice and I'd come up snake eyes. I took a step back, held up my hands and gibbered in panic, "I'll pay you back, I promise!"

They were halfway across the little garden now and barely a knife's thrust away from me. Then, there was a muffled crack, followed by another. The two men paused for a second and Franco looked down. His foot had sunk into the ground and he stumbled slightly. "Cazzo!" he muttered.

There were a few more snaps in quick succession, then Rizzo's legs plunged into the ground, right up to his thighs. He fell forward and his gun discharged – I heard the bullet crack into the wooden shack behind me, right past my left ear. "Don't shoot!" I squealed.

"Eeaargh!" shouted Rizzo, clearly dismayed. He had flung his hands forward to break his fall, but they sank into the ground too, up to his elbows.

Franco, caught off-balance, flailed his arms. The knife span out of his hand as his legs were sucked into the earth. He grabbed at the pink Wendy house, but it offered no support. As the ground enveloped his waist, the tent pinged from its moorings and engulfed him, unveiling the porcelain toilet and the neat little buckets of compost to the night sky.

Like a chunk of fruit dropped into an obscene breakfast cereal, Franco sank into the soil, consumed in a series of snapping, crackling and popping gurgles. A hideous smell of doo-doo and fermenting vegetables billowed from the ground. Franco's cries ceased, every trace of the man consumed by the hungry earth.

Rizzo looked up at me, eyes bulging. He extricated his left arm but the other, holding the gun, had sunk in up to the shoulder. He flung out his free arm and grabbed the toilet bowl, which tipped free of its pedestal and thumped to the ground. As his body sank further into the morass, he clung to it desperately. He was on his stomach now, both legs buried, as the filthy ooze crept across his back and his torso disappeared beneath the surface. He wailed like a child. "Help-a me! Help-a me!"

I was extremely disinclined to help. I watched in morbid fascination as his body was drawn into the sucking bog, only his head and arm now visible above the slurry. He hugged the upended toilet bowl to his face, then that too began to sink, dark liquid filling the porcelain, as the mud covered his chin. Rizzo's final sound was a hideous gurgle as the fermenting juices flowed into his mouth. Then the mud closed over his head and, apart from some gentle bubbling, all was quiet.

The sole trace of the struggle was a stray pink corner of the tent, protruding from the mud. A wide-eyed fairy princess with flowing blonde hair winked back at me, gold stars flying from her wand. I felt myself all over, checking whether I'd been penetrated by a stray bullet or thrusting knife point, but the Hart body had maintained its integrity. I was in the clear!

"Felix? Is that you dear?" Mrs Hodfurrough's voice floated over the garden fence.

"Ah, yes, Mrs Hodfurrough. Good evening! Hope you're well!"

"There's a lot of noise coming from your side of the fence, is everything all right?"

"Yes, everything's fine. Just joshing with my mates. Sorry to disturb."

"My husband said he heard a gunshot. We were going to call the police."

"Ah, no, just a firework left over from November the fifth! Nothing to worry about."

"Well, you're not supposed to let off fireworks after Guy Fawkes, Felix, are you? It's against the law. Unless you're Indian. Is it those Indian friends of yours? Is it Diwali?"

"No, I don't think so Mrs Hodfurrough. No Indians here, don't worry. Just letting off our last firework. We'd left it in a cupboard and didn't want to waste it."

"You do get up to some funny things over there, Felix!"

"Yes, sorry about that Mrs Hodfurrough. Won't happen again!"

"All right. Good night."

"Nighty night."

CHAPTER TWENTY SEVEN - BRAINSTORM

Fistule and Cawaale surveyed the wreckage of their composting toilet the next morning. "That will take a long time to rebuild, man. How did you manage to destroy it so completely?"

"Cannot build again. Not safe. Too much disease," said Cawaale, shaking his head.

"Sorry guys, I'd had a few glasses of wine and I knocked over the toilet. Next thing I knew, the whole thing had collapsed. I was lucky to jump clear in time.

The two of them started to shovel soil into the depression in the earth. They slowly advanced over the patch, stabbing their spades into the ground to ensure it was firm. As a mark of respect, I planted Mrs Spott-Hythe's Pinot Noir vine over the bodies of Rizzo and his friend.

That evening we sat in the lounge, pondering what to do. My old schoolmates Tariq and Dan had joined us, keen to drink some hundred-quid bottles of wine. It was a chilly December night and, as Mercedes placed more logs on the fire, I pulled a fine, first-growth Haut-Medoc from the rack.

It was clear we'd have to move our Somali friends on from Little Chalfont, and soon. Rizzo may well have shared our address with other members of his organisation, and one armed confrontation with Italy's finest was quite enough for me, thank you. There was also the horrendous Mrs Hall next door, causing trouble. Who would she complain to next? And might the unfortunate council inspectors return with a vindictive warrant, insisting on a more thorough inspection of the premises?

"We need to find a new home for our friends – it's not suitable here any longer. Besides, we'll be back to using the bath as a khazi by the end of the week."

"We need work," said Galad.

"But you need documents to work legally," said Mercedes. "And illegal work isn't a great option, unless you want to earn a quid an hour scrubbing the floors in a restaurant."

"And for the women, maybe much worse work than that," Galad muttered.

"Anyone got any bright ideas then?" asked Wodin.

"We need to brainstorm," suggested Dan, reaching over to take the bubbling water-pipe from Fistule.

"Ok, storm away," I sighed.

"No, you have to do it properly. I facilitate brainstorming sessions all the time at the office." After an unsuccessful couple of years auditioning for West End musicals, Dan had landed a job as Public Relations Officer at a charity called Jews for Goodwill. Their mission was to spread peace and light across the world, building friendly links with other communities and faith groups.

"Oh God, I came here for a smoke and a toot, not a middle-management frotting session," moaned Tariq, gesturing at Dan to pass the water pipe.

"No, we need to do this," he insisted. "I'm in a facilitating frame of mind. Do you have a flipchart?"

"No, of course we don't have a bloody flipchart," I said. "This is a radical squat, not a stationery office. Here, you can write on the wall, we'll paint over it." I threw Dan the felt-tip pen Wodin had used to stoke his reefer.

"First, everyone needs to get comfortable," he said. "And we need proper refreshments."

"Right, I'll put fresh whisky in the bong," said Fistule. "How about a thirty-year-old Balvenie?"

"Good work Fistule. Felix, line up some more wine."

I strolled over to the gigantic wine rack and picked out four more bottles of exquisite Bordeaux.

"Galad, would you like some khat from the fridge?" Fistule had made a special trip to a Somali grocery shop in Lambeth to procure the mildly narcotic herb.

"No, I'll have some wine, please."

"Wodin, get a couple of big joints rolled."

"Coming up."

Dan stood in the middle of the floor and limbered up, first rotating his shoulders, then tilting his head from side to side. He took the top off the felt tip and stood next to the fire.

"Ok people, here are the rules. Number one: there are no bad ideas. Number two: nobody is allowed to be negative about anyone else's ideas. Number three: just relax, keep it positive and put it out there!"

"Shoot me now," muttered Tariq. "Fistule, please get that water pipe smoking, I need to anaesthetise myself."

"On the way, man."

"Come on then, Dan, you corporate powerhouse," drawled Mercedes. "Let's get storming."

"Ok! Our opportunity – not problem, please note guys, opportunity – is to find a new home and decent work for our Somali friends upstairs." He scrawled 'home and work' on the wall above the fireplace.

"Ok, let's think about jobs first. Hit me."

"Cooking," said Wodin.

"Cleaning," said Mercedes.

"More creative guys, come on! We need somewhere they can be hidden away. Somewhere remote."

"Mining?" said Fistule.

"Mining?" scoffed Tariq. "What the hell are they going to mine, you muppet? Hashish?"

"No bad ideas, guys! This is a judgment-free zone!"

"You can say that again."

"Ok. We need creativity guys. Keep those ideas coming!" Dan whirled his arms in great circles above his head and stared at us each in turn.

"Gardening," said Fistule. "Cawaale is great at landscape gardening."

"Especially if you want a gigantic craphouse in the middle of your garden," said Wodin.

"Keep it positive guys, pos-it-ive! Gardening is a great idea, Fistule. Let's have more like that."

Dan wrote 'gardening' on the wall, below 'cooking' and 'cleaning'.

"Farming," suggested Galad. "Ten of us here are farmers."

"Ok, farming. Good." Dan wrote on the wall again.

"Farming what?" asked Mercedes.

"I want solutions, not questions, please!"

"Ok, cereal farming?"

"Fruit farming."

"Cannabis farming!" shouted Wodin. Everyone murmured their approval.

"I would like something that does not mean prison, please," said Galad.

"Now Galad, there are no bad ideas, remember," cautioned Dan, kindly.

"But that is a bad idea. I knew a man in Mogadishu who was a cannabis farmer – and the big boss killed his whole family."

There was a pause. "Ok, that kind of killed the creativity, Galad," said Dan. "Sorry to hear about your friend."

"Why does everything have to be about recreational drugs?" said Mercedes. "What about grape farming. You've made a start outside already." Mercedes took a smug draw on the joint. She'd spotted the Pinot Noir vine in its new home.

"Yeah, working in a vineyard, good idea." Dan wrote 'vineyard' on the wall.

An idea belly-flopped into my head, like a frog splashing into a summer pond. "That's it! A vineyard! Working in a vineyard," I said, staring at the wall.

"Er, yeah. We've had that one Felix. Anyone want to build on vineyard working … ?"

"No, that's perfect, a vineyard! In Pluckley, Kent. Harvesting Chardonnay grapes for ice-wine," I shouted.

"Ok. That's quite specific. Brainstorming works better when you keep things more general, so people can bounce ideas around."

"Listen. Jeremy Spott-Hythe needs people to harvest frozen grapes. Right now."

"Where will they live, man?"

"I don't know, Fistule. On the farm, I should think. He's got a huge estate. There must be outhouses or somewhere they can sleep."

"Will he let them work as irregulars?" asked Mercedes. "How will they obtain work permits?"

"They're pretty head in the clouds, but it would still be tricky. The other workers might be suspicious …"

"Really?" guffawed Tariq. "You mean forty-odd black Africans with limited English skills rock up at a vineyard offering to pick grapes – hi there, we're from Bromley, just popped by on the off-chance you had some work for us?"

"Ok guys," piped up Dan again, "so they're not just going to rock up … What could their story be? Get creative folks, come on!"

"A team of employment-law enforcers?" said Mercedes, sarcastically.

"I like it! You turned the whole thing on its head there! Keep the ideas coming, folks!"

"A team of consultant viticulturists … ?" I wondered aloud.

"A team of drunken students on a three-year bender, travelling around the vineyards of Europe?" Tariq chuckled. "Oh, sorry, that's your actual job, Felix."

"Students. That's a good one." Dan wrote 'students' next to 'law officers'.

"Do Somali students visit vineyards, Galad?" asked Mercedes.

"There are no students any more. They destroyed all the universities in the war."

"Ok … let's keep it positive, people."

"You wouldn't have to be Somali – you could be Nigerian," suggested Fistule.

"But we do not speak Hausa."

"I'm pretty sure the Spott-Hythes don't either," I said.

"You'd still need passports or ID, though," said Wodin. "Could they get some kind of student card?"

It might have been the effect of Fistule's billowing water pipe, which had filled the room with a sweet fug of hashish and aged Speyside malt, but Dan looked as though he'd had a Eureka moment. "Yes, international student ID cards!" Dan yelled. "You can get them through the Erasmus Plus programme if you're splitting your course across two universities in different countries."

"Look who's getting all specific now," I said. "Couldn't we buy a load of Nigerian passports?"

"Yeah, sure," said Tariq. "Anyone know any good Nigerian forgers?"

"But you don't need a Nigerian forger. I can get you an Erasmus Plus student letter of permission through my office."

"Er ... You work for Jews for Goodwill, Dan, not the Nigerian board of trade."

"Forget Nigeria, Felix. My charity has just associated with a foreign university. I can apply for international student IDs from our new partners for further education."

"Who's that then?" I asked.

"The Hebrew University of Jerusalem," said Dan.

There was a pause while everyone looked at Galad.

I cleared my throat. "I don't want to bring any negative vibes down on your freestyle brainstorming, Dan, but I don't think these guys look very Israeli."

"Well, at least they're circumcised," chimed in Fistule.

"Oh, well, that's fine then. One little peek down the pants and I'm sure they'll be waved through by the immigration service. Welcome to Britain, Mr Goldschmidt, I do hope your studies are going well."

"No," insisted Dan, "There *are* Africans in Israel."

"Yeah, selling knock-off Rolexes on Tel Aviv seafront," said Tariq. "I'm not sure their residency status is triple-A, to be honest."

"No, listen. There are Jewish Africans in Israel. One of the lost tribes. Academics believe they are descendants of the Tribe of Dan."

"The Tribe of Dan? What's that, your Middle Eastern fan club? Related to the Tribe of Kevin I suppose?" I put my head in my hands. "How many of those bongs have you smoked? Why don't we just white the guys up and pretend they're from Ashford?"

"I'm serious," persisted Dan. "There are a whole load of people from East Africa who can prove they have Jewish lineage. They are known as the Beta Israel. They're from Ethiopia rather than

Somalia but, you know, that's close enough. They've all moved to Israel and they're hanging around being totally kosher."

I peeped through my fingers at Dan. "Seriously? And you can get hold of some official student ID?"

"Yeah. We can say these guys are doing a course in vine growing or whatever. It's a big industry in Israel, they make loads of wine. We can say they're on a foreign internship as part of their course. I helped organise a student visa for some guy doing exactly that, just last week."

"So we're saying a bunch of black Israeli students want to come to England to study winemaking. In December?" said Mercedes, incredulously.

"They're here to make ice-wine, isn't that what you said Felix?" asked Dan. "They don't have ice-wine in Israel on account of it being very hot. So they're coming to England, in December, where it's miserable and cold. And icy. Lovely and icy. Yeah?"

"Yes, I suppose so," I said.

"Ok. I'll tell my charity I've had an approach from the Hebrew University of Jerusalem and they have a whole class of winemaking students who want to come to England to study. We're an official partner of the UK Accreditation Service for International Colleges – we handle all their enquiries for Israeli educational institutions. So, I can apply for proper papers from the Department of Education and we can make some official IDs. Yes! It's a plan!" He punched the air like a victorious athlete.

I drained my glass of fine Bordeaux and poured another large one. "That's great. But why are you doing this, Dan? Aren't you taking a risk?"

Dan sighed. "To be honest, I kind of need a break at work. Things haven't been going so well there. Mum keeps turning up at the office and haranguing me. My boss is losing patience."

Dan had complained for a while that his career was not developing well, mainly due to his radical communist mother regularly storming into his office, demanding to know whether he was collaborating with Israel. Despite being as Jewish as a smoked salmon bagel, Mrs Golden was also a fanatical anti-Zionist and implacably opposed to any accommodation, trade or cultural exchange with the State of Israel.

"It's not a good look when you're a Jewish PR Officer for a Jewish charity and your mother ties herself to the railings outside, calls the press and screams about Palestinian babies. This would be a really good news story for Jews for Goodwill. My boss would love it."

"We don't actually want any publicity, Dan," I said. "The whole situation needs to be kept under the radar, understand?"

"Yeah, of course! It's just an internal thing, so my boss can see I've achieved something."

"Will it work though?" asked Mercedes.

"Yeah, course it will," he said. "I can't think of anything that could go wrong."

"I can think of about eighty things without even trying," I pondered, "but I can't actually think of a better idea."

"I do not understand," said Galad, after a few seconds.

"Ah, yes, sorry Galad," I said. "Let me explain. You and your friends will pretend to be Jewish Israeli students so you can pick grapes and make wine on a farm in Kent. Do you think everyone will be ok with that?"

Galad thought for a minute. "No. They will not be ok with that."

"Oh dear. What's the problem?"

"It is our religion. We can pick grapes, but not the other things, like being Jewish or making wine."

"Ok...then don't mention those things to your friends, Galad. We'll work something out. Sounds like we have a plan. Dan, let's get those permits."

We took passport-style photos of everyone with Wodin's camera the next morning – Galad explained to his countrymen that they were for a grape picking licence – and I called Mr Spott-Hythe.

"Ears, Spott-Hythe here."

"Mr Spott-Hythe. It's Felix at Gatesave. How's the ice-wine harvest going?"

"Ah hello Felix. Not good I'm afraid. My workforce have scarpered. I'm not sure if it was my wife's poetry or the cold weather. I've had to do all the mouldy grape elimination myself. Got bloody frostbite last week, nearly lost a finger. No idea how I'll do the actual harvest, might have to let it all go to waste. Terrible shame."

"As it happens, I may be able to help, Jeremy. Gatesave has links with educational establishments around the world. We have forty viticulture students visiting from the Hebrew University of Jerusalem and they would love to pick grapes for your ice-wine. There's no salary required but you'll need to feed them."

"Good Lord, Felix – I'll bite your arm off. Hebrews eh? Who'd have thought it? When can they start?"

"Straight away. But you'll need to offer them accommodation too. Can you fit them in somewhere?"

"Forty people? Tricky. They'll have to sleep in the stables. We can put some straw down."

"Right … I'm sure that will be fine."

***

Dan was as good as his word – he brought us the laminated passes the following week, along with official-looking notes of permission from the Department of Education. We had to give everyone Jewish names for the passes, which Dan stole from a list of secondary school children visiting from Haifa as part of a cultural exchange.

Galad explained to his countrymen that, under English law, everyone had to have an official fruit-picking name as well as their normal name. None of the Somalis appeared to spot that there was an Israeli flag in the corner of their pass, nor that each one stated 'Hebrew University of Jerusalem' in both English and Hebrew. Astonishingly, our plan was on track.

We gave the job of transporting the Somalis to Carlos, of course. It was only right to give him the job after he'd helped bust them out of Braintree container depot the previous month.

"Hello again, chaps," he called brightly as they filed onto the Harlow Sunshine Tours coach once more. "Glad to see you've scrubbed up since last time!"

We'd also dipped into our drugs and armaments fund and spent several thousand pounds kitting everyone out with sleeping bags, camping beds and warm winter clothing – woolly hats, gloves, fleeces and thermal underwear.

A couple of hours later Carlos pulled up outside the entrance to Chateau Spott-Hythe. There was a banner over the front gate sporting a blue Star of David and the words 'Shalom and welcome to our guests from Israel!' A photographer took pictures as we disembarked from the coach. Dan jogged down the track from the farm, waving enthusiastically.

I grabbed him and took him to one side. "What the blinking hell's going on Dan? We didn't want any publicity!"

"Relax, Felix. I just need to generate a little PR so my boss can see I'm actually doing my job. It's only a guy from the Ashford & Maidstone Times, it won't go far."

We shepherded the Somalis in their woolly hats and gloves down the track to the farmhouse, each of them carrying their new sleeping bag. The Spott-Hythes were waiting for us at the door – both fully dressed, thank God.

"Welcome, welcome!" called Jeremy Spott-Hythe, clapping his hands. His face clouded slightly as our new vineyard team gathered around the farmhouse entrance. "Er…these are the students from Israel?" he asked, looking confused.

"Yes!" I said brightly.

"They don't look very Jewish," said Mrs Spott-Hythe.

"They're originally from Ethiopia, Mrs Spott-Hythe. There's a whole tribe of Jews there. This group was working on a factory assembly line in Addis Ababa, making plastic toys, before they were rescued and flown to Israel by the Ecological Youth League of Jerusalem, to work on a kibbutz. Now they are in love with the land, never happier than when out in the open air, picking fruit and communing with nature. When they were offered the opportunity to see Kent, they jumped at it!"

I thought I might have overplayed my hand slightly, but Mrs Spott-Hythe looked delighted. "How wonderful! I stayed on a kibbutz one summer in my youth. A liberating experience!"

"Excellent!" declared Jeremy Spott-Hythe. "Now then, it's a very chilly day, so we've made everyone mulled wine!" He revealed a steaming cauldron sitting on a table just inside the doorway, next to a pile of mis-matched mugs. "Right, let's get everyone warmed up before we hit the vineyard," he boomed, ladling the spicy brew into cups and handing it out.

I sidled over to Dan, who shrugged at me. "For pity's sake," I whispered. "Could you not have told them they're tea-total or something?"

"They're supposed to be wine students! How could I say that?"

"Why didn't you tell them they only drink kosher wine?"

"That's a good idea," he conceded. "Bit late though."

The Somalis were sniffing at their mugs, a few had taken a little sip. Nobody appeared to be causing a scene, thank God. It was bloody cold, though. I gratefully took a mug from Spott-Hythe and warmed my hands around it. I caught Galad's concerned eye and called out to him, "It's only grape juice, Abel. Nothing to worry about!"

Mrs Spott-Hythe laughed. "Indeed it is! Now, does everyone have a mug? Good! Right then – it's a very special day today, isn't it? Don't think we didn't know!"

I looked at Dan again, whose face was blank. He shrugged.

She ducked into the kitchen and returned with a lit candle. "Happy Hanukkah, Happy Hanukkah!"

"Dan! Dan!" I whispered savagely. "How in Methuselah's name did you not know it was Hanukkah? You're Jewish!"

"Ah. Yes, I'd forgotten. I'm not really that religious."

I dashed over to Galad. "Big smiles, Galad. We need everyone to give big smiles. Tell them it's an English grape festival. Everyone must look happy."

Galad passed on my instructions in hurried Somali. Thankfully, most of the team broke into a big grin, some swaying their mugs of mulled wine from side to side.

"And that's Hebrew they're speaking, of course?" asked Jeremy Spott-Hythe, a look of wonder on his face.

"Yes. Their English is very poor, unfortunately."

"We must ask Mr Wiseman, the dentist near the library, to pop down. He's Jewish isn't he darling? He could chat to them."

"Oh, don't go to any trouble. These African Jews speak a different dialect, anyway."

"Do they? Golly, I'm learning a lot today!"

After a little more awkward small talk, our Hebrew University students were shown to their lodgings. Spott-Hythe hadn't been joking, they really were stables – three long, wooden buildings with corrugated iron roofs and straw on the floor. A horse peered at us over a half-door, disapprovingly.

"You can't stay in that one, Bessie lives there," he said. "But the other two are empty. Should be dry and fairly clean. I sleep in there myself occasionally, when I have to be up early and don't want to disturb the wife."

Carlos gave me a hand carrying the camp beds down from the coach. We set them up in rows along each side of the stables, a sleeping bag on each. There was a building next door with several toilet cubicles over a sceptic tank – I was relieved to see they wouldn't have to dig another compostable latrine.

In the meantime, Spott-Hythe walked Dan and the students into the vineyards, together with the photographer from the local paper, to explain the finer points of ice-wine viticulture. I joined them and was pleased to see our team were diligent students, examining each bunch of grapes and carefully removing any that showed signs of mould, discarding the damaged fruit in a bucket. They fanned out across the vineyard, woolly hats bobbing up and down as they examined the vines, little puffs of breath rising in the cold December air.

Jeremy Spott-Hythe was delighted. "What an excellent bunch of workers, so much better than the locals! We just need to hold out now for a proper cold front. If we don't get one by the end of the month we'll have lost too much of the crop to mould. Fingers crossed for a big freeze!"

I bade him farewell and Carlos drove Dan and me back to Little Chalfont, where we rejoined Wodin, Fistule and Mercedes in the cosy lounge. Tariq had departed for a week of winter sun in Dubai and wasn't due back till Christmas Eve. It was very quiet in the house without all the praying, people running up and down the stairs and the constant clatter in the kitchen.

"What are they going to do when the grapes have been picked?" Mercedes asked me.

"There's always work to do in the vineyard. Winter pruning, then ploughing the vineyard, tying the young shoots in spring, guarding against frost..."

"At some point, isn't your wine-making friend going to wonder why his workers aren't going back to Israel to resume their studies?"

"Let's cross that bridge when we come to it. We can do another brainstorm," said Dan, confidently.

CHAPTER TWENTY EIGHT - THE PROMISED LAND

I t was Christmas Eve, the busiest day of the year for any food retailer, and Gatesave was having a bumper season. My Asti Spumante promotion was an outrageous success, pallet after pallet selling in every store across the country, customers filling their trolleys to the brim. We advertised the deal on television, a jaunty little ad showing bottles of Asti jumping into Christmas stockings, and customers responded by queuing round the block.

Jolly Trisha jumped out of her seat every ten minutes, announcing the latest sales figures to the trading floor. "That's two million bottles sold this week alone! Well done Felix!" she squeaked, as George Bolus glowered and Timmy Durange writhed and gurned with jealousy.

In a world-first, the Head of Margin actually came up to my desk to congratulate me in front of the entire floor. "Jingle bells!" he bellowed, pointing at me, "Back of the net!" before he strode off to scream at the mince-pie buyer for poor on-shelf availability.

As I basked in the universal glory from the trading floor, Bella from the media team stomped over. "I see you've generated another bit of interesting PR for us, Felix. Except this time it's interesting in a bad way. It would have been nice if you'd flagged it so we could have prepared for the calls from the media. We've had quite a few today already. Please tell me you can clear this mess up."

She threw this morning's Guardian on my desk and pointed to a story at the bottom of the front page, before stalking off.

Controversy as Gatesave supplier uses African Israelis to make Christmas wine

My bowels suddenly tightened. There was a picture of one of our Somalis, in woolly hat and gloves, carefully picking a grape from a vine. I scanned the article, panic rising.

Philomena Golden, of the 'Justice Israel: Zionism Is Murder!' campaign, has slammed Gatesave Supermarkets for associating with the Hebrew University of Jerusalem.

Dan, you useless bloody trollop, I thought. Why did you have to invite the press, let alone your lunatic mother? I read on:

We at JIZIM will campaign tirelessly against all association with the terrible, murderous Israeli regime until we see justice for the oppressed Palestinian masses. We will be demonstrating at Chateau Spott-Hythe on Christmas Eve to show our Palestinian comrades that we stand shoulder to shoulder with them on the brink of this so-called holy day.

I phoned Dan.

"Hi Felix, I know."

"Your insane mother is all over the papers, slagging off my employer and my wine supplier! For the love of God, I said no publicity! How did this happen?"

"Ah. Turned out the photographer for the Ashford & Maidstone Times was also a freelancer. He pitched the story to The Guardian and they went with it. Then they contacted my mum. They usually do, she's always good for a bloodcurdling quote when Israel's involved."

"Hell! I'm up the creek with *my* media team now. I'll be fired if this carries on! Can't you silence her? Call Mossad or something?"

"I can't really have my mother killed, Felix. Besides, we don't have an assassination arm at Jews for Goodwill."

"Well you bloody well should have. We need to get down to the vineyard now and supress this."

"How?"

"I don't know how. You're a PR Officer and she's your bloody mother! Call Wodin and get him down there too, we need some muscle. Maybe we can cause a riot and get all the protesters arrested."

"Oh dear, Felix, that's not very good is it?" gloated George Bolus, reading the article over my shoulder. "Be terrible if it took the shine off your Asti triumph. In fact, I'd be surprised if you make it into the New Year if that story keeps running. Middle Eastern politics…Palestinians…Israel…goodness gracious me, I think this might be the gift that keeps on giving! Anyway, nice working with you." He sauntered off, chuckling.

My phone rang. "Ears, hello Felix. There's a bit of a brouhaha at the farm gate. Do you know what's going on?"

"Nothing to worry about, Jeremy. Just some rabble rousers who've got the wrong end of the stick. I'm coming down now – I'll be with you in a couple of hours. Don't talk to the press."

"Oh. Well, I did have a chat to a very nice lady from the Daily Mail just now. Is that a problem?"

My stomach lurched. "Probably, Jeremy. What did you talk about?"

"She was interested to know about our employment practices. She was particularly interested in the stables."

Oh, mother of all bell-ends! "Kick them out. Don't talk to anyone. Don't show anyone else around. If they trespass, shoot them."

"Oh. Very good. Er … There's also a lady who's pregnant."

"What? Who?"

"One of your students. The one with the big stomach. She probably shouldn't be working in the vineyards. That's what the lady from the Daily Mail said anyway. She was very helpful. Her colleague took a few photos too."

I ran through the Somali women in my head. He must mean Khadro – she was rather on the large side but I'd thought nothing of it. "I thought she was just fat. How do you know she's pregnant?"

"She's complaining about cramps. We were going to call an ambulance, but she's insisting she's all right."

"Ah, yes. Don't do that. They're not insured for childbirth. They'll run up a huge bill if they go to hospital. A couple of the other students are midwives, they'll deal with it."

"Are you sure? Sounds a bit Heath Robinson to me, old chap."

"Just … don't do anything, I'll be there soon." I hung up and grabbed my coat.

This was bad. It wasn't just the PR embarrassment for Gatesave, of course. Our flimsy little conspiracy was about to be blasted wide open and it was probably a matter of hours before the police and immigration swooped on the winery and arrested the Somalis. Then they'd spill the beans on where they'd been staying and, as sure as night follows day, the authorities would turn up in Little Chalfont, search the premises, dig up the bodies of the Mafiosi … I'd probably be in Wormwood Scrubs by nightfall.

I was hurrying to the lift when my mobile rang. It was Tariq.

"Yo, Felix. Just got back from Dubai. Had a very interesting time."

"Wonderful, Tariq. I'm so pleased but I can't really talk. There appear to have been flaws in our plan. The whole bloody thing's coming apart at the seams and I'm properly in the cack-house."

"That's a surprise. But don't worry, I've got a much better plan."

"Oh, good," I panted, as I tore out of the Gatesave office and hailed a taxi. "Does it involve pretending they're Hindu holy men on a pilgrimage to the Ashford Shopping Centre? Or perhaps a posse of trainee monks searching Beckenham for the Arc of the Covenant?"

"They're great ideas, all of them. But no. Listen, have you ever heard the term *bidoun*?"

I hadn't. And as I sprinted from my taxi to the train at Waterloo station and sped through the Kent countryside, Tariq explained.

When I arrived at Chateau Spott-Hythe, there were two dozen shabby looking people gathered around the front gate, chanting. They had pulled down the little banner saying 'Shalom' and set fire to it – it now sat smouldering in a sad little pile. There was a tall woman in dungarees, with a huge head of bright red hair, right in the centre of the group. She held an open bottle of sparkling wine in one hand and a loudhailer in the other. I saw the bottle had a hand-made label that said 'Gatesave: Chateau Death'. I guessed the woman was Dan's mother.

She held the loudhailer to her mouth. "What do we want?"

"Justice!" shouted back the tawdry little group. Most of them were pale, greasy and wore cheap anoraks. A couple held banners saying 'JIZIM – End the Killing!'

"When do we want it?"

"Now!"

A photographer was down on one knee, pointing his camera up at the group, presumably to make them look larger, while another took pictures of the oblivious Somalis walking through the vines in the field above us. A woman in a beret was talking to the protesters, holding out a tape recorder.

I spotted Dan flapping his arms, miserably failing to pacify his wild, red-headed mother. As I got closer, I saw she had glued several dozen children's dolls' heads to her clothes. They swayed and bobbed obscenely as she jumped around.

Mrs Spott-Hythe stood on the other side of the gate in her kaftan, a large scythe in her hands and her face like thunder, looking like Death's angry mother-in-law. The demonstrators started to rock the gate, chanting slogans.

"Cross that gate, you urban hooligans, and I'll spill your blood!" she warned.

"Killer!" shouted back the red-headed woman.

"Hello folks," I called, "I'm from Gatesave Supermarkets. Can everyone calm down for a second?"

Dan's mother turned to me. "Down with the child-murdering occupiers!" she screamed through her loudhailer, right into my face, and poured the contents of the wine bottle, which contained a red liquid, over her clothes and the dolls' heads. The photographers took more pictures, zooming in as Mrs Golden flung herself to the ground and writhed around, screaming, "Justice for the dead babies!"

The lady in the beret approached. "Is it Gatesave policy to use pregnant illegal immigrants in their supply chain?" She thrust a small tape recorder in front of my face.

"Ah, er no. Not as such. Best if I refer you to my Press Office, I think."

"But as a representative of Gatesave, don't you agree that people trafficking is a serious crime?"

"Er, well, it depends really..."

"Would you be Mr Hart, by any chance?" asked an anxious voice behind me. I turned to see a neatly dressed middle-aged man in a grey suit and scarf.

"Yes..."

"Good afternoon. I'm George Cohen, the Commercial Attaché at the Embassy of Israel in London."

"Ah. Hello. Felix Hart."

Mr Cohen shook my hand and glanced over my shoulder. "Hello Dan." Dan joined us, looking very agitated. "I see your mother is causing us problems again Dan."

"Well, yes, it looks like it, Mr Cohen. Sorry about this."

"You two know each other … ?"

"Yes, Felix, we do," sighed Mr Cohen. "When I took this job I expected my fair share of invective from unhinged fundamentalists and pea-brained neo-Nazis. That's par for the course when working for the Israeli Embassy." He peered, dismayed, at the woman lying on the ground, her dungarees festooned with severed dolls' heads, broadcasting through her loudhailer to the heavens.

"Jus-tice, jus-tice, jus-tice!" she chanted.

"But I never expected my most implacable opponent to be one Mrs Philomena Golden of Hampstead Garden Suburb."

"What's your opinion of Gatesave using forced labour to make their wine, Mrs Golden?" asked the reporter, holding her tape recorder next to the woman's head.

"Their customers are literally drinking the blood of slaughtered infants!" she foamed from her position in the mud, shaking a smiling blood-soaked doll's head to make her point. She lifted her head and looked at me and Mr Cohen. "You're worse than the Nazis!" she screamed.

"Yes, hello Mrs Golden," he called back.

"Please calm down mother, you're not helping," pleaded Dan.

Mr Cohen turned back to me. "I wonder if you can help me understand what's going on, Mr Hart?"

"Well, it's complicated," I said.

"Hmmm. Yes, things often are in this world. I understand your supplier here is hosting a group of viticulture students from the Hebrew University of Jerusalem?"

"Yes, something like that," I said in a small voice.

"It's a great university. I know, because I studied there. Not viticulture, sadly, but ancient and modern languages."

"Oh. That's nice."

"Yes. So I was fascinated to hear about your little internship scheme. In fact, so was Professor Weitzman, the Head of the

Faculty of Agriculture, when I called him this morning. Most fascinated."

"Hmmm, yes," agreed Dan. "I can see why he might have been."

"I even took the liberty of speaking to a couple of your students earlier today, gentlemen. I tried English and Hebrew but they weren't too familiar with those languages. Which is strange, because students at the Hebrew University of Jerusalem tend to be pretty good at both. Their Arabic was far better, though. I suspect their Somali might be better still, although I confess my own Somali stretches to only a few words."

"Yes. Tricky old language, Somali."

"Indeed. Gentlemen, I don't really care what you're up to here. You could be running a gigantic crystal meth factory – it wouldn't concern me in the slightest." Mr Cohen raised his finger. "Except. Except, for some reason, you have involved the good name of Israel and simultaneously attracted the attention of Mrs Golden and the national press. And that, unfortunately, does make it my problem."

"Yes, I can see that."

"Good. Now then, I would be very grateful if you could extricate the good name of my country from this strange little scheme of yours. And I would like you to do it very quickly. Are you capable of doing that yourself or do you require my help?"

I had the feeling that Mr Cohen's help would involve flashing blue lights, men in uniforms and the inside of a cold, hard cell. Jeremy Spott-Hythe hove into view. He was naked and carrying a shotgun.

"Why is that man wearing no clothes, in the middle of winter?" asked Mr Cohen.

"He's trying to tell when the next frost is due," I explained.

"Felix! Your pregnant student has gone into labour!" Spott-Hythe called.

"Are you sure it's not just stomach cramps?"

"Well, the head's showing so…it's definitely looking like she's pregnant. For the moment."

Oh, Lordy! If we sent her to hospital she'd be questioned, we'd have the authorities down here in no time and I'd be locked up by the end of the day. I stared more closely at the Somalis up on the hillside. What on earth were they doing…? The group had taken a break from inspecting grapes and were arranged in a semi-circle on their knees. To my horror, I could see that Madar, the musical Somali who had led the call to prayer back in Little Chalfont, had sliced the end off a stray traffic cone and was holding it to his mouth.

"*Allāhu 'akbar. Allāhu 'akbar,*" he sang.

"Now, that's not a sound you often hear at the Hebrew University of Jerusalem," pondered Mr Cohen.

"Ah. No. Can you hold on for just a second?" I turned to Dan and whispered savagely, "For pity's sake, ask them to stop. Tell them they can do an extra-long prayer this evening or something."

"I can't interrupt. It would be rude!"

"Afternoon Felix!" called Wodin as he, Fistule and Mercedes emerged from a taxi. Wodin peered up at the praying Muslims on the hillside. "Oh dear. That's not part of the plan, is it?"

The crowd of protesters were rattling the gate more vigorously now – the chain was jangling and crashing against the wood.

I turned to Wodin. "Can you and the guys try to stop that rent-a-mob from vandalising the gate? We really don't want them invading the farm."

Wodin walked over to the protesters with Fistule, who held a large joint in his hand. "Hey, dudes. Why all the shouting? Let's just have a smoke and talk about this," called Wodin.

"Is it Gatesave policy to distribute illegal drugs, Mr Hart?" asked the journalist, her tape recorder hovering before my nose once more.

"*Ashhadu 'an lā ilāha 'illā-llāh,*" sang Madar from the hill-side above.

"Mr Hart. I can see you have a lot on your plate but I must ask, most respectfully, that you address my request," insisted Mr Cohen.

"Ah, yes, just hang on. With you in a minute."

At that moment, the crowd broke the chain around the gate post and pushed it open. "Get back! I know how to use this!" Mrs Spott-Hythe swept her scythe at the protesters, inserting a long, neat slash across the front of a small man's grubby anorak.

"Violated! I've been violated by the fascist agents of child murderers!" he whined. The photographer zoomed in on the unfortunate man's jacket. Sadly, the blade hadn't penetrated his chest.

"Police! Attempted murder! Call the police!" screamed Mrs Golden.

"I'm calling now!" shouted a tall, wet-looking man with bad acne.

"Don't you dare use those infernal machines on my property! They emit radiation!" Mrs Spott-Hythe flipped her scythe and jabbed the blunt end into the face of the spotty-faced protester. He dropped his phone in the mud and screamed, sinking to his knees and clutching his face.

"*Ashhadu 'anna Muḥammadan rasūlu-llāh,*" Madar's voice floated down from above.

"Murder! Murder!" screeched Mrs Golden.

"Close the gate! The alpacas will escape!" called Mrs Spott-Hythe. Sure enough, two llama-like creatures were jogging towards the open gate, friendly smiles on their furry faces.

"Good! Liberate them!" called a mousy-looking young woman from the crowd of protesters, opening her arms in a gesture of mammalian solidarity.

"*Ḥayya 'ala-ṣ-ṣalāh,*" sang Madar.

The alpacas ran through the open gate and careered into the crowd, knocking the mousy woman to the ground. Still smiling, one of them spat at the Daily Mail photographer while the other lowered its head and started to eat Mrs Golden's hair.

"Jesus Christ, my eyes!" shouted the man from the Mail, dropping his camera and pawing at his face.

"They're setting their animals on us!" screamed Mrs Golden, attempting to batter away the creature's head with her loudhailer.

"Mr Hart, please!" called Mr Cohen, tugging at my coat. "This must end now! I respectfully ask that you attend to my request!"

"*Ḥayya ʿala-l-falāḥ,*" sang Madar.

"Felix, we need a midwife, now!" shouted Jeremy Spott-Hythe, waving his shotgun, his dongle swinging in the frigid air. "None of the other students are qualified."

I turned to Dan, who was wringing his hands. "Go and do something useful, for God's sake! Wash your hands first!" Dan ran through the gate towards the stables.

Mrs Golden had grabbed hold of the alpaca's bridle and was now being shaken, flinging pouting, blood-stained dolls' heads in all directions. The animal began to walk backwards, dragging her like a sack of potatoes.

Despite Wodin and Fistule's best efforts to secure the gate, the crowd surged forward, pushing them aside. The press pack ran forward for a better shot.

"Back, you dogs!" shouted Spott-Hythe, discharging his shotgun into the air. Everyone ducked and the alpacas bolted in panic, dragging Mrs Golden, whose arm had become tangled in her animal's harness, through the mud and into a nearby vineyard.

"Don't shoot, man!" wailed Fistule, his arms outstretched in front of the crowd. "Everyone just chill!" Several of the protesters barged past Fistule, who fell on his back in the mud. They ran at Mrs Spott-Hythe, who swept the blunt end of her scythe across their legs, sending them toppling, howling to the ground.

"*Allāhu 'akbar. Allāhu 'akbar,*" sang Madar.

"Hold the front page and get down here, it's like the Alamo," shouted one of the photographers into his phone.

"Next time, I shoot to kill!" hollered Spott-Hythe, as his wife drove the end of her weapon into the buttocks of the acne-afflicted protester, who was rolling in the mud.

"Rape! I'm being raped!" he screamed.

"Mr Hart! Will you please address my concerns!" shouted Mr Cohen.

A siren sounded and a police car braked hard at the gate. Two policemen leapt out and ran up the track, the younger one shouting into his radio. "We are at the scene, Control. There's a disturbance in progress."

As they rushed past me and through the gate, they came upon Mrs Spott-Hythe, grey hair flying, spinning her scythe like a witch-ninja. "I survived the Mau-Mau, I can deal with you rabble!" she yelled.

"There's major public disorder here," advised the policeman. "Control, we're going to need backup!"

Then they caught sight of Jeremy Spott-Hythe, his dangling meat and potatoes and his loaded shotgun. The older policeman, a Sergeant, grasped his own radio. "We have an armed and naked man on the scene, highly agitated. Send armed backup, repeat armed backup. We need eyes in the sky, eyes in the sky!"

"*Lā 'ilāha 'illā-llāh,*" sang Madar through his traffic cone.

"Christ, Sarge, I think it's some kind of terrorist training camp!" wailed the younger policeman. "It's carnage here, Control! We need tactical!" he shouted, "Repeat, we need tactical! Send everything you've got!"

"Officers!" shouted Mr Cohen. "I am a diplomat in need of protection!" He held up an impressive looking piece of ID. The Sergeant's eyes bulged.

"We may have a diplomatic incident, Control, suggest you send Special Branch, I repeat, send Special Branch."

The other alpaca jogged over, a wide, dappy smile on its face. It grabbed Mr Cohen's ID in its teeth and swallowed it.

"Right, I'm not putting up with this anymore! I'm calling the Home Secretary," shouted Mr Cohen. He pulled out his phone.

"Put that devil's tool away or I'll smite you!" screamed Mrs Spott-Hythe, pointing her enormous blade at him.

"Suppress that woman please! You are obliged to protect me under the Vienna Convention," shouted Mr Cohen at the officers.

Another siren sounded and a police van skidded to a halt, blocking the road. Six more policemen piled out and ran up the track towards us. They were intercepted by Mrs Golden sprinting out of the adjacent vineyard, wailing like a banshee. She had managed to untangle herself from the alpaca, which cantered after her, a large tuft of her red hair in its happy mouth.

Mrs Golden was clearly in a highly distressed state, the remaining dolls' heads swinging wildly from her shredded, fake-blood-stained clothes, her hair a spiky mash of vine leaves and alpaca saliva. "Arrest everyone!" she screamed, "for rape, murder, assault with deadly animals, and oppression of the Palestinian nation!"

"Jesus Christ, Sarge, it's the zombie apocalypse!" shouted one of the officers, as the pack of policemen gave Mrs Golden an extremely wide berth.

"*Wa 'anaa 'ash-hadu 'an laa 'ilaaha 'illallaahu...*" chanted the Somalis in unison.

"What the hell's going on up there?" screamed one of the recently arrived officers. "It's a bloody al-Qaeda convention!"

"On me! On me!" shouted the Sergeant, crouching just inside the gate and beckoning furiously to his colleagues.

The police took up position around their colleague. Protesters were running back and forth trying to avoid Mrs Spott-Hythe's whirling scythe. Wodin and Mercedes were fighting a losing battle to prevent further protesters from invading the farm, while Jeremy Spott-Hythe spun around, waving his shotgun and winky at anyone who got too close. Fistule lay on his back, a muddy footprint on his face.

"Ok, we have a major incident here lads!" shouted the Sergeant. "Naked man with a firearm, probably mentally ill. Large number of Muslims praying, possibly in possession of explosives. Two mad women, one with a scythe, the other covered in dolls' heads, may be witches. VIP, possibly foreign diplomat, impossible to say, all evidence eaten by South American mammal. Miscellaneous members of the public, probably on drugs, definitely hostile. International media present. Have requested armed support, air support, bomb squad, Special Branch, RSPCA."

"My penis is on fire!" roared a deep voice. Everyone stopped and stared. Even the alpacas looked round. It was Tariq. He was accompanied by a very smart-looking man of Middle Eastern appearance carrying an attaché case. "Not really, my penis is fine. Just getting everyone's attention," he announced.

"Are you in authority here, sir?" asked the Sergeant.

"Yes I am, officer. My name is Tariq Hussein. I am a human rights activist. This is my lawyer, Mr Samara." The smart man nodded, rested his attaché case on the broken gate and flicked open the catches. "And this is my undercover colleague, Mr Felix Hart," he added, waving towards me. "He can explain."

I drew myself upright and thrust out my chest, nodding to the Sergeant.

The Sergeant folded his arms. "There's a lot that needs explaining here, Mr Hart. We'd be very grateful if you could shed a little light on the proceedings."

"You have arrived at the perfect time, officers," I began. "I thank you for your prompt and professional response." I extended my arm towards the Somalis on the slope above who, oblivious to the chaos below, had now finished their prayers.

"Standing before you, on the hills of Kent, are forty-two of the most benighted and oppressed individuals the world has ever seen."

"They are not Jews from the Hebrew University of Jerusalem!" declared Mr Cohen.

"Thank you sir, I'd worked that one out for myself," replied the Sergeant. "Please continue, Mr Hart."

"They are Zionist collaborators in the oppression of the Palestinian nation," shouted Mrs Golden, as she staggered through the gate, a few severed baby heads still swinging from her tattered dungarees.

"No madam, they are not," I said. "They are simple, honest Muslims, blameless pawns in a vicious game, way beyond their control."

"Oh," said Mrs Golden, looking rather deflated.

"These people have been subject to a life so wretched, so utterly foreign to us here, that it requires a strong mind to even comprehend such iniquity." Careful, better not bloody overdo it, I thought to myself.

"What's that then?" asked the Sergeant.

"Slavery!" I declared, dramatically. The protesters, Wodin and the Spott-Hythes had stopped fighting by now and moved closer. The whole crowd were rapt with attention.

"That's against human rights laws, Sarge," piped up the younger policeman. "I've never nicked anyone for slavery."

"Unfortunately, the offenders are not here, officer. They are far away, in their Dubai palaces, on the shores of the Persian Gulf." I flung out my arm, gesturing far beyond the rolling hills of Kent.

"I quite fancy a trip to Dubai," said one of the policemen.

"These men and women have been victims all their lives, officers. In Arabic, they are called *bidoun*, meaning 'without'. They are stateless. Their ancestors were simple African itinerant workers, stranded in Arabia decades ago when the maps of the region were redrawn around them. And there they remained, stranded, without passports, without permits, without hope."

Galad sidled up to me. "We are very happy here," he said. "Is everything ok?"

"Don't look happy, Galad, for God's sake," I whispered. "Tell everyone to look miserable. The police don't like happy people, it makes them suspicious."

I didn't have to worry. The Somalis had wandered down the hillside to join us, their now-frightened faces taking in the police, the wild, bloody Mrs Golden, and the naked Jeremy Spott-Hythe.

"Fear not, my friends, you are safe now!" I called. For Christ's sake, I prayed, keep looking oppressed and miserable. "Without passports they are not permitted to leave the Middle East to return to their ancestral homes. Without papers they cannot be officially employed. Without permits they cannot access healthcare, nor education. Generation after generation are condemned to a lifetime of irregular work as unpaid servants, slaves or prostitutes, in the palaces of the rich, shunned by the state and exploited by the powerful."

"How awful!" exclaimed Mrs Golden. "Something must be done!"

"Something has been done, madam, thanks to the brave efforts of the activists you see before you!"

"How did they get here then?" asked the Sergeant, frowning.

"Through the brave work of a dedicated network of human rights workers, including Dan Golden of Jews for Goodwill, and Tariq Hussein of Muslims For a Better World, who stand here before you." The protesters burst into applause.

"My son! How could I ever have doubted you?" wailed Mrs Golden, looking around. "Where is he?"

"I think he's delivering a baby," called Wodin.

Tariq's lawyer removed a sheaf of papers from his case and presented them with a flourish.

"We cannot reveal the exact route they took," explained Tariq, "but we have documentation showing that they were under the control of a certain Sheikh Rashid bin Salem, a vicious prince whose financial empire is built on a network of human misery!"

"He sounds like a beastly man!" shouted Mrs Golden, rattling her dolls' heads.

"He is indeed, madam," I replied. "But the good news is they are now safe from his clutches, thanks to the generous hospitality of the good people of this fine Chateau!" I gestured at the Spott-Hythes. The protesters applauded once more.

"Well, it was the least we could do!" piped up Jeremy Spott-Hythe, looking confused.

"Furthermore," called Tariq, waving the papers in the direction of the uncomprehending Somalis, "these poor people are now free! They are officially claiming asylum in the United Kingdom, as they are entitled, by the grace of her Majesty the Queen!"

"The Queen!" shouted Spott-Hythe, leaping in excitement and waving his shotgun, his old chap twirling in reply.

The police suddenly remembered Spott-Hythe was armed. "Can you place that weapon on the ground please, sir!" shouted the Sergeant.

"Don't worry officers, he's firing blanks," I explained. I was on a roll now. "It's a Kent University project to study bird-scaring techniques. Apparently, naked men are much more likely to scare crows than clothed men." Nevertheless, Jeremy placed his shotgun on the ground and raised his hands.

"I see. Well, just ensure you keep your research project to private land. We don't tolerate that kind of thing on the Queen's Highway."

"Ears, of course, officer."

I heard the chatter of a helicopter approaching over the hills. The sun had already set in the late mid-winter afternoon and a spotlight stabbed down through the gathering dusk.

"And what's the story with these scruffy types who've been rolling in the mud?" The Sergeant gestured at Fistule and the battered protesters.

"Misguided socialists, officer, who've grabbed the wrong end of the stick. But don't treat them too harshly – their hearts are in the right place. Besides, they've already had a good kicking."

"Did you say my son was delivering a baby?" asked Mrs Golden.

"Ah, yes. Would you be good enough to call an ambulance and social services?" I asked the Sergeant.

We all marched down to the stables in the fading light. And there, on a camp bed, surrounded by straw, lay Khadro, the new mother, a little baby in her arms.

Dan sat next to her, pulling a sleeping bag over the exhausted pair and dabbing her head with a sponge. He looked up as we entered. "It's a boy," he said, wonder in his eyes.

The policemen, Somalis and protesters all knelt before the camp bed, cooing and offering advice, while the press snapped away.

"This is pure gold, I'm going to make a fortune," sobbed the freelancer from the Ashford & Maidstone Times, tears of joy running down his cheeks. "It's a world-wide front pager and no mistake!"

"Bless the little blighter. Here's something to get the young chap on his way in the world," said Wodin, stepping forward and wedging a wad of used twenty pound notes under Khadro's sleeping bag.

"And here are your asylum papers madam," added Tariq, placing the official documentation next to her. "You won't be needing any for the little one – he's as British as a Yorkshire pudding!"

"And here are my brother's details, he's a top literary agent," said Mr Cohen, leaning over and giving her a card. "You've got one hell of a story, give him a call."

Bessie whinnied in approval from next door and the alpacas, still chewing Mrs Golden's hair, peered through the open stable door, all illuminated by the searchlight from the police helicopter shining overhead.

I stood back and surveyed the beautiful scene I had brought about.

And I saw that it was good.

***

The rest of the story is now wine folklore. As Jeremy Spott-Hythe's naked body attested, that night was the coldest of the year, and on the morning of Christmas Day the Somalis were hard at work, in their woolly hats and gloves, picking the frozen grapes. Jeremy Spott-Hythe was able to produce several hundred bottles of a magnificent Kentish ice-wine, the first ever, which he christened 'A Kentish Miracle'.

With the worldwide publicity from the story of the bidoun, and their intrepid escape from the evil Sheikh Rashid bin Salem, Jeremy Spott-Hythe was able to auction his bottles for over a thousand pounds apiece. He invested the money in upgrading the stables to a proper accommodation block and founding the Pluckley Institute of Viticulture and Islamic Thought, appointing Galad as vice-chancellor. To this day, it is the only Islamic institution housed in a winery, and it stands as a shining beacon of tolerance and hope in a dark, suspicious world.

Dan was promoted to Director of Public and Legal Affairs at Jews for Goodwill and, through the careful use of judicial injunctions, was able to effectively silence his mother's campaigning career. Tariq was rewarded handsomely by his father, who declared him the most loyal and successful of all his sons. He was gifted a large shareholding in one of his father's arms-dealing companies, allowing him to retire at the ripe old age of twenty-five.

Khadro, with the help of Mr Cohen's brother, published a best-selling account of her dramatic life which, as they say in the movies, was loosely based on a true story. She shared the royalties with the rest of her compatriots, allowing them to set up a thriving co-op selling freshly baked artisanal Somali flatbreads to the chattering classes of Notting Hill.

A few parties remained unhappy, but you can't please everyone. Sheikh Rashid bin Salem was furious, of course. But nobody gave him much sympathy as he raged in his palace on the shores of the Persian Gulf because he was indeed, to use Ms Golden's words, a beastly man.

He wasn't, however, as beastly as his sworn enemy, Tariq's father, who had secretly shafted him by forging all the bidoun papers supplied as evidence for the Somalis' asylum claim. The fraudulent, libellous paperwork caused the Sheikh a PR disaster back in Dubai, disqualifying him from a major public sector business tender, which was awarded to ... yes, Tariq's father.

You may think this a despicable state of affairs and no way to conduct business. I would have to concur, but I urge you to concentrate on the positive, particularly the relentless and virtuous advance of yours truly up the greasy pole of the international wine trade.

Gatesave's directors were delighted their supermarket was associated with the now world-famous Chateau Spott-Hythe, not to mention basking in the reflected glory of my recently revealed exploits as an undercover human-rights activist. Nor were my achievements limited to the world of ethics – my Asti Spumante sales triumph propelled Gatesave to an all-time high in market share, and we liberated hundreds of thousands of customers from exploitation at the hands of our competitors.

And so, following the management reshuffle that January, I was summoned to the tenth floor office by Roland Bonnaire himself. As I entered the plush office with its ankle-deep carpet, the perma-tanned CEO leapt from his seat, placed his guitar on his desk, and pumped my hand. "Congratulations Felix. A magnificent performance! You are promoted, with immediate effect, to Head of Wine, Beer, Spirits and Salted Snacks."

And that is the story of how I, a humble orphan, became a true connoisseur in a sea of sniffers and spitters, a champion of the down-trodden, and a titan of the retail trade. In short – and you know how I hate to boast – a god among mere mortals.

EPILOGUE - A CHEEKY DIGESTIF

There was a long pause. My interrogators stared, open-mouthed. Then the man pushed a button on the tape recorder. "I think that's probably all we need," he muttered, rolling his eyes. He fiddled with the wires running from the machine to the wall, then stood and stretched. The standard lamp in the corner flickered again – he walked over and felt under the shade, switching it off.

The woman put her pen down and yawned. "Yes, we can stop now. A litany of fraud, violence and subversion. The authorities will be most interested."

"But you promised you wouldn't say anything," I wailed.

"We promised nothing of the sort. And why should we?"

The big man by the door smirked and rose to his feet, massaging the back of his neck.

Oh hell. This was it then. Just as I'd reached the pinnacle of the wine trade I was to be shot out of the sky. I shook my head at the sheer injustice of it all. What came next? Arrest, extradition, electric shocks to the genitals and eighty years in a maximum-security penitentiary? Maybe if I sobbed and begged for mercy they'd take pity on me? It was a long shot but I could feel the tears welling up.

"Unless, Felix, you would care to work for us? You have unconventional methods but you do appear to be a man who gets things done."

I looked up, sharply.

"We see no reason why you shouldn't continue to work for Gatesave," the woman continued, "but we may require you to help us from time to time."

Hello. This sounded better. "What's the pay?"

"Don't be an arsehole, Hart!" shouted the man, as he adjusted the standard lamp.

"This is your remuneration, Felix," said the woman, tapping the recording machine.

Worth a try, I thought. I wondered whether I'd be given a gun. "Well, now that I'm working for Her Majesty's Government…"

"No, you've not quite understood, Felix," interrupted the woman. "We don't work for British Intelligence." She pulled a phone from her bag, pushed a couple of buttons and held it to her ear. "*Bonjour. Oui.*"

Mon Dieu! Not the bloody French Secret Service, surely? Still, the staff canteen was probably better than the one at MI6.

The woman moved the phone from her ear for a second. "What was it Sandra said? 'Not too bright, but intelligent enough to dress without help'. A certain peasant cunning, I think it's called." She spoke into the phone once more. "*Oui. D'accord.*"

"Sandra? Sandra who?" I demanded.

"Sandra from Paris-Blois Brands International, Felix."

Paris-Blois? I was extremely confused.

"We work for their research division. We're a thirty-billion-euro business, Felix. I think you'll find we're better resourced than most governments." She passed the phone to me. "Many people work for us, whether they want to or not. And now you work for us, too. Your new boss wants a word."

I took the phone and held it to my ear. "Hello?"

"Felix. Sandra here."

"What…? How…?"

"You're quite a talker, aren't you? I've had the dubious pleasure of listening to your life story half the night."

"I see. Well, I trust you enjoyed the racy bits?"

"Think of the past few hours as an audition, Felix. We're having this conversation because you've been successful. Congratulations. You've got the role."

"What role?"

"As an operative for Paris-Blois. There's no pay and I'm not suggesting it will be a satisfying or enjoyable job. But, thanks to that loose tongue of yours, you're going to do it anyway. Because the alternative will be considerably worse."

I tried to recall the more compromising parts of my confession. The corpses buried in the garden would be inconvenient to explain to the authorities, true, but it's not as if I bludgeoned them to death myself, was it? All the narcotics had been sold, bar a small chunk in the flat. And, according to my interrogator, Father Turk was dead. A recording wasn't enough on its own, surely?

"I'm calling your bluff Sandra. You've got nothing on me but a drunken audio tape."

Sandra sighed. "I wish I could be there Felix, to give your balls a good squeeze and engage that brain. We've no intention of telling the police. I only have to tell our Napoli office what you've been up to. We work very closely with the local families a little further south, their help is invaluable when it comes to, shall we say, stakeholder relations. Just imagine how they'll take the news of your involvement in their business affairs."

I remained silent. A Calabrian vendetta was not at the top of my Christmas present list. Sandra must have passed the phone over. A new, heavily accented voice growled from the handset. Sandra's boss.

"Felix 'Art! This is Pierre Boulle. Welcome to ze team, idiot. You dick me about, we 'ave enough to put you in an 'ole in ze ground. So, listen to my people and do what zey say, comprendre?"

The line went dead and my heart sank. I handed back the phone. The woman leant down and I heard the squeak of a metal box opening. She deposited my own phone on the desk and next to it placed a thick, expensive-looking white envelope bearing the crest of Paris-Blois Brands.

"It's the Brazilian Grand Prix next week. We require you to be in São Paulo the day before. These are your tickets. Flight details too."

A vision of tanned and athletic women floated before my eyes, all tousled dark hair and knowing smiles. I perked up. "How will I get the time off from Gatesave at such short notice? They're not going to let me just jet off to Brazil."

The woman rose and walked to the door. The big man stood aside and she retrieved a key from her pocket. "We employ you to find solutions, Felix, not problems."

She unlocked the latch and the door swung open. Sunlight flooded in from the lobby. It was morning. Time for Felix to go to work.

ACKNOWLEDGEMENTS

'd like to thank the following generous souls and lively mercenaries who made this book and its earlier, less respectable editions possible. In vaguely chronological order:

For providing a civilised and well-lubricated working environment: Dave Cope and the regulars at Publik Wine Bar, especially Markus and Ange.

For shaping the formative period: Mark Loudon, copy-editor and torch bearer; Patrick Latimer, illustrator par excellence; Leila & Ali Dewji, self-publishing gurus.

For beta-reading, literary encouragement and spreading the word: Curly, Paul, Glen, Blake, Rob J, Sasha, Heather, Jamie, Vicky Z, Macca, Beth K, Jonathan C.

For wine-infused, entrepreneurial support: Cliff Roberson, Jerry Lockspeiser, Justin Howard-Sneyd and Adrian Bridge. For spectacular guerrilla marketing: Alicia Mellish and her dynamic team at Stir PR, particularly Jessica B.

For taking a punt on an indie author: Muna Khogali at the sadly departed Book & Kitchen, Eric Treuille at Books for Cooks, Ed Barnard at W4 Love Books, Victoria at Segrue Books and the fabulous proprietors and teams at Queens Park Books, West End Lane Books, South Kensington Books, The Pitshanger Bookshop, Daunt Books and The Riverside Bookshop.

For contagious digital enthusiasm: Joey Casco 'The Wine Stalker', Jeff Eckles of 'We Like Drinking' (who doesn't?), Li

Valentine @TheWiningHour, Jo Diaz, Tamlyn Currin, Cindy Rynning, Neil Dubois, Dave Nershi, and Randy Smith.

For nudging me closer to the straight and narrow: David Haviland at the Andrew Lownie Literary Agency.

And finally, a huge thank you to all the purchasers and readers of the first, 'NSFW' edition of Corkscrew, most copies of which have, by now, been tracked down and quarantined. Without your fortitude, this slightly more respectable edition would not exist.

Raffaelo

Paoluculla
Natale

22648036R00246

Made in the USA
San Bernardino, CA
15 January 2019